MURDER OF A DEAD MAN

Also by Katherine John

Without Trace
Six Foot Under

MURDER OF A DEAD MAN

Katherine John

St. Martin's Press ❧ New York

A THOMAS DUNNE BOOK.
An imprint of St. Martin's Press.

MURDER OF A DEAD MAN. Copyright © 1994 by Katherine John.
All rights reserved. Printed in the United States of America.
No part of this book may be used or reproduced in any
manner whatsoever without written permission except in
the case of brief quotations embodied in critical articles or
reviews. For information, address St. Martin's Press,
175 Fifth Avenue, New York, N.Y. 10010.

Library of Congress Cataloging-in-Publication Data

John, Katherine.
    Murder of a dead man / Katherine John.
        p.   cm.
    "A Thomas Dunne book."
    ISBN 0-312-15369-4
    I. Title.
PR6060.O237M87   1997
823'.914—dc20   96-43319
                                            CIP

First published in Great Britain by
Headline Book Publishing

First U.S. Edition: January 1997

10 9 8 7 6 5 4 3 2 1

For Ross Michael Watkins

Prologue

A chill hush pervaded the basement of the General Hospital. Someone standing close to the lift shaft or to the staircase leading downwards into the entrails of the building could, by listening hard, make out the faint, distant hum of the boiler that fed scalding water into the heating system. The boiler worked well – too well. The temperature on the wards rarely dropped to a tolerable level.

The muffled clanking of a trolley being wheeled into an elevator, followed by the remote clatter of equipment on its way to a bedside, reverberated through the stairwells, but these sounds, far from reassuring, only served to remind that the general bustle of hospital life had no place down here. Even the corridors leading out of the brilliantly lit, white-tiled central hall that commanded three-quarters of the floor area were deserted. Shrouded in shadows lapping at the edges of sporadic puddles of dirty yellow light, they stretched into blind, secretive corners devoid of human presence.

When night fell, even seasoned staff, accustomed to death's presence on the wards, went out of their way to avoid the passages leading down to those steel double doors below ground level. For behind them were stowed the General's failures: the patients who'd succumbed despite all care, skill and technological advance.

A young man with an unhealthy pallor bent assiduously over one trolley. His hair fell forward over his face, his black spectacles slid precariously downwards, and his hands trembled as he concentrated on the task in hand. And all the while the powerful lamps, close overhead, burnt mercilessly: stinging his eyes and searing his neck.

1

He paused, glancing nervously around the deserted room. Shaking his head at his own foolishness, Simon flexed his rubber-clad fingers before resuming his kneading of the stomach of the cadaver he was engaged in laying out. He had watched this procedure many times, knowing his turn would come but never dreaming it would come so soon. That his colleague Jim would call in sick tonight, of all nights!

There had been nights when the two of them had spent the greater part of their shifts in the porters' station, drinking tea and scanning old copies of *Playboy*. But not tonight. By half-past eleven, three deaths already, and two calls from the wards warning of more to come.

Clenching his fists, he pressed down hard. Air wafted from the corpse's open mouth, to linger in the chill, bright air – a sad and final sigh that made the young attendant's blood run cold. He pushed down again, trying not to look at the face, or to think of the man this corpse had been. The tags attached to wrist and ankle detailed a name and number, but he could remember only the age inscribed there. *Twenty-seven*. Born the same month and year as himself. Even the casualty sister had seemed affected by the bleak futility of such early death, despite the brusque tones she habitually adopted to conceal her emotions.

Why hadn't he given some thought to his future when he had opted to read philosophy at university? If he'd studied accountancy or law at least he would have been equipped for a profession. He wouldn't be confined here in this bleak, modern house of the dead, all ceramic and steel. A repository where corpses were stowed – out of sight and out of mind – until the ceremonies were over and they could be forgotten.

He flinched as the telephone shrilled into the silence. Peeling off one rubber glove he left the corpse and picked up the receiver. 'Mortuary!'

'Ward 11. We need you immediately.'

'Can't you get a porter? I'm laying out.'

'No porters available.'

'Then a nurse.'

'We're short-staffed. Down to two here on the ward.'

'I'm working single-handed.'

'We all have our problems.'

Silence gnawed on the line.

'It's an old lady in a four-bedded ward. People are awake, and it's upsetting them.'

'I'll be there.' Simon replaced the receiver.

The twenty-seven-year-old lay flat on his back, legs straight, arms arranged parallel to his body. Someone, probably a casualty nurse, had half done the job for him. The corpse's eyes were closed, but not the mouth. As the attendant taped the jaw, he looked into the face for the first time. The features were regular, even: the kind his girlfriend admired when she wanted to tease. The man had been tall too, over six foot judging by the length of the trolley, and had thick, dark, wavy hair. What wouldn't he give to have hair like that? His own had always been thin, and was now showing marked signs of receding. He pulled off the second glove, tossed it into a nearby bin and picked up a fresh pair from the box. There wasn't anything so pressing that couldn't wait the quarter of an hour it would take to proceed to Ward 11 and return.

Simon moved towards the door, then an afterthought caused him to turn back. The sheet rustled as he draped it over the corpse. Silly to bother really, a case of childish phobia – of being afraid of the bogeyman. But he didn't want to be faced with the uncovered corpse on his return. Dark hair, pale skin; so lifelike – and so dead.

He pulled an empty trolley from a rank lined up against the wall and wheeled it out into the corridor. Regulations demanded that the mortuary be manned at all times, or else locked up. He'd read his contract carefully, and signed that rule among all the other hospital directives, but it didn't take him long to discover working practices were very different from rule-book ordinances. He had not forgotten the obligations of his contract, simply learned to ignore them, as did the other attendants and porters. There was often no other option since the place was now understaffed and run on a shoestring. Besides, it would be a real bind to have to dig his keys out of his pocket and lock the door when he would only have to repeat the entire procedure on his return.

The trolley rattled noisily on the corridor floor. The nurse had said there were other patients awake on her ward, so he'd specially chosen one of the new American-style carts, draped with a sheet. The body was deposited in a deep, box-like hollow and a lid dropped down to cover it. Then the sheet was replaced to conceal the box. Simple, but effective. A flat sheet didn't draw the same curious stares a shrouded corpse attracted. But these box carts never fooled any patient who'd already witnessed the disappearing act.

It was the visitors they didn't want to upset. Ward 11 always had relatives staying over: sitting by the beds, pacing the corridors, waiting for the end to come. And death nearly always came during the hours of darkness – or did it just seem that way?

Reaching the lift, he parked the trolley and pushed the call button. He didn't have long to wait. The elevator ascended smoothly to the seventh floor, then shuddered violently, finally jerking to a halt on the eighth.

'You took your time.'

'I came as quickly as I could. I'm the only attendant on duty tonight.'

The staff nurse made no pretence of listening to his excuse. 'This way.' She marched ahead, stiff and starched, clearly unable to see further than her own problems and her own domain. A woman stalked them, an anxious frown creasing her face. Clearly a relative.

'Staff . . .'

'I'll be with you in a moment, Mrs Smythe.' Nurse was as curt with the relative as she was with him. 'Here.' She pushed open the doors to a small ward.

Curtains were drawn around the bed nearest the door. As he wheeled his trolley through, it bumped against a student nurse who was dismantling a drip. She looked up silently, her eyes heavy from lack of sleep and unshed tears. Simon opened the box incorporated in the trolley, folding it down flat.

'She was a dear,' the student whispered after a minute. 'Never complained – not once.'

4

As she helped him lift the emaciated, slack-jawed figure from the bed on to the trolley, he made a decision. *Tomorrow!* He wouldn't go to bed right away; he'd shower and change, then take a walk to the job centre, look at the boards. If there was nothing there, he'd buy a newspaper, go through the situations-vacant column. There had to be *something* better than this.

'Thanks for your help. I'll take it from here.' He reassembled the box and straightened the sheet, ensuring its folds hung down to obscure most of the trolley. The staff nurse merely nodded as he made his way back towards the lifts. The woman he'd seen earlier – Mrs Smythe – stared at his load for a moment, then turned aside. Seeing the sick look on her face he wondered if the extra cost of these special wagons had been worth it.

The lift was still waiting on the eighth floor. There wasn't much call for movement between wards in the early hours. He wheeled in his load, and the same juddering was repeated as he descended to the basement. The door opened on to a deserted corridor.

He couldn't help looking over his shoulder as he headed the trolley down the corridor towards the mortuary. Stopping briefly, he backed against the wall and glanced around. There had been no sound, nothing unusual to alert him – only that general feeling of unease.

Fear trickled down his spine as he increased his speed. Then he realised what he was doing, and laughed. He was running towards a mortuary. Only a madman could equate a mortuary with safety.

He slowed his pace and took a deep breath. This was absurd. He was a grown man, a philosophy graduate. He knew all there was to know about the sane, logical order of the world. There was nothing to fear down here. Nothing at all.

As Jim had put it. 'Our clients may not be happy with their lot, but you'll never know any different. You won't get a peep out of them. And they can't do anything about it.' Then Jim had bitten into his midnight snack of a doorstep cheese-and-pickle sandwich.

Simon negotiated his way carefully through the mortuary doors, wedging them open with the front end of the trolley.

Then he froze. His mouth opened, but uttered no sound.

The young man's corpse was sitting bolt upright on its trolley facing him, the sheet now draped in folds around his waist.

Jim could have easily explained the phenomenon. All the air hadn't been expressed from the stomach. A common enough mistake for novices. But Simon was too horror-struck to wonder about the reason.

The torso facing him was white and finely muscled, with a mat of dark hair on the chest. But the porcelain gleam of the chest was in glaring contrast to the bloody, purple-blue pulp where the face had been. Only the eyes now remained: the irises dark, the whites bleached, staring out above close-scraped cheekbones. Below them, enormous teeth grinned inanely, in a vile, lipless aperture.

The young attendant continued to gaze, mesmerised, registering the stumps where the ears should be, the dark cavities between the eyes where the nose and nostrils had been torn away. The ragged hairline above the naked cranium – a reverse parody of scalping. One word echoed through his mind, as a scream finally tore from deep inside his throat.

Flayed!

The face had been skinned as neatly and completely as his father used to skin the rabbits he shot on their farm back home.

But why would anyone want to skin a dead man?

Chapter One

'Two, four, six, eight, who do we want to date . . . Turn – jump
– hop – scotch . . .'

The young girl hesitated for a moment, a serious expression
darkening her pretty face. Balancing on one leg she swooped
down and retrieved a flat piece of marble from within one of the
squares painted on to the surface of the playground. Placing it
next to her foot, she hopped – sending it skidding further down
the geometric pattern of white imposed on black tarmac.

'It's my turn after Hannah.' A short, plump, dark child
elbowed her way aggressively to the front of the queue.

'No, it's not!' The girl who had possession of the hop-scotch
hovered, one foot still in mid-air. 'It's Kelly's.'

'So there, Miss Bossy Boots.' The girl who'd been elbowed
aside reclaimed her place.

The children's voices, eager, high-pitched, carried across the
school yard and out through the railings to a narrow alleyway
where a tall, painfully thin man lurked, intently watching
their game. His face was dark with ingrained dirt, his chin
black with stubble, his shoulder-length hair matted in a thick
pelt. A rusty black overcoat flapped open at his knees, revealing
ragged trousers stiff with grease and filth. The only splash of
colour were his feet shod in incongruously bright red baseball
boots with luminous blue laces.

As he watched, he shrugged his shoulders to ease the weight
of a stained hessian knapsack on to his back. His dark eyes,
keen, feverish, watched every move of the young girl now on
the hop-scotch. She was an attractive child. Tall for a junior-
school pupil, slender with none of the puppy fat that
characterised her playmates. Her silver-blonde hair was

brushed away from her face and plaited into a rippling tail that reached her waist. Her eyes were blue, a deep cornflower blue that stood out like painted enamel in the drab surroundings of the school yard; her lips a natural pink that highlighted her glowing peaches-and-cream complexion.

She was the prettiest girl in her group: a swan in a sea of ducklings. The grace and beauty of the woman yet to emerge could already be seen in her slender, willowy figure. Features which would attract and enchant in later life were already budding in that sweet face.

'Miss! Miss! A dirty old man is watching us.' The voice was shrill, the speaker a small boy sitting apart from the others, on the tarmac beneath the railings.

A middle-aged woman, wearing a shapeless grey woollen dress and a lumpy home-knitted blue jacket, hurried towards the gate from the other side of the yard. Games were abandoned as all the children within earshot turned their attention and their heads towards the alleyway.

The man paused only a second longer, before turning to run off down the street.

'That's my Daddy!' Abandoning the precious stone that entitled her to take first turn in every game, Hannah tossed her plait over her shoulder and was darting out of the playground before the middle-aged woman could stop her. The child bolted across the narrow road, without a forward glance or thought. A squeal of brakes was followed by the muffled curses of a driver glaring through his car window.

'Daddy!' Hannah screamed, but the thin man kept moving. 'Daddy! Please stop. I can't keep up with you.'

He halted and looked back, with tears clearing grey-white tracks down his cheeks.

'You're not my Daddy.' Her voice dulled to a whisper.

Again the man broke into a run. The child now stood sobbing on the pavement behind him.

'Come on, Hannah. There's a good girl.' A young woman rushed towards her and, wrapping her arms around the child, tried to hug her.

'No!' Hannah fought against the embrace. 'I want my Daddy!'

She lashed out wildly, striking her teacher on the side of the face.

The woman didn't flinch. 'Come on, sweetheart. Whoever it was, he's gone now. Come back into school.'

'He looked just like my Daddy, but his face wasn't right.' The child's sobbing subsided into muted whimpers. 'I thought he was . . . I really thought he was . . .'

'Come on. You can sit with me while we send for your aunt. You can go home early. Would you like that, Hannah?' She guided the child across the road. The woman in the blue jacket tapped her colleague's arm. 'Police?' she mouthed.

The younger teacher shook her head. 'Ring the bell to get the children inside. Then we'll telephone Miss Davies.'

'Miss Davies?'

'Hannah's aunt, Blanche Davies. Only if Miss Davies thinks it's warranted should we contact the police.'

'Happy birthday to you, *dear* Trevor . . .' Peter Collins sang caustically at his colleague as Lyn Sullivan entered the darkened living room of Trevor Joseph's house, carrying a rich chocolate and cream gateau set ablaze with candles.

'He's not your dear Trevor, Sergeant Collins. He's mine.' Lyn set the cake on the table in front of the crowd gathered around the birthday boy.

'So he must be,' Peter agreed. 'No one's given *me* a cake since I was five years old.'

'Difficult to organise when you spend every off-duty minute in that disgusting White Hart,' snapped Sergeant Anna Bradley, Collins' colleague and companion for the evening.

'How do you know it's disgusting? You've never set foot in the place.'

'I don't need to step inside to guess what it's like. You've only got to look at the outside . . .'

'Time to blow out the candles, Trevor.' The smile on Lyn Sullivan's face was strained. Six months of living with Sergeant Trevor Joseph of the Serious Crimes Squad hadn't inured her to his colleagues' boisterous company, or their ways. The kindest thing she could think of saying to her other friends was that people who worked on the police force were 'different'. Different in the hours they kept, their habits, their lifestyle, their sense of humour – especially their sense of humour. And whatever went for the force in general applied doubly to Sergeant Peter Collins of the Drug Squad. Trevor Joseph's closest friend could be difficult company at the best of times – and it had been a while since she and Trevor had enjoyed the best of times. After only two months their relationship, begun with so much promise, had deteriorated into all-too-frequent days of separation due to grinding work schedules, interspersed with leisure periods mostly spent alone. No matter which nursing shift she opted for, she invariably returned to an empty house. Whether she worked days, mornings, afternoons or nights, Trevor's schedule rarely coincided with her own.

It had taken a mammoth amount of juggling at the psychiatric hospital, where she worked as a staff nurse, and endless liaison over the telephone with Trevor's immediate boss, Inspector Dan Evans, before she'd felt confident enough to arrange this party. Even now she felt on edge, waiting for the telephone to ring at any moment and summon half her guests away. In her anxiety she'd been unable to eat more than a mouthful from the buffet of cold salmon, sliced meats and salads she'd spent the last three days preparing.

Once the candles were blown out, the drinking would begin in earnest, and with luck Trevor would soon get too plastered to go out on duty even if he was called. Their first evening at home together for over six weeks, and she'd been stupid enough to invite thirty other people!

'Come on, Joseph. It's valuable drinking time you're wasting,' Collins grumbled.

Trevor took a deep breath and blew over the cake.

'I don't appreciate cream being blasted on to my best bib and tucker, mate, even by a birthday boy.' Andrew Murphy, who'd been a contented constable all his working life, and was now close to retirement age, flicked off a fleck that had landed on his tweed jacket.

'Stop moaning, Murphy. After some of the places you've worn that jacket, a spot of cream isn't going to make any difference. It might even disguise the blood and tooth marks.' Anna Bradley handed her plate to Lyn. 'Large piece, please – with a double helping of cream.'

'How do you put up with having her on your squad?' Collins asked Joseph, who was now cutting the cake into thick, uneven slices.

'More to the point, how does Anna put up with Dan and Trevor?' Lyn eased each slice on to a plate and handed it around.

'Three more promotions, and I'll be able to detail any sergeant in this town to clerical duties.' Anna smiled gleefully through a mouthful of chocolate and cream.

'Five more promotions, and I'll be able to order all policewomen back to what they're best suited to: paperwork, housework and bed work.' Collins touched his glass to Joseph's and then Murphy's. 'Here's to an all-male force.'

Anna stared Collins in the eye. 'Just wait until I'm your Super, Sergeant.'

'I doubt there's a man on that force who has the faintest notion what sexual equality means,' Lyn added scathingly.

'I give my women every opportunity to take their turn on top, as Bradley will soon find out.' Collins wrapped his arm around Anna's waist.

'I take it your past conquests used that position to watch for something better coming through the door?' Anna removed his hand from her waist and let it drop.

Bored with the banter, Lyn took the empty cake tray into the kitchen. Every inch of work surface was littered with abandoned plates, screwed-up paper napkins, half-eaten chicken wings, dirty glasses and knives and forks. She stared for a moment at the mess, before opening first the bin and then the dishwasher. After scraping the plates into the rubbish sack, she began to stack crockery and cutlery methodically into the machine. When it was full, she switched it on, debating whether to wait until the first load had finished, or wash up the residue by hand.

Trevor crept up behind and kissed her on the neck. 'I'm sorry.'
'For what?'

'For my tactless colleagues and their bad taste in jokes. You should have invited the nurses from the hospital.'

'This house isn't big enough for my friends as well as yours.'

'Then maybe you should have just invited your friends.'

'For *your* birthday?'

When he turned her around, her eyes were on a level with his own. At six foot, she was barely an inch below him in height. As he kissed her thoroughly and slowly on the mouth, her tension and irritation – with Peter Collins and the evening in general – began to dissipate, and she recalled exactly why she'd moved in with Trevor six months ago.

'Thank you.'

'For what?'

'For my birthday party – and for being here with me. Just one thing. On *your* birthday would you mind very much if I organised something for just the two of us?'

'If I could've been sure you'd make the effort to be here, I'd have done just that this evening.'

'Are you on duty this weekend?'

'Of course. Don't tell me you'll be off?'

'I was hoping we could go down to Devon.'

'To your mother's farm?' Her dark eyes sparkled at the prospect. She'd never met his family, though he'd told her about his mother, brother, sister-in-law, nieces and nephews. She'd even spoken to them on the telephone, but all of Trevor's protestations to the contrary had failed to reassure her that they approved of her living in his house.

'I want to show you off.'

'They might not like me.'

'They'll love you.' He kissed her again. 'And there'll be more time for this.'

'For an offer like that I'll swap my shifts.'

He pulled her closer, until the lengths of their bodies nestled against one another. 'We could go upstairs.'

'Someone might notice,' she demurred.

The kitchen door burst open, slamming painfully into Lyn's spine, and Peter Collins pushed past.

'We're dying of thirst out there, mate, while you're having it off with Florence Nightingale in here. Some bloody host you make.'

The drizzle-filled, saffron glow of the street lamps was neither soft nor kind enough to mask the muddy filth that stubbornly adhered to the rusty black overcoat, despite its sodden state. The trousers were more torn than when Hannah and her teachers had seen them earlier, only now a thick layer of slime from the dock end of the bay overlaid the starch of greasy dirt. Oblivious to his state, the derelict clutched his bottle, staggered, slipped and fell to his knees as he entered the seaward end of Jubilee Street.

Coarse laughter echoed eerily around the four-storey terrace of superficially elegant houses. Daylight would have revealed peeling paint on the graceful eighteenth-century facades, rotting wood, roofs dipping alarmingly in their centres, and more windows shored with wood than glass. But the drunk was in no state to evaluate his surroundings. He only knew he was in the vicinity of what he considered 'home'. The grand town houses, built on the wealth of merchant shipping, were now in their final stages of decay and degradation. The few still habitable had been leased by the Council to the churches and voluntary organisations that struggled to accommodate the town's homeless.

The drunk's cider bottle rolled from his grasp. A man appeared behind him and kicked it aside.

'Looks like you need some more to set you up.'

Still on his knees, the drunk reached for the fresh bottle the man offered. 'Good stuff,' was the only decipherable sound he uttered, as the unaccustomed warmth of whisky filled his throat.

'Nothing but the best for my friends.'

'You're a good mate. Never thought I'd say it, but you're a bloody good mate. One of the best . . . a bloody good . . .'

'Come on, let's get you behind this hoarding, and out of the rain.'

'Too bloody soft – that's your trouble. I'm fine out here.' The tone had become contentious. The man who'd given the bottle grew wary. He knew these men who lived on the streets. Drunk, the line between hostility and anger was easily crossed.

'For you perhaps,' he said easily. 'But then you've plenty inside you.'

'You complaining I've taken too much?' The drunk tried and failed to focus, as he passed the bottle back. He attempted to sit up, lost momentum and fell backwards, sprawling clumsily on the fouled and sodden pavement.

'I gave it to you because I want you to have it,' his companion explained patiently. 'But we're out in the open here, and you know what the others are like. One whiff of that bottle and it'll soon be gone.'

The fuddled mind digested and appreciated the gravity of this threat.

'Come on. Up you get.' A hand gripped the back of the grimy coat and the drunk managed to remain on his feet – but only with help. The owner of the bottle reeled at the fetid, sour stench of the filth his tottering companion had lived and slept with all winter.

'One more step. Here we are.'

The drunk crashed headlong, falling behind a hoarding which advertised a lager that would not only change your life but – if the image was to be believed – would also attract young, voluptuous females. Rolling over, he held up his arms.

'More,' he begged in a cracked whisper.

The whisky bottle again changed hands.

'Good stuff.' The words hung in the air as the bottle finally fell from his fingers. His companion watched it roll away over the rough ground, until it finally clattered to rest against a lump of concrete. There its contents gurgled out in a puddle, mixing with the rainwater.

The benefactor studied Jubilee Street from behind the shelter of the hoarding. It was deserted, just as he'd hoped. Its hostels for the homeless closed their doors early. They were forced to because the demand for beds greatly exceeded the supply. Anyone who'd been out on the streets for any length of time knew there was nothing for them in Jubilee Street at this late hour. Queues for accommodation started forming at five o'clock, and the Salvation Army and lay charity hostels were invariably full before six. The Catholic hostel, which was fighting a losing battle against lice and fleas, closed its doors a little later. At eight the police would come down and move on the stragglers. But, despite this intermittent police presence, Jubilee Street kept its hazardous reputation. Few had cause – or desire – to wander its precincts after dark. And tonight was no exception.

The pavements shone a dull, satin grey, except where the potholes hosted gleaming black puddles. The rain continued to fall, soft and silent. No footstep, no whine of a car engine disturbed the silence. Lights burned in the ground-floor windows of the various hostels, but no sound came from their precincts.

He exhaled through his nose, expelling twin plumes of warm misty breath into the chill night. Safe now! But there was no time to dawdle. He turned to look dispassionately at the drunken man lying at his feet. Eyes closed, legs wide apart, a snore ripping noisily from his throat, the vagrant was well and truly dead to the world.

The other man slung the haversack he had been carrying on to the ground. Quickly opening it, he took out a plastic litre bottle of clear liquid, then a tin gallon can, and finally a hunting knife with a six-inch hooked blade. Time to set to work.

Father Sam Mayberry, who'd been working late on the Catholic hostel's account books, heard the scream first. A piercing, bestial cry of pure agony. It took him precious minutes to unbar and unbolt the front door, and the first thing he saw was the flames soaring high behind the hoarding. As he ran closer, calling out behind him for someone to summon the fire brigade, he spotted a dark shape in the centre. The screaming ceased just moments after he reached it.

It came almost as a relief when the telephone finally rang. As Lyn picked it up, she looked across the room to where Trevor was talking intently with Anna Bradley and Peter Collins. He must have had a few, not to have even heard it ringing, she reflected acidly.

'Lyn, is Trevor there?'

She recognised the lilting Welsh tones of Trevor's superior.
'I'll get him for you.'

'I'm sorry to disturb you at home, but . . .'

'It's all right, Inspector Evans,' she interrupted, not wanting
to listen to any further excuses. As the live-in girlfriend of a
police officer the first thing she'd learnt was that 'buts' meant
cancelled plans. As a disgruntled wife had once complained to
her at the police ball, funerals, marriages and births – especially
births – came in second place to police procedures.

'I'm sorry Lyn. I really am.' Standing in the hallway Trevor slid
his arms into the sleeves of his quilted anorak. Anna Bradley
was already outside, waiting in the car the Inspector had sent
for them even before he'd telephoned.

'Stop apologising. I expected it.' Lyn stood back as the door to
the living room opened.

'But you've gone to so much trouble . . .'

'Don't worry, Joseph. We'll enjoy ourselves here without
you.' Collins stood in the living-room doorway, a drink in one
hand, a cigar in the other.

'I've no doubt you will.'

Collins picked up the sarcasm but chose to ignore it. He drew
on his cigar and retreated back into the noisy room, leaving a
trail of acrid smoke in his wake.

'I'll be back as soon as I can,' Trevor promised, reaching out
to embrace Lyn, but she stepped into the kitchen, away from
him.

'I won't wait up.' There was an edge to her voice he didn't
have time to soften.

Instead he opened the front door, and strode away. The car
stood, blue light flashing, at the bottom of the narrow driveway.

'You took your bloody time, Joseph,' Bradley grumbled.
'Needed one more double brandy to convince yourself it really
is your birthday?'

Twenty minutes later, it wasn't only Trevor who was wishing
he'd taken the time to have one more stiff drink. Dan Evans
was impatiently waiting for them in the middle of Jubilee

16

Street itself. The police cars and fire engines parked on either side of him had blocked the road until it couldn't accommodate anything wider than a motorbike.

Behind him the forensic squad was busy winding blue-on-white scene-of-crime tape around freestanding poles, to cordon off an area of wasteground and pavement the size of a football pitch. In the centre, behind a scorched hoarding, were the smouldering remains of a fire that had polluted the whole street with the stench of burning flesh. It still smoked defiantly, in the faces of the fire crew who stood impotently by.

'No more of your bloody foam, please!' Patrick O'Kelly, who'd been endowed with the dubious distinction of acting as police pathologist on call, glared at the firemen as he hoisted one leg over the tape.

'Sorry about your birthday party, Joseph,' Evans mumbled through a mouth stuffed with peppermints.

Anna Bradley followed Trevor out of the car. 'So am I,' she muttered. 'Hope this is worth it.'

'We've a body – or rather what's left of one.' Evans nodded towards the pile of smoking ashes that Patrick was studying from a distance, as he donned his rubber gloves. He was already wearing overboots and a sterile white paper overall.

'Doesn't look like there's much left?'

'Just a few cinders, from what I've seen.'

'Murder?' Bradley found herself asking all the questions. Maybe Joseph's thoughts were elsewhere – with Lyn Sullivan, she decided. Damn the girl for rendering a good detective useless.

'That's what O'Kelly is here to find out.' Evans led the way towards the barrier of tape, halting two foot from the line.

O'Kelly was squatting on his heels next to the ashes. 'Get that tent up here on the double, before these ashes are blown all over the docks,' the pathologist shouted to his assistant, who was heaving a heavy wooden box from his car. 'Any witnesses?' he asked, without looking up from the blackened mess.

'Sam Mayberry.'

'Father Sam Mayberry?'

Bradley was amazed. Joseph was with them after all.

'He heard a cry but it took him a few minutes to unbolt his door. By the time he got across the street, all he could see was a burning mass.'

'And saw no one else? Didn't hear anyone running away?'

'No.' Evans glanced towards the church hostel, where Sam Mayberry, short, round, diminutive by police standards, was standing in the doorway. He was talking with Captain Arkwright, who ran the Salvation Army shelter. 'But I only spoke to him briefly.'

'Is there anything to indicate murder?' Having worked with O'Kelly before, Joseph knew that in the initial stages of any investigation every judgement had to be dragged out of the man with constant prodding. The pathologist avoided making any firm pronouncements until he was one hundred per cent certain of his facts. This usually meant an infuriatingly slow start to investigations into 'suspicious deaths', where time could be of critical importance.

'I can tell you that if the victim was alive when this fire started, he or she didn't last long.' O'Kelly rose stiffly to his feet and straightened his back. 'And petrol was used.'

'How do you know that?' Evans asked.

'Can't you smell it?' Patrick waved the forensic people forward. 'Once this site's been tented and photographed, I'll take a closer look,' he murmured noncommittally. 'When the body's ready for moving, I might be able to tell you more.'

Bradley groaned, her hopes of returning to the party dashed. 'It's going to be a long night.'

'And that's before you begin questioning all the hostel inmates,' Evans said grimly.

Joseph didn't say a word. He'd been detailed to the Serious Crimes Squad for six months now – which was four months longer than Bradley. He knew exactly how long a 'long night' could be.

'You didn't hear anything else before the scream?'

Bradley wished Joseph was a video-recorder she could fast-forward. His slow, laborious method of questioning was irritating beyond measure. It was as much as she could do to refrain from

18

trying to take over. Biting her tongue, she stood idly by. As the junior on the team she knew better than to upstage any of the others. Even someone her own rank.

'As I've already told Inspector Evans,' Father Sam Mayberry continued, 'I was sitting in the office, trying to work out the accounts . . .'

'And the time?' Joseph felt dog-tired. There was a pain between his eyes that wouldn't go away. Already the dry, metallic taste of hangover tainted his mouth. His stomach heaved at the pervasive smell of burning flesh that persisted despite the onset of another shower of rain. He wanted to be home now, this minute, and in bed with Lyn. But, valiantly pushing that thought from his mind, he licked his pencil and forced himself to continue.

'After midnight. A quarter past twelve. I remember looking up at the clock in the hall, through the open door.' Mayberry's gnome-like features crumpled. 'There was a terrible scream . . .'

'And before that, nothing?'

'Nothing out of the ordinary. Just rain pattering . . .'

'It was raining?'

'Light but steady rain – like now. I got wet when I ran outside.'

The revelation warranted another scribble in the notebook.

'The scream sounded . . . well I wasn't even sure if it was human. I jumped up—'

'And ran to the door,' Bradley supplied, finally succumbing to temptation.

'And ran to open the front door,' Mayberry repeated unsmilingly. 'That's when I saw it.'

'What exactly did you see?' Joseph followed standard procedure.

'A dark shape in the centre of a fireball. Almost like the cartoon shape of a man.'

'Standing or sitting?'

Sam Mayberry frowned again. 'He must have been kneeling I suppose,' he declared after a moment's thought.

'Why kneeling?' Bradley interrupted, wondering at his uncertainty.

'Because the figure seemed too short, too close to the ground, to be standing upright. Because its arms were waving in the air, as if clawing wildly at its face.'

'At its face?' Joseph looked up from the notebook.

'It might have been the face or the back of the head. I really can't say which way he was turned. The fire was so bright he looked just like a cartoon silhouette.'

'And you noticed no one else in the street?'

'I didn't exactly look,' Sam murmured in his soft Irish brogue. 'I just ran back inside, shouted for help – for someone to dial 999. Afterwards, when I found the courage to go near, I gave the poor soul the last rites,' he concluded, apologetically.

'Thanks, Sam.' Joseph stowed his notebook and pencil in the top pocket of his shirt. He'd carried them there, even during his own birthday party. Habit? Lyn would have said conditioning. 'We'll need a formal statement, but it can wait until morning. Looks like we're going to be here all night, but in the meantime, if you remember anything else . . .'

'I'll call the station and ask to speak to you, or to Inspector Evans – or Sergeant Collins?'

'I don't work with Collins any more. He's still on the Drug Squad.'

'Then you've been promoted?'

'Just a sideways shift.'

Bradley moved closer. 'Was the victim still screaming while you gave the last rites?' The light from the street lamp fell full on her face. Harsh, unflattering, it threw her strong features into relief, emphasising the determined set of her jaw, the long line of her Roman nose, the hooded, deep-set eyes.

'Thankfully, no, the screaming had stopped. By then quite a crowd had gathered, including Captain Arkwright and Tom Morris. Naturally enough, everyone wanted to see what the commotion was about.'

'Did you notice anyone you wouldn't have expected?' Unlike Joseph, Bradley had no notebook to hand. Without asking, she reached into her colleague's pocket and removed both book and pencil.

'That depends on what you mean by "expected". The inmates

vary from night to night – especially in my hostel. We all have our regulars,' Sam explained. 'Captain Arkwright caters for the ladies, Tom Morris for the younger folk, I tend to get the old hands – but we all get casuals: those who stay for only one night. Some of them are looking for work, and when they don't find it they move on. Others, the lucky ones, have places to go to. A few will disappear from Jubilee Street and are never seen again. I like to think that for those, especially the youngsters, one taste of life on the streets is enough to make them swallow their pride and go back home.'

'But there *were* people in the crowd you didn't recognise?' Bradley persisted.

'Of course, but none from my own hostel. I've taken in only regulars tonight. But I can't speak for Tom Morris, or Captain Arkwright. Like me, they're fighting a losing battle against the authorities, just to keep their shelters open.'

'I read something about that,' Bradley said thoughtfully. 'Isn't the council trying to shut down the hostels so they can redevelop this whole area?'

Sam nodded. 'We're running these places on a wing and a prayer. The church leases my building from the Council, same as the Salvation Army. We pay a peppercorn rent, but they can close us down any time they choose. And as Tom there is seconded directly from Social Services, which is run by the Council, he's even more vulnerable than us.'

'Leaving the homeless with nothing but doorways and the underpasses in the town centre.'

'No disrespect intended, Sergeant Bradley, but seeing as how your colleagues regularly move them on from there, and since the pier was pulled down a while back, it will leave them with nowhere at all. They'll end up dying from hypothermia. One hard winter will be all that's needed to kill off most of them.'

'Perhaps that's what the Council wants,' she murmured cynically.

'I can't believe that any man truly wishes another man ill.'

'The Council's not a man, Sam. It's a hard, inhuman, faceless institution. I thought you'd have learnt that by now.' Joseph

21

retrieved his book and pencil from Bradley.

'O'Kelly's ready to move the body out. How about giving the boys a hand to push this crowd back? Then you can start listing and interrogating the hostel inmates.' The Inspector's massive six-foot-four frame loomed towards them, silhouetted against the spotlights trained on the cordoned area.

'Has O'Kelly found anything yet?' Joseph asked, once out of Mayberry's earshot.

'Precious little at the moment. The victim was human. Either doused with petrol, or had doused itself, prior to igniting. The only recognisable bits are a boot with a foot inside, and a charred skull. O'Kelly thinks that most of the petrol was splashed over the upper half of the body.'

They returned to where O'Kelly was preparing the pathetic remains for removal. A glistening black body-bag was laid out in front of the tent that had been pitched to protect the evidence against the wind. O'Kelly moved his gloved hand delicately among the warm embers, lifting each charred discovery carefully, painstakingly, as though it was an extremely precious object. He stared at one piece for a few moments then waved it in the air. 'Cheekbone,' he explained gleefully.

Joseph stared at the dark flattish bone. Unburnt flesh still clung to its contours.

'It was resting against this.' O'Kelly pointed to a piece of dressed stone already swathed in plastic. 'The weight of the body must have pressed down on it, to cut off any surrounding oxygen. It's barely singed.' He squinted at the fragment again, then produced a pencil torch from his top pocket, shining it directly on his find. 'These look like knife marks slicing diagonally into the bone.'

'What are you suggesting?' Evans queried.

'It could be that this portion of the victim's face was slashed with a knife before the fire was started. Which might account for the scream that was heard.' He took a plastic bag from his case and slipped the segment into it, holding it up against the light. 'Whoever it was did a good job. Look at that stump over on the side. It's clean cut, not singed. So that ear was probably removed before the burning even started.'

Chapter Two

'You must have known what it would be like before you moved in with him?' Peter Collins stacked the glasses he'd hunted down in the living room in the kitchen sink.

'Trevor did try to warn me,' Lyn conceded. 'Perhaps I just didn't want to believe him at the time.'

'They say love is blind. I didn't realise it was deaf as well.' He pulled out the unit that held the bin, hauled up the edges of the black plastic bag and tied them into a knot.

'How do *you* manage? With your girlfriends I mean.'

He glanced at her. The quip about 'not managing at all' remained unspoken. Despite her height and extremely desirable body, Lyn's long black hair and enormous dark eyes made her appear younger than her twenty-one years. She looked so clean and innocent – far too innocent to cope with the baggage which a detective the wrong side of thirty inevitably carries around with him.

'I don't manage,' he answered tersely, hauling the bag out of the bin.

'Anna . . .?'

'Anna and I fight with each other at the station – and occasionally, very occasionally, in my flat. But not in my bed. The biggest things between us are our differences. You invited us both, so we came.'

'There's nothing more to it than that?' She sounded genuinely disappointed, as though she wanted the whole world to enjoy a happy ending.

'Only banter.' Collins opened the back door, deposited the black bag in the dustbin, shut the lid firmly against marauding animals, and returned to the kitchen. He took his time over washing his hands, delaying the moment when he'd have to face her. He was policeman through and through: conditioned to interrogate, analyse, detect – and somewhere, in the process of conditioning, he had lost touch with his own emotions. The only thing he ran from was his feelings. It was bad enough when they surfaced in the form of sympathy for a victim during a case, but impossible when he tried to deal with them in his private life – or rather lack of it.

'You were married once.'

It was a statement, not a question, and he realised that Joseph must have told her. Damning Trevor, and Lyn's persistence, he finally turned and looked her in the eye. 'It was a disaster for both of us. All we succeeded in doing was driving one another mad.'

'Because you were never there for her when she needed you?'

'Because we were different. Because we wanted different things from life.'

'If you were different, why did you marry her?'

'Too much moonlight, too much booze – God only knows. Why does anyone ever get married? For her, I think it was the nesting instinct. She wanted a home, and with my salary taken into consideration she qualified for a larger mortgage and a better house.'

'That's a foul thing to say about someone you lived with.'

'Foul maybe, but true.' He looked at the clean, simplistic lines of the blue and white kitchen. 'I doubt you can comprehend just how ghastly her taste was – is,' he corrected himself. He'd become so used to relegating his ex-wife to the past, he sometimes had trouble remembering she was still alive. 'Fitted carpets with swirling patterns that knocked you in the eye. Fence-to-fence gnomes in the garden. Collections of knick-knacks that covered every inch of the house, even the kitchen worktops, and all inscribed with *A present from Brighton* in gold ink.'

'You're joking?'

This had to be better: at least she was smiling. 'I assure you I'm not. Less than a year after taking my trip down the aisle, I began drinking seriously in the White Hart. I had to find another home. I simply couldn't face all those gnomes every time I—'

'Peter!'

'In the end she found someone who understood her – and them – better than I did, so we split.'

'Trevor told me you gave her the house.'

'She needed it. I couldn't have lived with myself if I'd made all those gnomes homeless. Not even a jumble sale would have accepted them.' He folded a fresh bag into the bin. 'It's a sad story,' he said with a mock gravity that didn't quite come off. 'And in the force it's unfortunately a common one. You know the Super's wife left him?'

'I heard.'

'She's filing for divorce.'

'And Dan Evans is a widower.'

'I don't know anything about that. He was a widower when he joined us.'

'And Trevor lived with a girl for six years.'

Collins crossed his arms over his chest and leant back against the cupboard. So this was what she'd been building up to. He had no intention of revealing anything Trevor hadn't already. Lyn was Joseph's business not his. Just as Joseph's past was his own – and no one else's unless he chose to share it with them.

'He told me about her.' She rushed the words, sensing Peter's disapproval. 'Her name was Mags, and after she left him he couldn't even live in the flat they'd bought together . . .'

'*He* bought,' Peter corrected. 'Mags never contributed a penny piece. But then Joseph's always been a soft touch. He makes a point of paying all his ladies' bills.'

A deep blush spread over Lyn's face.

'Oh hell!' He opened a can of warm beer that had been standing on the work surface, and drank deeply. 'I didn't mean that in relation to you,' he apologised, wiping his mouth with the back of his hand.

'It's not about money.' She stared blankly at her reflection mirrored in the dark glass of the window. 'I would be happy to hand over my share of the mortgage every month. That would give our relationship some permanency. But I never see Trevor. I almost feel as though I'm in the way. As if I'm nothing more than an encumbrance.'

'You *are* important to him, Lyn. Probably the only thing that means anything in his life.' Peter spoke quietly, wanting, but not daring, to reach out and dry the tears that were welling in her eyes. 'And the plus side of living with Joseph is that he'll never look at another woman while he's with you.'

'How can you be so sure?' she demanded, wondering if he suspected the 'other woman' scenarios she painted in her mind's eye every time Trevor stayed out all night.

'You came to him after four years of celibacy. So much ardour isn't normal for a man of his advanced years, you know. It's the result of his living like a monk.'

'You're incorrigible.' Despite the derisive tone, her tears turned to smiles as she picked up the dishcloth and began to wipe down the work surfaces.

'Oh, he used to fancy women from afar from time to time, but after Mags and until you, fancying's all it ever was.'

'You know, you're not as bad as I thought you were.'

'Tell me where the Hoover is and I'll clean up the living room, and redeem myself even more.'

'It's three o'clock in the morning.'

'The wall between you and next-door is solid, isn't it?'

'Yes, but . . .'

'I hate to see a mess, woman.' He opened the broom cupboard in the hall, and called back, 'I've found it.'

Ten minutes later, their combined efforts had returned the house to pristine condition, and Collins was walking down the path towards the beach road – and his flat. He'd unbent enough to peck Lyn on the cheek as they'd said goodbye, but only when the door was open, and they were public enough to remove any temptation to grab her and give her what Joseph should have. That's if he'd had any sense.

After Collins had left, Lyn walked around the house, switching off lights, checking doors, adjusting ashtrays already set in their allotted places. Eventually she could find no more excuse to linger. Climbing the stairs she went into the master bedroom.

The present she'd intended to give Trevor at bedtime was still lying on his pillow – where she'd placed it before going downstairs to lay out the buffet. She picked up the small box, plumped out the blue velvet ribbon that held the silver wrapping in place, and laid it on his bedside table. In the bathroom she stripped off the short black dress that left little to the imagination, and stood under a hot shower for half an hour. She wouldn't admit it to anyone, especially Trevor, but she was spinning out time, waiting, hoping, that she'd still be up and awake when he returned.

As she finally slid beneath the duvet on the king-size bed, she picked up the book on Trevor's side of the bed. It was a guide to the West Country. Obviously bought with their intended trip to his mother's farm in mind. Perhaps he was aware how she felt after all.

She tried to read, but in the end sleep overtook her. When the alarm went off at six-thirty, the first thing she saw on opening her eyes was the untouched silver and blue package. Then she realised she'd spent yet another night alone.

'Is that the last one?' Trevor Joseph looked hopefully at the social worker seconded from the Council to help the voluntary organisation that ran the hostel. Joseph was already impressed by the man's gentle handling of the inmates, and the respect he clearly commanded from even the most difficult of them, despite his youth. No more than twenty-five or twenty-six at the most, Tom Morris was extremely good-looking, and personable with it. Fond references to a wife had caused Joseph to wonder just how well Mrs Morris coped with a husband who, on his own admission, slept out six nights of every week. Judging by the smile on Morris's face, she did so infinitely better than Lyn.

He watched wearily as Morris ran his finger down the list of names in a grease-stained ledger. 'Twenty-seven?'

Joseph shuffled through the papers in front of him. 'Twenty-seven,' he reiterated.

'Then that's it.'

'Am I glad that's done with.' No one had expected to gather anything significant from the inmates of the shelters other than their identities, but Evans had insisted that they take a hostel each and check everyone who'd slept that night in Jubilee Street, if only for purposes of elimination. Because Sam Mayberry had noticed the fire before any of the inmates had left their beds.

'Glad to see Serious Crimes being so thorough. Once these places open up in the morning, there's no telling where the guests will disperse to.' Superintendent Bill Mulcahy stood in the dilapidated hall, a miserable expression souring his face that originated in more than just the dismal surroundings. 'O'Kelly's waiting for us in the mortuary. Bradley and Evans are almost through. When you're ready?'

'I've finished, sir.' Joseph looked at his watch. Seven-thirty. He would have liked to go home, to see Lyn, get showered and changed, but he knew better than to ask for such a privilege in the middle of an investigation.

'Afterwards we'll set up a case conference at the station.'

'Sir.' Joseph walked wearily towards the door. He had a sudden craving for the brandy he'd left at home, and wondered if this was a sign of impending alcoholism. He'd never before wanted a drink in the morning. He realised it was morning as he followed the Superintendent out of the lamp-lit hall into drizzle-filled grey light, but his body clock was still set to night. Deep velvet night: time to go to bed and cuddle Lyn.

'I want everything discovered in Zone A tagged and in the laboratory within the hour.' Mulcahy's voice echoed across the taped area, where white-suited, rubber-gloved and booted figures had switched off their torches but continued to comb the ground in the growing light of dawn.

Joseph recognised Andrew Murphy and Chris Brooke among the searchers. Judging by the pained expressions on their faces, they'd stayed on at his party long enough to develop hangovers.

'Nothing in Zone A, sir, except a bottle.' Murphy held up a clear plastic bag that contained a whisky bottle.

'That's an expensive brand to find down here,' Joseph commented.

'Probably thieved from one of the bottle banks, just for the smell,' Mulcahy observed laconically as he walked away.

'Zone A everything within ten feet of the body?' Joseph asked Murphy.

"We had to go thirteen for this. We've been ordered to comb the ground down as far as the waterfront.'

Joseph took a last look at the damp, chilled searchers as he climbed into the back of the car. Rank did hold some privileges. At least it would be dry in the mortuary.

'Don't touch these. They're waiting to go to Forensics.'

'What are they?' Bradley squinted suspiciously at the blackened mess resembling a clump of burnt tree roots.

O'Kelly noted the bag that was claiming her attention. 'Hands.'

'You cut them off!' She retreated swiftly, crashing into Joseph.

'It's a slim hope, but we might be able to lift prints from them.'

'Off those!' Mulcahy studied the twig-like objects.

'Burnt and blistered, but some skin is still there in one or two places. You never know your luck. There may be an identifiable partial print.'

'I'll believe it when I see it.' Mulcahy turned away from the specimens destined for the forensic laboratory, towards the slab where O'Kelly had laid out the other remains of the incinerated corpse.

The pathologist pointed to one end of the slab. 'It's laid toe to head or as near as we could set it up, given what we've got. That foot was virtually intact inside the boot that's bagged behind you. I made out the position of the other foot, but that was reduced to a few spoonfuls of ash.' He touched another bag behind him. 'You can pick it up,' he said to Evans, who was trying to peer through the plastic. 'The surviving one's distinctive. I doubt that many men wear red baseball boots with blue laces, even in Jubilee Street.'

'You're certain it was a man?' Mulcahy questioned.

'That's no woman's foot.' He indicated the long, thin, splay-toed extremity balanced on its sole at the foot of the slab.

Thickly coated in black hairs, its upper parts were seared, covered by thick black scabs. Joseph felt as though he were looking at an exhibit in an art gallery, the toes and instep so lifelike, and so neatly severed at the ankle. 'The sock is next to the boot,' O'Kelly added.

Evans held up a bag containing a luminous green sock. 'Nylon – that's why it melted. You can see one or two bits attached here to the ankle bone. Also some rubber from the shoe has stuck to the sole of the foot. The little that didn't burn was badly affected by the heat.'

Bradley looked away from the slab towards the tiled wall. She'd never been very good at postmortems, so hadn't been very pleased with her transfer from Vice to the Serious Crimes Squad.

'Did you remove the foot or was it already severed?' Joseph asked, blanching at the sight of the splintered black bones arranged on the slab.

'It was severed by the burning. As you can see, we've had some fun trying to reassemble him. After such intense fire, it's never easy trying to work out which bit is what, particularly if the body was in a crouched position, like this one.'

The pattern of white tiles was making Bradley feel dizzy. She turned quickly and caught sight of O'Kelly's eyes. The gleeful look in them made her suddenly grateful for her empty stomach.

'Leg bones badly charred, virtually no flesh or muscle left.' O'Kelly continued to deliver his professional opinion on the state of the corpse. 'Pelvic bones badly burned, but enough's left to confirm a male, even without the foot. Torso . . .'

'Looks like a roast rib my wife once cremated over our barbecue.' Mulcahy frowned at the blackened breast cage O'Kelly had partially reassembled.

'Head – now that is interesting. As you can see the left side is completely burnt away, but not the right. It's my guess that the prior soaking in petrol was done haphazardly. Fire can be fickle. Petrol is highly inflammatory. It burns itself, and whatever it comes into contact with, but it goes for the soaked bits first, so when this body was doused by the firemen the flames hadn't quite got around to one or two places. This foot for instance, which was stretched away from the main body.'

'You said the body was in a crouched position?' Evans prompted.

'One knee drawn up to the chin, other leg extended; the hands over the head, which was face down, resting on the thighs.'

'For protection?'

'Possibly.'

'Sam Mayberry said something about seeing him moving his hands up to his head.' Until that point Joseph had viewed the remains laid out before them with equanimity. They hadn't been nearly as unpleasant to look at as one or two decomposed corpses he'd been forced to examine during his career. But now it suddenly struck him that a few short hours ago this had been a living, breathing human being. And anyone, himself included, was only a match and a can of petrol away from becoming one more such item in O'Kelly's overcrowded work schedule.

'And I found this, too.' The pathologist indicated yet another bag. 'Thick enough to be coat cloth. Wool and synthetic mix, black. I can't tell you any more, but the forensic boys might be able to judge.'

'Thanks a lot,' Evans groaned. 'Just about every vagrant in Jubilee Street wears a black overcoat. It seems to be the stock item offer from the charity shop.'

'And this is what I showed you earlier.' O'Kelly picked up a smaller bag that lay next to the brittle remnants of the skull.

'That the bit you said had knife marks?' Evans rummaged in his pocket, pulled out a bag of peppermints, and offered them around. O'Kelly and Mulcahy were the only ones unaffected enough to take up the offer.

'Which leads me to speculate that our subject here didn't kill himself. We've had plenty of suicides who torched themselves. There was a spate of them in the Seventies and early Eighties. We've even had a few who've mutilated themselves, but we've never had one who's done both.'

'There's a first time for everything,' Mulcahy chipped in, with the air of a man who's seen everything life has to offer.

31

'If he did it to himself, where's the knife?' O'Kelly asked practically. 'Even if the handle got burnt, we should still have found the blade. The marks are here, here and here. They're quite distinctive.' Joseph, Evans and Mulcahy peered closely at the diagonal slashes across the bone. Only Bradley refused to look. 'As you can see, there's not much flesh adhering to this section, although it's not as badly burnt as the rest. So it's my guess – and it is only a guess at this stage – that the flesh was actually scraped away before the fire even started. I've X-rayed these cuts, and I'd say they were made by something with a keen, honed, but not serrated edge, and a hooked blade. Possibly a hunting knife. But, whatever the implement, I think it also did this.' He poked his rubber-gloved finger into the plastic, and lifted a stump of cartilage at the side of the bone. Then they saw it: a deep gouge that sliced sideways. 'That almost certainly took the ear off.'

Evans stared at the fragment, and for the first time he was able to put it in the context of a face. He could even make out the rim of an eye socket at the top edge of the cheekbone.

'Mayberry said he heard the victim screaming as he ran into the street. Can you slice *that* much off a man's face without killing him outright?'

'Good lord, yes. Cases have been recorded where men have lost their faces in accidents and not even realised for a few minutes what's happened to them. These severe injuries could have prompted the first screams your witness heard.'

'Would the injuries have eventually killed him, if the fire hadn't?'

'Impossible to say on the little I've got here. The torso is so badly burnt, there's virtually nothing left of the lungs. We've tried freezing and slicing the couple of slivers we found, but there's not enough to tell whether smoke was inhaled. All I can say is that I don't think he'd have lasted long in an inferno that intense. The end of his screaming was almost definitely the end of the man.'

'So what we've got is male, wearing red baseball boots with blue laces, black woollen coat . . . possibly a vagrant . . .'

'In that get-up in Jubilee Street, I'd say undoubtedly a

vagrant.' Bradley felt she had to contribute something, if only to speed things up. She didn't know how much longer she could stay on her feet in this hideous formaldehyde-ridden atmosphere.

'All the homeless who hadn't found themselves a bed in one of the hostels would have moved on from Jubilee Street by that time of night,' Joseph mused.

'You an expert on down-and-outs?' Bradley regretted snapping at him the instant the words were out of her mouth.

'Not as much of an expert as Collins is.' Joseph felt every bit as exhausted as Bradley, but had learnt to keep his temper better, especially around his superiors.

'Age?' Evans queried hopefully.

'We can't tell much from this foot except that he was dark-haired, and white-skinned. The absence of any grey hair in itself can't be taken as an indication of age. Men can go grey anywhere between the ages of twenty and sixty-five, but from what is left of the skull I'd say we have someone aged between twenty-five and forty-five.'

'You can't assess any closer than that?'

'We may know more after I parcel up the teeth and what's left of his jaw and send it to the dental pathologist. The best I can do for you now is to tell you what we do know. He wore size ten boots, but his feet were eight and a half. And whoever owned those boots before him had stretched them, as his big toe had broken through the canvas, and the stitching on the side had split under the strain.'

'Beggars can't be choosers,' Bradley murmured.

'Hair colour? Eyes?' Evans probed automatically, not really expecting anything new.

'As I said, the hair on the upper part of the foot is very dark, almost black.'

'You have washed it?' Mulcahy demanded wryly.

'Yes.' O'Kelly glowered at him over his glasses. He'd never learnt to appreciate police humour. 'As for the eyes, I didn't find one.'

'Can we have a picture of this boot?' Evans asked.

O'Kelly called to his assistant, who handed over a selection of Polaroids. 'I'll send over my report as soon as it's typed. Then it's up to your boys.'

'Appreciate all you've done.'

'Any time, as long as it's not within the next four or five hours. I'm for bed.' O'Kelly yanked off his gloves and tossed them into a nearby bin.

'Tell you what,' Mulcahy conceded as they walked out of the mortuary into the fresh morning air. 'As you all look like hell' – he smiled tightly at Anna Bradley, whose white cheeks were decorated with smudges of rain-streaked mascara and green eye-shadow – 'and seeing as how the most pressing thing is to get a fix on the identity of the victim, I'll pass the photographs on to the day shift. That way you can all go home, get a couple of hours sleep, and meet back in the station for a briefing, say . . .' He glanced at his watch, and Joseph and Evans instinctively did the same. 'It's ten now. Five suit everybody?'

'Why not?' Bradley replied. 'Let's turn day into night.'

'When you've worked on Serious Crimes as long as I have, you'll be grateful for sleeping time whenever it comes,' Evans informed her, as he opened his car door.

As Trevor walked through his front door, he called out Lyn's name, although he knew there was little chance she'd still be in. He went from room to room, looking for a note, but there wasn't one. All evidence of the party had been cleared away, apart from leftover sausages, cold meats and salad in the fridge. He took a cold sausage and glared balefully at the salad. If that stuff was so good for you, why had so little of it been eaten?

Feeling guilty because he had left Lyn to tackle the mess on her own, he kicked off his shoes and climbed the stairs. If he'd lived alone he would have crashed out just as he was, clothes and all, but because he and Lyn shared the same bed, if not always at the same time, he took a shower first, although he was now so tired he actually nodded off for a moment or two as he leant against the cubicle door. A minute later, still damp and smelling of Lyn's cold-cream soap, he fell into bed –

instantly plunging into a dense, black unconsciousness that left no room for anything else. Not even thoughts of faceless burning men.

'I'm coming! I'm coming!' Anna Bradley tightened the belt of her towelling robe around her waist as she thundered down the stairs of her one-up, one-down starter home. She wrenched open the door to find Peter Collins standing on her doorstep, his new BMW parked on the kerbside behind him, an irritating smile on his face.

'I thought you might need a chauffeur.'

She frowned, sleep still numbing her mind. 'Why? There's nothing wrong with my car . . .'

'It went in for a service yesterday morning. I picked you up from the garage, remember, which is why Murphy gave you a lift to Trevor's party.'

'Oh hell!' It seemed as though this birthday party had taken place last year, rather than last night.

'Super's called a briefing,' he reminded her.

'It's not due to start until five.'

'It's a quarter to, now.'

'Blast!' She turned her back and plodded up the stairs.

'Want me to make you some coffee?'

'And food. I must have food. I'm starving.'

Collins shut the front door behind him. Negotiating the partition that screened off the entrance from the rest of her house, he stood stunned and disgusted by the mess that faced him. The previous night he hadn't helped Lyn clear up out of any altruistic feelings other than an overriding passion for order and cleanliness in all things domestic. As his wife had found out to her cost, he loathed clutter of any kind, and was paranoid about dust and dirt. The state of Anna Bradley's living room truly appalled him.

It was small – too small to hold the torn and grubby two-seater settee and matching chair she'd bought in a junk shop with the intention of re-upholstering, and never got around to doing. What areas of carpet could be seen beneath layers of abandoned newspapers, magazines and bulging plastic bags, appeared to be beige in colour, and in desperate need of a shampoo. Beer bottles, a half-empty bottle of whisky, three squashed Diet Coke cans, coats, towels and tea-towels were strewn over a folding table pushed into a corner next to two non-matching upright chairs. The brown and white Scandinavian-style curtains looked as though they hadn't been washed since they'd been hung, and the windowsill, like the window itself, was covered by a thick layer of grime that extended over two dead potted plants, assorted mummified insects and a dirty glass.

Remembering the coffee, he stepped over the newspapers to get to the kitchen area tucked in the corner behind a built-in breakfast bar. The rubber soles of his shoes stuck to the vinyl as he stepped off the litter-strewn carpet. A Venetian blind was drawn shut over a window above the sink. When he tried to raise it, it fell, crashing into the stainless-steel basin filled to the brim with cold, scummy water – plates and bowls breaking the surface like ship-wrecked vessels. This looked infinitely worse than the living room. Plates, cups and glasses, their surfaces thick with congealing food and furry mould, were piled high on the galley counter. He reached forward gingerly and opened the fridge that was set beneath the level of the counter, pulling at the handle with the tips of his fingers. The door swung slowly open, and the light flicked on to illuminate a shelf, bare except for a piece of hard yellow cheese delicately traced with a map of blue mould, and a bottle of greenish-coloured, separated milk.

'Coffee ready?' Anna was standing halfway up the stairs, pulling a sweater over her head.

'I'll buy you one to go in McDonald's.' He shut the fridge.

'Couldn't you find anything?'

'I was afraid of catching something if I left the door open any longer.'

'I suppose you think this place is a bit of a mess.' Her tone was defiant. His reply brutally honest.

'That's the understatement of the century. No wonder you always want to go back to my place.'

'I wanted to see how you lived before letting you in here, but, as I said last time I was there, your flat is sterile. It lacks character.'

'At least it's passed a health and safety inspection.'

'So would my bedroom and bathroom.'

'That an invitation?' He studied her critically. The place might be a mess, but she herself certainly wasn't. Her short blonde hair was brushed away from her face, still wet and gleaming from the shower. Her black slacks and grey pullover were clean, fresh and newly pressed, and she smelt of magnolias. But, despite her assurance to the contrary, he couldn't help wondering if chaos reigned upstairs as well as down.

'I suppose it is.'

He was surprised by her answer. Their four dates – two of them videos and take-aways in his own flat – had been surprisingly chaste affairs. He hadn't been able to quantify quite why until this moment. Bradley was obviously every bit as disorganised as his ex-wife and he'd been too stupid or too mesmerised by her body to notice before now. But it was nevertheless a magnificent body: well worth enduring a little squalor for.

'How about right now?' he suggested, his mouth dry in anticipation.

'Why not? I'm sure the Super won't mind us missing his briefing.'

'Cars break down all the time.'

'Even new BMWs?'

'Tyres blow out on BMWs same as Fords.'

'Seeing as how you disapprove of my housekeeping, sure you wouldn't prefer the blow-out to happen outside your place. That way you could enjoy a tussle on Collins-guaranteed clean sheets?' There was a peculiar glint in her green eyes, and he cursed softly under his breath. Was she or wasn't she leading him on? He simply couldn't be sure.

'Mulcahy's waiting,' he answered gruffly, cutting his losses. For the first time in his life he'd been put at a disadvantage by a woman. He actually felt intimidated, and he didn't like the sensation. Intimidation had always been his prerogative – especially where policewomen were concerned.

'Excuses, excuses. That's what I always get when I make a man an honest proposition. Seems to me, Collins, that in spite of all your promises you're terrified of a female getting on top of you. In more ways than one. Well, we going to this meeting or not?' She pulled her keys out of her shoulder bag, continued down the stairs and out through the front door, leaving him discomfited and slightly embarrassed, like an adolescent who'd just failed some important initiation rite.

'Sam Mayberry identified the shoes. Picked them out as soon as Murphy showed him a photograph of the one O'Kelly's holding.' Mulcahy pushed a set of Polaroids across the table, towards Evans and Joseph. 'As we suspected, they belong to a vagrant. He's known as Tony. And any minute now we're going to get a good look at him.' He stared expectantly at the door, as though waiting for the corpse to walk in.

'There's photographs of him?' Evans dipped a plastic stick into a polystyrene cup of grey coffee.

'Something better. Sam Mayberry mentioned that a team from the local television station was poking around Jubilee Street last month. They were filming a documentary on the Council's plans for the redevelopment of the area. They interviewed Sam, Tom Morris and Captain Arkwright, and a couple of the vagrants who weren't camera shy.'

'You've got the film?' Evans made a wry face on sipping the bitter brew.

'Man I spoke to says it's unfinished. I told him we weren't film critics, just needed to see whatever footage he took of this Tony character. Murphy's picking the film up now. He'll be bringing Mayberry along, too. I thought it might save time to have them all here together for the showing.'

'What about Morris and Arkwright?' Joseph asked.

'They knew about this Tony of course. Couldn't fail to, working where they do. But Sam knew him best, which is why he's coming and they're not. Good evening,' Mulcahy greeted Bradley and Collins with caustic courtesy. 'Nice of you to join us.'

'Collins?' Joseph raised an eyebrow at his unexpected presence.

'Seems our man might have been a small-time pusher,' Evans explained.

'And it seems like every time Serious Crimes Squad digs itself into a hole it can't get out of, it needs to requisition my help.' Collins grinned as he took a chair next to Bradley.

Chapter Three

'That's all there is. All there ever is. Drink, then oblivion. That's how we live. Drink, sleep, the next drink. Always looking for the next drink. Living in hope that we'll get it soon.' The voice was educated but flat, diluted by futility. The speaker was tall, thin – painfully thin – and unkempt, with the unwholesome look of those who lived rough. Skin weather-beaten to a light mahogany. Black hair so tangled it occurred to Joseph that it might owe much of its colour to grime. The curls may have been natural, or simply matted. Fully dilated pupils, with the thinnest border of brown iris, flashed uneasily, flicking from side to side – nervously searching . . . searching for what? The next drink? The next fix?

'And what happens when you haven't the money to buy drink, Tony?' The voice was female, professional.

'That's the worst. The absolute worst. You go out and look. You have to walk around and look . . .'

The camera panned down over the filthy clothes that hung loosely on his emaciated body. A long, black overcoat, threadbare, torn and stained. A crumpled, horizontally striped shirt that must have cost someone money before it had been pushed into a charity sack. Jeans, scabrous and torn. Feet clad in bright red baseball boots with blue laces. The camera climbed again, focusing on a pair of skeletal, fidgety hands; the nails split and blackened. Someone, out of camera sight, handed over a cigarette. Clean hands passing swiftly over grimy ones, careful not to touch. The lens followed the cigarette being lifted to the man's mouth. Dry, cracked lips opened to display the chipped edges of yellowed, neglected teeth. The eyes closed as smoke was drawn deeply into anticipating lungs. The following

41

exhalation was slow, every moment of nicotine sensation being savoured to the full.

'A man who makes the most of every little pleasure.' Nigel Valance, the freelance producer for the local television company, shifted uneasily on his chair.

'A man who *made* the most of every little pleasure,' Collins corrected.

'Quiet!' Mulcahy hissed, pausing the remote control until silence once more reigned in the room.

'And tonight, Tony?' The same female voice, with an additionally sympathetic note.

'Tonight?' No matter what angle the camera took, Tony's eyes refused to meet the scrutinising gaze of the lens.

'You went to the DSS this morning, for your payment,' she reminded. 'Do you have enough left for a bed in the shelter tonight?'

'Bastards wouldn't give me nothing. Said I had to wait.' He gripped the glowing end of the cigarette tensely between his thumb and forefinger. 'Until tomorrow.' He suddenly swayed on his feet, and might have fallen if the interviewer hadn't nudged him back against the wall with the head of her microphone.

Sickened, Joseph shook his head. He'd spent enough time in Jubilee Street to profile this man and a hundred like him. If it *had* been Tony's day to visit the DSS the money he received would have been off-loaded in the first off-licence prepared to serve him. That's if he was on drink. The pupil dilation suggested otherwise, and there were enough varieties of cheap dope on offer down in the dock area to buy not only Tony, but all his fellow 'guests' in the hostels, at least a few hours of oblivion.

But what he'd been taking wasn't important. Tony had clearly organised himself an escape out of the misery of his existence for a few hours. Judging by the look of him, he wouldn't even have been awake for the filming if someone hadn't shaken him for the benefit of the rolling camera. Whoever had planned this documentary had needed a dosser to give an Oscar-winning performance of a man at the end of his rope, and they'd settled on Tony because someone knew addicts. Catch a man sleeping after a trip, and you've got compliance. Wake him, and he'll jump through hoops if he thinks it will finance his next fix. What had they offered? Money or dope? Something beyond the usual price range of the inhabitants of Jubilee Street?

Pity they hadn't seen fit to film him when whatever he was high on was wearing off. Another couple of hours and it would have been a different story. Watch the raving lunatic who'd kill his grandmother for a ticket to temporary oblivion.

He looked along the table. Mulcahy, Evans, Bradley, Murphy, Sam Mayberry and the documentary maker, Nigel Valance, were closely watching the screen as though they were due to sit an examination on what was flashing up there. Only Collins' eye caught his. That quick glance was enough to tell him his friend's mind was running along similar lines of thought. But Collins' patience was shorter than his.

'Do you really expect people to fall for this "poor lost soul" crap?'

'Pardon?' Nigel turned his pony-tailed head and stared at Collins through weak blue eyes rimmed by gold wire spectacles.

'You want the world to feel sorry for a junkie who's an hour off a downer, when he'd be prepared to do anything or anyone to fund his next trip?'

'He told us it was just drink.'

'And I'm Santa Claus. Don't they teach you to read pupils down that TV station before they let you loose on the streets with your cameras?'

'That might explain . . .'

'What?' Mulcahy paused the tape.

'What comes next. You see, Detective Murphy asked if we had any shots of a man, wearing red boots . . .'

'Constable Murphy,' Mulcahy corrected.

'And Tony is the man?'

'He is,' Evans agreed.

'I put all the footage I could find of him on this tape.'

'If there's more to come, let's watch it,' Mulcahy said testily, as he released the pause button.

'We were in Jubilee Street for two weeks . . .'

'Quiet!' Mulcahy ordered sharply, as all eyes focused again on the large-screen TV.

Another interview, this time with Captain Arkwright, who gruffly pleaded for more understanding – and financial support – from the community. Then a longer session with Tom Morris, who reiterated the Salvation Army worker's message more compassionately and forcibly. Even Collins was tempted to put his hand in his pocket.

'He's very pretty,' Bradley commented.

'He's married,' Joseph warned.

'With looks like that, who cares.' Bradley glanced slyly at Collins.

'Doesn't he simply *exude* sincerity. He was a treasure. An absolute gift to a documentary maker like me,' Valance enthused. 'Blond hair and blue eyes are often photogenic, but Tom has something more. He's wasted where he is. I told him to go for a career in advertising or presenting. Those looks, coupled with that marvellous manner, could take him all the way to the top.'

'Perhaps he's "exuding sincerity" because he believes in what he's doing,' Collins suggested coldly.

A shot of Andy – one of the better known vagrants in the town – came on to the screen, fading to a close-up of another long-term resident of Jubilee Street, a one-legged tramp who went by the name of 'Gramps'. He was telling a yarn longer, and taller, than even Collins or Joseph had heard him spin before.

'You're a better listener than me,' Collins said drily to Valance.

Then the film cut to a queue forming outside the hostel. It was still daylight. Mid-afternoon? A pan along the queue. Tony, huddled into his long black overcoat and wearing incongruously bright red baseball boots, stood between two other men. One, who could have been any age between thirty and fifty, had dirty blond hair, a round face and a cheerful smile. The other was as tall and dark as Tony himself, but, unlike Tony, his eyes were static in his lean face, heavy and dull with disinterest or – drug damage?

'Know them, Sam?' Mulcahy paused the tape again, and looked over at the priest.

'The blond one's name is Vince. His companion usually avoids the staff in the hostel. We've learned to tread carefully with our guests, but that one is particularly withdrawn.'

'They still around?' Evans asked.

Sam thought for a moment. 'Didn't see either of them last night, but that doesn't mean anything. They're regular casuals, if you know what I mean. They sleep with us when they can afford it, and out on the streets when they can't. We can go for days at a time without seeing them.'

'They a pair?' Collins leant forward on his elbows.

'They're usually together. The dark one is . . . well, shall we say, not quite himself.'

'Mental case?'

'From what I've gleaned from Vince, I believe they've both been discharged from Compton Castle.'

'Into our kindly, caring community,' Collins sneered.

Joseph clenched his fists and said nothing. He'd had first-hand experience of Compton Castle, and some of his colleagues' attitudes to his brief incarceration in a psychiatric ward had been anything but supportive or understanding. It was the sideways glances when he walked into some of the station offices that hurt the most.

The camera continued to roll along the queue, the same soft, syrupy female voice droning on in the background. It fell silent as a grey, foam-topped microphone came into focus in the centre of the screen. Out of shot, Valance addressed Tony and the two men standing next to him.

'There's only beds for twenty-seven in this hostel. Do you realise you're the fiftieth in line?'

'Of course he bloody realises! We all bloody realise.' Tony, no longer shambling and incoherent, but aggressive, high on something that had pumped him full of adrenaline, stepped close to the camera. 'What the hell are you doing here, anyway? Haven't you the decency to leave us alone? Some of us have families: people who don't know how low we've sunk. And we'd like to keep it that way.'

'Please . . .' Nigel's voice was no longer authoritative, questioning, but pitched high with fear.

The camera swung alarmingly. A heaving, sickening shot of uneven ground speckled with dog mess was followed by a fuzzy blackout – then sky: beautifully clear blue sky adorned by white fluffy clouds that ended sharply in black nothingness.

'He smashed the camera,' Nigel divulged remorsefully. 'The station was absolutely furious. It was beyond repair.'

'Serves you right for playing with junkies,' Collins interjected.

'We were trying to make an honest social statement.'

'About what? The depths that those forced to live on our streets are capable of sinking to? Let's visit the dossers, they're more amusing than monkeys, and they have the added spice of being more dangerous. And watching this programme will make you, the viewer, feel superior to the common herd for an hour or two.'

'Collins!' Mulcahy warned.

'There's nothing worse than a bloody armchair do-gooder. Try approaching it his way.' Collins pointed to Sam Mayberry. 'You might accomplish a bit more than just talk, for once.'

'We're raising consciousness . . .'

'By turning your audience into voyeurs? You and your kind make me sick.' Ignoring the NO SMOKING sign on the wall Collins filched a cigar from the top pocket of his shirt, and rammed it between his lips.

Mulcahy waited in a silence pregnant with hostility, until he was sure that Collins had finally burnt out his anger. Only then did he take his finger off the pause button. Shots of a hostel interior came into view, dark with shadows and poor lighting. Scenes of men undressing in a dismal corridor that led into a communal shower room were interspersed with frames of broken vinyl tiles badly laid on an uneven concrete floor. They were followed by lingering close-ups of black mould growing between cracked white wall tiles. Then the filthy showers themselves, plug-holes blocked by gobs of dirt.

'How the other half live?' Collins lifted his eyebrows.

'I didn't give you permission to film inside,' Sam protested. 'I explained to you that, with so many men going through, it's impossible to clean up the showers while they're constantly in use.'

'I should imagine it's impossible to keep a shower room of that age clean, full stop.' Bradley uncrossed her legs and sat back in her chair. After seeing the grubby clutter of her living room, Collins couldn't help wondering how *her* bathroom would fare in close-up.

Lines of naked men, wrapped only in cheap striped towels, queued to hand over their clothes to the volunteers. The camera followed their bundles as they were pushed through the enamel doors of several large machines.

'Since when did you start washing their clothes for them, Sam?' Joseph asked.

'I only wish we could. There isn't time. Our customers generally have only what they're standing up in. We're always on the look-out for donations, but men's clothing never comes into the charity shops in sufficient quantities for us to kit out our clients. Plenty of women's and children's, but never men's.'

'Then what are those if not washing machines?' Evans asked.

'Tumble dryers. Their clothes don't get wet, so they can be put straight back on, and the heat kills off the lice.'

'Fried lice?'

'Collins!' Mulcahy's glare shifted from Collins' unapologetic face to Valance's bewildered expression.

'Just trying to add some levity to the proceedings.' The unlit cigar still dangled between his lips, but even Collins knew better than to antagonise Mulcahy by lighting it.

Pan out on the dilapidated buildings of Jubilee Street, marooned like abandoned ships in a sea of debris and rubbish. Pan in on the new marina: clean, white, gleaming concrete walkways, three- and six-storey red-brick buildings sporting shining UVPC windows. Neatly dressed, law-abiding citizens, smiling, walking, standing, chatting, and generally not doing very much of anything. Girls wearing bright summer T-shirts and jeans, women in print dresses and straw hats, men showing off pale, hairy arms in short-sleeved shirts. Children licking ice-cream cornets as they gazed in toyshop windows. White plastic tables outside pubs, people eating steak and salads, drinking long cool pints of lager, loud music, a fade to credits . . .

'That's it?' Mulcahy fast-forwarded the credits to the end.

'That's the first rough. It's still got to be cut to half of that length. I left some stuff in the cutting-room, but no clips of any of the vagrants.'

'None?' Collins raised his eyebrows.

'Just shots of the hostel interiors, interviews with Father Mayberry, Captain Arkwright, Tom Morris, and their staff,' Murphy broke in. 'I went through them with the researcher.'

'But I brought along the out-takes, just in case you wanted to look at them as well.' Valance pointed to a second videotape resting on top of the machine.

'We can keep both these tapes?' Mulcahy asked.

'As long as you like. I've booked them out to you.'

'You ever talk to Tony away from the cameras?' Joseph questioned.

'Only a few words. The film was my idea,' he added superfluously. 'I produced and directed it, as well as doing some of the interviewing. But Tony didn't say much more than you just saw.'

'What about the rest of the people who worked with you?'

'The rest of us?' Nigel laughed deprecatingly. 'You mean the camera man – and Joanne who doubles as researcher and second interviewer.'

'That's it?'

'The whole team. It's about average for a television station our size, since we had to buy the franchises.'

'No wonder we get so many old films and repeats.'

'You won't have any free time to worry about the quality of television in this posting, Bradley,' Mulcahy said flatly.

'You sure there's nothing else you can tell us about this Tony?' Evans pressed.

'Nothing I can think of,' Valance asserted. 'That first interview took place the minute we saw him, and we knew nothing about him before.'

'When you woke him up, you mean.'

'How did . . .' Valance looked from Collins to the

Superintendent. 'On the second occasion, as you saw, he went berserk the moment he spotted the camera,' he finished quickly.

'Did you ever see him after that?'

'Once or twice, but we went out of our way to avoid him.'

'So you didn't talk to him again?'

'You kidding?'

'Did you give him anything after that first interview?' Collins asked shrewdly.

'Like what?'

'Money? Booze?'

'We may have given him a couple of quid.'

'May have?'

'I can't remember.'

'Sure those quids didn't come wrapped in little plastic packets.'

'I'm not a drug dealer, Sergeant Collins,' Valance protested. 'What made you think I was talking about drugs?'

'It's obvious.'

'You might have given him money. Nothing else?' Remembering Lyn, Joseph tried to press on.

'Maybe a bottle of whisky.'

'Mr Valance! You promised, no drink,' Sam Mayberry reproached.

'Constable Murphy will take down your statement, Mr Valence.' Mulcahy wound up the interview. 'Thank you for your time.'

'If there's anything else I can do, Superintendent.' Nigel Valance rose slowly from his seat, reluctant to leave. He had just conceived an idea for a documentary on the local police force, and was tempted to bring up the subject. He glanced at the faces around the table, wondering if it was a good time.

'We'll call you if we need you again, Mr Valance,' Mulcahy replied. 'And I assume you'll contact us if you do remember anything else, no matter how trivial or insignificant. In a case like this we need every crumb of information we can get.'

Mulcahy's dismissal decided Valance. He turned and headed out of the door that Murphy was already holding open for him.

'Well?' Mulcahy looked expectantly around the table.

'A row between two dossers over a bottle?' Bradley suggested.

'It might explain the knife injuries to the face, but not the petrol. That sounds premeditated to me.' Collins pulled the cigar from his mouth.

'I agree,' Joseph concurred. 'Vagrants don't carry petrol. My money's on kids looking for kicks.'

'Anyone ever tried to drink it?'

'Meths, but never petrol, to my knowledge,' Sam Mayberry said slowly.

'If they were gone enough, they might siphon some out of the tank of a car,' Bradley suggested.

'You saw Tony on that downer,' Collins mused, ignoring Bradley. 'And most of the old hands carry knives. I wish I had a fiver for every weapon Joseph and I've had to take off them.'

'You ever see Tony armed, Sam?' Joseph asked the priest.

Sam shook his head. 'They all know the rules. If they're seen carrying a weapon inside the hostel, they're quickly disarmed and shown the door – permanently.'

'Supposing it's as Bradley suggests,' Evans reflected. 'Tony had acquired a bottle, and another dosser wanted it. So one of them pulled a knife, they fought . . .'

'And the other one just happened to be carrying a can of petrol?' Trevor finished for him.

'Perhaps the knifing came first, the petrol later. Supposing Tony was killed in a brawl, and the other man panicked when he realised Tony was dead. Then he fetched the petrol and used it to try and cover his tracks.'

'Tony was still screaming when Sam got to the door of the hostel,' Joseph reminded him. 'And that scenario doesn't fit with dope-induced or drunken stupor.'

'Some of our customers can get very violent when provoked,' Sam contributed, 'but I can't see many of them going to such complicated lengths to cover their tracks.'

'Finding out what happened is our problem, Sam, and so far this is all pure conjecture.' Mulcahy rose to his feet. 'If there's anything else you can add to what's already been said . . .'

'I'll get in touch, Superintendent.'

'One last thing, was Tony a regular?'

'On and off. We wouldn't see him every night. A couple of

times a week for about a year, maybe a year and half, according to the book. I checked before I left.' Sam produced a folded piece of paper from his trouser pocket. 'I made a list of the precise dates. Thought you might find it useful.'

'That's saved someone a bit of leg work.' Evans unfolded the sheet and laid it flat on the table in front of him. 'Any idea where he went on the other nights?'

'Same as all the others who can't raise our seventy-five pence fee. Cardboard boxes and blankets on the beach, or a shakedown in the underpasses or the multi-storeys. You people should have a better idea than me.'

'Only when we're young and out on the beat. When you start working from an office, you forget about the streets.'

After Mulcahy and Mayberry had left, Evans picked up the remote control. He rewound the film, then pressed PLAY. On the screen, Tony drew on his cigarette again, his eyes darting uneasily in their sockets.

'I'd give a great deal to know what ghosts were chasing that man.' Making the most of Mulcahy's absence, Collins finally lit his cigar.

'We releasing that film, sir?' Bradley asked. 'There could be a witness out there.'

'Too damned right,' growled Collins. 'The murderer for one.'

'We can book a slot on the ten-minute local spot at ten-thirty, after the national news.'

Evans rose stiffly to his feet. 'If anything comes up after that film is shown . . .'

'We know,' Collins said drily. 'You'll telephone.'

'They'll be telephoned, Collins. *You*'re still on duty,' Mulcahy corrected.

'What have I done to deserve this?'

'You slept last night.' Evans yawned and stretched. 'See you in the morning.'

'Can I beg a lift to my place?' Bradley asked Joseph, as he walked out of the room.

Left to his own devices in the conference room, Collins poured himself another cup from the coffee jug that was standing on the hot-plate. He re-ran the tape of Tony's second interview.

'There's people out there who know us. Don't want to see us like this . . .'

He scribbled a note on the back of Sam's list. There had to be a way of finding out just who, if anyone, really knew Tony.

Trevor went straight to his desk and picked up the telephone. Dialling nine for an outside line, he then called home. He allowed it to ring eight times. No answer. Lyn had probably given up on him and gone out. That's if she'd returned home at all. He debated whether to stop off on his way and pick up a take-away – then he remembered the party leftovers in the fridge.

'You eaten?' he asked Bradley, as she climbed into his car.

'No, and I'm bloody ravenous.'

'What about some cold party food?'

'Take me to it.'

The telephone stopped ringing just as Lyn had come to enough to roll to the edge of the king-sized bed and grasp the receiver. Cursing, she slammed it down and looked around her. She found she was still dressed in her uniform.

As soon as she'd reached the end of the street, she'd realised Trevor wouldn't be home. There had been no car in the drive, and she'd opened the front door to the unmistakeable signs of an empty house. No shoes kicked off in the hall, no coat hanging over the bannisters. She'd even checked the kitchen in case he'd come in and gone out again. But there were no dirty dishes on the work surface, and the unemptied dishwasher was full of clean dishes, just as she'd left it that morning. That's when she'd climbed the stairs to lie on the bed . . . just for a few minutes.

She rubbed her eyes and read the clock. Half-past eight, and she felt like hell. Stiff, aching and hungry, she showered, then dressed for bed in silk pyjamas, the ones Trevor had given her for Christmas.

Subtly perfumed, warm and comfortable, she put on a dressing gown and made her way downstairs. Taking a clean plate out of the dishwasher, she foraged in the fridge – getting herself liberal helpings of pasta and green salad, coleslaw and Mexican bean salad. Healthy lot the police, she noted; the pork pies, gateau and crisps had all been consumed. Two pieces of spiced chicken and half a scotch egg completed her meal. She balked at the few remaining cold sausages. She couldn't stand their greasy taste, but Trevor would dispose of them if he ever got home while they were still edible.

There was even half a bottle of Chardonnay with a cork rammed in the neck; so she picked it up and put it on the tray with the food. Removing a glass from the top shelf of the dishwasher, she carried her feast into the living room. Switching on the television, she curled up on the sofa, the tray on her lap.

Flicking channels, she settled for an old wartime black-and-white film. She'd seen it before, and it had an unhappy ending, the hero dying in a blazing plane crash. But it was preferable to the two channels of football and sitcom repeat she'd rejected. She was about to take her first forkful of pasta when she heard a key in the door. Pushing the tray to one side, she leapt to her feet – the smile dying on her lips when she saw Anna Bradley step into the hall.

'I rang.' Trevor followed her in.

She didn't see the weariness, only the apologetic look on his face as he brushed his hair from his eyes.

'I was asleep, and I didn't get to the phone in time.'

'If you two would rather be alone, I'll call a taxi,' Anna interrupted. 'I need a shower anyway.'

'You can take one here,' Lyn offered abruptly.

'After we've eaten,' Trevor suggested. 'We're both ravenous.'

'I'll get you something.'

'The fridge is full. We'll help ourselves.'

Lyn returned to the living room. The food on her plate now tasted like sawdust, and even the film had lost what little attraction it had held.

'You sure you don't mind me barging in like this?' Anna returned, carrying a plate heaped high with leftovers.

'Not at all,' Lyn lied.

'I know what it's like not having any time alone with the person you're living with.'

Lyn felt like screaming: *Then why are you bloody well here?* But what she actually said was, 'Have you finished for the day?'

'Hopefully.' Trevor laid his plate and a couple of beers on the coffee table. Walking over to the sofa, he pecked Lyn's cheek, but sensing her mood he moved away to share the second sofa with Anna.

'They're putting out photographs of the victim after the ten o'clock news,' Anna volunteered. 'If something comes of it, we may have to go back to the station.'

'I see.' Lyn looked across at Trevor. 'We going to have to cancel Devon?'

'Not if I can help it.'

'This case . . .'

'Is probably just one vagrant killing another. It's simply a question of tracking down which one. Should be easy enough as his clothes must be bloodstained.'

'After this time?'

'They don't have anywhere to change them?' He picked up a forkful of salad and put it in his mouth, almost choking on the dry lettuce.

'News is about due,' Anna hinted.

Lyn switched channels. They ate mechanically through the horrors of Bosnia, Somalia, South Africa, the rowdy name-calling antics of MPs in Parliament, two celebrity deaths including a film star. A clip of the wartime film Lyn had been watching on the other channel came on the screen, and then she realised why it had been repeated so soon after its last showing.

A woman walking alone on a beach. Planes flying overhead, dipping their wings. A superimposing of two ghostly figures embracing on the skyline.

'Darling, forever . . .'

Lyn knew Trevor was eyeing her. She looked away. The weatherman now stood in front of his chart covered with arrows and lines. Cold, rain turning to snow on high ground . . . Then music, the local station cutting in . . .

'Murder . . . Jubilee Street . . .'

Lyn concentrated on her plate. The local news broadcast finished. An American detective series began. The credits had barely stopped rolling when the telephone rang.

Trevor picked up the receiver. 'Are you sure? When? We'll be right there.'

'You're going out *again?*' Lyn glared at him with accusing eyes.

'That was Collins.' Trevor wasn't looking at Lyn, but at Anna Bradley.

'They've now got more of a handle on the victim than just "Tony"?'

'He's been identified as Anthony George, a solicitor from Crawley Woods.'

'A name and a place?' Anna wiped her mouth with a paper napkin.

'The only problem is he died two years ago, in hospital. Of a heart attack.'

Chapter Four

'Did many calls come in after the broadcast?' Joseph asked Constable Sarah Merchant, as he passed by the switchboard on his way into the station.

She glanced at the notepad beside her. 'Nine so far: one retired policeman, one doctor, seven general public.'

'All with different IDs?'

'All the same.'

He frowned, recalling Collins' peculiar telephone call.

'Seems we have a real-life mystery on our hands.' Merchant had always retained a soft spot for Joseph, who was more polite and considerate than any of the other sergeants who worked out of the station – including Anna Bradley.

'I'm sure it's nothing Sergeant Collins can't handle. But thanks for the information.'

He pushed open the door separating the reception area from the inner sanctum of offices, and headed down the corridor towards the room he shared with Bradley. She caught up with him there, with two polystyrene cups in her hands.

'Machine coffee?' He made a face as she handed him one.

'Latest economy measure. No more free filter unless the Super's around or we're entertaining.'

'Great!'

She pushed open the door with her elbow. Collins was sitting behind Joseph's desk, on a swivel chair tilted to its limit.

'Comfortable?' Joseph inquired as Peter shifted the in-tray so he could rest his feet on the corner of the desk.

'Chair could be softer.'

'Where's the fire?' Bradley demanded, dumping her handbag and setting the coffee on her desk.

'No fire. Boss wants to sort out work schedules for tomorrow in the light of information received.'

'Speak English.' Bradley sipped her coffee, and made the same face as Joseph had done when she'd handed him his cup.

'You ready for this?' Collins picked up a sheet of paper from the desk. 'Our victim is one Anthony George, solicitor. The casualty doctor who treated him originally, telephoned to identify the man. Colleagues from his office phoned, as did his mother's cleaner, not to mention three of his friends, and the policeman, now retired, who investigated the mutilation of George's face in the mortuary of the hospital where he died.'

'Mutilation?' Bradley sat down on her chair and began to rummage through her desk drawers.

'Mutilation,' Collins repeated carefully, checking the notes he'd made. 'According to our informants, there's absolutely no doubt as to the victim's identity. Anthony George, twenty-eight years old at the time of his death two years ago, cause a heart attack following a vigorous game of squash. No doubt about his death either. It was verified by the attending doctor in casualty, and by two others. His body was also identified by his boss and by the family solicitor, due to the ill-health of his mother who was his closest living relative. I got all that from a certain Inspector Edwards who investigated the case at the time.'

'Then it's obvious our victim's got to be a close relative.' Ousted from his own desk, Joseph sat on the edge of Bradley's.

'Anthony George was an only child.'

'Then a cousin, or a look-alike. We're all supposed to have a double somewhere.'

'So close nine people feel its worthwhile phoning in to tell us that our victim is a man already dead?'

'Couldn't this have waited until tomorrow?'

'Where's your dedication, Joseph? "Strike while the iron's hot" always used to be your motto.' Collins pulled out the inevitable cigar. 'Couldn't stop you putting in the extra hours on your last case, when your lady love was at risk.'

'Joseph, Bradley, thanks for coming in.' Evans strode into the office, several sheets of fax paper in his hand. 'I got the Crawley Woods station to send us their files on the George case.' Pushing the clutter – and Collins' feet – aside on Joseph's desk he spread out the faxes. 'Anthony George's face was removed from his corpse shortly after his death.'

'Removed?' Bradley looked at Collins. 'I thought you said it was mutilated?'

'According to the pathologist's report it was skinned.' Evans read swiftly.

'As in rabbit?'

'There was no question of a suspicious death. According to this, Anthony George died in a casualty unit. After his death was certified, his body was taken to the hospital mortuary. The attendant there was halfway through laying it out when he was called away to pick up another corpse. Contrary to hospital regulations, he didn't lock the mortuary door behind him when he left, and on his return he found that Anthony George was minus his face.'

'But surely you can't think that our "Tony" and this Anthony George are one and the same?' Joseph protested.

'Obviously not.' Evans continued to flick through the faxes. 'But there's something else here, something the Super at the Crawley Woods station particularly mentioned . . . Here we are. It's a clipping from a newspaper.'

'Giving a clairvoyant's number?'

'What would we do without your humour, Collins.' Bradley made a concertina of her cup and tossed it into the bin.

'It's a report on a plastic-surgery technique being pioneered in America. Face transplants for burns and accident victims. It explains here that a complete face transplant can save years of surgery. That a face from a suitable donor could be grafted on all in one, ears, nose and all, which would be a vast improvement on the bone grafts and screw-in ears they're using for burns victims at the moment.'

'Spare us the details.'

'Squeamish, Bradley?' Collins needled.

'I've just eaten.'

'So what are you saying?' Joseph slid off Bradley's desk and paced over to the window. 'That this Tony was wearing Anthony George's face?'

'It's an interesting theory. Interesting enough for the people who held the open file on the George case to consider.'

'Science fiction.'

'Science fact, once articles like these are published,' Evans replied seriously. 'You can bet your last pound that, before publication of this article, there'd already been one or two cases of the technique being tried and tested. Right, let's start planning for an early start tomorrow. First thing, Joseph, you and I check with O'Kelly to see if he's come up with anything new on our victim – and we'll also run this,' he held up the report, 'by him. Then we go to the police laboratory. Collins, you and Bradley drive to Crawley Woods – interview as many of these informants as you can. Oh, and if you have time, check around the hospital in which Anthony George died.'

'After two years, what do you expect us to find?'

'Even if you are Drug Squad, you're experienced enough to recognise it when you see it, Collins.'

'I thought I'd been drafted in to check this Tony's drug-pushing activities.'

'Will this warrant an overnight?' Bradley asked.

'If you've any leads to follow. So best pack a bag.'

'Goody.'

'This is *work*.' Evans looked sternly from Bradley to Collins.

'I can't speak for Bradley, but my intentions are strictly honourable,' Collins protested. 'Besides, by the time the force has finished with me I'm only good for sleeping anyway.'

'All sleeping time cancelled until this case is solved. Pick you up at eight tomorrow, Joseph?'

'No one rang in yet from Jubilee Street?' Joseph abandoned his untouched coffee on the windowsill.

'No one has a television down there,' Collins reminded him.

'Before you go, Joseph, there's one last job before bedtime. You can interview that retired policeman, Inspector Edwards. He lives on the Marina, just across the road from your place.'

'It's midnight.'

'I checked with him and it's all right. He's an ex-copper, so he knows the score. He's expecting you.'

60

'Serves you right for leaving me to hold the fort all alone this evening.'

'Collins, you and Bradley come with me to Jubilee Street. We'll take one hostel each, and interview all the inmates who weren't around last night.'

'You weren't joking about cancelling our sleeping time, were you, Inspector?'

'The one thing you'll learn, Bradley, is that there are no jokes on the Serious Crimes Squad, except the ones played on us by the punters.' Evans ushered them out the door.

Inspector Edwards lived on the third floor of a luxury block set between the Marina and the open sea. It was barely five minutes walk from Joseph's own house, so he was tempted to call in on Lyn. But then he remembered Evans. The Inspector knew where he was going and, being a careful and methodical man, had undoubtedly made a note of Edwards' telephone number. If anything relevant cropped up Evans was quite capable of phoning there – and if he was found to be sitting at home with Lyn there'd be hell to pay.

So, turning the steering wheel left instead of right, he pulled up in the *Residents Only* parking bay of Grenville Court, and cut the engine. He stepped out of his car and locked it, then turned to look across to the sea, and the short, renovated, early-Victorian terrace that fronted it. His own house was the third in the row, all the windows were shrouded in darkness. There was no point in rushing this interview. Lyn had clearly gone to bed.

Pocketing his car keys, he walked up to the foyer. The night porter had locked the internal doors, but he could see him, sitting behind a desk, peaked cap pushed to the back of his head, reading the *Sun*. Trevor pressed the buzzer.

Without bothering with the intercom, the porter rose from his chair and unlocked the door.

'Sergeant Joseph?'

'Yes.'

'Mr Edwards said to expect you. Third floor, apartment eleven.'

Joseph took the stairs. Six months ago he hadn't been capable of taking a single step unaided. He'd discarded his walking stick only three weeks ago, and there were still occasions when he missed it. Multiple leg fractures didn't heal easily, but exercise was supposed to quicken the process.

'Sergeant Joseph?'

'It's good of you to see me at this hour, Inspector Edwards.'

'Plain "Mr" will do now, Sergeant. Come in.'

The ex-Inspector was a tall, spare, upright man. His apartment, for all the pretensions of luxury, three-inch-deep grey carpeting, long, elegant navy-blue velvet drapes, and enormous picture windows designed to make the most of the view over both the sea and Marina, was simply furnished in a strictly masculine style. It contained three enormous leather recliner chairs, a television and video recorder housed above a small cabinet which presumably held tapes, and an ultra-modern glass coffee table. There was nothing else. Not a single picture or photograph, nothing to give a hint as to the character of the owner.

Typical retired policeman, Joseph decided cynically. Casualty of the force in the relationship stakes. Nothing to do, nowhere to go, no partner to love, just television to watch, and public-spirited telephone calls to make in the hope that he could be of use to his ex-colleagues. This man had lived for his work, and now had nothing to live for at all.

'I remember only too well what it's like, starting a new investigation. Would you like something to eat or drink?' Edwards offered. 'Coffee? Tea? Or, if it's the end of a long day, something stronger?'

'Coffee would be fine, thank you.'

'I've made some sandwiches,' Edwards called back as he disappeared into the kitchen. 'We don't often use this place and when we do we tend to eat out, so I can't offer you anything substantial.'

We! Joseph looked around again for evidence of a woman's touch.

Edwards reappeared with a tray set out with plates, knives, mustard, milk, sugar and two porcelain cups and saucers. He set it down and returned to the kitchen, emerging again with a steaming, hot jugful of ground coffee and the sandwiches.

'Milk and sugar?'

'Neither, thank you. This isn't your home?' Knowing what apartments on the Marina cost, and what inspectors on the force earned, Trevor was surprised at the mention of another place.

'My wife calls it our summer place, but after living on a farm all her life she can't stand it here. I think it's the thought of people, as opposed to animals, all around her. We rent it out a lot, and use it for house exchanges abroad. Now that I've retired, we do a fair amount of travelling. My wife handed over management of her farm to her son, but she still breeds dogs and horses, so when we're here in the UK we tend to live in the country.'

Her son? A second marriage?

'But it *is* useful during the sailing season.'

'You have a yacht?' Suddenly Joseph was very interested in Edwards. He represented a rare glimpse of how life could be after the force.

'Racing dinghy. My interest – not my wife's. But when she inherited this place from her father, the two seemed to go together. He bought the apartment as an investment just three months before he died, and never set foot in it. He would have hated it, anyway. Like my wife he was more a country dweller than a water-and-concrete person.'

'That's *one* way of describing the Marina.' Joseph sipped the coffee and set about revising his initial impressions of this man.

'I've just had my boat overhauled in dry dock, ready for the first race of the season, so I wanted to see it put in the water myself. Stupid, really. Chap who looks after it for me is more than capable. It was a long, cold day so I thought I'd have a few drinks' – he got up and opened the cabinet, and pulled out a brandy bottle – 'watch some TV and have an early night. Then I saw that newsflash.'

'You headed the team on the Anthony George case?'

'Yes – not that we gave it all the manpower or attention it

63

deserved. The George case cropped up at a time when we were already working on half-a-dozen top priorities. Like everyone else, I assumed that whoever did it was a nut. One of the tabloids even mentioned black magic, and the rumours started flying thick and fast. Then, about a year after it happened, I spotted an interesting article.'

'Inspector Evans has a copy of it.'

'Says something for my old station that it's still there in the file.' He poured a generous measure of brandy into his coffee, then offered the bottle to Trevor who shook his head. 'I thought there might be something in that, but our investigations drew a blank. There was no programme of face transplants in the UK at the time. I checked with a plastic surgeon in Harley Street: top man in his field. He agreed that face transplants were possible, in theory, but he said that you'd need to remove the donor face with total precision, and keep it in exactly the right conditions until it could be used. When I showed him photographs of Anthony George's corpse minus the face, he agreed it could have been a surgical removal. But it could also have been done by someone with a sound knowledge of skinning animals. Without first-hand examination, it was impossible to tell.'

'Wasn't there a postmortem?'

'For the heart attack, yes. But we didn't even consider the possibility that the face had been surgically removed until I saw that article later, and by then George had been dead and cremated for twelve months. The pathologist who examined the body decided that the face had probably been removed with a scalpel. I studied his report then, but the case wasn't homicide, although it held a certain macabre interest, and with three full-blown murder investigations then on my hands, the theft of Anthony George's face didn't seem all that important at the time. I'm not making any apologies for relegating it to open-file, low-importance status. We were short-staffed, and had received our orders to prioritise.'

'What about George's relatives?'

'There were none to speak of. His mother was terminally ill with cancer. Her doctor wouldn't even allow us to interview her. He said the upset might prove too much. She died not long after, anyway.'

'Girlfriend?'

'I believe he was of the other persuasion. We interviewed the man who ran a pub around the corner from George's office. At the time, he appeared distraught, but when I called in there again just before I retired there was another young fellow around.'

'His name? The first man?'

Edwards shook his head. 'I can't remember, but that will be in the file, too.'

'What about an inheritance?'

'If you're thinking about someone going to all this trouble to impersonate him, forget it. I've already travelled down that road and ran into a stone wall. Anthony George was comfortably off, and with insurance policies he left about two hundred thousand, but it all went to the mother.'

'And when the mother died?'

'I checked on that, too. She left half a million. It was divided equally between the British Heart Foundation and various cancer charities.'

'No other beneficiaries?'

'Nothing to speak of. I think the housekeeper and the cleaner got something. But nothing spectacular.' Edwards heaped three of the sandwiches on his plate and sat back in his chair. 'It was really eerie seeing that face again tonight.'

'You're that sure it was George's?'

'Absolutely,' he replied with the confidence of a trained eye. 'I studied that same face for weeks after that newspaper article was published. I sifted through dozens of photographs of Anthony George . . . I was winding down to retirement, and things were going at a slower pace then,' he explained in answer to Joseph's quizzical glance. 'I even had one photograph pinned above my desk. The man in that video had the same mole high on his right cheek, the same scar below the bottom lip. It was listed in his passport as a distinguishing mark. Someone – I think it may have been his mother's solicitor – told us he'd banged his chin and put his teeth through his lip as a child.'

'You really do know that face.' Joseph pushed his pencil into his notebook and took a sandwich.

'If you'd studied it as long as I had, Sergeant, you would know it, too.'

'I have a feeling I may be doing just that,' Joseph replied drily, before biting into his sandwich.

It was one-thirty before Joseph reached home. Remembering that the Inspector was picking him up in the morning, he left his car in the road so Lyn would be able to get hers out of the drive if she was working an early shift. He opened the front door and stole softly inside. Lyn had emptied and restacked the dishwasher, the kitchen work surfaces had been cleared, including the remains of the meal they had eaten earlier.

Creeping up the stairs, he quietly opened the bedroom door. Light shone through the French windows, throwing the shadows of the balcony's wrought-iron scrollwork over the carpet and on to the bed. Lyn was lying on her side, the duvet pulled close to her chin, her eyes closed, her breathing slow and steady.

Treading stealthily, Trevor picked up the alarm clock from his bedside table and carried it into the bathroom, lest the noise of setting it disturb her. Too tired to shower, he stripped off his clothes, threw them into the linen basket, and cleaned his teeth.

Inching back the duvet he lay alongside her, waiting for his body to warm up to her temperature before daring to touch her. But sleep overtook him long before he summoned up the courage to place his arm around her waist . . .

The alarm woke him. He fumbled for his clock, only to realise the ringing had come from Lyn's side of the bed. He turned over just in time to see her back disappearing through the bathroom door.

He headed down the passage into the other bathroom. Since early-morning shifts had started creating problems, he had got into the habit of keeping a spare selection of toiletries there. Perhaps if he managed to make breakfast, it would go some way towards appeasing her.

Five minutes later, dressed in light-coloured slacks and dark open-necked shirt, he opened the fridge door. Nothing but party leftovers.

He moved the clingfilm back from a salad bowl. It might last today but no longer. He then took out four eggs and the butter. Rapidly he ground coffee, scrambled eggs, put toast in the toaster – and had it all ready waiting on the table just as she came downstairs.

'Breakfast?' He held his breath, hoping to evoke a smile from her.

'I haven't time.'

'It's only six-thirty.'

'I promised to pick up one of the girls whose car broke down.'

'How about a piece of toast?' He offered her the plate.

She reached out and took a slice. 'What time will you be home tonight?'

'I don't know.'

'Then you won't mind if I go to the cinema with the girls.'

'No, of course I won't mind. Lyn . . .?'

'Talk to me another time. Must go.' Leaving half the slice of toast on the table, she hurried out through the door.

He stood and stared at the breakfast he'd prepared, then slowly picked up the plates and scraped them into the bin. It wasn't until he went upstairs to make the bed that he noticed the gift box on the bedside table. He left it where it was.

'Where first?' Anna Bradley looked up from the map she was using to plot a route.

'The station for a courtesy call,' Collins suggested. 'We'll be operating in their territory.'

'I thought the Inspector had all their files last night.'

'He did, but you know as well as I do there's always things that aren't in the files. Joseph got some of them last night from the chap who'd originally been in charge of the investigation.'

'You telephoned Joseph?'

'At seven.'

'Disturbing the love birds?'

'Disturbing nothing. Lyn was already at work.'

'I've a feeling that one's about to fly the nest.'

'That's Joseph's business, not ours.'

'But it has been our business, and it still is. We're all in the same boat. I've four long-term but broken relationships behind me. Word is you've been married . . .'

'What's this? Auntie Anna's marital guidance hour?'

'Don't you ever wish you were a civilian with a nice, normal job and a regular home life?'

'Only when I'm sharing a car with a female sergeant who practises psychology for beginners.'

'Go on, Collins, admit it. You miss a woman in your life.'

'Only sexually, and if you're offering . . .'

'I'm not offering anything at this hour.'

'Pity, I know of a nice little lay-by.'

'I outgrew car sex in my teens.'

'A staid lady.'

'Staid nothing . . .'

'We're here.' He steered the car through a set of low gates into a parking bay. 'Right, first stop the files – just to check nothing was missed last night.'

'I hate "just checking",' she grumbled.

'Then you should have stuck to housework, Bradley, instead of joining the force.'

'Just the people I want to see.' Mulcahy had waylaid Evans and Joseph as they entered the station.

'Not for long, I hope,' Evans demurred. 'We're on our way to the mortuary.'

'Aren't we all?' Mulcahy quipped.

'Not this week, I hope.'

'Forensic reports came in.' Mulcahy waved a sheaf of paper at his office door, and they followed him inside.

'Did they get any prints off the hands?' Joseph asked.

'They're still working on them. Trying out a new technique, nothing useable has come of it so far. But they did come up with a set of smudges and a beautiful set of clear prints from the bottle.'

'Smudges as in gloves?' Evans questioned.

'As in gloves,' Mulcahy agreed. 'Looks like it was handled by two people. The prints are being checked through the computer now.'

'Did they come up with anything else?'

'They're running the boot past possible manufacturers, but even if they track down the maker, I've a feeling it's not going to be that useful. We've circulated the charity shops with a description, in the hope that someone will remember selling them.'

'He could have picked them up directly from the hostel or from a clothing skip.'

'I'm aware of that, Joseph,' Mulcahy said irritably. 'I'm also aware that the press are having a field day.' He pushed a newspaper across his desk towards them. The headlines were three inches high: WHO CARES? 'According to them, not the police,' Mulcahy continued acidly. 'Graphic descriptions of lingering death by burning, and screams – and us not trying very hard.'

'Looks about par for the course to me.' Evans slid the paper back to Mulcahy.

'Upstairs isn't happy.'

Joseph crossed his arms and leant against the door, wondering how much of this Evans was going to stand. In his experience, upstairs was never happy. And the pressure always came with the impossible cases. He'd never heard of an officer receiving a pat on the back for solving a case quickly, but they sure as hell always got a kick in the rear for some reporter's vivid imagination, as though the officer in question had personally written the article.

'I'll get back to you after we've had a word with O'Kelly.' Evans put his hand on the door.

'Where are Collins and Bradley?'

'Checking out the leads we had in after last night's screening.'

'The dead man?' Mulcahy dismissed, scornfully. 'Surely you're not wasting time on that?'

'We've had no other positive ID.'

'It could be a look-alike relative,' Joseph suggested.

'Keep me informed.'

'We will, sir,' Evans said evenly, as he finally opened the door.

'I thought you'd be around this morning.' O'Kelly delved into the abdominal cavity of the corpse laid out before him, and snipped. Moments later he lifted out an entire liver.

'Found anything else?' Evans asked.

'Alcohol in the bloodstream. There was even enough left in the foot to test.'

'High?'

'Yes, but the reading we took can't be taken as gospel. Some blood sugars turn to alcohol after death.'

'Given that we found a whisky bottle nearby, was there enough to assume he was drunk?'

'At least more than double the drink-drive limit.'

'Forensics found one set of prints and a few smudges on the whisky bottle.'

'Killer wore gloves?'

'Could be – if the bottle is connected to the case.'

'I came across a couple of other things that might interest you.' Patrick dumped the liver into a tray, and handed it to his assistant. 'Freeze, then slice for cross-sections.'

'Nice job,' Evans commented.

'Evidence in an industrial compensation case.' Patrick pulled off his gloves, binned them, and put on a fresh pair, before walking to the bank of drawers against the far wall. He pulled out the one holding the charred remains of the victim.

'Here we are.' He picked up the piece of cheekbone with the shreds of flesh still clinging to it, then another sliver which resembled a slice of dried bark. 'This is, or rather was, facial skin. Though we peeled it off the kneecap. Under the microscope we found a series of slashes running across it.'

'Like a skinning?' Joseph suggested.

'Not like a skinning at all. Some of these slashes can be matched with cuts running across the skull. I think whoever did this went berserk. Cut the face to ribbons! Even if the victim hadn't been burnt, I think identification would have been pretty difficult.'

Dan looked up from the notes he was making. 'Anything else?'

'Some people are never satisfied.'

'Can we run something by you?'

'As long as it's in my office over coffee. I've been on my feet all night.'

'Nothing for me, thanks.' Joseph had been served O'Kelly's specimen-beaker coffee before. No matter how many times Patrick and his assistants assured him that a few beakers were kept aside just for coffee, he couldn't bring himself to drink from them.

'Inspector?'

'Nothing for me either, thanks.'

'Just one, then,' O'Kelly called to his assistant, before slumping in the chair behind the desk.

'You ever heard of face transplants?'

'Is the force now keeping up with the latest developments in plastic surgery?'

'Only since our victim was identified as a dead man.'

'That's interesting.'

'Did you notice any signs of surgery on his face?'

'You saw what was left. I've showed you what I've got. I'm not a miracle worker.'

'But, you reckon face transplants are possible?'

'Oh, yes.'

'In America?'

'Here.'

'London?'

'Here,' O'Kelly repeated. 'In the Severe Burns Unit.'

'In the General?'

'Burns Unit was relocated here two weeks ago. Don't you read the papers? There was an official opening. Royalty . . .'

'And they've actually carried out face transplants?'

'I had a drink with the chap in charge the other night. Nice fellow. We were talking over the procedures for harvesting material from donors via the morgue. He's only attempted two so far, but apparently they've been quite spectacularly successful.'

71

'He's done them *here*?'

O'Kelly shook his head. 'London. Both on women. One born with malformations; the other a burns victim.'

'And the press hasn't reported them.'

'Apart from a couple of general articles printed in America, which one of the Sundays picked up and reprinted here, the press has been quite deliberately kept in the dark about the programme. As I mentioned, both transplants were physically successful, but *mentally* appears to be another matter. Both recipients have suffered severe psychological problems in adapting to their new image.'

'I can understand that,' Joseph said. 'Must be quite a shock to look in the mirror and see another face staring back at you.'

'You sure there's been no case yet of a male face transplant here?' Evans probed.

'Until last week I didn't know anything except what I'd picked up from the odd item printed in the press. You'd be better off speaking to the chap in charge of the Burns Unit. It's easy enough to find. It cost forty million to build, and thirty-six of those went on the foyer alone.'

'What's his name?'

'Smith. Mark Smith. But you won't get him this week. He flew out to a conference in America this morning. His assistant should be around, though. Dr Randall.' He glanced at Joseph. 'She'll be able to tell you all you want to know. She got the job because she's already familiar with the procedures involved. Before she came here, she was assisting the chap who pioneered the surgery in the States. It seems the first operations were carried out in a leper colony in Africa. Good place to try out experimental medical techniques.'

'No one with money enough to sue when things go wrong, you mean.'

'You've got it in one, Inspector.'

Chapter Five

'Mr Marks will see you now, Sergeant Collins, Sergeant Bradley.'

Brian Marks' officious, middle-aged secretary picked up their empty coffee cups from the solicitor's impersonal cream-and-brown waiting room. 'But I must warn you he is giving you what is left of his lunch hour, and he has an appointment with a client in fifteen minutes. If you had rung ahead, we could have arranged a time more suited to both yourselves and Mr Marks.'

'Fifteen minutes will be more than sufficient,' Bradley interrupted, wary of Collins cutting in with something likely to upset the woman. 'We appreciate him fitting us in at such short notice.'

Brian Marks turned out to be a tall, balding and surprisingly handsome man in his late sixties. He rose from his desk and ushered them to seats set around a low coffee table standing in front of a window which overlooked a vista of budding and blooming parkland. The office was vast. High-ceilinged, oak-panelled, it had once been the drawing-room or dining-room of a well-to-do Victorian gentleman. Now it was lined with bookshelves designed to complement the panelling. These held the usual selection of law tomes Bradley expected to find in a solicitor's office, plus a few books on art and antiques that she hadn't.

'Coffee?' he enquired.

'Your secretary's already given us some, thank you.'

'Did she tell you I can unfortunately only allow you fifteen minutes? Normally I'd be only too delighted to assist the police, but this meeting is something I simply cannot postpone. However, if you'd like to come back later . . .'

'I doubt that will be necessary.' Collins flipped through the notes he'd prepared at the station. 'You were Anthony George's solicitor, and his mother's too, I believe?'

'I was.' A frown darkened the bland, businesslike features. 'Such a tragedy.'

'In what way, Mr Marks?'

'Anthony dying the way he did – on the threshold of life. He had so much to look forward to. And then there was that terrible business in the hospital.'

'You're referring to the mutilation of his corpse in the mortuary?'

'Indeed.'

'How did his mother react to the news?' Joseph had discovered that the inspector in charge had never even interviewed the mother, and he'd found no mention of her in the notes covering the George case at the local police station.

'I'm afraid we never told her, Sergeant.'

'We?'

'I was executor of both Mrs George's and her husband's wills. Anthony's father predeceased her by some twenty years, and there were no close relatives. As Anthony was only ten when his father died, Mrs George turned to this firm, and consequently myself, for advice on personal matters as well as legal and financial affairs. When Anthony died, I took it upon myself to arrange the identification of his body, to organise his funeral and, as executor of his will, to settle his estate. However, I was very ably and generously assisted by Anthony's employer, who was aware of the extent of Mrs George's ill health at the time. She herself was in no state to attend to the details, or even join the mourners at Anthony's funeral.'

'I understand she inherited the bulk of her son's estate?'

'All of it, Sergeant Collins. His father left him one hundred thousand pounds in trust. By dint of judicial investment, we saw him through college and doubled that initial investment. It all reverted to his mother on his death.'

'There were no other bequests?'

'I believe we gave one or two items to his close friends, as mementoes. There is a list in the file but, as I remember, there was nothing of any great value.'

Collins referred to the notes he'd made earlier and there was no mention of any bequests. 'If it's not too much trouble, I'd like to see that list.'

'It may take Miss Wilkinson a little time to locate the file, but if you call back at the end of the day, she should have it ready for you.'

'I'd appreciate that. Can you confirm that Mrs George died shortly after her son?'

'Less than two months after.'

'And her estate?'

'It was divided between the charities specified in her will. Both her and her husband's wills were quite specific. They left their entire estates to each other and, in the event of their death, everything reverted to their son Anthony. Unfortunately we then had to resort to a clause specifying certain charities in the event of the untimely demise of the entire family.'

'And *they* were?' Collins had them written down in his notebook, but he wanted to hear it from Marks.

'Medical research charities – heart disease and cancer.'

'They split everything between them?'

'Apart from three separate bequests, one of twenty thousand pounds and two of five which Mrs George added in a codicil the year before her death.'

'The recipients?'

'Her live-in housekeeper who had worked for the George family for over thirty years, and a daily cleaner and a jobbing gardener who had worked for Mrs George's mother for ten years before joining her.' Marks gave Collins a withering look that might have intimidated a lesser man. 'Sergeant, I answered all these questions two years ago, when the police investigated the mutilation of Anthony George's body subsequent to his death. Has this case been reopened?'

'Not exactly.'

'Then may I ask why you are here?' The words were polite but couched in steel.

'I take it you don't watch much television, Mr Marks?' Collins reached into his inside pocket and extracted a brown card folder. He laid it on the table in front of the solicitor.

'I don't watch *any* television, Sergeant. Neither my eyes nor the programmes are what they used to be. I prefer listening to the radio.' He picked up the folder and opened it. The colour instantly drained from his face.

'We have reason to believe that man was murdered in a run-down dock area seventy miles from here two nights ago. As far as we can ascertain, he was a homeless vagrant who was in the habit of frequenting hostels. To the people who manage the hostels he was known only as "Tony",' Collins continued flatly, making no allowances for the shock etched on Marks' face. 'When the video clip those stills were lifted from was shown on the news last night, nine members of the public telephoned the hotline. All of them said they recognised the man as Anthony George.'

'But that's impossible. I identified Anthony George's body myself, more than two years ago.' Marks dropped the photographs on to the table and leant back in his chair, pale and trembling.

'I understand his face was completely removed after death. Under the circumstances, could you have made a mistake?'

'No, Sergeant. There is no possibility that I made a mistake. Anthony George suffered his first heart attack in the squash club. He was driven to the hospital by a friend, who, knowing of his mother's condition, then contacted me and Fraser Caldwell . . .'

'Fraser Caldwell?'

'I spoke of him earlier. He employed Anthony in his practice. Caldwell, Caldwell and Buckingham, solicitors. Anthony died of a second heart attack in casualty, before either of us arrived. We were, however, both in time to formally identify him before his body was removed to the mortuary.'

'Then how do you explain this, Mr Marks?'

'I can't, Sergeant Collins, other than to say that we are all supposed to have a double somewhere.'

'One with the same mole on the cheek, and the same scar below the bottom lip?'

'I noticed,' Marks countered frigidly. 'But one thing I do

know, Sergeant' – he leaned forward in his chair and closed the folder – 'is that Anthony George was most definitely dead when I last saw him.'

'Then you do not identify this man as Anthony George?'

'I agree that, whoever he is—'

'Was,' Bradley corrected.

'He certainly looks like him,' Marks continued swiftly. 'But I also know that dead men are not in the habit of walking the streets.'

'So you can offer no explanation for the marked similarity?'

'Other than to say I believe someone is playing a very sick joke. Both Anthony and his mother are clients of mine.'

'Were, Mr Marks.' Collins stared at him coolly. 'Surely you must have closed their files by now.'

'I administered the family's affairs for many years. I watched Anthony grow up. It's not easy to come to terms with the premature death of someone you knew as a child.' He glanced ostentatiously at his watch. 'I'm sorry, Sergeant, but I did mention another appointment.' He left his chair and walked to the door.

'So you did.' Collins rose from his seat. 'If you would like to keep those photographs, Mr Marks, you may.'

'No, but thank you for offering, Sergeant Collins. Actually, I find them quite disconcerting.'

'If you remember anything, anything at all . . .'

'I have had two years to remember, Sergeant. I hardly think I am going to come up with anything new now.'

'He was in love with the mother.'

'What?' Collins slammed on the brakes when a car cut in front of him as he pulled out of the car park.

'Brian Marks. He was in love with the mother,' Anna Bradley pronounced authoritatively. 'Didn't you notice his expression whenever he mentioned her name. How it grew softer . . .'

'You sound like an advert for washing-up liquid.'

'Take my word for it. There was something going on between that man and Mrs George.'

'The day I accept a female's intuition as hard evidence is the day I retire from the force.'

'I may hold you to that.'

'Try me.'

'I intend to – tonight, if we stay over. Turn left up ahead, for the hospital.'

Collins glanced at her out of the corner of his eye, as he rounded the corner. He had to admit Bradley was different: the first woman he'd ever worked with who could be counted on to answer back.

Trevor Joseph stood in the foyer of the new burns unit, and reflected that Patrick O'Kelly's comments about cost had not been understated. On a Saturday you couldn't move in the town for community-spirited people collecting signatures in an attempt to keep the General's casualty unit operational twenty-four hours a day. Six months ago, as part of a cost-cutting exercise, the Health Authority had diverted all night-time emergencies to another hospital eight miles, and a delaying network of small roads, out of town; and as well as the petitions against this economy, collecting boxes were waved under every passing nose in an effort to raise money to buy vital equipment for the ITU or the premature-baby unit. In the light of such desperate, life-threatening deficiencies, it seemed obscene to spend so much money on white and silvered marble tiles, chrome-plated staircase rails, gushing fountains, and more potted plants than he'd seen outside of the botanical gardens attached to the university.

'Can I help you, sir?'

Even the receptionists were dressed in tailored blue uniforms trimmed with silver, no doubt carefully and expensively designed to co-ordinate with their surroundings.

'I'm here to see Dr Randall.'

'Do you have an appointment?'

'She's expecting me.'

'Your name, sir?'

'Joseph. Sergeant Trevor Joseph.' He flashed his identity card.

'There's nothing booked for Dr Randall under that name.' The receptionist was young, attractive. He wondered what training procedures hospital bureaucracy used in order to turn people like this into automatons.

'Mr O'Kelly's just made the appointment for me. He phoned through from the mortuary.'

'Sergeant Joseph, it *is* good to see you again.'

It was a voice from his past, and one he'd never expected to hear again outside of his dreams. He turned his back on the reception desk and drank in her image. Five foot eight, slim, dark-haired, and very, very beautiful. The looks matched the voice. It was her. Only the name, Randall, was unfamiliar.

'There's no appointment booked for Sergeant Joseph, Dr Randall,' the receptionist reproached.

'There wouldn't be, Mary. It's just been made.'

'We can't be expected to keep a check—'

'There was no time to inform you, Mary.' Polite, charming, but firm – exactly as he remembered her. 'If you'd like to come this way, Sergeant.'

At that moment Joseph would have followed her, blindly and trustingly, to the ends of the earth. He climbed the stairs slowly behind her, admiring the long, black-stockinged legs, just as he'd done two years before. She had not cut her hair shorter, or changed the style, but still wore it in a knot twisted low at the nape of her neck. Once, he had seen it hanging loose, and it descended almost to her waist.

'Coffee?' She showed him into a magnificent office furnished, like the foyer, in a mixture of bleached white wood trimmed with chrome, and pale grey carpeting.

'Yes, please.'

She pressed a button on the desk telephone and ordered coffee through the intercom. 'You're looking fine. Much better than the last time I saw you.'

'When was that?'

'On the beach, just after you'd been thrown off the pier. None of us thought you'd make it.'

'There were times when I wondered if I would, myself.' He took a deep breath, wishing for the first time in his life that he

79

had one of Collins' cigars in his hand. 'Peter Collins told me you went to Africa.'

'I did. I worked in a leper colony there.'

He remembered O'Kelly's briefing. 'Then you're the assistant who carried out face transplants?'

'Partial ones,' she qualified. 'We started with ears, noses, and lips. But I've only assisted at two full-blown transplants. Come in,' she called in reply to a knock at the door, clearing a space on her desk for the tray of coffee her secretary brought in.

'Hold all my calls for half an hour, Julie,' she ordered. 'Black with no sugar?'

'You remember.' He was barely aware of the secretary closing the door on them.

'I remember a great deal about you, Sergeant Joseph. You made the most difficult time of my life just about bearable.'

'You've married again?'

'No.' She frowned slightly, then smiled, her silver-grey eyes lighting up in amusement. 'When I went to Africa, I reverted to my maiden name. The name Sherringham held too many memories, both personal and within the medical establishment.'

'That I can believe.'

'And you?'

'Me?' he asked in bewilderment, forgetting everything, including his reason for visiting, in the face of her sudden and totally unexpected reappearance in his life.

'Are you here on business, or just looking up an old friend?'

He recalled that peculiar glint in O'Kelly's eye when Dr Randall's name had first been mentioned. He must have been wearing his heart on his sleeve when he'd investigated the disappearance of Daisy Sherringham's husband, for the pathologist to have eyed him that way now.

'Business,' he replied quickly. But even as he launched into a brief description of the facts of the case as he understood them, and the possible, if far-fetched, theory of face transplant, he couldn't stop studying her. Noting the changes. The tan on her face and hands, the loss of weight that had thrown her cheekbones into greater prominence, the appearance of the first fine lines around her eyes. There had been a time, and not that long ago, when all his wildest, most cherished dreams had centred around Daisy Sherringham. And, now she was actually in front of him, he was gabbling out the facts of his current investigation like an idiot. It would be a miracle if she understood what he was telling her. He wasn't even sure he understood it himself.

'This man's face was surgically removed two years ago.' Daisy stopped him mid-flow.

'Yes.'

'There wasn't anyone carrying out face transplants in this country two years ago.'

'Are you sure?'

'Of course, I can't be sure. But, as far as I'm aware, most of the pioneering work was carried out in America – and, for legal reasons, Africa.'

'No one likely to sue in Africa?'

'That sounds like one of Sergeant Collins' remarks.'

'I still work with him occasionally.'

'On this case, too?'

Joseph nodded.

'Let's say that the Americans have gone litigation-crazy over medical matters in the last few years. It's getting to the stage where doctors are afraid to treat any patients in case they decide to sue at a later date for something that wasn't even taken into consideration at the time. And lepers, more than most, are generally prepared to take the risk of pioneering surgery to improve their lot.'

'So how many face transplants have been carried out in *this* unit?'

'None so far, but we have three possible recipients waiting for suitable donors.'

'Men or women?'

'Two men, one woman.'

'And two have already been carried out in London – both on women?'

'I suppose Patrick O'Kelly told you that. The senior consultant, Mark Smith, has become quite friendly with him. There are other plastic surgeons operating similar programmes in this country but, as far as I know, none of them has transplanted a full face as yet, apart from Mark.'

'You're in touch with these other teams?'

'Yes. Contrary to what the newspapers may think, we do actually try to co-operate with one another. Most doctors do, when they're practising techniques still in the experimental stage. That way our failures can become someone's else's successes, and vice-versa.'

'Could you give me the names of the other teams – and which hospitals they're operating from?'

'I can do better than that. If there's nothing top secret about what you've just told me, I can run the scenario by them and see if they come up with any ideas.'

'Would you?'

'For you, Sergeant Joseph, anything.'

'You used to call me Trevor.'

'And you used to call me Daisy.' She looked away from him towards the panorama of sand and sea framed in the window. The tide was out. The vast expanse of beach was speckled with the miniature figures of lugworm diggers. 'If you give me your telephone number, I'll get back to you.'

'How long will it take you to get the information?'

'That's what I like about the police. You offer to do them a favour, and they want it yesterday.'

'I won't deny we would like the information as soon as possible, but I thought perhaps you could give it to me over dinner.'

'You've changed. Eighteen months ago it would have taken you eight weeks of acquaintanceship to make a proposition like that.'

'Since I last knew you, I've begun to live more like a normal person and less like a hermit.'

'I don't want to disrupt your life.'

'You wouldn't be.'

'In that case, why don't we have dinner tomorrow night? If there's any news, I should have it by then.'

'I'll pick you up about eight.'

'I'm living in the same block of hospital flats I stayed in last time I worked here.'

'I'll be there.'

He shook her hand, resisting the temptation to hold it a fraction longer than necessary.

'Look, Sergeant . . .'

'I'm Collins. She's Bradley.' Collins ground the stub of his cigar to dust in the ashtray in front of him. It was the tail end of a long and – what was even worse – fruitless day. They'd got no joy at the hospital, not that he'd really expected any, after two years. The shift on which that mortuary attendant had discovered Anthony George's faceless corpse had been his last. The casualty doctor, who'd telephoned the hotline, had tried to be helpful, but he could only endorse the same statement he'd made two years ago. The George family GP had dropped a few hints which Bradley had snatched as verification of a suspected affair between Mrs George and Brian Marks, a theory which did nothing to take their case any further forward. Anthony George's friends all confirmed that the man featured on television had definitely been Anthony George – which didn't help at all. And now they were at their last port of call: the pub where Inspector Edwards had found Anthony George's boyfriend, Luke Davies. He was an effeminate gay to whom Collins had taken an instant dislike but with whom Bradley had established instant rapport.

Davies, the bar manager, snapped the folder shut and handed it back to Bradley. 'All I can say is that, whoever he is, he bears an uncanny resemblance to the Anthony George I knew, and' – he glared defiantly at Collins – 'loved. But it simply can't be him.'

'Why?' Collins twirled the remaining beer around his pint glass, and downed it. It was his second, and he now intended to have a third, which would either mean Bradley driving them back, or them staying over, and at that moment he didn't give a damn which.

'Because I drove Anthony to the hospital after his first heart attack. I sat in the waiting room while they tried to resuscitate him. And I held his hand just after he died.'

'And that was definitely George?' Bradley probed.

'No doubt about it.'

There was another young man in evidence, just as Inspector Edwards had said. While serving drinks behind the bar, he bestowed frequent glances in their direction, but his close attentions didn't stop Luke Davies from blotting away the tears he'd shed over Tony's' photograph with a napkin.

'All right. So let's accept that Anthony George is dead,' Collins agreed. After all these positive identifications of the corpse, that fact's been established to a point where even the Super would have to treat it as gospel. 'But you *are* aware that someone subsequently removed his face?'

'Sick bastards. If I could get hold of them, I'd kill them.' Surprisingly, neither Collins nor Bradley found anything humorous in Davies' high-pitched threat.

'Inspector Edwards suggested that you were closer to Anthony George than anyone else?'

Davies nodded, then motioned to the young man along the bar to refill their glasses.

'Have you any idea why anyone would want to impersonate him?'

'Impersonate him?' Davies gazed blankly at Collins, as the barman set a large gin and tonic before him and fresh pints in front of Bradley and Collins.

'You've agreed that the man in that video looks very like Anthony George.'

'Looks like, nothing more. From what was said on television last night, this "Tony" person was a down-and-out who lived rough and slept in hostels.'

'As far as we know.'

'Funny attempt at impersonation that lands a man out on the streets. Now, if he'd tried to take over Anthony's house and money, I could understand it. Anthony's mother had a nice place, and a few bob.'

'You got nothing after he died?' Collins probed for signs of resentment.

'I got a great deal more than I deserved. Anthony lent me the money to buy this place. I gave him a full partnership in return for his cash, but it was a private arrangement. I wanted Anthony to draw up a legal contract, but he never did. Said we didn't need one.'

'And when he died?'

'His solicitor, nice elderly chap . . .'

'Brian Marks,' Bradley supplied.

'That's him. I met him briefly at the hospital, then afterwards . . . after the funeral, that is, I visited him. I told him about our arrangement, but he said that, as there was nothing documented about any loan in Anthony's will or in his papers, the best thing for me to do was forget about it.'

'Generous of him.'

'He insisted it was what Anthony himself would have wanted. Being a solicitor, Anthony must have realised what would happen in the event of his death. A few weeks later, Mr Marks himself called in here. He brought along some of Anthony's private things from the house. Told me to take my pick. He obviously knew about us.'

'What sort of things?' Collins had taken a copy of the list that Brian Marks had compiled, but it contained no mention of any loan to Luke Davies.

'His silver hairbrushes . . . a few paintings he'd bought. Modern art, nothing very valuable – but he patronised the students at the art college, and he had a good eye.'

As this description tallied with Marks' list, Collins didn't press any further. They sipped their drinks in silence for a while.

'You know, I've been thinking about that man on TV ever since I saw the news last night. Even if I hadn't seen Anthony lying dead, there's still no way I'd believe it was him.'

'Why not?'

'He would have shot himself sooner than dress in the filthy rags that man was wearing. Anthony was fastidious to the point of annoyance. He abhorred dirt of any kind.'

'So, you don't think he could have survived Jubilee Street?'

'Jubilee Street?' Davies looked quizzically at Collins.

'The area where the down-and-out was murdered,' Bradley furnished for him.

'I don't know about Jubilee Street. But I do know he wouldn't even sleep in my bed until I'd changed the sheets and showered to rid myself of the smell of cigarettes and food.' He looked at their empty glasses. 'Another?'

'We've got to drive.'

'No one's driving anywhere,' Collins said emphatically. 'We've both just drunk three pints.'

'I've a room upstairs I can let you have.'

'As long as you bill us for it – and the drinks. This trip's on expenses.'

'Glad to.'

'In that case, another round, barman.'

Both Collins and Bradley were much the worse for wear when they finally climbed the stairs that night. The only difference between them was in the way they held their beer. Collins became slow and deliberate in speech and movement, Bradley slurred and swayed on her feet.

'We should have asked him for two rooms as it's going on our expenses,' Collins complained, as he attempted to insert the key in the lock and steady Bradley at the same time.

'I didn't hear him say he had two available.'

'I don't think you've heard anything that's been said, for the last half hour at least.' Collins finally turned the key, and kicked the door open.

'I've been thinking about this case,' Bradley complained resentfully, almost falling over Collins' feet as she tried to enter the room.

'Here, wait until I find the light switch.'

'Very nice,' she murmured, sinking down on to the king-sized bed covered in pink satin.

Collins walked across to the room's second door and opened it. The bathroom had a pale pink suite, gilt taps and green tiles. He glanced at the disposable toothbrushes, small tubes of toothpaste, and sample-sized bars of soap, and decided he could live with this for one night.

'Do you want to take first shower?' He turned around. Bradley had fallen asleep where she lay, sideways on the bed.

'Bloody women, never can hold their booze,' he grumbled, as he stripped off her shoes. The jacket was easy enough, but her blouse and skirt more complicated, with buttons and hooks in unexpected places. Either women's clothes had changed recently, or he was very out of practice. He tried not to look as he peeled off her tights, but found that impossible. She had a stunning figure. He was surprised he hadn't noticed her legs before but, then, she always wore trousers or long skirts. Not that she had any reason to.

Resisting temptation, he stopped at her bra and pants. Turning down the bedclothes, he rolled her over so her head reached the top of the bed, then covered her with the sheets and blankets. Just his luck. First time he'd been alone in a bedroom with a woman for months, and she was out cold.

Exhausted after a brainstorming session with Dan Evans and Bill Mulcahy, which had produced absolutely nothing, Trevor Joseph walked into his empty house. As he closed the door behind him, he was more preoccupied with thoughts of Daisy Sherringham – Randall, he corrected himself – than corpses without faces.

His birthday cards were still displayed on the windowsill of the living room, so he gathered them up – hesitating only as he picked up the one that Lyn had sent him. It was a humorous greetings card depicting pink and blue hippopotamuses wallowing in mud. What was he doing now thinking about one woman while living with another? He had no right to ask Daisy out to dinner. That was the kind of behaviour he'd always silently criticised Collins and other male colleagues for. It was the *screw them all; anything goes as long as we're not found out* attitude that so many men on the force adopted as a defence mechanism against the pain and trauma of constantly broken relationships.

Until now Trevor had prided himself on being honest with the women in his life – not that there'd been that many. Just two, really – Mags and Lyn. But he'd been the one to ask Lyn to move in with him, after he'd come to rely on her totally and absolutely during his darkest months in hospital. Lyn had found him at his lowest ebb, and steered him professionally, caringly, and later lovingly, back to health and what passed for normality. What right had he to forget their recent life together in order to chase rainbows. Because, whichever way he looked at it, that's what Daisy Randall represented: the brightest rainbow that ever sparkled over his horizon. And he'd never really known her – never as much as held hands with her, let alone kissed her.

He went into the kitchen and opened the fridge. Seeing there were still party leftovers, he opened the bin and shovelled the debris into it before stacking the dirty plates in the dishwasher. Then he opened the door of the freezer. What was Lyn's favourite meal? She liked light, tasty snacks: paté on toast, tuna and pasta salad, Chinese . . . that was an idea. He went to the telephone table in the hall and pulled out the drawer. Underneath a pile of business cards and leaflets that Lyn irritatingly hoarded, because they might come in 'useful', he found the menu card of the Marina takeaway. He glanced at his watch: ten-thirty. Even if Lyn had gone out for a drink, she'd be home in half an hour. He ordered a special for two, to be ready in twenty minutes. Unimaginative but quick. Then he laid the table in the dining room, with candles and the best linen he could find.

At half-past eleven the takeaway was drying up in the oven, and he was two-thirds of his way through a bottle of wine, when he heard her car pull up outside. He poured himself the last glass from the bottle as he waited.

'You're home?' She looked at him in surprise, as she opened the hall cupboard to hang her coat away.

'I ordered a takeaway. It should still be edible.'

'If only I'd known, I would have been here earlier.' The edge to her voice reminded him that she was usually the one who sat waiting – for him to return from duty.

'I don't think it's spoiled. You ready to eat now?'

She looked at the table, the candles, the empty wine bottle, and something snapped.

'I'm not hungry!'

'A drink, then?'

'There's no need to open another bottle just for me.'

'Lyn, I'm sorry. I don't like working these hours, any more than you do. But I'm a copper. It's what I do for a living. I thought you understood.'

'I do . . . I . . .' It would have been easy for her to take a step forward and fall into his arms, but pride held her back. 'I'm tired. I'm going to bed,' she said shortly. 'Don't forget to turn the oven off before you come up.'

Chapter Six

'Good morning.'

Anna Bradley opened a bleary eye to see Peter Collins, damp from the shower, a towel wrapped around his waist, and a tray of coffee in his hands.

'I rang down for this. Thought you might need it.'

'What time is it?' she slurred, her tongue suddenly feeling too large for her mouth.

'Eight.'

'Thank God for that.'

'They'll expect us back at the station in a couple of hours.'

'They can expect all they like.'

'The trouble with you, Sergeant, is you can't take your drink.'

'The last thing I remember is witnessing you in the same state.'

'Sorry to disillusion you, but it was me who undressed you.'

She lifted the bedclothes and looked down. 'You enjoy necrophilia?'

'No, which is why I stopped where I did.' He took one of the continental bowl-shaped cups and placed it on the bedside cabinet next to her.

Tucking the sheets under her arms she sat up and plumped up the pillows behind her head. 'I hope you folded my clothes neatly.'

'Neater than you would have, judging by the state of your house. Do you fancy breakfast up here or downstairs?'

'I'm not sure I can face breakfast.'

'I thought you were always hungry.'

'Did we solve anything last night?'

'Only your craving for drink.'

'What a waste of a day.'

'And night.'

'Speak for yourself, Collins. I slept.'

'Didn't we all?'

'What did you do with my handbag?'

He looked around blankly.

'You *did* bring it upstairs?'

He found it lying in the corner by the door.

'Good. Now I can dress.' She opened it and extracted a clean set of underclothes, a pair of tights, some toothpaste and a toothbrush.

'Now I know why women have suitcase-size handbags.'

'Did you check in with the station last night?'

He shook his head as he sipped his own coffee.

'Hadn't you better do so before they report us missing?' She stepped out of bed, and he ran an appraising eye over her slender, finely muscled figure.

'I'd rather stay missing for another hour or two.'

'You were the one in a hurry.'

'Not any more.'

'Work comes first, Sergeant. Go and order us some bacon and eggs. I'll eat them downstairs in ten minutes.'

'Happy birthday. It's two days late now, but it's been there in the bedroom.'

'I know. I saw it, but I didn't want to open it without you.'

'I'm here now.' Lyn was seated at the breakfast table. Trevor hadn't bothered to cook, but he had made some coffee, so she helped herself from the jug.

'Lyn . . .'

'I have to be at work in half an hour.'

'We need to talk.'

'Not first thing in the morning.'

'How many times, and in how many ways, need I apologise and explain before you'll accept that this is the way it has to be when I'm working on a case.'

'It just takes a bit of getting used to. The loneliness, the broken dates . . .'

'Broken dates?' In answer to her hard stare, he finally began to untie the ribbon on the parcel.

'Wasn't it today we were supposed to be going to the West Country?'

'There'll be other weekends.'

'When, Trevor?'

He lifted the lid of the box. Nestling on a bed of pale blue cottonwool lay a pocket watch: a silver antique. 'What can I say?' He looked at her miserably.

'Open it,' she demanded curtly.

He pressed down on the top and the cover flew open. Engraved on the inside was a dedication: *To Trevor, thank you for the happiest six months of my life.*

'I only wish that were true.'

'As I said, it just takes getting used to. Will you be home tonight?'

'No, there's a doctor I have to interview. But perhaps tomorrow.'

'Perhaps.' She slammed the front door on her way out.

'We've had a positive ID of the prints on that bottle.' Dan Evans looked across at Joseph, who sat slumped at his desk.

'Tell me they match Anthony George's, and I'll book a car to hell. Collins can drive.'

'They belong to one Philip Matthews.' Evans paced over to the window as he continued to read out the details. 'Ex-army private and deserter who ran off after laying out a superior officer. He was cashiered from the service, after serving his time in the glasshouse, then he embarked on an interesting civvy career: breaking and entering, fraudulent use of cheques and credit cards, and demanding money with menaces. Take a look. See if the same thing strikes you as struck me.' He tossed the papers over to Joseph.

'Height six-one, medium build, thirteen stone, black hair, brown eyes . . . Apart from the mole and scar, this could be Tony.'

'Descriptions match,' Evans agreed.

'Have we a picture of this Matthews?'

'Only the one faxed down the line with his record. It's pinned to the back.'

Joseph flipped over the sheets of waxy paper. The face that stared up at him, although blurred, was most definitely not the vagrant they knew as 'Tony'. It looked older, the eyes further apart, the chin longer, the mouth not as wide. 'Our killer?'

'Possibly, if that bottle actually had anything to do with the crime. But that would mean the victim himself wore gloves, and O'Kelly made no mention of them.'

'Could be they didn't survive the fire?'

'Could be. I've ordered mug-shots of Matthews. As soon as they arrive, I want you to take them down Jubilee Street and show them around. See if anyone remembers seeing Matthews there.'

'Collins and Bradley come up with anything?'

'Not even themselves.'

Joseph raised an eyebrow.

'I can hardly see Bradley succumbing to Collins' charms,' Evans commented flatly.

'Oh I don't know. He has his moments.'

'If he's having them on my squad's time, I'll make sure he won't see his bed again until this villain's caught.'

'Want me to start down Jubilee Street now?' Joseph held up the fax. 'I can photocopy this – show it to Sam Mayberry, Tom Morris, and that Salvation Army captain.'

'May as well, there's nothing else needs doing urgently. I'll be here if you need me.'

'You think we've reached a dead end?'

'Unless you can see a turning point I can't, yes.'

It was a dark, damp morning. After the sun and its brief promise of spring the day before, Joseph found the drive to the dock area more than usually depressing. Grey street followed grey street, endless rows of terraced houses shining damp and forlorn in the rain, looking ever more neglected, derelict and decaying the closer he drew to Jubilee Street.

The surroundings matched his mood. He felt that Lyn's deliberate move to distance herself from him, just when Daisy had reappeared in his life, must be a bad omen. He knew he should have forced Lyn to listen to him, talked to her about the case, tried to involve her, but he was ridiculously naive when it came to women's moods. How had he once handled similar situations with Mags? Looking back, he realised he hadn't. She, like Lyn, had absented herself with increasing frequency, both mentally and physically, until one day Collins had taken him aside and told him brutally what Mags should have told him months before: that she was embroiled in an affair with another man.

Trevor drew up outside Mayberry's hostel. Picking up one of the photocopies of the fax from the passenger seat, he stuffed it into the inside pocket of his anorak, then walked towards the battle-scarred front door.

'We're closed,' proclaimed an irate voice from inside, before he had even reached the doorstep.

'Sergeant Trevor Joseph to see Sam Mayberry,' he called back.

The sounds of feet shuffling down a passage were overtaken by swifter, surer steps. Bolts grated back inside the door.

'Trevor, it's always good to see you.' Mayberry swung the door wide open. 'Come in. Come in,' he repeated, as though he were the genial host of a pub. 'Let's go into my office. One of the boys has just lit a fire there. Would you like some tea?'

'Tea will be fine, thank you, Sam.' Trevor settled in one of the springless, hand-me-down chairs that had been repaired with slabs of foam by some job-creation scheme.

'Have you any more news on the poor soul who died?' asked Sam, as he sat down opposite him.

'We're working on it, but it's difficult.' Joseph thrust his hand into his pocket. 'I know his picture's blurred, but have you ever seen this man around the hostels?'

Sam picked up a pair of rimless spectacles from his desk, perched them on the end of his nose, and squinted through the lenses. 'Yes, I think I can say I've seen him around. But not this place. No, I've seen him queuing to get into Tom Morris's hostel across the way. If you check with him, I'm sure he'll be able to tell you something. Tom's very dedicated, and spends hours talking to his customers. He gave up a high-ranking post in Social Services – with two years secondment on a lower salary – to come down here.'

'I take it he's an idealist.'

'I prefer to call him a man who saw a need and tried to fulfil it.'

'How long has he been here, then?' Joseph asked, as a young priest carried in two cups of tea.

'Let me see . . . not all that long. Round about Christmas time, I think it was. He came down originally as part of a Social Services' working party, who were looking at the Council hostel with a view to closing it down permanently. Ben Proctor, who'd been running it, had just retired. I heard that the official line in County Hall was they could well do without the place. Fortunately that wasn't Tom Morris's opinion. He took one look at the queues for beds, and asked to be given a transfer. The reason his place looks better than ours – inside, that is – is he really knows how to put pressure on the local charity groups. He has a lot of friends who sit on the committees of voluntary bodies. In the four months since he's been here, he's managed to find money to redecorate the place from top to bottom, and put in new showers and new mattresses. It's a pity those television people didn't see fit to film inside his hostel instead of mine.'

'Wouldn't have offered the same shock value.'

'Perhaps. Tom does a good job over there. Not the same as ours, of course. It's odd, but we all seem to have specialised in some way. Captain Arkwright caters for the ladies and the young girls – God help them, they seem so much more vulnerable than the men. I get the drunks and the hopeless cases. Tom looked around, saw what was needed most, and set out to make his place a halfway house for those who really want or have the drive to get back on their feet. *And* he's succeeded. Since January he's got six young men on to training schemes and into bedsits in the town.' Sam rose from his chair and knocked out the ashes from his pipe against the grate. 'That may not sound many to you, but for each of those young men it's a triumph over odds that seemed impossibly stacked against them – before Tom arrived here.'

'I can imagine.' Joseph looked out of the window at two shambling figures wheeling a supermarket trolley towards the underpass that led into the town centre.

'Shall we go then?' Sam smiled. 'Across the street and up a social stratum?'

The hostel run by Tom Morris stank of fresh paint. The ceilings, walls and woodwork were covered in blinding white emulsion and gloss. Inexpertly applied, thick white streaks and splashes garnished a fair proportion of the cracked quarry floor-tiles; and the boundaries between gloss and emulsion wavered in places, shining on walls and dulling doors.

Tom Morris himself came down the stairs to greet them, casually dressed in an immaculate white Aran sweater and pleated brown trousers. He extended his hand, smiling when he saw Joseph studying his surroundings.

'As you see, Sergeant, this place has been decorated with more enthusiasm than expertise. The local Rotary club supplied the materials, and some of our younger inmates did the work.'

'I've been asking Tom when he's going to start on my place,' Sam chipped in.

'As soon as I've got this place straight.' Morris led the way up the stairs, and past a room on the first floor that had been turned into a makeshift café. 'Rough beginnings of a day centre,' he explained. 'It's no use giving a man somewhere to sleep, only to turf him out into the cold all day long. It's little wonder so many turn to drink and drugs.'

'A café's a beginning,' Joseph agreed.

'Oh, we have a lot more going than that. We try to persuade our regulars to improve their prospects – attending the free literacy and numeracy classes in the YMCA is a start. Two even embarked on a computer course last week.'

'See what I mean about dedication,' Sam murmured, as Morris led them into his large, cold, cluttered office.

Tom sat behind his desk, and motioned them towards the only other two chairs in the room.

'I take it you've come to ask more questions?'

'Sam thought you might know *this* man?' Joseph handed him the now crumpled photocopy.

Morris stared at it.

'I told Trevor I'd occasionally seen him queuing to get into your hostel.'

'I know the face, but he's not one of our regulars. Quite a hard man, as I recall. I threw him out four . . . no . . .' – he picked up a ledger from his desk and flicked through the pages – 'five nights ago, for hitting one of the other lads. He slammed him so hard against the wall, it's a wonder the boy wasn't seriously hurt. This man was drunk as a lord at the time.'

'Can you remember his name?'

'The boys call him "The General", but I can't tell you why. He signed in here as Philip Smith.'

'Do you know if he was ex-army?'

'No. You looking for him in connection with the murder?'

'Just want to question him at this stage, that's all.' Trevor returned the photocopy to his pocket.

'Do you think he's the killer, Trevor?' Sam Mayberry asked bluntly.

'We haven't got that far down the line yet, Sam.'

'Should we warn our clients that he's dangerous?' Morris asked.

'I thought you said you'd thrown him out.'

'I have, and banned him from the hostel, but that's not to say they won't bump into him on the streets.'

'Just ask around, if you would. Get word back to us if anyone sees him.'

'I will, but shouldn't I also warn them to stay away from him?'

'Might be just as well.' Trevor rose to his feet.

'It's a cold, miserable day out there, Sergeant. Can I offer you something before you go. Coffee, tea?'

'Nothing, thank you. I really must be going.'

'I'll have a cup of tea if I may, Tom.' Sam Mayberry settled back into his chair. 'I really would enjoy a chat with you about some free paint.'

* * *

Joseph left the hostel and walked across to his parked car. The street wasn't as deserted as it had been when he'd arrived. A group of four young men and a girl were standing close to his car looking in, staring at the phone.

'You're a pig, aren't you?' The question came from a boy Joseph gauged to be about sixteen. His head was shaved, and covered in thick blue, amateurly drawn tattoos. A swastika radiated out from the crown of his skull, a dagger lovingly embraced by a serpent graced one cheek, a rampant dragon the other.

Joseph's instinct was to back off: to climb into his car, lock the doors and drive away. Then he remembered the look on Evans' face as he had left the office. Five minutes probably wouldn't make any difference. Not with this crowd. But with no other leads to follow, it was worth a try.

'I'm investigating a murder that took place here three nights ago.'

'Why?' the girl demanded truculently. She was no older than the boy, but definitely grubbier. Her grey miniskirt was streaked with mud, her blue anorak torn and grimy. Her bare legs were bruised, her shoes down at heel, and her blonde, thin, greasy hair was tied back with a piece of string. 'No one gives a damn what happens down here,' she asserted forcefully.

'I do – and those people who run the hostels do.' Joseph pulled out the fax likeness and the folder in which he kept the 'Tony' photographs. 'Have any of you seen either of these two men around?'

'Naw.' The boy with the shaved head turned his back, and pulled a cigarette paper from his pocket.

Joseph pointed a finger at the girl. 'You just said no one gives a damn what happens down here. If that's true, have you ever thought it's because people like you won't allow anyone close enough to try.'

'What's it to you what happens to us?'

'I'm looking for a killer who's already struck once in this street. If he isn't caught, any one of you could be next. Are you telling me you don't mind who he picks as his next victim?'

99

'Just let him try anything.' One boy, with a purple Mohican haircut, had produced a horn-handled hunting knife. Removing it from its sheath, he ran his fingers down the edge of the six-inch blade. Joseph studied it, trying to recall exactly what O'Kelly had said about a knife. Had his first guess of kids out for sick kicks been right? Could he be looking at the murder weapon?

'What you staring at?' the boy demanded truculently.

'Nothing,' Joseph replied easily. 'But from what I saw on the mortuary slab you're going to need a lot more than that to save yourself' – he nodded towards the knife – 'if you ever come up against the villain who burnt that poor bastard to death behind that hoarding. A burnt-up corpse is not a pretty sight. I've seen more meat on a barbecued spare-rib,' he added brutally, trying to provoke one of them into a response.

'Tell us what we should do if we run into him?' the girl demanded nervously.

'Run for help as fast as you can. But it might not come to that if you help us find him now. Just look at these photographs.' Joseph risked handing them over to her. 'Tell me if you've seen either of these men around.'

This time the girl accepted them. She looked closely at the blurred fax photograph, but shook her head.

'Here, let me look.' The boy with the shaved head and swastika took it from her. 'You expect us to recognise him from *this*?' He tossed it back to Joseph in disgust.

'Try the other one. It's a clearer print.'

The girl opened the folder. She eventually pointed to the photograph of Tony. 'I know this one.'

'Yeah, we know him,' the boy with the tattoos asserted. 'He the killer, then?'

'We think he's the victim.'

'The one that got burned?' The boy glanced over at the waste ground, looking cleaner than it had done in years, after the intensive police search.

'Yes.' Trevor folded the fax back into his pocket.

'*He* wasn't burned a couple of nights ago.' The girl held up the photograph, so the boy with the Mohican could see it. 'We saw him last night.'

'Where?' Joseph demanded urgently.

They exchanged glances.

'In the underpass,' the boy said quickly, too quickly.

Trevor sensed he was lying. 'What time?'

'I don't know. Late, I suppose.'

'Was he sleeping?'

'Naw. Just walking through,' the lad with the Mohican haircut interrupted.

'He walked through before . . . before . . .'

'Before what?' Joseph demanded of the girl.

She clammed up at a signal from the shaven boy.

'Please. This could be very important. *Where* did he go?'

'If we tell you, you'll take us all in. We know your kind.'

'I swear, whatever you've done, if it's short of murder I'll turn a blind eye.'

'You're only saying that. You pigs are all the same. Once we've told you what you want to know, you'll turn us in.'

'Do you want me to put it in writing?'

'Yeah, go on, give us a letter saying no copper will take us in.'

'For anything you've done up until now,' Joseph qualified, patting his pockets in search of paper. He found only a telephone bill he'd been meaning to pay all week. Pulling it out of its envelope, he filched a pen from his top pocket.

'That's not legal,' contended the boy with the tattoos. 'You're all bloody mugs . . .'

'It could be one of *you* next.' Joseph spoke directly to the girl, hazarding a guess that the boy with the tattoos had a soft spot for her.

'What if that man we saw is the murderer?' the girl appealed to the boys.

'What if we loose our squat?'

'Is that all this involves?' Joseph asked incredulously. 'You're trying to protect a squat. Don't you know the law? It would take us weeks to get you out if the place was empty when you moved in. That's always providing you didn't break in.'

'See, I told you,' the girl said.

'Wherever it is, I promise no one from the force will go near the place unless someone else reports it.'

'It's the old factory by the port buildings.' The girl blasted a defiant look at the four boys.

'And you're sure you saw this same man in there?'

'Last night.'

'You wouldn't like to show me exactly where?'

The girl looked around.

'You're on your own in this, Dell. We don't talk to pigs.' Three of the boys moved off.

'Jason?' she pleaded with the boy with the tattoos. 'Come on, you know I can't get in there by myself.'

He looked from her to Joseph. 'You sure this guy is a murderer?'

'He could well be,' Joseph replied ambiguously.

'I never thought I'd see the day I'd help a pig. Come on, then, if you're coming.'

Joseph looked wistfully at his car. It was a two-minute drive to the port buildings, and a ten-minute walk, but he couldn't see either of the kids willingly climbing into it. Pushing his keys back into his pocket, he followed them.

They walked quickly. He found it difficult to keep up with them, particularly when the cracked paving stones gave way to rough ground. Legs aching, he finally stood in front of a huge square building. Once white, it was now covered with green slime. All the windows were boarded over, and the ground-floor doors sported huge iron bars fastened with massive padlocks.

'How the hell do you get in here?'

'Around this way.' The girl led the way over a carpet of broken glass and rubble to one side of the building. The forty-foot wall was punctuated by rows of windows that ran symmetrically upwards on every floor except the ground. She stopped halfway along the sides and looked up.

'Next one,' the boy said curtly. He aligned his body in front of the high, narrow, boarded window on the first floor, then he held out his hands. 'Dell?'

She looked at him and glanced at the window above. In one swift easy movement, she took his hands into hers and climbed up the length of his body on to his shoulders. He clasped his hands firmly over her ankles as she balanced precariously and reached above her to the window. She pulled at the bottom of the covering board, and it swung outwards. Hooking her hands inside, on to the windowsill, she hauled herself off the boy's shoulders and upwards. Ducking her head, she wriggled inside. Joseph held his breath until her feet finally disappeared beneath the board. Moments later a thick, knotted rope fell heavily from above, one end secured inside the building.

'You promise. No pigs around here evicting us?'

'I'll do all I can,' Joseph murmured, as the boy pulled himself up towards the window on the rope.

Ten sweating minutes later, Trevor eased himself inside, tumbling over the windowsill into a black, shadowless void.

'Light a candle, Dell,' came a disembodied voice from his left.

'I can't find the bloody things.'

'Here, I'll strike a match.' A brief glare was followed by a small flickering flame that did little to dispel the gloom.

'No electricity?' Joseph joked badly.

'It's got running water,' the girl retorted defensively. 'Which is more than most squats I've been in.'

'You wanted to see where that man was dossing.' Taking the candle Jason led them across what could have been a vast hall, but, without even a chink of light coming in from the outside, it was difficult to gauge the size of the place. He opened a door, and the rank, musty odour of rodent droppings wafted in the atmosphere. A scurrying up ahead confirmed Joseph's suspicions.

'Rats,' the girl murmured. 'They usually run away from any light.'

Jason walked confidently ahead, holding the candle high, shielding its flickering flame with his fingers. As his eyes grew accustomed to the darkness, Joseph saw bundles of rags and piles of newspapers and cardboard boxes heaped along the sides of the corridor. There were still plaques on some of the doors: WOMEN'S WC, MEN'S WC, MANAGER, GENERAL OFFICE. Turning a corner, they were faced by an old-fashioned iron lift-cage stranded in the centre of a stairwell. Jason paused at the foot of the stairs leading upwards.

'The higher you go, the fewer rats there are,' the girl assured him as they began to climb.

'We live down there.' Dell pointed down a corridor that led away on the next floor. 'And we saw him going in here.' She pushed open the first door on their right. It creaked open.

Joseph held out a hand to Jason.

'You want the candle?'

'Only for a moment.'

Jason reluctantly gave it to him.

Trevor moved forward. The room was small, with benches around the side and hooks on the wall. Probably designed as a cloakroom. He wondered how many years it had been since workers had hung their coats on these pegs. He had lived in the town for close on fifteen years, and couldn't remember this factory ever being operational. The air was cold, dank. He raised the candle higher and peered around, spotting a bundle lying on a bench in the corner. He moved towards it, checking the floor as he went. It was dusty, but there were so many scuff marks in the dirt already that his own would never be noticed.

What he had seen was a sleeping-bag. Next to it stood an empty tin, jaggedly opened, its baked-bean wrapper still intact. On the separate lid of the tin, glued by a puddle of wax, was a stub of candle, smaller than the one he was holding. Both tin and lid were laid out on a small, battered suitcase. He tried to open it, and found it locked, but one look at the mechanism was enough. He could spring the clasps in an instant with his penknife if he chose to, but there were two witnesses standing behind him, and legally he had no right to investigate, or even to be here. Not without a search warrant. And, then again, caution told him to handle the suitcase carefully. If there were any prints to be found on it, they might finally produce an answer to the riddle of who exactly 'Tony' was, that's if he had a criminal record.

'Seen all you want to?' Jason's voice startled him.

'For now.'

'You'll be back, won't you?' the girl insisted. 'To arrest him.'

Trevor reflected that, now the kids knew what he looked like, it wouldn't be him who returned.

'We'll be keeping an eye on the outside of this building, in case he comes back to pick up his things. But you have my word: you won't be evicted or bothered.'

'Your word,' Jason sneered.

'Here.' Trevor returned the candle to the boy, and again removed the envelope from his pocket. 'My name is Trevor Joseph. Sergeant Trevor Joseph.' He wrote it on the back, scribbling his office direct-line number, with his home telephone number beneath it. Taking his wallet out of the inside pocket of his anorak, he removed fifteen pounds, all the notes he was carrying. He pushed them into the envelope and handed it to the girl. 'Here's my telephone number, in case you see that man again. Or if you need help, I promise I'll try and do all I can.'

She took the envelope and pushed it down the front of her sweater.

As Jason led the way out, Joseph checked the door of the room. There was no identifying nameplate, but it was the first door on the right at the top of the stairs on the second floor. He noted how long it took to walk from the cloakroom back to the room with the loose window board. Someone else would need those directions tonight. He'd try to ensure that his promise to these kids was kept but, whatever time 'Tony' returned, there'd be a reception committee waiting. And then, with luck, they should have the answer as to who exactly had been killed – and why.

Chapter Seven

Trevor Joseph rubbed his leg as he climbed stiffly out of his car. He'd landed awkwardly when he'd jumped that last foot down from the rope the kids used as an access to the old factory. Momentarily crippled, and cursing soundly, he'd stood back and watched Jason pull the rope back in, then jump to the ground. There'd been a time, and not that long ago, he reflected regretfully, when he could have done the same *and* run a mile afterwards. Limping, he hobbled into the station.

'You all right, sir?' Sarah Merchant asked, as he passed her desk.

'Fine,' he grimaced, heading down the corridor towards his office. There, Collins had taken possession of his desk yet again, Bradley sat behind hers, and Evans was standing in the doorway that opened into his own office.

'We were just thinking of putting out a missing persons report on you,' Collins commented caustically.

'You were the one who was lost this morning.'

'Not as lost as I'd like to have been,' Collins retorted irritably. Over breakfast, he'd spent a fruitless ten minutes trying to persuade Bradley that staying an extra hour at the pub could make a great deal of difference to their blossoming relationship without making any inroads into the time they owed the force. But she'd remained unconvinced, and had insisted on their driving back here as soon as the coffee pot was empty. Which left him exasperated and, infinitely worse, frustrated.

'Was your trip worth it?' Joseph looked from Collins' long face to Bradley's impassive one.

'We didn't come up with one single, solitary, useful thing that Inspector Edwards didn't document two years ago.'

'Except confirmation from Anthony George's boyfriend . . .'

'You met him?'

'Didn't we just,' Collins asserted. 'He told us he bought his pub with a long-term loan from Anthony George, which George's solicitor cancelled after his death.'

'Very generous of him, considering it was someone else's money.'

'There was no legal document to substantiate the loan. The solicitor probably didn't think that the thirty thousand pounds figured largely in the scheme of things. Particularly when you consider that the two hundred thousand Anthony left to his mother was passed on to charity less than six months later, along with the half a million she herself left when she died.' Bradley crossed her arms on the desk and sunk her chin on to them.

'Did this solicitor have the right to distribute George's money?'

'Every right. He was sole executor of the will. The boyfriend also insisted that the Anthony he knew couldn't possibly be the "Tony" in our film, because his Anthony George would rather be seen dead than wearing filthy rags outside a hostel for the homeless. Apparently he was far too fastidious to end up on skid row.'

'Well, if it was him, he certainly *did* end up dead.'

Collins watched Joseph hobble across to the filter coffee machine which the Inspector had set up in defiance of the Super's money-saving decree. 'You're crippled again,' he observed acidly.

'All in the line of duty.'

'You've got something, haven't you?'

'Yes.' Joseph pulled out a chair, and sat in front of his desk. 'I've located "Tony".' He smiled triumphantly.

'You've taken him out of the mortuary?'

'No.'

'Come on. Out with it, man.'

'I came across some kids who are squatting in the old factory down the docks.'

'The weaving mill?'

'Is that what it used to be?'

'Get to the point.'

'They said our man slept there last night.'

'Kids? Down-and-outs?' Collins rattled off scornfully. 'And you believed them?'

'It took me a while to get them to trust me, and I only really succeeded with one girl. Young, no more than fifteen or sixteen – probably a runaway. I think this murder's shaken her. Anyway, they identified our man from these.' He removed the wad of photographs from his inside pocket. 'Then they took me to the factory.'

'You went in there?'

'Yes.'

'We'd better get the security firm in charge of the place to check it out.'

'I gave them my word I'd turn a blind eye.'

'You did what?' Collins shook his head.

'This is a murder investigation, and we on Serious Crimes have to bend the rules from time to time. Not like you lot on the Drug Squad.' Joseph's lecture was tongue-in-cheek; he was only too aware that Collins had bent the rules more frequently than any other copper on the local force.

'Joseph's right,' Evans concurred, misinterpreting Joseph's sarcasm. 'We'd never get any information if we didn't compromise with our narks.'

'And God bless our narks, and keep them coming.'

'The kids showed me the room he used. He's left some stuff there. A suitcase, a sleeping bag . . .'

'All ready for a stake-out,' Evans mused.

'Unfortunately, those kids know me now.'

'And someone my size can't hide that easily.' Evans deposited his six-foot-four, twenty-stone bulk in a visitor's chair.

'Which leaves me?' suggested Collins.

'Us,' Bradley corrected.

'Women don't go undercover on Jubilee Street.'

'You're out of touch,' Joseph reprimanded him. 'There's a women's hostel down there now, remember.'

'Equality in all things.' Bradley gave Collins her most radiant and insincere smile.

'Even destitution?'

Evans read his watch. He was hungry, and it was almost one o'clock – time for lunch. 'Did those kids say what time they expected this fellow back?'

'It's not a hotel down there, with special hours, although they do have running water.'

'In which case, the sooner you go in, the better. I take it you both have suitable clothes?'

'At home, yes.'

'Pity there's no time for you to grow stubble, Collins.'

'He looks disreputable enough the way he is.' Bradley left her chair.

'I'm for food.' Evans looked to the others.

'I may as well go along to the canteen with you.' Joseph stretched his aching legs.

'Back here in two hours?'

'Give us time to eat as well as change,' Collins protested.

'An hour to transform yourselves, and an hour for lunch, what more do you want? You don't even need to wash.'

Collins looked across at Bradley. Strange that he hadn't noticed just how attractive she was before last night. He felt tempted to add an extra hour to their timetable for seduction.

'Eat first, transformation later?' Collins suggested, as he drove Bradley away from the station.

'If it's to be anything in the nature of the last meal, there's an expensive but brilliant Italian place down the road.'

'Make it a Chinese takeaway and we can eat at my place.'

She looked at him coolly. 'As long as it is just *eat*.'

'What else could I possibly have in mind at this hour?'

'Don't tempt me to answer that. If you stop off at my place first, I'll pick up my things.'

'Do you really live here, or just keep the place to impress gullible girls with your clean living habits?' asked Anna Bradley, as she wandered around the clinically clean, beautifully proportioned but Spartan living room of Collins' flat. It was furnished simply and severely with standard brown cord carpet, unimaginative three-piece suite and a coffee table. The curtains, like the suite, were gold, to coordinate with the carpet. But the view they framed, out over the sands and the sea, was spectacular. There wasn't a single ornament on the mantelpiece, and only one picture: a rather macabre gold-framed print of Breughel's 'Triumph of Death'.

'I do live here, and you're looking at the proof. That's one of my few superfluous possessions, and the only thing my wife ever gave me that I liked,' he said, as she studied the print.

'I think she must have been trying to tell you something.'

'All things come to an end – even rotten marriages. It gave me the hope and strength I needed to file for divorce.'

'You must have loved her once, to marry her.'

'I didn't relish the idea of living alone.'

'But you do now.'

'She cured me of my fear of the dark.'

'Are you never serious?'

'What's there to be serious about?'

'Life?' She walked around to join him in the kitchen, which was built into a windowless alcove off the living room. It had an air vent instead of a window, but the under-cupboard lighting was bright enough to show that the cream worktops, on which Collins was now setting out plates, were sparkling clean. 'Every time I come here, I wonder what you do with your routine mess and dirt.'

'I haven't any. The lady who comes in twice a week to give the place a going-over sees to that.'

'Perhaps you ought to give me her telephone number.'

'You'd have to call a fumigation squad before Betty would set foot inside your living room.'

He loaded everything they needed, including the carrier bag they'd brought from the Chinese, on to a tray. Carrying it into the living room, he laid the table with a clean cloth, and unpacked the bag.

'Your chop suey, ma'am.'

'I could get used to that.'

'Chinese takeaways?'

'No, you calling me ma'am.'

111

'You should be so lucky. I'll make Super before you do.'

'What makes you so sure?'

'I'm a man, and, as every selection committee knows, we're cooler, calmer, less emotional and better managers than women.'

'And I'm a member of a minority group. And everyone knows that a policy of positive discrimination operates in the force these days.'

'Not on Super selection committees.'

'You know you should never do that.' She changed the subject abruptly as she watched him lift the cardboard lid from one of the foil containers.

'Do what?'

'Order curry at a Chinese takeaway. It's not one of their traditional dishes. The Indians do it much better.'

'It always tastes good to me.'

'You know something, Collins? You're the legendary cartoon copper. Temper worse than a two-year-old, and a psyche to match. You live on slabs of grease and spices strong enough to blow your mind, and you think you're hard, but all you really succeed in is being boorish.'

'I congratulate you on your insight.' He refused to let her annoy him. 'Tell me, have you always preferred rabbit food.'

'Since I was old enough to make my own decisions.'

'When was that? Last week?'

'Cheap remark, Collins.' She pushed a fork into her vegetable mess and stirred it around. 'You ever gone undercover in Jubilee Street before?'

'Joseph and I have had the misfortune to itch there on many occasions. This your first time?'

'Undercover? No.'

'Where was the last time?'

'A pub. I went in to act as a barmaid, when I was detailed to the Vice Squad.'

'You were involved in the Dog and Whistle case?'

'I was.'

'Cracking piece of work that.'

'You're telling me. It earned me my sergeant's stripes.'

'Did it, now?' He shovelled down the last of his curry. 'Want a beer?'

'We're on duty.'

'We're eating lunch now. Besides, if we're going down Jubilee Street we should smell like the natives.'

'I'd still prefer coffee.'

'While it's brewing I'll go and change. You can use the bathroom.'

'You really have given up on me, haven't you, Collins?' She pushed her plate aside. Standing up from the table she walked round towards him. Throwing down his napkin, he rose warily to meet her. Wrapping her arms around his neck, she looked up into his eyes. Disentangling her embraces he held her by the wrists, then pushed her away.

'I don't like women who tease,' he said thickly, furious at his inability to control his own physical responses.

'Who's teasing?'

'As you said, we're on duty.'

'Not for another . . .' She swivelled her arm to look at her watch . . . 'hour and a quarter.'

'If you're serious, there's always tonight.'

'Isn't an hour and a quarter enough for you?' She thrust herself forward again. His grip on her wrists relaxed as she meshed her body close to his.

'Bradley . . .'

'Don't you think you could call me Anna? Just while we're making love?'

Collins was whistling as he opened his wardrobe door and extracted a black plastic sack. He rarely threw out any old clothes. When he had to dress for undercover, he preferred to wear his own cast-offs. Tipping the contents on to the floor, he rummaged through and finally selected a pair of jeans with the back pocket hanging off and a hole in one knee. Pulling these on, over a pair of black boxer shorts that Bradley found amusing for some unaccountable reason, he viewed himself critically in the mirror fixed on the wardrobe door. From what he'd seen out on the streets, the holes certainly weren't in fashionable places. He then pulled on a pair of faded cotton socks; the threads had gone in the back of one heel, and the ribs on both were frayed. He next found a nightmare of a blue-and-purple patterned shirt his ex-wife had bought him before they were married, and a black brushed cotton sweatshirt that had once been his favourite, but had been relegated to the rag-bag when the holes had appeared at the elbows. At the very bottom of the bag he found his old navy-blue anorak. It was faded but clean. The last time he'd come out from undercover, he'd taken it along to a dry-cleaner's, who had agreed to deal with it only after a fierce argument. Slipping on a pair of old cracked trainers, he completely pulled out the bottom drawer in his bedside cabinet. On the floor beneath it lay a ten-inch silver rod. Pressing a button on its base, he stared at the long, thin, stiletto blade that shot out of the tip. Retracting the blade, he tucked the knife into the back of his shoe. Ruffling his hair, he returned to the kitchen and poured them both some coffee. Carrying the mugs into the bedroom, he knocked on the bathroom door.

Bradley opened it and looked him up and down.

'You look like a Hollywood version of a tramp. Where's the best place for off-the-peg designer rags these days?'

When he saw her, he almost dropped the mugs. She didn't just look like a vagrant; she *was* one – right down to the all too realistic filth on her jeans. Her cropped blonde hair was no longer sleek and shining. It stuck out in greasy tufts, at right-angles to her head. Her face looked pinched with exhaustion, and was grey as though she hadn't washed it for a month. The man's shirt she wore over a torn black vest had lost most of its buttons, and it sported an enormous rent in the back.

'God, do you look like an authentic bag lady!'

'I used to be an actress.'

'You're kidding.'

'Three years in drama school, and I have the papers to prove it. When I left it, I found work as a chorus girl in a summer show in Blackpool. But that was it: my only time in the spotlight. After six months of sitting on my rear end waiting for something to turn up, I decided that summer season was all there was ever going to be for me, and, having a gut feeling there had to be a better future than starving on benefit, I went to police college.'

'After the bag-lady part, we'll have to see if we can elevate you to romantic lead.'

'If you're playing as well, I'd prefer soft porn.' She kissed him, then pushed him away as his hands began to wander beneath her shirt. 'Down boy. Here, you need a dirty face.' She picked up her make-up purse from the bathroom shelf.

'As long as *you* take it off afterwards,' he muttered, as she pushed him into a chair and began to rub grey greasepaint over his cheeks.

'Yes – and more if you're good.'

'I could get used to you being around, Bradley,' he murmured, wanting but not daring to put things more clearly.

'One step at a time, Collins.'

'Does that mean you'll run another marathon with me tonight?'

His eyes appeared naked without the habitual veneer of cynicism he used to cloak his emotions. Bradley looked away and smudged a dark line on his forehead. She knew already that what they had now was good. But it was also very new – and fragile. She didn't want to rush it. She wanted it to be right. To last. But there was no guarantee that whichever way she played it would be the right way. And if a week or two was the most there was going to be, why shouldn't she take all he had to offer?

'Marathon or pentathlon?' she smiled as she zipped the bag closed.

'Got it?'

Collins stood over the rough map Joseph had sketched on a sheet of paper covering his desk. 'Think so. It's the right side of the building as you face it from the front. Fifth window along, second floor, has loose boards covering it. Climb up . . .'

'There's a rope tied to the radiator below the windowsill, but the chances are, if you wait around until the kids come along, they'll lower it and you can move in.' Joseph looked out of the window at the rain teeming down relentlessly. 'An evening like this one promises to be, and they won't waste much time hanging around the streets.'

'The Inspector got the place under surveillance?'

Joseph nodded. 'Murphy's watching the side wall from the Port Offices. Chris Brooke is sitting in with the security guard at the dock gates. Murphy telephoned half an hour ago to say a couple of kids have already gone inside, but they've pulled the rope up behind them. Neither he nor Brooke has yet seen anyone answering the description of our man.'

'I've a feeling this is going to be a long night.'

'Where do you go, once you're inside, Bradley?' Joseph prompted. She seemed distant for once, and he couldn't help wondering if she'd heard a word he'd said so far.

She closed her eyes and conjured up the plan Joseph had drawn into her memory.

'Walk straight across the room from the window. The door leading into the corridor is directly opposite. Once through the door, turn left, walk along the passageway past the men's toilet, the ladies', and the manager's office, until you come to a stairwell with a metal lift-cage in the centre. Up one flight. First door on right.'

'Good. Just remember, though, it seemed like bloody miles to me.'

'You're crippled.'

'I wasn't then,' Joseph bit back at Collins. 'Got your torches?'

Bradley pulled one out of a pocket stitched inside her anorak, and held it up.

'Candles, matches?'

'And this.' Dan Evans entered the room and laid a gun on the pile of forms arranged on Bradley's desk.

'We're dealing with a down-and-out,' Collins protested.

'A down-and-out who may have already burned one man to death. It would look bad for the force if either of you became the next victim. Got your radios?'

'Yes, sir,' Bradley answered.

'Has Joseph told you that you'll have back-up in the Port Authority Buildings and at the security booth at the entrance to the docks?'

'Yes, sir.'

'Once you're inside, try to make radio contact with us every half hour. Remember, that'll be your only point of contact. We won't be able to watch you through those windows.'

'They're unlikely to forget that fact,' Joseph countered. 'It's like the black hole of Calcutta in there.'

'Who'll be outside, Inspector?' Bradley asked.

'Murphy, Brooke and myself: all the men the Super could spare for something that may not be anything. But if you hit trouble, we'll radio for back-up.'

'Sergeant Joseph's night off to cuddle his lady love?' Collins needled.

'Sergeant Joseph's night for interviewing doctors who carry out face transplants.'

'In a nice warm office. Want to play swops?'

'Not tonight, but thank you for the offer.' Joseph couldn't help wondering just what Collins would say if he knew that this 'interview' was going to be held in a restaurant rather than an office. And the precise identity of the doctor.

Rain-laden winds lashed inland, harsh, penetrating and salty from the sea, as Collins and Bradley walked along the quayside towards the old factory. Evans had dropped them off at the gates which stood at the sea end of the docks, on the supposition that no native of Jubilee Street would go anywhere near a security booth. Huddled, shivering in their anoraks, they kept their heads down and their hands in their pockets as they made their way towards the port offices.

'You imagining a cosy room with a glowing fire and a comfortable bed?'

'The one thing I learned early on, in this line of work, Bradley, is never imagine anywhere other than where you are on nights like this.' Collins shuddered as a particular vicious gust slapped him soundly across the face, bringing tears to his eyes.

'A nice mug of spiced mulled wine, a blanket and . . .'

'You're a bloody sadist.'

'I'll show you just how much of one, later.'

'That a promise?'

'Work first.' She switched quickly into her professional mode as the old factory loomed before them.

'Let's hope this'll be a short shift.' Wrapping his arms around his chest, Collins rubbed his shoulders briskly in an effort to warm himself. But he realised that, for the first time in months, if not years, he actually had something worth looking forward to at the end of a shift. 'See anyone?' he asked, as they rounded the corner and out of the worst of the howling gale.

'Like who? Jack Frost?'

'Like anyone who could see or hear me contacting Murphy.'

She glanced around the waste ground that surrounded the factory. It was deserted. 'You're safe.'

Collins whispered into the radio receiver tucked inside his pocket. Seconds later, Murphy's voice crackled thinly back.

'Eighteen people in the building so far, but no sign of our man. Over and out.'

'Do we stay outside until he shows?' Bradley asked.

'Do we, hell! I'm not standing around here freezing my balls off to no purpose, when you've promised me I'll need them later.'

They rounded the next corner. The rope was exactly where Joseph said it would be. Collins eyed the young girl who was shinning up it.

'Nice legs,' he murmured appreciatively, standing back. 'Ladies first.'

Bradley climbed the rope even quicker than the young girl had done. He watched her disappear inside. As soon as her legs vanished beneath the board, he followed her.

His arms were aching from the unaccustomed exertion by the time he'd finally hauled himself up as far as the windowsill. He scraped skin off his hands as he pulled out the board and scrambled inside. Bradley had lit her stub of candle, and he saw her face illuminated in its delicate glow. Behind her, further back in the room, two other lights flickered.

'How did you find out about this place?' The voice was angry, challenging. The speaker was the young girl whose legs Collins had been admiring a minute ago.

'Fellow told us about it in the Social. Bloody bastards wouldn't give us an emergency cheque when we came in today.'

'In from where?' a masculine voice demanded.

'London.' Bradley's cockney twang was good. Very good. 'We thought we'd stay with my brother for a bit. But he's shacked up again with his girlfriend and, seeing as how we can't stand one another, there was nothing for it but to hitch back down here. This is my boyfriend, Eddie.' She turned as Collins stepped further into the room. 'Eddie comes from round here, so we thought we might sort something out.'

'Like what?' the man sneered.

'What's it to you?' Collins snapped.

'We don't like strangers butting in on our squat.' The young man stepped threateningly towards them.

'We heard this was an open squat.' As his eyes became accustomed to the gloom, Collins looked around. The huge room was empty apart from the two men and the girl. 'It looks big enough to take all of us.'

'Looks can be deceiving.' The young bruiser took another step forward.

Collins pulled out the flick-knife he'd pushed into his trainer, and pressed the button. The blade shot out. 'You mess with me,' he snarled, 'and I'll mess with you. All we want is to be left alone, to doss down for a night or two. Now, if you've got something to say about that, you'd better say it here to my face right now.'

'Just as long as you keep away from us,' the youth conceded.

'We will. We don't like the way you smell.'

'Say that again!'

'You heard the first time.' Collins gestured to Bradley. 'Come on, love.'

'Next time, you go up first,' she hissed as they passed through the door.

'Do I hear the great women's libber admitting she needs a man to protect her?'

'Only to take the first knock. It's generally the hardest.'

Trevor Joseph drove home, where he showered and shaved,

and spent ten minutes flicking through the rails in his wardrobes before changing into a pair of cream slacks and a cream silk shirt. Picking out a light-grey silk tie and a lightweight grey jacket, he stepped back to gauge the effect. Deciding he liked it, he knotted the tie while brooding over the choice of restaurants the town had to offer. He first considered then rejected the two most expensive ones. He'd never felt comfortable in them and, as he couldn't read French and didn't know much about wine, it didn't take much for the head waiter of either establishment to make him feel small. But that narrowed the prospects. He didn't want to take Daisy to any of the Indian or Chinese places, where they were likely to run into someone from the police force, or worse still from the hospital. Relations with Lyn were strained enough without the added problem of a well-meaning soul carrying gossip back to her. There was a good Greek restaurant – would Daisy like Greek food? – a couple of Italian places, a Mexican place that was about as Mexican as an Italian western . . .

After slapping on a generous application of the most expensive aftershave he could find, he hurried down the stairs. Lyn had left a copy of the local paper folded on the coffee table. He flicked through its pages, searching for any feature on eating out. There, in the corner, was an advertisement for a new Turkish restaurant on the Marina. Picking up his car keys, he headed out. He'd already started the engine before he remembered his wallet was still in his work jacket. The telephone rang just as he was closing the front door for the second time.

'Trevor? I was hoping you'd come home to change.'

'I did, and I'm just on my way out.'

'I won't keep you long. I just wanted to say I'm sorry about this morning.'

He glanced at his watch. It was five minutes to eight. It was a ten-minute drive to the hospital from the Marina at best, and he'd told Daisy he'd be with her at eight.

'I'm sorry, too.'

'I'll try to be more understanding about your hours. It's just that—'

'Can we talk about this tonight, Lyn,' he interrupted. 'I'm running late.'

'I'll make us supper.'

'I'm taking the doctor to dinner, so I won't be eating, but how about we share a bottle of wine.'

'Red or white.'

'Red.'

'I'll have it open. Love you.'

'Me too,' he murmured as he hung up the receiver. Yesterday he wouldn't have stopped to wonder if he'd really meant what he'd said. But, then, yesterday Daisy hadn't walked back into his life.

'Carry on to the end of the corridor . . .'

'How many do you reckon kip here?'

'Your guess is as good as mine.' Collins was preoccupied with the black, clustering shadows beyond the range of his torch beam, and the light from the guttering flames of candles he could see flickering beneath one or two of the doors. Rags, papers and all sorts of rubbish were strewn over the wooden floors, and heaped high against doors that were as dry as firelighters. All it would take was one candle knocked sideways by one derelict in a drunken stupor, and the whole place would go up. He wondered how secure the boards were that covered the windows, and hoped they'd be easy to knock out of place in an emergency.

'There's the stairwell.'

Collins shone his torch beam up and down it. White graffiti was plastered over the dark-brown and green paintwork.

Dee loves Richie . . . Anarchy for the masses . . . and the inevitable *Fuck off pigs.*

'Think that's meant for us?'

'Not personally.' Anna made an effort to sound braver than she felt. This eerie silent building, with its hidden occupants, bothered her. Even Collins' reassuring bulk alongside her failed to quieten her fears.

'Up the stairs, and . . .'

'First door on the right,' she finished for him.

'Here we go, into the lion's den.'

Collins led the way up the stairs. Before they reached the top, he put his hand inside his anorak and unbuttoned the shoulder holster. The knife was fine for scaring off thugs – although he was aware Evans and Mulcahy would have a fit if they knew just what he carried around on his undercover assignments – but, if the man they were after was the same one who'd carved up then burnt that victim in Jubilee Street, he was in a very different league from the lad who'd challenged him downstairs. He should have insisted on getting in some practice earlier that afternoon, as he hadn't fired a gun for over six months, and even then he hadn't scored well on the range. Now both his own and Bradley's lives might depend on it. His own safety he could cope with but, after the events of that afternoon, he was worried about having to take responsibility for hers. Suddenly their relationship was no longer just professional. It was much, much more.

Slipping the barrel half out of its holster, he proceeded slowly up the last few stairs.

'First door on the right.' As Bradley swept her torch beam towards it, Collins jerked down her hand. Murphy was adamant that he hadn't seen the man enter, but that didn't mean there couldn't be another entrance to the building. Here there was no flicker of candlelight down at floor level. He put his hand to the door and thrust it open. The room yawned black before them.

'What now?' Bradley shone her torch over benches and coat hooks.

'We wait.'

'In here?'

'Can you think of a better place?' He turned around and glanced behind the door. There was a pile of newspapers on the nearest bench. He kicked them to the floor. Something scuttled across the room.

'What the hell was that?' Bradley whispered urgently.

'It looked fairly small. Big mouse or baby rat? Would ma'am care to be seated?'

She shone her torch below the bench and only when she was certain nothing was lurking there, did she sit with her hands clasped tightly around her knees.

Collins sat down next to her.

'Right, this is where we conserve energy by switching off our torches.'

She reluctantly pushed down the off button.

'Joseph was right: it *is* as black as the hole of Calcutta.'

'Here.' He pushed something metallic into her hands.

'What's this?'

'A flask. Seeing as how you turned down my offer of beer, I thought you might appreciate something stronger later on. And, as we all know, no down-and-out should be without his bottle.'

She lifted it unsteadily to her lips. 'No vagrant I know drinks best brandy.'

'This one does. Right, silence now. And if you get scared you can cuddle up close.'

'I'm not scared,' she asserted. 'But I am bloody frozen.'

'Give me your hand.'

She did as he bid, and he blew on her fingers.

'I've a horrible feeling this is going to be a bloody long night. Damn Joseph for ever finding this place. If that had been me, *he'd* be here with you now,' she whispered.

'And look at the opportunity for togetherness we'd be missing.'

'I'd rather we were together in your bed.'

'So would I, love, but think of the pluses. All the fantasising we can do while we wait – and act out later.'

Chapter Eight

'He did tell you he'd like red wine?'

'Yes.' Lyn turned a miserable face to the other staff nurse working on her ward.

'Well, there you are, then.'

'It's just that a couple of months ago it was all so marvellous, and now—'

'And now he's busy working on a police case. You only see each other during the boring parts of the day, when neither of you is at your best. The excitement's gone, the glitter's worn off, and you're beginning to wonder if there was anything between you, other than lust, in the first place.'

'How do you know?'

'Been there, seen it, done it – with my ex, unfortunately, who was never as good-looking as Trevor, even in his prime. Your generation is luckier than mine. If we'd moved in together it would have given both our mothers heart failure, so when lust struck we dutifully trailed to the altar. Marriage lasted about as long as the sex did. What did that psychologist say the other day? The length of time that sexual attraction lasts was set by nature to give cave-women the timescale they needed to bring up a child to semi-independent status. Four years is about average, but I don't think we made it even that long.'

'But at least you did get married. You had something . . .'

'Something incredibly messy and tangled to get out of. Just be grateful that you haven't got to resort to the courts, or end up paying a solicitor to sort out your mistakes for you. You don't even have a share in the house, do you?'

'No, but that's not the point. I think there's still something left between Trevor and me.'

'Twenty-one to thirty-six – I make it fifteen years.'

'Fourteen and a half,' Lyn contradicted vehemently.

'And that six months makes all the difference?' She laughed. 'Look, forget about it for one night. Come on out with the rest of us. It's Richard's birthday. He might be a worm, but it's a night out, and everyone who's off duty will be there.'

'I don't feel like it.'

'So what else are you going to do? Sit alone in Trevor's house and mope waiting for him to come home. That's how resentments build up. Listen to Auntie . . .'

'I won't be good company.'

'Who said anything about company? You'll have your car so you'll have to stay sober. That means whatever you contribute to the wine kitty has to be a plus for the rest of us, and seeing as how you're driving anyway, you won't mind taking me home.'

When Trevor rang the doorbell of the hospital flat it was opened immediately, as though Daisy had been waiting behind the door for him to arrive.

'The traffic was dreadful,' he apologised.

'That's all right,' she smiled. 'I've only just finished dressing.'

'You look beautiful.' Not given to paying compliments, he really meant it. She was wearing a calf-length black skirt and black silk polo sweater that made her pale skin glow. Her long dark hair hung loose, brushed back from her face.

'I like a man who knows how to flatter.' She picked up a wool wrap and an enormous handbag from the table next to the door, and stepped out to join him in the corridor.

'I wasn't sure of your taste in food, so I haven't booked anywhere. But there's a new Turkish restaurant just opened.'

'Turkish sounds fine.'

He led the way down to his car. Opening the passenger door, he waited until she climbed in, then he closed it.

'I've had a very successful couple of days on your behalf.' She opened her handbag and pulled out a folder. 'My secretary typed up the notes I made.'

'You didn't have to go to all that trouble.'

'Yes, I did. You've never seen my handwriting.'

'Doctor's handwriting.' He stopped at the traffic lights that marked the entrance to the network of hospital roads, and glanced across at her. She sat very poised and very still. His mouth went dry; his heart pounded erratically. What would he have given to have this happen eighteen months ago? Then he remembered how, eighteen months ago, she'd just lost her husband and he himself was a physical wreck.

'As far as I can make out, there's only four surgeons working on the transplant programmes. I'm talking internationally. Three of those programmes are funded from America: one in Mexico, one in Los Angeles, one in New York – which is the one that also operates in Africa.'

'The one *you* were working on?'

'Before I came here, yes. And, of course, there's also the programme I'm working on now.'

As the lights changed, he slammed the car into gear and drove on. 'Is your current boss British or American?'

'British. But then so are the consultants leading the New York and Los Angeles teams. You'd be surprised how much expertise we humble islanders provide for international medical programmes. Oh, and I also found out that the first documented face transplant took place in America twenty months ago.'

'There was nothing before then?'

'Nothing official that anyone will admit to. It might help if you told me a little about this case you're working on. It is a case, isn't it?'

'It is.' The thought crossed his mind that, ever since she'd walked across the foyer of that new unit to meet him, it had seemed more of an excuse to see her than a serious case. He'd done no work that afternoon – nothing at all except think about the evening that lay ahead.

'Is it classified information?'

'What?'

'Your case?'

'We try to keep some aspects of every case out of the press. It gives us an edge over the villain.'

'So I recall, but I'm not the press.'

'No, you're what's called an expert witness.'

'I haven't seen a crime.'

The lights of the Marina loomed ahead, so he turned into the right-hand lane that led away from the main road.

'You don't need to be an eyewitness to a crime to know something about it.' He drove slowly along the street looking at the signs above pubs and restaurants.

'We looking for the "Turkish Delight"?'

'Excruciating name, isn't it?'

'The first thing you learn as a doctor is to never judge the inside by the outside. The ugliest people often have the most beautiful kidneys and livers.'

'That's a disgusting thought.'

There was a parking spot free just outside the restaurant.

'Good omen?' she commented as he reversed into it.

'Or everyone else has already tried this place and they're staying away.'

'I thought you said they'd just opened.'

'First time I noticed their advert was tonight.'

They stepped out of the car and he locked it. Staring up at the restaurant's facade, he realised that the last time he had eaten here it had been an Indian curry-house. Inside, the decorative changes were minimal. The banquettes in the booths were now covered with Turkish tapestry as opposed to red silk damask. The pictures on the wall comprised enlarged Turkish miniatures of men wearing impossibly massive turbans, or dancing women who were uniformly bell-shaped and cross-eyed. But, on the plus side, an appetising smell was wafting from the kitchens at the back and, at thirty-five minutes past eight on a week night, it was blessedly, wonderfully quiet.

The black-suited waiter directed them to a table set in pride of place in the centre of the room, but Trevor stood his ground and they finally settled in a quiet booth behind a screen, at the back.

'You do realise you've ruined his advertising plans for the evening,' Daisy whispered as the waiter left them to study the wine list, while he carried off her wrap.

'I don't think it's a good idea to be overheard discussing what we're going to be in the middle of a restaurant.'

'You mean replacing tissue, rebuilding noses and ears, dovetailing eyebrows around eyes.' She smiled at him mischievously, and he stared helplessly back.

'Wine, sir?'

Trevor looked down the list. 'Red or white?' he asked Daisy.

'A very dry white, please.'

Trevor chose the most expensive, in the hope it would be the best. The food was easier. They opted for the specialty of the house: a mix of Turkish meze, followed by Circassian chicken, oriental rice and salads.

Hoping the waiter would have the sensitivity to leave them alone, when the wine came Trevor insisted on pouring it himself.

'You ever eaten Turkish food before?' Daisy asked him.

'No, have you?'

'Only in Turkey.'

'I might have known you'd been there.'

'Only as a student. Tim took me there the year before we got married.'

Her dead husband's name was spoken easily, but he wondered if she had really had come to terms with his death.

'Our meze's arrived.'

'Lady's thigh meatballs, fried meat fingers, gardener's meatballs, sardines in vineleaves, sir.'

'Sounds like a cannibal's feast.'

'They look delicious,' said Daisy in an attempt to mollify the hurt apparent on the waiter's face.

'What you said earlier, about no one carrying out a transplant *officially* before twenty months ago, how definite is that?'

'It isn't. There always has to be a guinea-pig in every new procedure, and very often a doctor will jump the gun in an attempt to stay ahead of the media. There's nothing worse than a negative press, and adverse publicity has been known to stem the flow of funding, and close down entire research programmes. First attempts inevitably run the greatest risk of going wrong. If the initial transplant turned out to be a disaster, the surgeon involved might attempt to cover up his mistakes, although it wouldn't really be ethical to do so. With new programmes like these, the different teams try to learn from one another's mistakes.'

'Pooling ideas?'

'Through conferences, yes. And believe you me, there have been problems – even on the programmes I've been working on. Give someone a new face through plastic surgery and it's generally accepted, even though it doesn't quite match their previous appearance. Give a man or woman a face that once belonged to someone else, and you can end up with a full-blown identity crisis. At least, that's what reports from the clinic in Los Angeles are suggesting.'

'That's the only problem?'

'Frankly, as long as it doesn't go any further than this table, it's the biggest obstacle we've encountered so far. And it can prove very serious for the person and family concerned.'

'Personality changes?'

'Drastic. Just imagine that your face is wrecked in a car crash, a fire, whatever. You wake up swathed in bandages like the invisible man. Eventually they come off, and you look like Frankenstein. Then along comes a doctor offering a miracle: a completely new face. Please note, not the old one remodelled, but someone else's. It can take four or five operations just to rebuild a nose, if the cartilage has been smashed or burnt away. With a transplant, it all goes on in one, along with ears, lips, cheeks, and eyebrows.'

'And you look in the mirror and see someone else.'

'Exactly. Someone who has lived previously with friends, family and a life of their own. Everyone involved in the programme agreed from the outset that one of the most important things is for us to be totally honest with our patients. We try to keep the donor/recipient arrangement totally anonymous, but there is always an off-chance that the recipient may meet someone from the donor's past.'

'Could be hard on a widow or widower.'

'We warn the donor's relatives that if they should ever meet the recipient, they should look at them carefully. What they will see is not an exact copy of their loved one's face. It can't be.

For a start, I've yet to come across a case where there's been an exact match of skull size. And, no matter how meticulously the tissues are grafted, there always seems to be a slight slip to one side or the other.'

'But if the donor has scars . . .'

'Then they'll turn up on the recipient's face. On the other hand, even with a new face there are some things that never change.'

'Such as?'

'If the recipient's eyes are left intact, they remain the same, and everyone has something that's uniquely their own that isn't dependent on looks. A way of walking, of holding themselves, or an inflection in the voice. We've learned to concentrate on mannerisms and on the indefinable part of a person some people call the soul. But all the early studies still suggest that face-transplant recipients will need more protracted and in-depth counselling than those receiving organ transplants. This morning I heard that the Los Angeles team is currently working on a face transplant for someone who has not only lost their face but was blinded in the fire. Psychologically that may be easier; at least he'll never see himself as someone else.'

'Is that by nature of an experiment?'

'Probably,' she admitted cautiously, helping herself to a slice of Turkish bread.

He shuddered involuntarily as he poked his fork into the batter-covered meatball on his plate.

'If doctors had never experimented, people would still be dying of appendicitis and gangrene – and that's without the more sophisticated transplants of heart, lungs, and liver. I believe in what I do, Trevor. The first time I saw a leper smile with new lips that we'd grafted on to his mouth, it seemed like a miracle.'

'From his point of view, it probably was.'

'Can't you tell me what's this all about?'

He pushed the meatball aside and pulled out the folder of photographs from his inside pocket. 'This man' – he extracted the pictures of 'Tony' that had been lifted from the video – 'was photographed just a month ago in Jubilee Street.'

131

'So?'

'He died two years ago in a hospital seventy miles from here. There's no doubt about it. We checked it out. His death was verified by two doctors. His body was identified by people who knew him well. His closest friend held his hand just after he died.'

'And you're thinking face transplant instead of look-alike?'

'We're thinking face transplant because his face was skinned from his corpse as it lay in the mortuary. It was peeled off, right down to the bone, less than an hour after he died.'

'I see.'

'Was there anyone working on transplants here in the UK two years ago?'

'As I said, not officially.'

'Was anyone capable of carrying out this operation living here at the time?'

'I'd have to check.'

'You said there *are* British personnel working on these projects?'

'At least four, including two of the consultants.'

'We'd appreciate a list.'

'I'll get you one.'

The waiter, who'd been hovering at a distance, noticed they'd stopped eating and swooped down to remove their plates. Trevor sat back. He wasn't hungry, but he was beginning to wish his meal would never end. Sooner or later, when it did, he'd have to go home to Lyn. He was conscious of the debt he owed her, for his sanity and a great deal more. There *had* been some happy times. It was just that here, sitting opposite Daisy, it was difficult to remember them.

'What time is it?'

Bradley's whisper, echoing out of absolute darkness, jolted Collins like an electric shock. He stretched his cramped legs, and leant back against the bench. He was aching all over, especially the shoulder where she had rested her head for the last hour and a half. Pulling back the knitted sleeve of his anorak, he pressed the button on his digital watch.

'Ten minutes to ten.'

'It feels like we've been here forever.'

A cackle of insane laughter echoed up the stairs from the floor below.

'Welcome to the house of fun. One dose of crack, and you too can join in the merrymaking.'

'I'd rather not. God, this place is bloody freezing.'

'I thought women didn't feel the cold.'

'This one does.'

'Ssh!'

She heard it the same time as Collins: a barely perceptible shuffle. Like soft carpet slippers skidding over a hardwood floor. The sound crept closer – up the stairs. They both held their breath, and tensed their bodies in readiness. A yellow glow shone beneath the door, a thin sharp line of brilliance slashing the darkness, dispelling the gloom into clumps of grey shadows. Then came a sighing of slow, laboured breath. The door opened a crack. After a moment it was flung back, slamming into the bench barely an inch from Bradley's head. She shrank back, knocking the curve of her spine hard against the bench. A hand closed over one of her clenched fists. Collins might be a bastard at times, but he also knew when to reassure.

For an infinite moment, time hung suspended. Bradley was left with the eerie impression that someone had pressed the pause button on a video-recording she'd suddenly become part of. Light streaked in through the open door, illuminating the suitcase, the sleeping bag and the bean tin opposite them. The breathing continued to pant in short quick gasps, each identical to the preceding one. A black-booted foot came into view.

Bradley's trained eye registered height – six foot two inches. Hair dark, curling, long and matted. Black overcoat, black trousers, lighter-coloured knapsack slung over shoulder. Was it khaki? The figure bent over the suitcase, unclipped the locks, and removed a moth-eaten blanket from its depths. He straightened up, shook out the blanket, spread it on the floor, then turned.

Peter Collins was on his feet before her. She'd reckoned without the cramp and stiffness that had entered her limbs and joints during four long hours spent hunched in the bitingly cold, tomb-dark blackness.

Even in the half-light of the scuttering candle he was carrying, she registered that Joseph's information had been correct. It was 'Tony' from the video.

Then he saw them.

Collins spoke first. 'Anthony George?'

There was no time for anything else. The man lunged forward. There was a blinding flash. A cry. Pain exploded on the crest of a crimson tide that flooded Bradley's head. She was conscious of the door slamming shut. Then there was only a swift sinking feeling – and darkness.

'If you looked carefully at the video we have, would you be able to tell if this man has had a face transplant?' Trevor Joseph and Daisy Randall had finished their second course. As neither of them had wanted dessert, he had ordered Turkish coffee. The wine was going down slowly, and he couldn't help wondering if Daisy was as anxious as him to protract the evening or if there was someone waiting for her – if not in her flat, then on the end of a telephone. A special person who now meant as much to her as Tim Sherringham once had.

'Obviously there are scars. They fade in time, but they never entirely disappear. We try to hide them in the hairline, and below the neck-line. How detailed are your shots of this man?'

'Not very,' he admitted, 'There's only one or two close-ups.'

'I'll take a look at them, if you like.'

'Thank you. I'll give you a ring tomorrow and arrange it.'

The restaurant had gradually filled up, which was hardly surprising as the food was excellent and the service, if anything, too attentive for Trevor's liking. A large raucous party was sitting at the centre table they'd rejected: the women shrieking with laughter, the men noisily demanding more wine and beer from the waiters.

Trevor listened to the din and debated whether or not to suggest moving on to a pub. Daisy might take it as a hint that the evening had come to an end, and ask to be driven back to the hospital. He didn't want to lose whatever time they had left together, but then neither did he want to continue sitting in a noisy restaurant. The excuse of talking business was no longer valid, as they'd long since exhausted the topic of face transplants, and the file she'd prepared for him detailed all the information he would need to continue his investigation, and more besides.

He looked at her hand resting on the linen tablecloth close to his own. He would have liked to close his fingers over it, look into her eyes, and ask her how she really was, but something held him back. Fear of starting something he couldn't finish – or guilt over Lyn perhaps? He took the bottle and poured the last of the wine into their glasses.

'Would you like anything else?'

'No, thank you. It's been a lovely evening, thank you, Trevor, but I have to think of getting back. I'm due in the operating theatre first thing tomorrow, and no, before you ask, it's not a transplant.'

'I'll get the bill.' He turned and motioned to the waiter, then froze. Sitting amongst the boisterous party at the centre table were people he recognised as Compton hospital staff – and they included Lyn.

'Someone you know?' Daisy asked intuitively.

'The girl I'm living with,' he replied, making a swift decision that honesty was the only policy in this case. 'Would you like to meet her?'

'Yes, I would.'

The waiter blocked his view of Lyn. He handed over his credit card, and led Daisy towards the central table.

'Hello, Lyn,' he said quietly, below the hubbub.

'Hello.' The expression in her eyes told him she had seen him long before he'd spotted her.

'I'd like you to meet Dr Randall. She's helping us with the case.'

'Pleased to meet you.' Daisy extended her hand, and Lyn took it. 'Trevor told me that you're together. You're a lucky lady.'

'I think so.' Some of the animosity faded from Lyn's eyes.

A high-pitched electronic bleep screeched, audible even above the noise of Lyn's party.

'Is that yours, Trevor, or mine?' Daisy asked.

Lyn's eyes narrowed again. 'Trevor.' There was something about this doctor. Something familiar. Then she recalled those endless sketches Trevor had produced during art-therapy classes when he'd been a patient on her ward. A woman with long dark hair and an obscure face. A woman he had once said he could have loved, if there'd been time to develop a relationship.

'It's mine.' Trevor fumbled in his pocket, and the bleeping ceased. He stopped a waiter. 'Is there a telephone here?'

'By the desk, sir.'

'Excuse me.' He nodded to Daisy before looking at Lyn.

'Why don't you sit down and have a drink with us?' shouted Richard, seated next to Lyn. He was too drunk to notice anything beyond a new and attractive face.

'Thank you, but as soon as Sergeant Joseph comes back I have to go.'

'Have you known Trevor long?' Lyn probed.

'We met about a year and a half ago when he was working on another case.'

'Before his accident?'

'It was just before his accident,' Daisy concurred, disturbed by the signs of jealousy Lyn was clearly exhibiting.

'You didn't go to visit him when he was in hospital.' It was statement not a question. Lyn would have remembered Daisy if she'd walked into her ward.

'I've been out of the country.'

Lyn recalled a conversation she'd had with Trevor about the mysterious woman in his sketches. *'She isn't in the country. I couldn't get hold of her even if I wanted to.'*

'Then you lost touch.'

'There was no reason for us to keep in contact.'

Trevor returned. Scribbling his signature on the credit-card slip on the waiter's tray, he turned to Daisy. 'A fire's broken out in a disused factory down the Marina. They've sent for ambulances.'

'I'll come with you.'

'You don't mind?'

'Not in an emergency.'

'I'm sorry, Lyn. This probably means another late night.'

Before Lyn had an opportunity to reply, they were gone, leaving her to her vivid imaginings of the beautiful, elegant Dr Randall ending up in bed with Trevor.

'Collins! Collins!' Unnerved by the silence in the room, Bradley was shouting as loud as she could. From below came the panic-stricken sounds of people screaming, and the thick, acrid smell of smoke.

'Collins!' She clambered up on to her hands and knees, cursing the blackness tinged with a red which she sensed derived from the blinding pain inside her head. She had to keep calm, cool – think clearly and incisively. Summon those qualities they'd tried to instill into her in police college. From somewhere at the back of her numbed, aching head came the memory of a torch. The Inspector had insisted they both carry torches. She fumbled inside her anorak for the pouch she had sewn close to her armpit. It was still there, she could feel the shape. 'Collins, damn you!' she shouted angrily. 'For Christ's sake, why won't you answer me?'

It took an age, and two broken fingernails, for her to remove the torch. She switched it on and swept the room with its beam. The heap of rags, the suitcase and the blanket the man had shaken out were still lying on the floor in front of the opposite wall.

'Collins!' She gripped the bench and rose unsteadily to her feet. The screams downstairs were growing louder, the smell of smoke intensifying, lung-searingly suffocating. She took a step forward, and stumbled over something large and soft.

'Collins?' She fell to her knees and shook his shoulder. Her hand felt damp as she lifted it away. Examining it, she saw it was wet and sticky. Blood! Looking all the more ghastly in the sickly yellow beam of the torch. Carefully she rolled him on to his back. There was a bullet hole high on the left shoulder of his anorak. Damn it, that man must have been armed. But, then, so was Collins – why hadn't he got in first? A siren screeched faintly from somewhere outside the boarded windows. She wondered if it signified an ambulance or a police car – then the smell of burning wafting into the room from under the door cleared all extraneous thoughts from her mind.

She followed the grey, billowing wraiths of smoke with the torch beam. Misty like the ghost trails of childhood fears.

'Collins!' She sank to her knees and lifted his head on to her lap, but his eyes remained obstinately closed. She laid fingers over his mouth and could feel his breath breeze over her fingers. He was still alive! She went over to the door and opened it unthinkingly, in defiance of all fire-drill advice.

A voice shouted below, calm yet commanding. It was Tom Morris's voice, and there was no time for her to wonder what he was doing inside the building. A gust of scalding air propelled her sharply backwards, but not before she'd seen flames licking at the bannister, and dancing up the stairs towards her.

She banged the door shut again. Coughing and spluttering, she ran across the room and picked up the sleeping bag. Rolling it tightly, she jammed it against the foot of the door. She had to get a grip on herself. That last mistake could well have proved hers – and Collins' – last.

A crash, followed by a single loud scream, echoed above the crackling of the flames. Smoke still seeped into the room through the badly fitting door-frame. If only she didn't have this sick, blinding headache that made every move sheer agony. If only she was able to think.

Head and heart pounding, she stood in the centre of the room and swept the torch beam around the walls. Collins groaned, but she fought the instinct to go to him. It wasn't mothering he needed now, but an escape route.

Her beam picked up the glint of glass, blacked out by a wood panel behind it. It was high up on the wall: a tall, narrow window no more than two foot wide. She ran towards it, leaping up on a bench to get as close as she could. Taking off her shoe, she pounded hard, wielding its heel like a hammer.

It took half a dozen blows before a hail of glass splinters finally showered over her. No reinforced glass in buildings this age, she reflected sourly, shaking the larger fragments from her arm and shoulder. Snatching up the blanket from the floor, she wrapped it around her arm and pounded against the exposed wood. From the sides of the frame more glass splinters showered over her, but she kept hammering. Two lung-bursting, smoke-laden minutes later, she realised this was useless. Whatever had been used to fasten the wood in place on the outside, it was holding firm. How the hell had those kids Joseph had encountered got into this building?

Stooping right down to the floor level, she took a deep breath of relatively clean air before resuming her study of the window, running the torch beam along its top and down the sides. She'd broken the small panes in the lower sash, but the top ones still held firm. Climbing up on to the sill she gripped the centre bar, ignoring the bite of broken glass into her finger joints. Hoping and praying the sash would take her weight, she levered herself up on it, swung back and then kicked forward with all her might.

Chapter Nine

The skyline visible above the shining gabled roofs of the Marina pubs, restaurants and apartments was tinged with a radiant golden glow, lending the street the theatrical aura of a stage set. If it hadn't been for the acrid tang of smoke in the air, Joseph might almost have believed that dawn was breaking eight hours early. But even before he and Daisy had driven to the end of the street, they could see flames shooting through the roof of the old factory in a brilliant show of sparking crimson-and-blue pyrotechnics.

'There shouldn't be any casualties in a disused factory,' Daisy said, as Trevor tried, and failed, to contain his anger at the traffic now ground to a standstill, as the road was clogged by sightseers who'd spilled out of every adjoining street that led into the dock quarter.

'It's being used as a squat for the homeless.'

'How many?' Daisy turned an anxious face to his.

'You know what the housing situation is like in this town.'

'There's someone else in there, isn't there?'

'Two of my colleagues. Or at least they were there when the station paged me.'

'Clearing the place out?'

'Working undercover,' he answered briefly, refusing to be drawn. 'Looks like we're going to have to get out here.' He halted his car behind a line of fire engines, police cars and ambulances.

'You can't park here, sir.'

'It's all right. He's one of us, lad.'

Joseph recognised Murphy and ran over towards him, without bothering to lock his car. 'She's with me. She's a doctor,' he

141

shouted as Chris Brooke tried to block Daisy's progress towards an open space in front of the wall, where a row of injured were laid out to be treated by paramedics. 'Where's the Inspector?'

'With the Super, over there.' Murphy pointed to a spot behind the old factory, where a tight-knit group of firemen and police were standing just within the 'safety lines', watching the boarded windows blow out on the first floor of the building, one by one. Slightly to one side, and behind them, Joseph could see the crouched figure of Nigel Valance, camera on shoulder, as he panned his lens upwards along the frontage of the burning building.

'Bloody ghouls,' Murphy muttered under his breath. 'They were already here when we arrived, jamming their cameras and microphones into the faces of the casualties before the paramedics could even . . .'

The rest of Murphy's complaint was drowned out by a roar of flame breaking through the roof. Sickened by the thought that time might have already run out for Collins and Bradley, Joseph sprinted forward.

'Collins?' he asked breathlessly as soon as he was within hailing distance of the Inspector.

'No sign of him, or Bradley.' Evans was devouring a tube of peppermints at a rate of knots, blindly pushing them into his mouth as he scrutinised the building.

'South side's ready to go,' a fireman shouted, just moments before flames burst simultaneously from three first-floor windows.

'What a shot,' Valance screamed in excitement, as he caught this action on film.

'This isn't a bloody spectator sport,' the chief fireman shouted angrily, turning on him.

'Just doing my job,' Valance protested, backing away from the combined wrath of the Super and the Chief.

'Do we know how it started?' Joseph croaked, inhaling a gust of black smoke as Murphy dragged the cameraman away.

'Murphy radioed that someone answering the description of our man was going in. Ten minutes later we saw the first smoke, then people started screaming, and jumping out of the windows . . .' Evans' voice trailed off as an axe blade hacked through one of the boarded windows on the ground-floor. A spear of shimmering, multi-coloured flame erupted from the shattered wood. Then the stocky, clumsy, spaceman silhouettes of two firemen, wearing protective clothing and breathing apparatus, emerged from the inferno. Each carried a dead-weight bundle in his arms.

Joseph watched as the first one shook his head at another colleague.

Tom Morris appeared, helping a smoke-blackened, injured girl around the side of the building. They staggered slowly towards the firemen.

'That's it, Mr Morris. You've done more than enough for a civilian,' the leading fireman called out. 'Back with the paramedics now, or we won't be able to guarantee your safety.'

'We've got to tell them about Collins,' Joseph insisted urgently.

'We have, lad.' Mulcahy's accent always reverted to its North Country roots under stress. 'There's men in the building searching for him and Bradley right now.'

'I should go in. I know where to look. They don't.'

'The second floor's completely gone, Inspector.' A senior fireman, weighed down by equipment pushed back his breathing mask as he waddled towards them with an awkward gait. 'If your people are still in there, we've no way of getting to them except from above.'

'I have to go in.' Joseph pushed forward. All he could think of was Collins and Bradley trapped in that blazing conflagration. If it hadn't been for his morning's expedition they would be safe in the station right now. They shouldn't have gone in, he should have. He could have avoided the kids who knew him, gone up to that cloakroom . . .

'Other side of the building, sir.' Chris Brooke raced up to them, his dark eyes gleaming with excitement and the light of the flames. Evans and Mulcahy led the way around the side. More sheltered than the back, the wind wasn't as fierce here, and neither was the fire. But most of the second- and third-floor windows were ablaze, and smoke poured from every available crack in the fourth- and ground-floor covering boards.

A fire engine was parked perilously close to the smouldering facade. Its ladder, with one man perched in the wire-cage basket on top, was moving slowly, infinitely slowly, upwards. Joseph followed the line it was taking. Then he saw her. A slight, vulnerable figure poised on the sill of a small corner window on the third floor, framed in the jagged edges of a shattered board, and wreathed by the smoke that was pouring out of the room behind her.

'Bradley.' Evans breathed.

'But not Collins,' Joseph said uneasily.

'Can't your people move any quicker?' the Super barked at the fireman who'd come along with them.

'I'd say we're doing all we can.' A troubled expression creased his face as he stared intently at the fireman aloft in the basket.

The ladders swayed precariously as they rose, meeting great surges of heat escaping from the building. The fireman stood poised, ready, in his cage. He reached out to Bradley, went to take her hand, but she shook her head and clung to the shattered sides of the window-frame.

'For Christ's sake, now what?' Mulcahy cursed.

'She's frozen, traumatised,' the fireman muttered.

The fireman on the ladder leaned forward, closer to Bradley. Pushing his breathing apparatus over his nose and mouth, he unfastened the door of the cage and stepped on to the sill, just as Bradley turned.

'She can't be going back inside!' Joseph exclaimed in disbelief. 'She has no protection, no oxygen . . .'

'It has to be Collins,' Mulcahy snarled, furious at having to stand by and watch, impotent and helpless.

'If Collins is in there, I'd have thought he would have been getting ready to jump by now,' Evans muttered.

'Probably getting used to the temperature, in preparation for eternity.' Mulcahy's knuckles were every bit as white as Evans' and Joseph's.

'He's hurt!' Joseph shouted, as the fireman finally emerged with Collins slung over his shoulder. The man looked at the basket fixed on top of the ladder, judged the distance between it and the narrow windowsill, then jumped.

'They made it,' Evans grunted.

The fireman laid Collins' inert figure at the back of the basket, then looked up at the window as Bradley staggered out. Even from that distance, they could see her shoulders hunching as she coughed violently to rid her lungs of the noxious fumes. The fireman motioned her forwards, but still she turned back.

'Now what the hell is the stupid woman doing?' Joseph asked impatiently, squinting upwards to judge whether or not Collins was alive.

. She re-emerged moments later with a suitcase under one arm.

'Luggage?' Evans asked, as the fireman pulled her forward. She fell into the basket. He then wasted no time in refastening the side, and giving the signal for the ladder to retract.

Mulcahy stepped back – and tripped over Valance, who had crept up behind them yet again with camera running. 'Get this bloodsucking bastard out of my sight,' he bellowed to Brooke. 'And get an ambulance up here on the double, and whatever medical help you can. I want those two in hospital as soon as possible. And you,' he glared at Evans and Joseph, 'go with them. See if you can find out what happened here before he' – he jerked his head towards Valance – 'delivers his story. The last thing we need is upstairs finding out about this mess from the television news before we put in our reports.'

'A few weeks and he'll be back to his usual, charming self.' Daisy Randall stood outside the emergency room and pulled away the paper mask that had covered her mouth. As Daisy was on the staff of the General, the doctor in charge of the casualty department had welcomed her assistance gratefully and unquestioningly. His department had been stretched to breaking point by the influx of burnt and injured brought in from the old factory. And not all of them were squatters either. Two firemen were on the critical list, and one was dead. The body count now stood at four, but both Evans and Joseph realised it was likely to rise steeply once the building was cool enough to be searched. And, given the speed with which the fire had spread, and the difficulty of getting out of the building, the mortality list could grow drastically. Which said something about the number of youngsters living rough on the streets of the town. Practically all of the civilian casualties brought in had been under twenty-five.

'What's the extent of his damage?' Joseph asked, as he leant against the wall. His legs were still giving him trouble after his unaccustomed acrobatics.

'He's been shot, but it's only a flesh wound in the shoulder.'

'Collins always has had the devil's own luck.'

'He certainly has this time,' Daisy concurred. 'The bullet didn't do much more than graze him, although he's lost a lot of blood. He probably passed out from shock at first, then succumbed to smoke inhalation, but I think he may have hit his head on the way down. That would explain the lump on his crown, and also why he was laid out cold. No doubt the headache he'll enjoy for the next couple of days will make him more irritable – but that's your problem, not ours. Depending on how he goes overnight, he'll most likely be discharged tomorrow.'

Evans was curious how this extremely attractive female doctor knew so much about Collins, and also why she and Joseph seemed so friendly, but he put his curiosity aside for the moment. There were more important questions to ask.

'And Sergeant Bradley?'

'She's in the room next door, having her hands sewn back together. She'll be coming out in a moment.'

'Will you be keeping her in, too?'

'I doubt it. The wards are packed to capacity. We've had to send all non-urgent cases home, as it is. The administrator's postponing routine operations for the next few days. Someone just mentioned that we've admitted sixty-five patients in the last hour alone. Even for a hospital this size, that's some going.'

'Can we see Collins?' Joseph asked.

'For a few minutes. He's a bit dozy from the anaesthetic and the concussion, so don't press him too hard. A porter will be along soon to take him up on to the ward. I'll try to see you before you go, but in the meantime I've a feeling I'm needed elsewhere.'

'Thanks, Daisy.'

'Any time. I enjoyed the meal. I'm not too sure about the dessert, though. I prefer a less eventful life.'

Joseph watched her walk away.

'Nice lady,' Evans observed.

'Very.' Joseph went into the emergency room. Collins lay stretched out on a trolley, a red blanket covering his legs, his face as white as the bandages wound around his upper right arm and shoulder.

'Seems I ended up here once before, when I was working for your Serious Crimes squad, Inspector.' The voice was husky and raw from smoke inhalation, but sounded as cocky as ever.

'Serious Crimes a bit strong for you perhaps, Collins?'

'What happened?' Joseph hovered at the foot of the trolley, needing to reassure himself that Collins was indeed as intact as Daisy had diagnosed.

'I didn't expect the bastard to have a gun.'

'Sloppy work. You'd been issued with one, you should have been prepared to use it.'

'Have a heart, Inspector. I thought I was tackling a down-and-out, not Al Capone. Did you get him?'

'No.'

'And you accuse me of sloppy work. Bloody hell, that means we have to keep looking.'

'Did you see him properly?'

'Enough to know he's our "Tony" all right. No doubt about it.'

'Then our dead man isn't dead.'

'Which leaves us a problem with the corpse.'

'The doctor' – Collins gave Joseph a telling look – 'told me I'll be out of here tomorrow. I can be back at work the day after.'

'See how you go. If we're desperate for manpower, we'll find you a cushy number behind a desk, answering the phone.'

'Thank you, thank you very much indeed.'

'I'll be round tomorrow to pick you up and take you home.' Joseph hesitated in the doorway as Evans left.

'Daisy told me you'd just finished dinner when you were paged. How long has she been back in the country?'

'Not long. I only met here for the first time yesterday. She's working on the face-transplant programme.'

'Never thought I'd see the day when *you* had two females on the go, Casanova.'

'It was work, pure and simple.'

'Where the female of the species is concerned, nothing is ever pure and simple. Save the lies for the expense-account clerks – and Lyn,' Collins croaked.

'Look . . .'

Collins held up his hand. 'I don't want to hear. It's *your* life. I only wish I had your problems. It must be a hard choice to make. Youth and naivety or sophistication and maturity. I wonder which one I'd plump for.'

'If you've any sense, the blonde who saved your life.'

'Daisy told me that, apart from her hands, she's fine. You seen her?'

'Not yet.'

'Did she carry me out?'

'Out of a third-floor window?'

'I don't remember anything.'

'A fireman did the actual humping, but if she hadn't battered the boards off one of those windows, you'd both be barbecue by now.'

'Tell her I'd like to see her.'

'I will.' Joseph suppressed a smile as he left the cubicle. It couldn't be! Not hard-bitten Collins falling for a woman. It simply couldn't be.

'So that's why you went back, you little darling.'

Joseph pulled back the curtains of the cubicle in time to see Dan Evans lift Bradley bodily out of a wheelchair and plant a kiss on her forehead.

'There's a sick man in emergency asking for you.' Joseph blanched at the extent of the bandages covering Bradley's hands and forearms.

'They told me his injuries aren't serious.'

'Apart from a bang on the head and a flesh wound to his shoulder, he's in one piece, thanks to you.'

'And look what she brought out with her.' Evans held up the suitcase.

'It belongs to our man?'

Bradley nodded. 'Collins and I watched him take a blanket out of it.'

'Run it over to the laboratory, Joseph.'

'Aren't you going to open the case?'

'The lab boys can do that after they've checked for fingerprints. This man operates like a seasoned villain, so with luck his prints will be on file somewhere.'

'The outside of this case has been handled by half the fire service, and most of the staff in this hospital, so tell them the exterior isn't worth bothering with,' Bradley advised.

'I'll phone ahead and warn them you're on your way.'

'I'll be gone just as soon as I've said goodbye to Dr Randall.' Joseph took the suitcase from Evans.

'A *quick* goodbye,' Evans called after him, planning to ask Joseph more about his relationship with Dr Randall in the morning.

'Sorry our evening had to end this way.'

'It was bad enough being married to a doctor. After tonight, I believe a policeman could be worse.' Daisy looked up at him from the report card she was filling in.

'Dinner again next week?'

'You're living with someone.'

'Daisy . . .'

'It doesn't take a genius to work out you have problems there, Trevor. I'd rather not become part of them.'

'And when they're resolved?'

'If I were you I'd think about resolving them, and no further at the moment, Sergeant Joseph. I'll send you the next lot of information I get.'

'Daisy . . .' He looked around. The reception area was crowded with police, paramedics, firemen, injured bodies suffering varying degrees of burns, cuts, sprained ankles and smoke inhalation. 'Sometime, Dr Randall, there will be a time and place for us.'

'Perhaps.' She put down the form she'd filled in and picked up another. 'But have you ever thought it might not be in this lifetime?'

From the hospital it was a thirty-mile drive to the police laboratory, and a thirty-mile journey back home. True to his word, Evans had telephoned ahead, and two men from the forensic team were waiting in the lobby to take the suitcase from Joseph.

'Top priority?'

'Top priority,' he echoed, realising that his own top priority at that moment was bed and sleep.

He finally pulled up outside his house at three o'clock in the morning. As he opened the car door, he looked down at the remains of his finery. His cream silk shirt and slacks were covered with black smuts from the fire, his shoes and socks were sodden from the puddles left by the fire hoses, and he stank of smoke. So much for any further romantic intentions.

He glanced up at the house. Something white moved on the balcony outside his bedroom. Three a.m., and Lyn had waited up – tonight of all nights! He sank his head into his hands. He was tired, aching, and he had developed a foul headache. All he wanted was to stretch out and enjoy a couple of hours sleep, until he had to start all over again. What on earth had happened to sour the relationship between them, to the extent that he was now reluctant to enter his own house and face her?

He experienced a sudden pang of regret for the peace and quiet of his old bachelor flat. When he had lived alone, he had often felt lonely, but perhaps loneliness was preferable to the trauma of sulks and arguments.

He climbed slowly out of the car, wincing as the muscles in his ankles protested at taking his weight. He stretched his aching back, only just remembering to lock the car doors before walking up the short drive. Shrugging his shoulders out of his jacket, he hung it over the bannister in the hall. Kicking his sodden shoes into a corner, he headed straight upstairs. The lights were on, but Lyn was still standing outside on the balcony.

'You're going to be exhausted tomorrow.'

'I'm not working, so I can have a lie-in.' She turned to face him. The rain had stopped, but the wind was still blowing in cold from the sea. Her face was white and frozen, but she appeared to be oblivious to any discomfort.

'I wish I had the day off too, so we could spend it together.'

'Do you?'

'Of course I do. It seems weeks since we spent any time with each other.'

'Then why don't you just *take* the day off?'

'Because we're in the middle of a case, we're short-handed...'

'The police are always short-handed,' she snapped. 'Let Peter Collins take some of the load for a change.'

'He can't. He's in hospital.'

'Is he all right?' She came in from outside, and closed the French doors.

'He should be OK in a couple of days.' He sank down on the bed and slipped the knot of his tie. 'He and Anna Bradley were trapped inside that factory down the docks when it went up. I suppose you heard about it.'

'We heard the sirens. We couldn't hear anything else in that restaurant at one stage. My God, look at you. You weren't with him ...?'

'No. I'm fine. Just got a bit messed up, watching from outside, that's all.'

'Is Peter badly hurt?'

'Concussion, smoke inhalation, and a bullet wound that hit nothing vital.'

'He was shot?'

Trevor nodded, conscious that he hadn't told her anything that wouldn't appear in the press tomorrow. Wasn't it possible to stop thinking as a policeman – even in the bedroom?

'But he *is* going to be all right?'

'Both he and Anna, yes. Her hands were badly cut when she smashed a window to get them both out of the building.' He almost made a gibe about the great male chauvinist being rescued by a mere woman. If it had been another evening, or one early on in their relationship, they might have laughed about it before rolling on the bed and making love. As it was, he couldn't even remember the last time he'd touched her.

'That woman you were with?'

'Dr Daisy Randall.'

'Is she the one you told me about in Compton Castle? The one you were in love with?'

'Nothing has ever happened between us.'

'That doesn't make any difference, Trevor. It's obvious you wish it had, and in some ways that's even worse. If you'd had the sense to fuck her when you first met, you'd probably have forgotten all about her by now.'

'I doubt it,' he replied with unintentional cruelty.

'I'll move out tomorrow.'

'Lyn.' He pleaded. 'It's late, and I'm tired. This is neither the time nor the place to start another row.'

'I'm trying to tell you that, if you love her, you're free to go to her.'

'I can't to go her, because I was never with her,' he said vehemently. 'She was the wife of a murder victim. It was a traumatic case for her and for me. You saw the state I was in at the end of it.' He grimaced at the pain in his legs, as he forced himself to rise and take the steps he needed to stand beside her. 'Lyn.' He reached out and touched a strand of her hair. 'I'm sorry. But it's always difficult when we're working flat out on a case. I tried to warn you.'

She looked up at him through bruised, tear-stained eyes. He bent his head and kissed away the tears, before kissing her on the lips. She tasted of salt, brandy and toothpaste. It took five minutes of whispered endearments and caresses to evoke a response.

As he pulled her down on to the bed, and began to undress her, he reflected that if men and women never had to talk to one another, life would be wonderfully uncomplicated. Making love to Lyn was so much easier than making conversation with her. But when passion finally triumphed, and they rolled naked between the sheets, he remembered Daisy Randall and how easy conversation had always been with her.

Lost in a jumbled dream-world of blazing fires and injured colleagues, Joseph reached for the telephone on his bedside table.

'Don't tell me you're still in bed?' Dan Evans' voice growled down the line.

Trevor opened an eye and tried to focus on the clock beside the telephone. Ten o'clock.

'It was a hard night,' he apologised drowsily.

'You're telling me? I didn't leave the hospital until two, and I was still in here at seven.'

'I'm obviously not as robust.'

'We've had the results back from the lab.'

'And?' Trevor sat up in bed, shuddering as a cold draught blew across his shoulder-blades from the open bathroom window. He'd forgotten to close the connecting door last night.

'A complete and beautifully clear set of prints. They're being run through the computer now. How soon can you get here?'

'Twenty minutes.'

'Make it ten.'

'I have to shower.'

'*I* won't mind if you smell.' Evans hung up.

'Work?' Lyn stirred beside him.

'Afraid so, love.' He leant over and kissed her. 'I'll be back as soon as I can.'

'See you next week.' Even half asleep, she was capable of sarcasm.

Having compromised on food, but not on the shower, Joseph walked into the station fifteen, not ten, minutes after receiving Evans' call.

'Sergeant Collins telephoned,' Sarah Merchant informed him. 'He told me to let you know they'll probably discharge him after the doctor's rounds at two o'clock.'

'Do me a favour?'

'For you, anything.'

'Ring them at two, and see if I can pick him up.'

She nodded as the telephone buzzed again.

When Trevor entered the office he was amazed to see Anna Bradley sitting at her desk.

'You sure you should be here?'

'No. But as I can't do anything at home with these' – she held up her bandaged hands – 'I thought I may as well come in. I need someone to feed me, and at least with the aid of the intercom I can answer the telephone.'

As if to prove a point, the telephone buzzed and she pressed down on the button with her elbow.

Joseph walked over to the wall where Evans was pinning photographs on to a cork board.

'Philip Matthews?'

'We had these photographs collected from records. I'd like you to run them over to O'Kelly in the mortuary some time today, together with a full description, to see if he can match him to our victim.'

'Nothing from forensics on the victim's fingerprints?'

'You saw those hands. Did you really expect anything?'

'I live in hope and bow to science.'

'You'd be better off bowing to leg-work. That's what usually solves these cases. But, talking about hope, I've asked for Philip Matthews' dental records to be sent to forensics, to see if we can match them to the remaining teeth.'

'That jaw was pretty badly burnt.'

'According to O'Kelly, there should be enough to facilitate a match. And, of course, thanks to Joan of Arc here' – he smiled fondly at Bradley – 'we have this.' He handed Trevor a faxed report from the laboratory. 'They not only found prints inside the suitcase, they've also matched them. Now they've finished with it. Chris Brooke has gone over to fetch it. He should be back around eleven.'

'Adam Weaver . . .' Joseph frowned. 'Why should I know that name?'

'He was that actor who killed his wife.'

'I remember. He played a detective in some series . . .'

'And for a curtain call he murdered his wife in real life. The tabloids loved it.'

'Did he have a good reason?' Joseph flicked over the first page of the fax.

'The best. She wanted to leave him because he was having an affair.' The telephone rang. 'Do you want me to get that?' Evans asked Bradley, who was staring blankly into space.

'No, I can manage,' she said hastily.

'As you can see, it was an interesting case,' Evans continued as Joseph read the sordid details.

'He dismembered her body in the bath . . .'

'Weaver insisted he had nothing to do with it. Claimed he was in London at the time, but couldn't come up with one single witness to substantiate his alibi.'

'Unusual for London.'

'His defence sent people to ask questions in the off-licence Weaver claimed to have visited that night. They also interrogated the porter who'd been on duty in his building, combed the streets looking for people who'd been in the area at the time, put out an appeal in the press and on TV, and drew a complete blank.'

'There's some people who never see anything beyond their noses, especially assistants in urban off-licences,' Bradley contributed.

'The pathologist who carried out the PM never entirely established the cause of death. Although he did say that in his opinion it was strangulation.'

'Because the upper horn of the thyroid cartilage on the right side of the neck was fractured,' Joseph read. 'And there was a blot clot around it, which meant it couldn't have happened after death.'

'That's the small bone in the neck that can only be broken when the neck is gripped hard by someone's hand?'

'I thought you'd read this?' Joseph held up the report.

'I only received it ten minutes ago.'

'The jury saw fit to believe the prosecution. Adam Weaver was sentenced to life imprisonment three years ago.' Joseph flicked over the last page.

'And he escaped one year later, to the day,' Bradley murmured half to herself.

'How come you know so much about this case, Bradley?'

'Would you believe I once had a crush on Adam Weaver?'

'A hardened policewoman like you?'

'I was a teenager before I became a hardened police officer.' Bradley didn't say any more. She realised her explanation sounded ridiculous, but not as ridiculous as the truth. That she had in fact met Adam Weaver in drama college. That she had fallen head over heels in love with him. That she had moved in with him the very day he had asked her to. And had taken an overdose the day he had left.

Chapter Ten

'The suitcase, sir.' Chris Brooke, fresh-faced, young, keen and wearyingly eager, knocked before carrying the case he'd collected from the forensic laboratory into Joseph's office. He pulled an envelope out of his pocket and handed it to the Inspector. 'They made a full inventory of everything they found inside, sir.'

'Quick driving, Brooke,' Evans complimented, as he glanced at the clock. 'Now you can telephone this station, and see if you can pick up full copies of those two files.' He handed Brooke the initial pages of the Adam Weaver fax, and what details he had collected of the investigation into Weaver's escape from prison.

'Right away, sir.'

'It makes me tired just to look at him,' Bradley sighed, as he left the room.

'Now that you and Collins are laid up, we could do with some of that lad's energy,' Evans said thoughtfully. 'I think I'll have a word with the Super.'

'As long as you keep him on a leash whenever I'm near.'

'You sure you don't want to go home, Bradley?'

'I told you, there's no one there to feed me.'

'We can always tip some beans into a bowl, so you can lap them up cat-fashion.' Joseph picked up the suitcase and laid it on his desk. He sprung the locks, lifted the lid, and stood back as the rancid smell of damp, dirty clothes wafted into the room.

'If our man really is Adam Weaver, he's not thinking any straighter than when he carved up his wife in the bathroom and did a runner, hoping no one would notice. Someone should have told him that there's no point in locking a cardboard suitcase. All you need is a good penknife to cut through the back.' With his thumbnail, Evans slit open the envelope Brooke had given him.

'I don't think he kept the crown jewels in here.' Joseph lifted out a brown wool sweater. It was covered with a thin film of the greyish-white fingerprint powder the forensic team had applied to every hard surface inside the suitcase. The wool felt thick and greasy to the touch. He held it gingerly between his fingertips, looking around for somewhere to put it.

'Not on *my* desk.' Bradley leant protectively forward.

'One sweater, brown wool.' Evans ticked it off the list, as Joseph finally dropped it to the floor at his feet.

'It doesn't look as though he quite got around to doing his laundry.' Catching sight of an empty plastic bag in the bin next to Bradley's desk, Joseph pulled it out and thrust it on to his hand.

'Four socks?'

'Four socks.' Joseph held them at arm's length with the bagged hand, then dropped them on top of the sweater.

'Two pairs of underpants.'

'This is getting sick.' Bradley turned her back so she wouldn't have to look at the grey rags Joseph had removed from the suitcase.

'What did you expect? Silk boxer shorts?' Joseph discarded them on top of the growing pile.

'Newspapers?' Evans queried.

Joseph pulled out a brittle yellow bundle, rolled up with an elastic band. He checked the date on the first one. 'This goes back two years.' He opened it out to show headlines two inches high: ESCAPED KILLER ON THE RUN.

'Weaver?' Evans asked.

'Who else?' Trevor unrolled the others. All of them carried variations on the same theme. He deposited the newspapers next to the clothes. There was now very little else left in the case. Two tins of beans, one of sausages, a rusted, lethal-looking tin-opener with a spiked end, a plastic bag that had once held bread but now contained half a bar of gelatinous soap, and an extremely unsanitary piece of ragged towelling.

'Is that it?' Joseph looked over at the Inspector.

'No, it says here they found some photographs in the lining.'

Joseph rummaged in the case.

'Try inside,' Bradley suggested. 'They may have replaced everything exactly as they found it.'

It was stuffed into the spine of the suitcase: a grubby brown envelope containing two photographs. One was a studio portrait of a beautiful blonde wearing a beguiling smile and a plunging neckline. Bradley knew exactly who she was. She'd torn a similar photograph to shreds when she'd found it in Adam's wallet just before he'd walked out on her ten years ago. The other showed a child about six or seven years of age. She'd inherited her mother's exquisite blonde hair, blue eyes, and captivating smile – only the smile was minus a few baby teeth.

'Weaver's family?'

'Presumably the wife he murdered. By the looks of it, they must have had a daughter, or perhaps it was her daughter and not his.' Evans took the photographs from Joseph, and moved over to the wall-board. 'We'll know more when we get that file.'

'Where do you want to go from here?'

'Wait for the files, and comb through them for anything that was missed at the time.'

'And Adam Weaver?'

'I have every man on the beat and every undercover officer on the force out looking for him. Or rather for him with Anthony George's face,' Evans amended.

'How did he escape from prison?'

'From what I gather, no one ever found out. The when is easier, and it could be significant. He disappeared from his cell in the early hours of the morning on the day after Anthony George died.'

'Good timing, then, for a transplant operation using George's face.'

'What exactly did your doctor friend say about the conditions required for these face transplants?'

'They're similar to those that apply to organ transplants. The face has to be *very* carefully removed, and there also has to be a tissue match between donor and recipient.'

'Do we have medical details for George and Weaver?'

'They should be included in their files. If not, these socks should provide forensics with a head-start. I should think there's more than enough sweat and other secretions soaked into them.'

'If you give me the file, and a pencil with a blob of Blu-Tack on the end, I'll start looking.'

'Why the pencil?' Joseph asked her in puzzlement.

'To turn the pages. I think you're forgetting I have no hands. Only a mouth.'

'You took your time getting here.' Collins was sitting dressed and impatient in the ward's day-room when Joseph walked in. He was wearing the same clothes he had used to infiltrate the squat the day before, only now they were covered with soot, and stank of smoke.

'Sarah telephoned at two. It's only twenty past now.'

'You were due here at ten past.'

'I was, but the sister wanted to discuss your condition.'

'Really? How many complaints did she have?'

'A few.'

Collins held up a newspaper he'd bought that morning. 'I see we're painted as the town villains again. We do nothing constructive when one vagrant is burned. So will we do anything when an entire squat-full go up in smoke?'

'I try not to read those rags.'

'I should have more sense, too.' Collins tossed the paper into the bin on their way out.

'How about I drive you back to my place?' Joseph suggested, as they took the lift to the ground floor.

'Need a lodger to help pay the mortgage?'

'The sister said you shouldn't be left on your own. That your concussion needs watching.'

'And you'd rather watch it than quarrel with Lyn?'

'I'm trying to help.'

'And I'm too streetwise to get caught up in an argument between you and your lady love.'

'Collins . . .'

'Take me to my flat. I'll do a quick change, then you can drive me to the office.'

Joseph looked at the bandage that bulged beneath Collins' shirt and sweater, the sling he wore on his right arm, and the visible signs of pain in his face. 'You're in no condition to work.'

'You'd rather I died of boredom in my flat?'

'We're running an investigation, not a hospital. We've already got Bradley there demanding nursing care as it is.'

'She turned up this morning?'

'By taxi. Her excuse is that with her hands bandaged she can't feed herself. When I left, Evans was pushing a sandwich into her mouth.'

'That's one task I can take off your hands, seeing as how I've still got a hand left.'

'What is going on between you and Bradley?'

'Nothing that need concern you.'

'I thought we were mates.'

'This coming from the man who doesn't drop a hint about spare females when he's got them queuing for his favours.'

'It's not like that.'

'It never was like anything between you and Daisy Sherringham, if I remember rightly. You were always content to worship her from afar.'

'Her name is now Dr Randall, and last night was strictly business.'

'Since when has dinner been business?'

'This may come as a surprise to you, Collins, but some people can contrive to take a lady to dinner without tumbling in the sack with her afterwards.' Joseph opened the central locking of his car.

'You must tell me how you manage it, sometime.'

'Didn't you take Bradley out to dinner that time you booked an overnight?' Joseph asked in an attempt to deflect Collins' attention away from himself.

'Liquid dinner.'

'And that's different?'

'Everything I do is different from what you do. For a start, I'm a lot wiser, especially when it comes to women. Come on, then, give me an update on the case, so I'll know exactly what's what when I get in.'

Joseph picked up the file on Adam Weaver as soon as it arrived, and moved into Evans' office to read it – out of sight of Collins and Bradley, who were sitting side by side at Bradley's desk, checking on the findings of the inquiry that had investigated Adam Weaver's breakout from prison. Evans had been called into an emergency meeting with the Super, which probably meant that 'upstairs' were furious at implied criticisms of the police appearing in early press reports on the fire in the old factory.

Leaving the connecting door open so that he could hear any incoming telephone calls, Joseph propped his feet on a spare chair, opened the file and began to read. The murder case had received heavy press coverage because of Adam Weaver's television connections, and whoever had investigated it had been meticulous in keeping newspaper cuttings. There was a thick wad of them, liberally spattered with theatrical studio photographs. Adam Weaver had possessed the typical leading man's good looks. Tall, rugged, dark-haired and dark-eyed, he had contrived to look more American than British, possibly deliberately because the network had been trying to sell his series to American television before tragedy and scandal had put paid to the whole venture. The photographs of his wife matched the photograph they'd found in the suitcase, and Joseph found himself speculating on the mental state of a convicted killer who carried a photograph of his victim around with him. The child had also been his own, and her photographs in the press cuttings also matched the one discovered in the suitcase lining. Joseph scribbled a note reminding himself to check where she was now, just in case Adam/Tony made an attempt to contact her. Checking her age in the file, he realised she'd be nine years old now. He wondered if she'd been told about her father, or the way her mother had died.

'If Weaver and this "Tony" are one and the same,' Collins shouted suddenly through the open door, 'and with the fingerprint evidence I don't see how he can be anyone else, the key's got to lie in a face transplant.'

'Daisy Randall checked for me, and no official face-transplant operations were carried out in this country until eighteen months ago.'

'Then there has to have been an unofficial one.'

'Obviously,' Bradley added drily.

'You thought to tackle it from the angle of doctors capable of carrying out this operation, Joseph?'

'Dr Randall's compiling a list for me.'

'Call in on your way home and check if she's made any progress,' Evans ordered, as he walked into the room.

'Nice meeting?' Collins asked.

'Isn't it always, with upstairs and the Super. Particularly when they've learnt more from the local TV midday news than we've been able to tell them. You'll no doubt be pleased to hear that some of Valance's shots are going out on the early-evening nationwide network. I've seen the tape, and you looked very heroic, Bradley. And you, Collins, made a *very* helpless victim.'

'We should have smashed Valance's camera while we had the chance,' Joseph muttered angrily.

'Anything come of it besides a dressing-down for this department, sir?' Bradley enquired.

'Not from Valance's tape – the way that was put together, I've no doubt he'll be offering it to Hollywood next. But the Fire Service has reported that the source of the blaze was on the central, second-floor staircase.'

'Cardboard boxes and newspapers.' Bradley recalled the pile of rubbish they'd passed on the way up.

'Hang about.' Collins stared at Evans. '*Central* staircase?'

'That's right. There were three serving each floor. One at each end of the building and one in the middle.'

'Bradley and I used the one to the right as you face the front of the building?'

'That's certainly the end you were hauled out of,' Evans agreed.

'How long after this Tony ran out on us did you smell smoke?' Collins asked Bradley.

'I'm not sure, it was dark, confusing, probably not more than five minutes.'

'Wouldn't it take longer than five minutes to set a fire?' Collins demanded.

'I have no idea, I've never had pyromaniac tendencies,' Joseph said flatly.

'What was set alight?'

'That's anyone's guess now. All the fire department could tell us was the blaze was hot enough to melt the ironwork on the staircase, so if it was set in rubbish . . .'

'With petrol?'

Evans pursed his lips as he looked at Collins. 'Could be,' he mused carefully, following Collins' train of thought. 'They're still carrying out tests. I'll mention the possibility.'

'And if our "Tony" was responsible, and petrol *was* used, then it's a fair bet he's got a couple of containers stashed away somewhere.' Joseph carried the file he'd been reading out of Evans' office and over to his desk.

'There has to be a connection. The victim in Jubilee Street, whoever he was, was wearing clothes Tony had been seen in.'

'But why would Tony exchange one set of rags for another?' Bradley asked.

'To make everyone think he was dead. Those boots were quite distinctive.'

'What I'd like to know is did he have time to set the fire between entering the building, attacking us and leaving?' Bradley questioned seriously.

'Don't ask me.' Collins rubbed his aching arm. 'I was out cold, remember.'

'We could try asking the man,' Evans suggested.

'First we've got to find him.'

'Exactly, and that's just what the Super wants – preferably before Valance gets hold of him, and puts him on a television chat show.'

'Which means we're all out on the streets tonight?'

'That's right, Joseph. But not you two.' He gazed from Bradley to Collins. 'In fact the pair of you should get off home right now. After a good night's rest you might even be of some use to me in the morning.'

'Nice to know you really care, sir,' Bradley muttered, heading towards the door, her bandaged arms stretched out in front of her like a tapdancer's.

'What I'm trying to say,' continued Evans, 'is that, although I appreciate your help, we can manage without you. I've succeeded in getting Murphy and Brooke co-opted on to the team – and the Super's promised more.'

'Mr Keen and Eager . . .'

'And Mr Over the Hill,' Collins chimed.

'Now that our original murder inquiry has expanded to take in arson – and more victims . . .'

'How many more?' Joseph asked.

'They found another five in the wreckage this morning.'

'That's nine, including the ones from last night.'

'Ten,' Evans corrected. 'Another died in the hospital this morning.'

'That's one way of clearing the streets.'

'Collins, I don't want to hear you saying that outside of these four walls,' Evans warned.

'Why not? It's the truth. You know as well as I do that no one gives a damn about homeless kids – not even their parents. If they did, those poor sods would spend their nights tucked up in warm, dry beds at home, not dossing down in squats.'

'You're talking about kids . . .'

'Reject kids who were going nowhere.'

'Maybe not all of them, but now we'll never know different, will we?' Silence reigned heavily in the room, while the Inspector glanced at his subordinates. 'Right, Joseph, your doctor,' he reminded, 'then back here. We'll work in pairs tonight. Murphy with me, Brooke with you. All officers on duty to report into Central Control every ten minutes. I suggest you do the same. Every available man will be out tonight.'

'Then we'll expect to see our "Tony" here tomorrow morning,' Collins sneered, as he opened the door.

After dropping Bradley and Collins off outside the latter's flat,

Joseph drove straight to the General Hospital. He parked in a bay marked 'Residents Only,' entered the palatial foyer of the burns unit and asked at reception for Dr Randall.

'Dr Randall isn't in the building,' the girl manning the desk informed him stiffly.

'Is she at home?'

'I really wouldn't know.'

He walked across the car park to the hospital staff quarters and climbed the stairs leading to Daisy's door. There he rang the bell, and waited. Minutes ticked past. He rang again, not really expecting a reply. The flats were tiny, and there was no way it would take so long to answer. Turning his back, he began to walk away.

'Trevor!' She opened the door, and stood with her head and body swathed in towels.

'I'm sorry, I didn't mean to inconvenience you. I'll come back later.'

'I know how busy you are, so please come in.' She disappeared back inside, leaving the door ajar, and he followed. 'Give me a couple of minutes to put something on, and I'll be with you. Help yourself to a drink.'

As she returned to the bedroom, he looked around him. A pretty, cream lace cloth covered a table which, if the legs were anything to go by, was ripe for a jumble sale. A two-seater couch and chairs had been transformed by bright Indian cotton throwovers. A bunch of daffodils stood in a cut-glass vase on a side table, and next to it was a silver tray set out with four glasses, a soda syphon and bottles of brandy and whisky. Trevor reached for the brandy bottle and poured himself a small one.

'I'll have one of those too, please.' Daisy stood in the doorway. She was wearing a black and silver kaftan, but with a towel still wrapped round her head.

'I called in at the hospital, but they said you'd left for the day. I wondered if you'd come up with anything yet?'

'I put in calls to all the relevant surgeons, giving the dates you suggested last night. Two have already responded in the negative, but those in the States haven't got back to me yet. They could be at the conference.'

166

'The one your boss is attending?'

'Yes.' She took the glass he handed her, and curled up on the sofa. 'But I did manage to get through to him last night. He mentioned that there was a doctor practising in London two years ago who had worked on the initial research programme involving face transplants. Given his expertise, it's possible that he was in a position to carry one out himself. But if – and it is an "if" – he did, it certainly isn't documented.'

'Does this doctor have a name?'

'Yes, but I'm not sure I should tell you without conclusive evidence that he's actually involved – or at least until I can contact him to discuss it. It wouldn't be ethical.'

'Neither was that fire last night.'

'You think it was set by the man who seems to have had a face transplant?'

'It could have been. The most I can say at the moment is that he's top of our suspect list. Truth be known, he's our only suspect.'

'Trevor . . .'

'Look, I know you'll keep this to yourself, but there's a strong possibility that this man walking around with Anthony George's face is an escaped prisoner who was convicted of murder.'

'How can you possibly know that?'

'Bradley picked up a suitcase from the factory yesterday. Both she and Peter Collins witnessed the man who resembles Anthony George handling it, but the only fingerprints found inside are on file as belonging to this villain who broke out of prison two years ago.'

'Who's Bradley?'

'You met her last night, while she was having her hands sewn up.'

'The brave lady who saved Collins.'

'You look as though you disapprove.'

Daisy laughed. 'No, no, I would never wish Sergeant Collins ill. In fact, after you were injured, he was quite decent to me. In his own way,' she added dryly.

'I've never known Peter do anything other than in his own way.'

'I can imagine.'

She leant back against the sofa and pulled the towel from her hair. As damp hair cascaded down her neck, a dry, astringent scent he remembered so well flooded into the atmosphere. It was so very different from the light flowery perfume Lyn usually wore.

'So, what you're saying is we have a killer running loose on the streets of this town?'

'And the key to tracking him down probably lies with the doctor who performed the face transplant that transformed his appearance.'

'Killer or not, it still wouldn't be ethical for me to implicate a fellow doctor without some form of confirmation.'

'No one need ever know it was you who told us.'

'Can't you give me until tomorrow morning?'

'Time could be of the essence.'

'I found out a year and a half ago that time is *always* of the essence, where the police are concerned. It seems to mean more to them than integrity, people or feelings.'

'I'm just trying to do my job, and hopefully prevent a maniac from taking further innocent lives.' He finished the brandy and set down the glass on the table.

'Would you like another?'

'Yes, but I haven't time.'

'You're on duty?'

'All night, or until we find our man.'

'I hope you do find him.' She rose unsteadily to her feet. He reached out and touched her arm.

'Are you all right?'

'Perfectly, apart from drinking on an empty stomach.'

'You haven't eaten today?'

'Not since last night. It's been one of those days.'

'You should take better care of yourself.' His voice was grave with concern.

'Don't worry, I've already got something waiting in the microwave.'

'I'm glad to hear it.' He pulled her towards him, and she came quietly, unresistingly.

'Trevor . . .'

He silenced her by placing his mouth over hers. She stiffened, as though about to protest, then suddenly he realised she was kissing him back.

'I've wondered what that would feel like for a long time,' he confessed as they finally drew away from one another.

'And?' Her eyes glittered mischievously.

'And, I'd like to take it a step further.'

'You're forgetting you're spoken for.'

He remembered Lyn – and work. 'I'll be back, and we'll talk about it then.'

'It's Laurence Marks.'

'Who?'

'You wanted the name of that transplant surgeon practising in London two years ago. It's Laurence Marks.'

'Marks?' He tried to think where he had heard the name recently, but was now incapable of thinking about anything except Daisy, and the fact she was finally in his arms.

'If you give me until tomorrow, I'll contact him.'

'No one will be doing anything much before tomorrow,' he murmured as he made his way to the door.

'This is marvellous. I never thought you'd be home this early. I've prepared dinner, and it will only take half an hour to cook.' Lyn stood in the hall watching as Trevor took off his jacket and threw his keys on the hall table.

'I'm sorry, but I've got to go out again as soon as I've changed.'

'With her?'

'Don't be ridiculous. Mulcahy's posted every available man out on the streets tonight to look for . . .'

'Don't lie, Trevor. Please don't lie,' she whispered. 'Whatever else you do, give me credit for some intelligence. You stink of her perfume. I could smell it yesterday in the restaurant. Her lipstick is all over your mouth . . .'

Trevor glanced in the mirror. There was no lipstick there.

Then he remembered there wouldn't be, as Daisy had just come out of the bath. But that one quick glance was enough to damn him.

'What's the matter, Trevor? Thought you hadn't wiped it all off?' she taunted.

'I have to get going,' he said brusquely.

'And so do I. Right now.'

'Lyn, please.' He hurried up the stairs after her, but she had locked herself into the bathroom. He looked at the clock: there was no time to reason with her. Not if he wanted to make Mulcahy's briefing. Instead he opened his wardrobe door and pulled out his oldest pair of jeans. Dressing 'down' was a problem for Trevor. After he'd been discharged from hospital he'd got rid of most of his older clothes. Eventually he found a shirt with a tear in it, and also an old pair of trainers. A suitable coat was going to be a problem. He'd just have to freeze. He looked around quickly; he really didn't have any more excuse to linger. Just Lyn . . .

He hammered on the bathroom door.

'Lyn, please. I have to go out now. If you'd only open the door, you'd see how I'm dressed. It's work, I swear it. No women are involved, not even Bradley.'

Not a sound came from inside. It would have to wait until morning. Slamming the bedroom door behind him, he walked down the stairs and out of the house.

The problem was that, even if Lyn had opened the door, he still wouldn't have known what to say to her. She'd been right: he was totally besotted with Daisy Randall – and was finding it increasingly difficult to see anything beyond her.

Chapter Eleven

'One thing's certain, we're not going to find "Tony" hanging around the hostels now,' Joseph commented, when he and Brooke met up with the Inspector and Murphy, after parking their respective cars outside the Port Offices.

'It's still worth checking with the inmates in case any of them have encountered him since yesterday. With that fire putting paid to what was probably the largest squat in town, the homeless will be out in force, looking for a replacement. If we find that place before our man, we may even catch him moving in.'

'I have a feeling he's unlikely to be running with the pack.' Murphy stamped his feet in an effort to warm himself. Signs of spring were evident in the buds appearing on the trees, and the multi-coloured tips of daffodils and tulips pushing up from the flowerbeds in the nearby roundabout. But the encroaching night air still bore the chill hallmark of winter.

'Murphy and I will take the hostels.' Evans glanced at his watch. 'The doors will be closing on them by now. The Super's detailed a squad to check the underpasses and the multi-storey car parks. Think of anywhere else, lad?'

'Me, sir?' asked Brooke, amazed at being consulted by a superior officer.

'You were out on the beat last week. The Sergeant and I haven't done that in years.'

'It's like you said, sir: the car parks, the underpasses. Some of them used to squat in that old pub down the bottom end of High Street.'

'The Drunken Sailor?' Joseph asked.

'That's the one.'

'I thought the owners had boarded it up.' Murphy's foot-stamping had become more energetic.

'The old factory was boarded up, too, not that it achieved much.'

'After yesterday, every abandoned building in town is worth checking,' Evans said firmly. 'Joseph, you and Brooke take everything west of High Street. Murphy and I'll take the east side, after we've visited the hostels in Jubilee Street. Don't forget, you make contact with HQ every ten minutes, giving position and progress, and details of any other officers you've met and compared notes with.'

Joseph returned to his car and picked up his anorak. To hell with freezing. He glanced at Brooke as he zipped it against the biting wind. In his jeans and leather jacket he looked more like a scared teenager than an officer of the law. Trevor gave him an encouraging nod and set off down a deserted quayside that bordered the Marina.

Brooke stared out at the berthed yachts.

'There's dozens of hiding places there, sir.' He had to shout above the ringing of the masts.

'Owners pay the Marina security guards to check their vessels every day. And even if they didn't, a place like that would be much too open for our man. He'd be seen the minute he made a move to find food or water. Whatever else he is, this fellow's not stupid. He'll realise we're out looking for him by now.'

The pubs and wine bars on the Marina were crowded. As the two officers passed, a couple of women swung open the door of one of the more popular establishments. Joseph caught a glimpse of men standing at the bar, drinking pints and watching the news on a TV set high on the wall in a corner. Too early for the night revellers; these were probably office workers stopping for a pint on their way home. He remembered Lyn, and wondered if they, too, were heading back for a confrontation with their wives and girlfriends, or if their partners were more understanding. He turned his collar up to his ears in an effort to combat the increasing cold, which was now peppered with stinging moisture carried on the inshore breeze. For tonight, the best thing he could do was forget Lyn. Tomorrow, somehow or other, he'd make the time to sit down and talk to her properly. To settle the problems between them once and for all.

'We're not likely to find him here, are we, sir?' Brooke enquired hesitantly.

Joseph stopped and looked around. Lost in thoughts of his recent argument with Lyn, he'd headed blindly for the Marina's golden waterfront mile, where property prices were at their highest. The most expensive and exclusive nightclubs, pubs and restaurants lay just up ahead, and the homeless elements of the town were not encouraged to linger.

'I think it's worth checking out the back of these buildings,' he replied, in a face-saving exercise. 'That will take us to the edge of town, then we can systematically comb the side roads that lead into High Street.' He turned the corner and entered an alleyway running parallel to the waterfront. He didn't need the torch he carried in his pocket, as all the pubs and restaurants had installed security lights that flashed on as the two men approached the back yards.

'So this is what it's like to be in the spotlight,' Joseph commented as they walked on past the fifth or sixth restaurant. A chef looked out at them from his kitchen window, before continuing to chop vegetables on a board slung over a sink. Another light flashed on up ahead, but too far for either of them to have set it off. Startled, both Brooke and Joseph stepped into the shadows, only to see a cat scurrying towards them.

'No vagrant with any sense in his head would come wandering around here before morning.' Feeling rather foolish, Joseph walked on. 'And then only for a quick scavenge.'

'I've seen them at it, sir. They come around six or seven, pick up one or two parcels the cooks leave out for them, then they scarper.'

'You walk this beat?'

'Walked most of them in the town by now, sir.'

'You ever noticed this man we're after?'

'Not that I remember, sir.'

'That's the problem with this job. You only have time to register the obvious villains.'

At the end of the alley they paused, looking out towards the network of narrow terraces that fringed the oldest quarter of the town.

'If *you* were homeless, and your squat had burned down, Brooke, where would you head?'

'Probably for one of the farms on the outskirts, sir.'

'Given intensive farming methods, nowadays you'd soon be noticed and sent packing.'

'There's one or two derelict places, too, sir. I've been looking at them with a view to doing one up.'

'Fancy yourself as a farmer?'

'Only in retirement.'

'Good God, how old are you: nineteen, twenty? And you're already making plans for retirement?' Retirement was something Joseph only thought of in passing, and never in any great depth. Probably because he didn't have a clue what he'd do with his time if he didn't have to go into the station.

'Sometimes I cycle for miles around the farms without seeing a soul.'

'If that's the case, you'd better get a list of all those uninhabited places from the estate agents tomorrow, so we can search them.'

'Yes, sir.' Brooke's voice had lost some of its enthusiasm.

'Didn't they warn you that ninety per cent of detection is boring, repetitive leg-work, Brooke? Believe you me, there are times when I look back on my own time on the beat with nostalgia. Then, no two days were ever the same.'

They checked streets, they checked alleyways, they peered into narrow, walled-in back gardens. They joined the beat constables and checked the multi-storey car parks. They encountered more vagrants than they would have given the town credit for. The more sheltered floors of the multi-storey furthest from the town centre – and consequently the least favoured by motorists – looked more like an African shantytown than a suburban car park. Joseph chose one side of the square, Brooke and a PC took the other. They peered into cardboard boxes, unravelled bundles of rags, shook sleeping bodies awake, shone torches into comatose faces, but none bore even a slight resemblance to the one they sought. And although they flashed photographs of 'Tony' at the more lucid of those they disturbed, none would admit to ever seeing him at all, let alone recently.

It was three o'clock in the morning when, footsore, weary and chilled to the bone, Joseph and Brooke finally made it to High Street.

'Where to now, sir?' Brooke asked, wondering if they were going to work all through the night without a break.

'We check out the underpass – and hopefully meet up with the Inspector.'

'Which point do we start at?'

'The first one we come to.' The underpass in High Street had as many legs as a spider. It was built at a crossroads, and sunk below a high-walled roundabout. The planners had drawn up a detailed blueprint for a sunken garden twelve foot below the wall, which the council had meticulously laid out right down to the stone nymph at the centre of the flowerbeds; but the whole area had long since degenerated into a dumping ground for drinks cans, general rubbish and dog mess. The spider's arms leading out from the centre towards the feeder roads had originally been smartly tiled in pastel colours, but these had quickly become hidden beneath layer after layer of graffiti, and the tunnels themselves stank of urine and worse. Each side street sported two entrances: one with steps, one with a ramp. Linking all of them was a circular walkway that fed into the central garden. The parts of the tunnels that were best sheltered from the windy access ramps and steps and the central open area were the spaces most prized by the homeless. Like at the hostel, these spaces had to be claimed early, but not too early, as the police tried to keep the area clear at least until the cinemas and pubs had closed their doors.

As Joseph and Brooke descended the ramp closest to the High Street, they could hear a soft hubbub of voices.

'Gentlemen, you look frozen. Can I interest you in a cup of soup?' Standing behind a makeshift barrow stand, and surrounded by a group of teenagers, Tom Morris and Captain Arkwright had set up a soup kitchen.

'What kind of soup?' Brooke asked a Salvation Army officer who managed to look young and attractive despite her sombre uniform.

'Tinned vegetable. One of the larger manufacturers has kindly donated catering packs to our little project,' she explained. 'They've been most generous.'

Joseph watched as a young girl held a steaming polystyrene cup to the mouth of a toothless old man who was blue and shaking with cold. He pulled a pound coin out of his pocket.

'We'll have two.'

'It's not for sale,' Captain Arkwright protested.

'Call it a donation.'

As he dropped the coin into her collecting box, Morris ladled soup into two cups and handed them over.

'As you can see, Sergeant, we're trying to do our own bit to help.' He pointed to the photograph of 'Tony' that he'd pasted on the side of his barrow.

'That the Inspector's idea – or yours?'

'Bit of both. We thought it might save time. We've pinned copies up in all the hostels, too. After the terrible events of yesterday, it's the least we can do.' He handed his ladle over to one of the teenagers, and accompanied Joseph and Brooke deeper into the tunnel.

'I saw you outside the burning factory yesterday.'

'Captain Arkwright and myself were actually inside when it went up. Late yesterday afternoon someone snapped through the steel padlock on one of the ground-floor doors. Captain Arkwright and I thought it a good idea to go and see if we could persuade any of the youngsters to come with us into the hostels. I'm afraid we got a good deal more than we bargained for.'

'Have you told anyone – about your being there?'

'Oh yes. I told your Constable Murphy in the hospital last night, but I didn't really see anything. One minute I was talking to a couple of young lads who'd made their way down from Scotland to find work, the next the place was full of smoke and screaming.'

'I saw you helping a young girl out of the place.'

'Not out of the building, Sergeant. Only away from it. The

176

firemen rescued those trapped inside, then I led them to the paramedics. Captain Arkwright was the real heroine. She actually went on up to the second floor, looking for people to guide out through the open door. If it hadn't been for her bravery, I think the death toll would have been higher.'

'I had no idea,' Joseph mused, resolving to check with the Inspector if it was worth putting all the statements that had been taken after the fire on to a computer, in order to provide an overview of who exactly had been in that building when the blaze had started.

'I was sorry to hear about your two colleagues being injured,' Morris commiserated.

'They're just walking wounded. They'll both be fine. Tell me, do you organise this kind of thing often?' Joseph nodded in the direction of the soup wagon.

'Captain Arkwright and I try to make sure that someone goes out with the cart every night during the winter, and also a couple of times a week in summer.'

'Who are your helpers?'

'Most of them are either young Salvationists from the citadel, or Christians from the local evangelical church. They've put a lot of effort in: raising money for this wagon, begging manufacturers or the Chamber of Commerce for food donations. It wasn't easy, as most of the town's retailers were wary at first. They feared that vandalism would escalate if we attracted more homeless into the centre of town this late at night. I don't think they realised most of them were already here. And, even after the retailers had been won over, our customers remained sceptical of our motives. They expected us to give out Bible tracts and hymns along with the food.'

'You've forgotten to mention the police.'

'We've never had any hassle from the bobbies on the beat – only assistance. I think that's fair comment, Constable Brooke, don't you?'

Joseph looked at Brooke. 'You've worked this area too?'

'Once or twice.'

'The Inspector was here about half an hour ago, and he checked everyone then.'

'In that case there's not much point in us doing it again. Needless to say, you've seen no sign of our man?'

'If I do, you'll be the first to know. The Inspector has loaned me a police radio, just for tonight.'

'Then we'd better move on. There's a few more places we need to look at before dawn.' They turned and began to walk away. As they rounded the corner, Joseph recognised a small group of teenagers huddled on the ground as the same one he had encountered in Jubilee Street the day before. He walked towards them. They each had a blanket, thick grey, old army issue of the type the evangelical volunteers had been handing out.

'You got a bloody nerve coming near us after what you did to our squat.'

'Ssh.' Joseph crouched down beside them. 'You all right?'

'Fine in this bloody freezing hole,' the boy with the bald head retorted angrily. 'And before you ask, no we haven't seen that bloody man you're after. That's the last time you'll talk us into helping the fucking pigs.'

'It's possible that same man set your factory on fire. And if we hadn't been watching the building, a lot more people might have been hurt.'

'Ten are dead now.' The girl looked at him with dark, accusing eyes.

'I know, and I'm really sorry, but with all those people and all those candles, it was likely to happen sooner or later.'

'Burn inside or freeze out here, what's the bloody difference? We'll all end up dead now that, thanks to you, we've nowhere to go.'

'I know an agency where you can rent bedsits without a deposit.'

'Oh, yeah. Where's that, then? Never-never land?'

'Here.' Joseph handed the girl a piece of paper with an address written on it. 'Go and see that lady in the morning, and mention my name. She's expecting you and she can help all of you. I've seen the place. Those bedsits aren't up to much, but they're a start, and you can stay together if you want.'

'Why you doing this?' the girl asked suspiciously.

'Like your friend said, I could be the reason your squat burned down.'

'Pig?' Jason called after him as he moved away.

'What.'

'You're not as bad as most of your kind. If we see your man, we'll let you know.'

'Thanks.' Joseph smiled as he walked back towards his colleague.

'Nice place,' Joseph commented, as he dropped Brooke off outside the gates of an expensive suburban mansion.

'It's my parents' house,' he said without much enthusiasm. 'I'm saving for a place of my own.'

'I wouldn't be in a hurry to leave this one, if I were you.' Joseph revved the engine and drove away.

There were no lights on in his own house, and none of the curtains were drawn. Fighting a sinking feeling in the pit of his stomach, he walked up the drive and let himself in. A crushing silence greeted him as he closed the front door and headed into the living room, switching on the light. Everything seemed in its place, exactly as it should be. It was the same in the kitchen and dining room. Leaving his coat and shoes at the foot of the stairs, he raced up them. The bed was neatly made, with clean bedclothes. He opened the communicating door between the bedroom and dressing room. His own clothes were hanging exactly as he'd left them, but the left-hand rail, which Lyn had used was empty.

The bathroom shelf where she had kept her cosmetics and perfume was bare, and wiped clean. There had never been anything else of hers on display in the place. Perhaps that was part of the problem. Nothing in the house had ever belonged to Lyn, or been chosen by her, other than her own few personal possessions.

He remembered someone, somewhere in his past, saying that people could get used to anything, given time. Experience had taught him that wasn't true. He'd never really grown accustomed to living on the streets. He was constantly waiting to move on to better times, and better places, without consciously making an effort to change his situation. It was almost as though he were playing a role in a long-running television series. He had been given the part of a *vagrant*, and at first he'd treated this in the same way he'd approached a role when acting. He'd immersed himself in the character of a down-and-out, ready to play the part to the absolute hilt. So he'd frozen in winter, baked during a heat wave and, apart from the odd shower taken when he'd slept in a hostel, he'd barely washed. As a result he was verminous, his hair so thickly matted that a comb would never run through it again until it was cut. And he stank. He knew he stank, because he'd seen people recoil from him in the streets, though he could no longer smell the stench of vagrancy on himself – or on others. He simply lived minute by minute, hour by hour, day by day, waiting for the man in charge of this particular production to shout 'Cut!' so he could go back to his old, clean, comfortable way of life.

In the meantime he tried to survive as best he could, by not thinking too hard about his present situation. He had learned to cope with counting for nothing in the eyes of the public. It was as though living on the streets had endowed him with the power of invisibility. If he put out a cardboard tray, with *Homeless, please help* written on it, people passed by as though he wasn't there. If he slept in a doorway or the underpass, the only ones aware of him were the police when they wanted to move him on. But now suddenly everything had changed, and not into the bright cosy world he'd been waiting for. Now he felt as though he could never again be invisible *enough*.

He paused on the corner of the alleyway. The street in front was a narrow cul-de-sac. Purely residential. Well away from the usual haunts of vagrants and destitutes, but he dare not risk going back where the down-and-outs gathered, because he knew he'd soon be found. And, once found, he'd be finished.

He shivered, pulling his thin shirt close around his shoulders. It was cold, he was hungry, but he couldn't even go to the DHSS and ask for the no fixed abode allowance, not since his picture had been plastered all over the local newspaper stands, with the headline ARMED AND DANGEROUS. SHOULD NOT BE

APPROACHED BY ANY MEMBER OF THE PUBLIC.

He stepped back into the shadows and looked around him. There were lights on in most of the houses, but one or two of them were in darkness. Would it be easy to get into one? Would they be empty? And would one contain enough food and warm clothes to set him up for another day or two? He crept along the alley, carefully keeping his back hunched below the level of the garden walls. Once or twice he peered cautiously over the brickwork. Darkness was no guarantee that a house would be empty. The occupants could be sitting in a front room, lights off, television on.

In one house the curtains were open, and he could see that the whole of the downstairs area had been knocked into one open-plan room. A woman was washing dishes at the sink in front of a window facing him; behind her he could see a music centre close to the opposite window. The house next door was in darkness – empty, or still divided by its original walls with a presence sitting in a front room beyond? He shuddered. He felt cold and sick. How long had it been since he'd last eaten? There'd been nothing yesterday – and just baked beans cold from the tin the day before. Strange, he didn't feel hungry; only thirsty. Terribly thirsty. Even if someone was home, they weren't anywhere close to the back of the house and there might be an outside tap. Lots of houses had outside taps to supply garden hoses.

He pressed down on the latch of a garden door set into the back wall. The click it made sounded alarmingly loud. He paused, ready to run. A dog barked further down the street – then there was silence. He risked stepping on to the garden path. Shutting the door behind him, he crouched low, edging closer and closer to the house, which was shrouded in darkness. The only light on it was the glint of the full moon on window glass. He inched slowly and stealthily forward, listening hard for the slightest sound from inside.

A cloud drifted across the face of the moon. When it had sailed gently past, he could see that the kitchen window was closed but not latched. The handle was at a right angle. He took out his penknife and slid it beneath the plastic frame. He didn't have to exert much pressure for it to swing out towards him. So he was right: it hadn't been properly latched. The windowsill inside was bare. He paused again, until his ears almost hurt from the strain of listening. A clock ticked from the room within, music blared from a television next door. A voice echoed from the end of the street.

Heaving himself up on his hands, he tried to haul himself inside, but he was so weak it took an eternity. His arms alone couldn't bear his weight but, by dint of scraping his knee against the wall and gaining toeholds, he finally crouched on the sill. Then, losing his balance, he fell awkwardly into the sink. There was a shattering sound as it started to give way. He jumped off quickly, and turned on his ankle. Wincing with pain, he stood still and looked around. Even in the shadowy moonlight, he could see that this was no modern fitted kitchen. The sink he'd almost wrenched off the wall was free-standing stainless steel, with a pronounced hollow in the draining board. Probably one he'd just caused. He hobbled over to the fridge and opened the door. The light illuminated a small piece of cheese carefully wrapped in greaseproof paper, a jar of jam, half a pint of milk, and a tub of low-fat margarine. Nothing else. Beset by a pang of guilt, he closed the door. It looked and felt like the house of someone trying to survive on very little money. A pensioner perhaps?

Next he opened a Formica dresser. It contained half a loaf of bread, cut-side down on a breadboard. Higher up was a cupboard. Opening it he found glasses and plates. Taking a glass he filled it with water from the sink, and drank deeply. After three thirsty refills he risked leaving the kitchen. The passage outside led to a cramped living-room crammed with heavy, old-fashioned furniture. On a sofa covered by a woollen blanket, he spotted a sleeping cat. He scooped up the animal in his arms, intending to move it to a chair. It hissed and spat at him before running off, but left him in possession of what he wanted. Draping the blanket around his shoulders, his chilled body gratefully absorbed the residual warmth of the cat. He'd stayed long enough; there was nothing for him here. He left by the back door.

Further down the lane he found a garage with a broken door. The place was cold, draughty, and stank of oil. But, huddled in a corner with the blanket wrapped around his shoulders, he slept warmer than the night before.

'Could I speak to Sergeant Trevor Joseph, please.'

'Speaking.'

Evans and Collins exchanged glances. Joseph had been acting like a snake with back trouble since he'd put an appearance in the office at nine. That was far earlier than was strictly necessary after a night combing the streets.

'Trevor, it's Daisy.'

'Hello there.'

As Trevor's whole tone changed, Collins lifted his eyebrows at Anna Bradley.

'Have you done anything about that information I gave you yesterday?'

'About Marks? No.'

'I've found some old records that might be of interest to you, in our files. All experimental projects carry information on the early transplants. That goes back to what I was telling you about exchange of information. The first transplant detailed here was carried out on a male patient in his late twenties. And the donor was twenty-eight. Might that tie in with your case?'

'It could well do. What are the dates?'

'That's just it – there are none. And, what's even more unusual, no photographs. For obvious reasons, all files should carry detailed shots of a patient before and after the transplant has been performed.'

'These files, they're in your office?'

'Yes.'

'I'll be with you in ten minutes.'

'You mentioned someone called Marks?' Collins was quick to question Joseph.

'Last night Daisy Randall told me that the only person experienced enough to carry out a face transplant in this country two years ago was a surgeon called Laurence Marks.'

'And you didn't think to tell us!'

'I only found that out late last night, before we went looking for "Tony".'

'You bloody fool,' said Collins angrily. 'He could be related to Brian Marks.'

'Bloody hell, the solicitor? I knew I'd heard that name before.'

'Joseph, you're turning sloppy in your old age,' Collins reprimanded him, angrily.

'We've only lost twelve hours at the most.'

'I could have interviewed the fellow last night.'

'You couldn't. He's in America.'

Chapter Twelve

'As you can see, full and detailed files on all partial and total face transplants that have been carried out, abroad as well as here. Twenty-eight so far.' Daisy heaped the files, one on top of the other, on her desk, before finally tossing a file thinner than the others on to the summit of the pile. 'The telephone number and address of Laurence Marks' current project in the States is in this one.'

Joseph picked the file up and opened it.

'Would you like coffee?'

'Yes, please,' Joseph murmured, already engrossed in the file.

'Coffee would be fine.' Collins smiled at Daisy.

'I'll ask my secretary to fetch it. You can use this office for the next hour or so, if you like. I've got ward rounds now.'

'I'm sorry we've been keeping you,' Joseph apologised.

'Not really. If you have any questions, I should be through in an hour and a half.'

Collins picked up one of the other files, as Daisy left. He blanched at the photograph pinned to the first sheet: a detailed study of the face of a corpse in the process of being peeled away from the skull. The second was no better: a badly burned face being prepared for surgery.

'Real bedtime-story stuff this. I think I'd rather have the grown-up version.'

Joseph looked up quizzically.

'The one without pictures,' Collins explained wearily.

'I wish this one did have pictures,' Joseph complained. 'All I've got is a list of dimensions. Centimetres from eyebrow to eye, from tip of nose to chin.'

'Sounds like O'Kelly's province.'

'Until we find our "Tony", we have nothing to compare these with.'

'We have enough photographs of Weaver to paper the station.'

'Colouring of skin, dark,' Joseph read out. 'Weaver's skin was light.'

'Presumably you can graft a darker shade of skin on top of a face that was originally lighter, but then it would show at the join. I wonder if they have stitches around the neck, like Boris Karloff in *Frankenstein*?'

'Can't you ever be serious for more than five minutes at a time?'

'Just trying to help. When "Tony" is eventually found, it should be easy to check him out. I can see it now. "Excuse me, sir, would you mind removing your tie and unbuttoning your collar so we can look for the stitch line."'

'Have you thought through the implications of this case?' Joseph sat back in Daisy's chair as her secretary carried in a tray of coffee and biscuits.

'Thank you, darling.' Collins winked at the girl, eying her legs as she left the room. 'What implications?' he asked after she had closed the door. 'You mean, if you fancy someone's face you'll . . .'

'I mean for terrorists and criminals.'

'Criminals as in Adam Weaver?'

'Exactly.'

'We caught up with Weaver through his fingerprints.'

'And if they transplant those next?'

'You're a real bloody pessimist, aren't you?' Collins pulled out his pen and notebook. 'Let's start. Name of doctor: Laurence Marks, right?'

'Yes.'

'Dates?'

'None that I've seen yet.'

'What have you got there?'

Joseph pushed over the piece of paper with Laurence's US address and telephone number.

'What else you got?'

Joseph continued to pore over the file. 'The transplant occurred two days after the face was lifted from the donor.'

'I hate to risk ridiculous questions, but how do you store a face until you need it? Next to the beefburgers in the freezer?'

'We'll have to check that with Daisy.'

'Anything on the recipient?'

'Only that his own face was removed after the anaesthetic was administered.'

'Nothing on its condition?'

'No.'

'What I can't understand is why the hell a man like Adam Weaver would want to have his face changed? With his looks, he could have pulled any bird he wanted?'

'In jail? Aren't you forgetting he was a convicted murderer serving a life sentence, with a judge's recommendation of a minimum of thirty years. That can seem like a long time to someone who's twenty-eight going on twenty-nine.'

'So, you're thinking that he agreed to a new face in exchange for a new life.' Collins heaped three sugars into his coffee. 'All I can say is he didn't get very far, if that was his intention. Jubilee Street isn't exactly the kind of new life anyone in their right mind would want for themselves.'

'Then something must have gone wrong somewhere along the line.'

'Very wrong,' Collins echoed. 'I wonder what it was.'

'Have you got through to America yet?' Collins asked Evans as he and Joseph walked through the door of the incident room.

'Yes, but not to Laurence Marks himself.'

'I'm not surprised. If I was Marks, I'd keep my head down for a while.'

'Why?' Evans asked. 'No one's accusing him of anything.'

'Like stealing a face?'

'We've no evidence to link him with the mutilation of Anthony George.'

'Only those transplant notes.'

'Nothing in them suggests he knew where that face originated.'

'You believe in fairies, too, Joseph?' Collins asked caustically. 'You heard Daisy, same as me. Those faces have to be removed by experts.'

Evans slammed down the telephone. 'All I'm getting is "Mr Marks is in conference, and won't be available for some time". And the "some time" doesn't include a date.'

'You really do expect him to talk to you, don't you?' Collins looked from Joseph to Evans.

'I expect some degree of co-operation from an intelligent man – yes.'

'Someone's going to have to go over there,' Mulcahy predicted.

'Me, please. Want to come?' Collins asked Bradley.

'Not this time, Collins.' Mulcahy turned to the Inspector. 'I take it you have a current passport?'

'Yes, sir.'

'Get Merchant to book tickets for you, now. When you find Marks, offer immunity, whatever it takes, but get the truth out of him. Preferably one that will stand up in court. Once we know exactly who and what we're looking for, we might be in a position to clear up this mess.'

'It would be a step in the right direction,' Collins agreed drily.

'Any other leads being followed?' Mulcahy barked.

'Adam Weaver has a daughter, Hannah, who's living here.' Bradley indicated the Weaver file that Joseph had put in front of her before he'd left for the hospital.

'Here as in this town?'

'Yes, sir. On the modern estate on the outskirts.'

'Cowslip Road?'

'That's it. She's living with her aunt, her mother's sister, who's called Blanche Davies. The aunt is twenty-seven, single, and a social worker.'

'If you're up to it, you and Joseph can go round there tonight, just to check if the father's tried to get in touch.'

'Why not me?'

'Because I've something else in mind for you, Collins.' Mulcahy smiled coldly. 'In the Inspector's absence, you can co-ordinate the ongoing search for "Tony". Day and night. May I suggest a systematic approach. I'll give you all the men I can spare.'

'Systematic? We can't search and tag off every area in a town this size.'

'No, but we can search and then move on.'

'And if he moves in behind us?'

'Stop being so bloody awkward, Collins. Use your imagination. Given enough men, you can herd all the vagrants into the underpass in the centre of town. Then you can interrogate them. They live in places we don't even know about. If our man is still in the area, one of them must have seen him.'

'And even if they have, do you really think they're going to want to tell us about it?'

'With your powers of persuasion, Collins, it should be a piece of cake.'

'I telephoned her, but she doesn't get home until six o'clock. The little girl is picked up from school by a neighbour, who sits with her until the aunt gets home. I told her we'd get there around eight. I thought it would be best to let them have their tea and settle down before we go in.'

'Good thinking,' Joseph replied absently, his mind half on the case and half on Lyn. For the first time in six months, it didn't matter what time he got off his shift. He'd been wrong: it wasn't better to go back to an empty house. Even the prospect of Lyn in a bad mood was better than no Lyn at all.

The first thing Joseph and Bradley noticed as they drove up Cowslip Road was a gleaming grey Mercedes, complete with capped and uniformed chauffeur. It looked slightly ludicrous parked outside a semi-detached house which was small even by the standards of the modern housing estate. Pristine and neat, it's white UVPC windows shone in the darkness, the lights within highlighting rose-patterned, cotton-lace curtains. The mock-Victorian lamp next to the front door illuminated a neat square of turf surrounded by a border of sprouting bulbs.

'Social workers must get better pay than we do,' Bradley observed looking at the car.

'I doubt that's hers.' Joseph eyed the chauffeur.

Before Trevor had time to switch off the engine, the front

door opened and a man came out of the house.

'That's Marks.'

'The solicitor?'

'Yes!'

'I wonder why he's such a long way from home?'

'Do you want me to ask him?'

'No, we're not here to question him. Whatever his reasons, we'll find them out in our own good time. Nice cashmere coat,' Joseph observed, as they continued to watch the man. A few months ago, he wouldn't have known cashmere from worsted. Just one more thing he had Lyn to thank for.

An attractive blonde appeared in the doorway as Brian Marks stepped out on to the pavement.

Bradley caught her breath. 'My god, she's the spitting image of her sister!'

'Isn't she just.'

Marks held out his hand, and the woman took it. Then the solicitor leant forward and kissed her on the cheek.

'Very friendly.'

'Come on, Joseph. That's all it is: friendship. Look at their age difference.'

'Age difference doesn't stop some men.'

'You're forgetting I've interviewed Marks. A gap of forty years *would* bother someone of the old-school type like him.' As the solicitor turned and walked towards his car, Bradley slid down in her seat, though she needn't have bothered. Looking neither left nor right, Marks climbed into the back seat, and moments later the Mercedes slid noiselessly away from the kerb.

'Well, well, well.'

'The story of the three wells.'

'I'd forgotten that one.' Joseph smiled hollowly at her. 'Shall we go inside?'

'Miss Davies? Miss Blanche Davies?' Bradley asked as the blonde re-opened the door for them. Joseph stood back. When, minutes earlier, he had seen Blanche Davies under the light of the carriage lamp in her porch, he had thought her pretty. Now, close up, he could see that she was beautiful. Headturningly beautiful, with the same kind of looks that had launched her sister on a theatrical career.

'Yes, I'm Blanche Davies. You must be Sergeant Bradley.' She looked from Bradley to Joseph, her brilliant blue eyes searching, appraising.

'I am – and this is Sergeant Joseph.'

'Please come in.' She opened the door wide. A half-grown girl from the same astonishingly beautiful mould was sitting at a table in the living room. Both Bradley and Joseph instantly recognised Adam Weaver's daughter from the photographs discovered in the suitcase. But if they hadn't seen those, they would have taken her for Blanche Davies' daughter. The resemblance was remarkable.

'This is my niece, Hannah.' Blanche ushered them towards a small wooden-framed three-piece suite. 'Have you finished your homework, Hannah?'

'Yes, Auntie.'

'These police officers have come to discuss a case with me, so why not go upstairs and watch television?'

As the girl packed away her schoolbooks into a small rucksack, Joseph had a sudden pang of nostalgia for the family life he hadn't experienced since he'd left home. He couldn't help wondering what a daughter of him and Lyn would look like, should they ever be lucky enough to produce one. She would be dark of course, with brown eyes. Both he and Lyn had brown eyes, although his hair was nowhere as dark as hers. It was most peculiar that recently, while he'd been living with Lyn, all he could think about was Daisy. And now that she had left him, all he could think about was Lyn.

'Pretty girl,' Bradley murmured after Hannah had left the room.

'How long has she lived with you?'

'Two and a half years, now.' There was no need to ask further about the time-span. It was almost two and half years to the day since Laura Weaver's hacked and dismembered body had been discovered by the postman whose curiosity had prompted him to walk through the open front door of the Weavers' cottage. 'Would you like some coffee?'

'No, thank you. We've just eaten.'

Blanche picked up a tray with coffee cups and uneaten biscuits from the table and carried it through to the kitchen. When she returned, she sat down opposite them in an armchair.

'You said on the phone this was something to do with my brother-in-law.'

'Have you heard from him since he escaped from prison?' Joseph decided on a direct approach.

'No, Sergeant Joseph.' She crossed her legs demurely at the ankles, and relaxed back into her chair. 'No, I haven't, although I must admit that has surprised me.'

'Why?'

'Whatever else he was, and whatever faults he had, and I must admit there were quite a few, Adam was a completely devoted father. And I also have to concede that, right up until the end, as far as I could tell he remained a devoted husband.'

'But he *did* kill your sister?'

Blanche looked Trevor straight in the eye. 'That's what the jury decided. Although, if you had asked me, I'd have said he was incapable of killing a mouse, let alone another human being.'

'Are you saying you don't think he killed your sister?'

She thought carefully before she answered. 'No, Sergeant Joseph. What I'm saying is that, from what I could see, Adam and Laura's relationship was no better and no worse than any other married couples of my acquaintance, particularly when you consider the precarious nature of their chosen profession. If anything, Laura was the more highly-strung and volatile of the two. When the police came knocking on my door to tell me they suspected Adam of killing her, I found it very hard to believe. And later, when I heard the sordid, brutal details of how Laura died, I found it impossible. I always considered Adam a singularly gentle person, but of course, like most actors, he could be charming as and when he chose to be. Utterly charming, in fact,' she murmured softly, as though mulling over fond memories. 'As with most actors, including my sister, it was sometimes difficult to differentiate between the real person and the role-playing. But, for all of that, the

Adam *I* knew could not have killed any other living creature,' she stressed emphatically, 'and certainly not in the way described in court.'

'It must have been a difficult time for you – and for Hannah,' Bradley sympathised.

'It wasn't simply Laura's murder or the trial. My father died of a heart attack a month before Laura, and my mother was terminally ill with cancer at the time. She died shortly after the trial finished, and my brother, who had to identify Laura's body, suffered a complete nervous breakdown.'

'Leaving you to cope?'

'Someone had to. There was Hannah, you see.'

'Where was Hannah when it happened?'

'She was staying with a school friend. It was the friend's birthday party and she'd been invited to spend the night.'

Joseph tried to remember the Weaver family's movements on the night Laura had been murdered. Laura Weaver had been killed in their country cottage, and Adam had been unable to account for his movements other than to claim that he'd visited an off-licence and slept at their London flat. He'd admitted that he and his wife had been having problems, and that they'd quarrelled earlier that day.

'Did your sister say anything to you about another man in her life?'

'As I told the police at the time, Laura didn't really confide in me to that extent. I knew little more than what appeared in the gossip columns. My sister was successful in her own right, and the theatrical world is a very social one. Both she and Adam went to a lot of parties. The chances are that, if Hannah hadn't been staying over at a friend's that night, she would have been left in the London flat with her nanny. Hannah often only saw her parents at weekends, particularly when they were both filming.'

'I seem to remember Laura Weaver being a hostess on a game show.'

'If you recall that much, Sergeant Bradley, you must also remember that her name was linked with that of the show's presenter.'

'Just as Adam Weaver's was linked with that of his co-star.'

'That rumour was started by a tabloid journalist who needed a story.'

'Did your niece come to live with you directly after the murder?'

'Yes, the day after. The police had already taken Adam into custody to "help with their inquiries", so I went up to London to fetch her.' Blanche opened a cigarette box on the coffee table at her side. Taking one, she offered the box around. When the others declined she apologised. 'I know I shouldn't, but since the murder I succumb now and again. Laura and I weren't close, but we shared a lot of things – like our childhood.'

'I'm sorry. We must be bringing back painful memories.'

'Yes, you are,' she replied honestly. 'And I'd like to know where all these questions are leading.'

'We have reason to believe that your brother-in-law may be living in this area.'

Blanche stared at Joseph in disbelief. 'So that's why you're asking if he's contacted us?'

'His fingerprints were identified inside a suitcase found in the town yesterday. Are you absolutely sure he hasn't tried to contact you or his daughter?'

'I'd know if Adam came anywhere near us, Sergeant.'

Anna Bradley gave Joseph a hard look, and he knew what she was thinking. Just how much should Blanche Davies be told about Adam Weaver's change in appearance? He shifted forward on the edge of his seat.

'There's just one thing,' he said softly. 'We don't think Adam Weaver looks at all like he did two years ago.'

'Sergeant, Adam was an actor.' Blanche flicked her cigarette into the ashtray at her side. 'I went to see him in *The Merchant of Venice* at the Theatre Royal in Bristol four years ago. The first act was over before I even realised it was him who was playing Shylock.'

'I don't mean just a theatrical disguise.' Joseph pulled the folder of 'Tony' photographs from his inside pocket, and handed them to Blanche. 'We think this is what he looks like now.'

She opened the folder. 'But that's impossible. The mouth is

entirely different, the nose . . .' She looked up. 'You think he's had plastic surgery?'

'Sort of,' Joseph hedged evasively.

'But this looks nothing like him. Nothing at all.' She thumbed through the prints, then she paused at the full-length one of 'Tony' taken from the video film. Shabby red canvas baseball boots provided the only splash of colour in an otherwise uniformly drab scene. A pinched, grey face was framed by long matted hair, and a black coat swept down to the knees of the pathetically gaunt frame. 'You really think this man could be Adam?'

'I know it's hard to believe, but yes.'

'It's not just the face, it's the body. This man is so thin.'

'Would you mind very much if Hannah looked at these photographs?' Anna Bradley proposed quietly.

Blanche drew heavily on her cigarette and thought for a moment before answering. 'Would she have to be told why?'

'Not if you didn't want us to tell her.'

'Then how could you explain your reason for showing them to her?'

'That we're looking for the man. That we're hoping she might have seen him.'

'She's a bright child.'

'You said yourself he looks nothing at all like Adam Weaver.'

Blanche stubbed out her cigarette in the ashtray before going to the foot of the stairs and calling her niece.

'Haven't you done enough bloody damage,' Collins hissed as he bumped into Valance in the doorway of Tom Morris's hostel.

'The public have a right to know the facts.'

'If it hadn't been for the number of victims who died in that fire, the public wouldn't give a bloody damn about the facts. You're a ghoul, pandering to ghouls, Valance. The lowest life-form on earth . . .'

'Come in, Sergeant, Constable.' Tom Morris stood above them on the stairs. He stepped back to make room for Collins and Murphy to pass.

Valance continued out through the front door.

'You get a lot of trouble with him?' Collins asked.

'Valance? Not much. All I have to do is steer him towards one or two of our more vociferous and aggressive clients.'

'I'll remember that technique the next time I bump into him.'

'He won't be hanging around here much longer.' Tom showed them into his office. 'The fire's over, the dead are dead, and the injured are out of sight in hospital. There's nothing left to hold the media's interest, although we do have one thing to thank them for. Since the national news coverage of the fire, donations of cash and food have been flooding into this street.'

'I hope you're making the most of them.'

'We are, Sergeant,' Morris answered dryly. 'Everyone who works here is only too aware of how short the public's memory can be when it comes to deserving causes.'

'We called in to see if you'd heard any more about our man?'

'If we had, we would have contacted you. Have you tried Sam Mayberry?'

'We've tried everyone including Captain Arkwright.'

'Not likely to find him there.'

'Unless he's wearing drag,' Collins suggested facetiously.

'I hear some of the squatters from that factory have moved into a derelict pub down the bottom end of High Street.'

'We checked the place out last night. In fact we combed the whole bloody town last night,' Murphy grumbled miserably.

'And we'll be doing the same tonight,' Collins echoed. 'Can we run through all the places your soup kitchen covers, Tom. It might save us some leg-work if we leave a radio with your people again.'

'As Constable Murphy saw last night, we cover the underpass, the multi-storeys, the docks – that's about it, really. We try to avoid the squats, as we can't be seen to be condoning possible law-breaking. All the volunteers have seen the photographs. We have one on our barrow. Tell us what more we can do, and we'll do it.'

Hannah, hands behind her back, stared at the photograph, bit her bottom lip to stop it from trembling, and nodded.

'You're sure, Hannah?' Blanche asked gently.

'That's the man,' Hannah whispered. 'The man who was outside my school. The one Miss Phillips telephoned you about. Who is he?'

'Just a man who's been sleeping out on the streets,' Bradley answered.

'Has he done anything wrong?'

'We can't be sure, not yet. But we want to talk to him about a fire in a building.'

'He lit it?'

'Perhaps not, but we do know he was in the building at the time, and there's a possibility he might have seen the person who did.'

Hannah nodded sagely, laying the photograph on the coffee table. 'Then he *is* just a dirty old man?'

They all picked up on the disappointment in her voice.

'I'm afraid it looks like it, Hannah.' Blanche Davies' voice was unsteady as she reached for another cigarette. 'You can go back upstairs now, we won't be much longer.'

'Can I get myself a glass of milk?'

'Of course, darling.'

Hannah skipped off into the kitchen, leaving all three adults very conscious that she was still within earshot.

Joseph picked up the table lighter next to the cigarette box and lit Blanche's cigarette for her.

'I should have remembered, I'm sorry. I never connected the incident to Adam,' Blanche apologised after she'd heard the kitchen door closing. 'Hannah's headmistress telephoned me at work, last week. She said that a vagrant had been seen outside the playground watching the children. When someone noticed him, Hannah ran out. She . . . she thought it was her father . . .' her voice tailed.

'Why would Hannah have thought that? You just said yourself that this man looks nothing like Adam Weaver?'

'She followed his back. Apparently when he turned and Hannah saw his face she stopped running after him.'

'Surely the local constables have been given this description?' Joseph looked to Bradley for confirmation.

'The young policeman who interviewed Hannah and the

teachers at the school said there wasn't much he could do other than keep an eye out for the down-and-out and ask him what he was doing there. It's not a criminal offence for vagrants to stand on street corners or watch school playgrounds.'

'Did you get the name of the policeman?'

'He told me, but I really can't remember. No doubt the headmistress will have it. It's Cowslip Primary School.'

'You said that Hannah believed this man was her father until he turned around?' Bradley pressed.

'I assumed that was wishful thinking. I told you, Adam was a good father. Hannah misses him. The mind can play curious tricks.' She looked Trevor squarely in the eye. 'You're absolutely sure this *is* Adam?'

'He has his fingerprints.'

'Then what happens now?' Blanche asked.

'We have his description, so we keep looking until we find him.'

'Was that the solicitor Brian Marks we saw leaving here just as we arrived?' Joseph asked suddenly.

'Yes,' Blanche answered, surprised at the change of subject.

'May I ask what he was doing here?'

'He's our family solicitor. He handled Laura's estate after the . . . accident.' She nodded towards the kitchen to remind Joseph that Hannah was still nearby.

'It must be rather a long drive for him to get over here.'

'When my sister first engaged him, her cottage was only four miles from his office.'

'Was that the cottage where . . .'

'Where the accident happened,' Blanche furnished quickly as Hannah returned to the living room with her glass of milk and a plate of toast which explained the time she'd taken. 'Be with you soon, darling.'

Blanche waited until she heard Hannah's feet ascending the stairs.

'His firm also handled my brother-in-law's defence. I've always found Mr Marks to be a man of the highest integrity.'

'I'm not questioning his integrity, Miss Davies,' Joseph said gravely.

'But you seem to know him?'

'Only in connection with another case,' Bradley interposed.

'To be honest I don't know what I would have done without him after Laura died. He settled all the business, paid all the bills, even the ones for the funeral. And he handled the sale of the cottage and the London flat as well as Adam's defence. In fact I've now put my own estate in his hands, and made his firm executors of Hannah's affairs. You see, my sister left Hannah far better provided for than I would have given her credit. One day Hannah is going to be quite a wealthy lady.'

'Your sister took out insurance policies?' Joseph asked.

'Yes. It amazed me when Mr Marks first mentioned them. That seemed quite out of character for Laura, but she'd taken out a substantial lump-sum insurance policy payable on her death, as well as an annuity which more than covers Hannah's living expenses – and that will continue until Hannah finishes her full-time education. Mr Marks has taken an almost fatherly interest in poor Hannah. He calls in to see us quite regularly. Yet it's strange . . .'

'What is?'

'He admits he never actually met Laura. It was one of his partners who drew up her will. But then of course his firm did organise Adam's defence. As I said, my brother-in-law is an intelligent man and he can be delightful company when he wants to be. Perhaps he simply charmed Brian Marks into taking care of Hannah for him.'

'Perhaps.' Joseph rose from his seat. 'Thank you very much for your time, Miss Davies.'

'Thank you for coming, Sergeant. It's funny, really, but you've succeeded in putting my mind at rest. I was rather worried when I heard that a tramp had been watching the school-yard. I know this sounds strange, with Adam being convicted of murdering my sister, but I find it reassuring to think that it might have been him watching Hannah, and not some dirty old man.'

'Something strike you as peculiar, Joseph?' Anna asked, as they sat in his car at a set of traffic lights.

'Nothing in particular.' He wondered if her hands were giving her trouble. She had seemed very preoccupied ever since the fire.

'Brian Marks took a paternal interest in Anthony George, and visited Mrs George regularly in her home. Now he's doing much the same with Blanche Davies and young Hannah.'

'Could be just business. He's an old-fashioned family solicitor.'

'Maybe,' Bradley conceded grudgingly. 'But Adam Weaver's a convicted murderer. He killed Blanche Davies' sister, and she's looking after his daughter, so you'd think she'd be petrified at the thought of him coming near them, for the child's sake at least. Instead she seemed to almost welcome the idea of Weaver getting in touch with them.'

'She also said he could be very charming. Perhaps he simply charmed her too. They say most psychopaths are intelligent, endearing souls.'

She wanted to shout that, whatever else Adam Weaver might be, he wasn't a psychopath, but she managed to contain herself. If she revealed her past relationship with the actor, she'd risk being taken off this case. And that she didn't want, at least until she'd had a chance to prove herself every bit as good a detective as the men she worked with.

'There could be something fishy there. Blanche Davies certainly seems to be very taken with Adam Weaver. Let's just hope she won't have to pay a heavy price for her infatuation.'

'You heard her, she doesn't believe Weaver killed her sister.'

'He's been tried, convicted and sentenced. That's good enough for me. I'll ask the Super to give her and the child round-the-clock protection, just in case.'

Chapter Thirteen

Trevor drove directly to the central underpass. He and Bradley left the car on double yellow lines and walked down one of the ramps. Tom Morris's evangelists were there with their soup kitchen, but there was no sign of Tom himself.

'They have a rota,' Collins explained, when they finally tracked him and a shivering, blue-faced Murphy down.

'No sign of "Tony"?'

'It wouldn't surprise me if he's halfway to Moscow by now. That's where I'd be, if I was him.'

Bradley held up her bandaged hands and shook her head at one of the youngsters who was offering her soup.

'How's the hands, Sarge?' Murphy asked.

'They've promised me they'll be almost serviceable after one more dressing in out-patients.'

'As it doesn't look like we're going to be doing very much here, I think it's time all sick people were put to bed. That way we can at least put in a full day tomorrow. Come on, Sergeant.' Joseph laid a hand on Bradley's shoulder. 'You too, Collins. Eight tomorrow suit everyone?' He glanced at Murphy, who was detailed to an all-night shift again.

'Great, a lie-in.' Collins murmured caustically.

'Lift?'

Collins nodded. 'Supper for two at my place?' he whispered to Bradley. She shook her head.

'I really am very tired. Perhaps tomorrow.' After interviewing Blanche Davies, all she wanted now was the peace and quiet of her own bed, and time to think about her present – and her past.

* * *

Joseph led the way up the ramp, back to his car. Across the road a narrow lane separated a furniture store from a burger bar. At the far end, the gleaming yellow outline of a skip shimmered in the darkness. The sea of glistening black bags filling it heaved slightly as Trevor Joseph reached his car ahead of the others. A dark head peered cautiously over the edge. Feverish brown eyes searched the narrow prospect of the main street, before finally focusing on Anna Bradley – watching intently as all three figures climbed into Joseph's car. The engine turned, there was a puff of smoke from the exhaust, and suddenly the street was empty.

Ten minutes later Murphy emerged from the underpass with Brooke in tow. The head burrowed beneath the bags again. The rubbish stank, but only of stale, greasy food. And that was a small price to pay for security, and warmth of a kind on a cold night.

The centre of town was deserted as dawn broke. The soup kitchen had long since packed up and departed. The young volunteers were now at home, sleeping in their soft, comfortable beds. The town's homeless, huddled in rags, newspapers and cardboard boxes, were just beginning to crawl out of whatever sheltered corners they had found. A milk-float rattled around the high-walled roundabout, the clinking of its bottles diminishing with distance, until silence once more reigned in the streets.

Before the fingers of chilly light reached the nooks and crannies in the lane, the shiny bags in the skip throbbed and shuddered. A man emerged from their billowing mass. Dropping over the side, he landed lightly, low on the soles of his feet. Discarding his coat, he darted across to the shelter of the shadows fringing the wall of the furniture shop. He moved out cautiously on to the main street. Pulling up the collar of a thick denim shirt he'd scavenged from the second-hand clothing skip, he put his head down and walked swiftly towards the YMCA. It opened early, and its top-floor rooms were rented out to students. They used the showers and bathrooms up on that floor, which meant he could slip into the bathroom on the ground floor and lock the door. He read the clock as he passed the church tower. Three and a half hours – that's all he had to wait.

At eight-thirty, the caretaker unlocked the door to the bleak hall that housed the Job Club. Its first members weren't due in until after nine o'clock, but some – the keen ones – often came in early. They dropped their kids off at school, and continued on into town, hoping that this would be their lucky day. Hugh Grant felt in just such a mood. He'd sent his CV off to thirty-six different firms in a fortnight. Something was going to break – and soon – he just knew it. He opened the door, then stood and stared.

'Hey, you, you don't belong to the Job Club!' he shouted at the filthy individual who was standing at a table flicking through the local telephone directory. As the man looked up, Grant registered sunken cheeks covered with stubble, and dark, haunted eyes; also trembling hands and the foul stink of sweat and unwashed clothes.

'Sorry, mate, just looking for someone's number. Didn't mean no harm.' The man moved towards him. Repelled by the thought of being touched by him, Hugh stepped smartly sideways. The man carried on out through the door. Barging into the corridor, he almost knocked over the next arrival.

'Hey, doesn't that look like . . .'

The vagrant didn't wait around to hear any more. He had to find somewhere to hole up. Just for today. Thanks to the phone-book, he had somewhere to go at nightfall – but not sooner. Where now? The question seethed in his mind. There simply wasn't a safe bolthole left. Since the fire down at the old factory, the police were everywhere, checking and double-checking every abandoned and empty building. The usual haunts were out, therefore. But there had to be somewhere! He tried to think clearly, logically, but conflicting thoughts whirled round his mind like dead leaves in an autumn wind, without rhyme, reason or clarity. He was no longer capable of reasoning, only feeling. Cold, hunger, exhaustion held sway, paralysing his mind, rendering it impotent. He couldn't recall ever feeling this wretched before. Not even the first night he had been forced to sleep on the street.

A police car hurtled around the corner, siren blaring. Behind the YMCA stretched rows of terrace houses, including the one he had broken into the night before. Covering the same ground twice was risky, but staying here invited arrest. Looking the way he did, it was only a matter of time before he was picked up. One or two of those houses had to be empty. Some people still went out to work, didn't they?

He headed down the first back alley he came to. In an adjoining garden, a woman, dressed smartly in a tailored suit, was hanging out washing on a line: men's trousers, shirts, towels, a pullover. When she finished, she called a dog into the house, and he heard her lock the back door. After five minutes he risked a closer look. Seeing no movement, he leapt over the wall. The dog began to bark, hurling itself against patio doors. He froze, waiting and watching, but no one came to investigate. He'd struck lucky. There was a shed and a greenhouse. The shed was locked, but the greenhouse wasn't, and it had reed screens against the glass to shade the plants from the sun. He went inside, closed the door and lowered the blinds. Now no one could see him.

Daring to relax, he looked around. A gravel path ran down the centre of the greenhouse, bisecting the growing area into two. It was dry, gritty, and the stones pressed into his skin as he lay down on them, but he was so tired it didn't matter. Experience had taught him that this discomfort would wake him up before too much time passed. From the look of the woman, she was dressed for work, so he hoped it was a full-time, not part-time, job. A couple of hours – that's all he needed. The weather was good, her washing would dry, and he'd noticed an outside tap. Later he could clean himself up, take a change of clothes from the line, then head out of town. But for now all he needed was sleep.

'Evans called yet?' asked Bradley, as she entered the office. Collins and Joseph were sitting at opposite ends of the latter's desk, both poring over reports from the night before.

'Have a heart? He's probably only just landed – and New York is five hours behind us,' Joseph answered.

'And I still say you can't believe a bloody word a junkie says,' Collins protested, continuing an argument that had been raging before she arrived.

'What's this?' Bradley sat down at her own desk and attempted to flex her bandaged fingers.

'We have some spaced-out junkie who *thinks* that he saw our "Tony" sleeping in a skip at the back of the burger bar last night.'

'Was the area properly searched?'

'From one end to the other – twice,' Collins asserted forcefully.

'Inside the skip, too?'

'That I don't know.'

'If you were a constable on the beat, would you climb up to your neck in half-eaten chips and rotting burgers to check out a skip for a mere suspect?' Joseph asked.

'If it had to be done.'

'Then all I can say is that it's a pity not all officers on the beat are as conscientious as you, Collins.'

'I tell you, that guy wasn't compos mentis.'

'That's as may be, but as I'm the senior permanent sergeant assigned to this squad, that makes me officer in charge now the Inspector's away, and I say we empty that skip and search it thoroughly. You never know your luck, he might have left something behind.'

'If he was ever in it in the first place.'

'Look at it this way, Collins, it's not as if we're inundated with leads crying out to be followed.'

'And I don't suppose for one minute, now you've elected yourself bwana, you want to dirty your hands doing the actual work involved.'

'Someone has to wait here for the Inspector's call.'

'So it's my job?'

'Seeing as how you want it.'

'From the look on your face something tells me I'm going to get it, whether I want it or not. Give me two constables' – Collins held up his still-bandaged arm – 'and I'll do the supervising for you.'

'Sadist.'

'Has any copper earned his stripes without a little of that tendency?'

'A little?' Bradley mocked.

'Sir!' Murphy, exhausted, red-faced and looking hot under the collar, knocked at the door and walked in accompanied by Brooke. 'Our man was spotted in a Job Club in the YMCA this morning, at about a quarter to nine.'

Joseph glanced instinctively at the clock on the wall. 'Three-quarters of an hour ago?'

'You sure?' Collins demanded.

'No doubt about it, a Job Club member' – Murphy consulted his notebook – 'by the name of Grant – Hugh Grant – dropped in early and found him reading the telephone directory.'

'I'll ask the Super to put more men into that area.'

'The whole town's crawling with men as it is.'

'Then it will crawl some more, Murphy, won't it!'

Even Bradley looked up at this uncharacteristic outburst from Trevor Joseph.

'I don't suppose anyone noticed what he was looking for in that phone-book?' she asked.

'Unfortunately our man closed the book before he left,' Brooke explained. 'But Mr Grant did say that it looked as though he was looking at something near the beginning.'

'The beginning . . .?' Joseph glanced at Bradley. 'Davies, maybe?'

'You *did* ask the Super to give Blanche and Hannah round-the-clock protection?'

'Yes.' Joseph reached for the telephone on his desk. 'But I think I'll up their cover to two men each, just in case.'

'I know my rights, Inspector Evans. I don't have to speak to you.'

'You don't, Dr Marks, but—'

'*Mr* Marks. I'm a surgeon.'

'Mr Marks . . .'

'You are a British police officer, and I am now a permanent resident of the United States of America. Events in the UK really don't concern me.'

Dan Evans shifted awkwardly on the hard vinyl chair in an attempt to get comfortable. Marks had been thoroughly uncooperative from the outset. It had taken the threat of adverse publicity to get him to even sit down with him out in the foyer of the hotel where the conference was being held. They were an odd couple by anyone's standards. The Inspector's massive frame dressed in a suit more crumpled than usual after a journey of more than fourteen hours via two airports and a New York police station, and the small, dark surgeon with his manicured hands, neatly trimmed beard and moustache, and immaculately tailored Savile Row suit.

'Mr Marks' – Dan Evans leant closer to the surgeon, causing him to jerk backwards – 'last week I was investigating a murder. A singularly brutal one. A man had his face removed while he was semi-conscious and alive, then his body was soaked in petrol and set alight. He was found still screaming in the centre of his personal fireball minutes later. Have you any idea what it must be like to be burned alive, Mr Marks?'

'No, Inspector. But I fail to see what interest this brutal crime can hold for me.'

'That was just the first murder, Mr Marks. As I said earlier, I began by investigating just one killing. Now I am investigating eleven. Ten more people burnt to death or asphyxiated when a derelict building was deliberately set ablaze. One of those victims was a fireman.'

'So, you're looking for an arsonist who has been active in Britain during the past few weeks. I've been here all that time, so what has it to do with me?'

'The man we're looking for, Mr Marks, is this one.' Evans handed him a photograph of 'Tony'. 'And I can see from your reaction that you know who he is.'

'You're seeing a reaction that isn't there, Inspector.'

'Were you aware that he was a convicted murderer when you operated on this man? Was that why he agreed to go along with your little experiment? The promise of a new face, and a ticket to a new life? What else did you offer him, Mr Marks? Money? A job? But then, of course, that was before you dumped him, and before he ended up on what I believe the Americans call skid row.'

'You have evidence to substantiate these allegations, Inspector? Because you'll soon be hearing from my lawyer.'

Evans opened the briefcase and pulled out a photocopy of the file Daisy had located in the hospital, giving medical details of the face transplant carried out on a twenty-eight-year-old male.

'There's no date on this – or any indication of who the surgeon was.' Marks barely glanced at the papers before tossing them aside.

'Perhaps you should look at the end of the document.'

Marks picked up the file and flicked through it. A date was scrawled at the bottom of the last page. 'But this isn't my writing . . . This isn't . . .' he stammered. 'It could have been added at any time,' he concluded, quickly regaining his composure.

'Then you agree this document originated with you?'

'I don't have to stay and listen to this.' Marks rose from his chair.

'No you don't, Mr Marks. But I have to warn you there's enough evidence in these papers for the British authorities to apply for your extradition.'

'On what charge?'

'Perverting the course of justice, to begin with. That's a serious offence in a murder case. Particularly one involving eleven dead and thirty injured. All I'm asking is for you to spare me an hour or two of your time. Your conference has broken up for the day. I promise you that any information you give me relevant to the face transplant you carried out on this man' – he tapped the photograph of 'Tony' – 'will remain strictly confidential.'

Laurence Marks hesitated for a moment. 'Are you promising me immunity from prosecution?'

'Only from any charges that might arise relating to the actual transplant. Not the subsequent or prior events.'

'And the harvesting of the face?'

Evans took a deep breath, he'd already stretched his authority beyond its limits. 'No, not the harvesting,' he murmured.

Laurence Marks led the way upstairs to the privacy of his hotel suite. It proved to be a characterless, impersonal series of rooms. The air-conditioning kept the atmosphere at a comfortable, and constant temperature; the double glazing effectively shut out any noises from the street; the beige and blue decor neither pleased nor displeased. They could have been in a four-star hotel in any city in the world.

'Drink?' Marks offered as he closed the door and walked over to the bar.

'No thank you.'

'Please, sit down, make yourself comfortable. You don't mind if I indulge?' Marks poured himself a large bourbon without waiting for an answer. 'Now, Inspector, tell me exactly how you think I can help with your inquiries?'

'Perhaps it would be better, Mr Marks, if I began by telling you what we *do* know. Then you can correct me when I go wrong. For instance, we're aware that you operated on a perfectly healthy young man, first removing his face, then transplanting on to him the face of one Anthony George who had recently died of natural causes. We also know there was no medical reason for the surgery you performed, and that shortly afterwards your guinea-pig patient began living rough on the streets.'

'You say there was no medical reason for the transplant, Inspector. Supposing I told you that the operation was experimental and pioneering in nature? That because of its success at that crucial time in the development of the face-transplant programme, it has since proved to be of incalculable benefit to subsequent patients. Would that be reason enough for you?'

'My approval or disapproval is immaterial, Mr Marks. Suppose you begin by telling me who approached you to carry out this particular face transplant – and why?'

'There is such a thing as patient/doctor confidentiality.'

'There is also such a thing as extradition,' Evans replied dryly. 'We have already established that you were working in the same hospital that Anthony George died in. Also that you were on duty the night the face was removed from his corpse in the mortuary; and that you had both opportunity, and motive to do just that.'

'I may have been on duty at the hospital that night, but I was hardly the only surgeon on the premises capable of carrying out that procedure.'

'But you were the only consultant plastic surgeon on duty that night. The inspector who took charge of the George case was extremely thorough. We have statements taken from every member of staff in that hospital, detailing exactly where they were, and what they were doing during the crucial half hour when Anthony George's face was removed. Even two years later, it should be fairly easy to establish that you had every opportunity.'

Marks carried his glass over to a chair, and made himself comfortable. 'So did others.'

'A scandal could affect your career and the whole transplant programme you're involved in.'

'I pioneered,' Marks corrected harshly, and Evans knew he was finally getting through to the man. 'You'd risk sabotaging, perhaps even halting a programme capable of playing a vital role in the rehabilitation of damaged people, simply to carry out a personal witch-hunt against me?'

'I'll do whatever is necessary to remove a vicious murderer from the streets.'

'If I tell you everything I know, will you give me your word that you won't contact the press about our programme?'

'I believe I can guarantee that.'

'Very well, then. The operation was performed in a private clinic. I rented the room, the theatre facilities, and engaged an anaesthetist and a nurse to look after my subject.'

Evans winced at the use of the world 'subject'. It had the advantage of instantly dehumanising Weaver.

'The recipient?'

'His name wasn't important. If I ever knew it, I've since forgotten it.'

Evans produced the folder of photographs from his inside

pocket. He pulled out a studio shot of Adam Weaver, one that had been released to coincide with the transmission of Adam's first detective series. 'Was this the man?'

'It was.'

'You're absolutely certain?'

'Absolutely. I needed to study that face before grafting on the new one.'

'There was nothing wrong with it?'

'No.'

'Didn't you think to ask why a man with apparently perfect facial features should want a transplant?'

'Neither his wishes, nor his life were of any importance. He was a convicted killer serving a life sentence.'

'You knew that much about him?'

'Of course. That's how I came across him. He'd put his name forward to the authorities as a subject prepared to assist in medical research.'

Evans shifted uncomfortably on his seat. He'd heard of medical research programmes being carried out in prisons. The testing of new antibiotics, and cures for the common cold. But there was a world of moral difference between those programmes and what Marks had done to Weaver. 'Did you discuss the nature of the surgery your "subject" was about to undergo, with him beforehand?'

'I saw no need to. I required a guinea-pig. The man had volunteered.'

'Earlier you said his name wasn't important, yet you knew he was a prisoner serving a life sentence?'

'I could hardly not know. His face had been splashed across the front pages of all the newspapers. He was considering an appeal.'

Evans had heard no mention of an appeal, but his features remained impassive. 'You spoke to Adam Weaver's solicitor?'

'Adam Weaver?'

'Your subject.'

'Why should I?'

'Because there was no mention in the press at the time of an appeal. But if there was to have been one, his solicitor would have undoubtably known about it; and then again' – Evans raised his eyes to Marks – 'Weaver's solicitor has the same surname as you.'

Laurence Marks drained his glass and walked over to the bar. 'Brian Marks is my uncle. I was living in his house at the time I carried out the transplant.'

'And Brian Marks was both Anthony George's and Adam Weaver's solicitor.'

'I did not inform my uncle of my plans, nor discuss the transplant programme with him.'

Evans remained sceptically silent.

'I needed a donor and I needed a subject. I was working in conjunction with the prison authorities, my subject had already signed a medical release form enabling him to take part in research programmes. The donor face was available. If I hadn't taken it that night, it would have been cremated along with the rest of the corpse a few days later. And Anthony George was carrying a donor card. I checked with the casualty sister.'

'A card that has no validity unless it is endorsed by next-of-kin,' Evans said calmly.

'Research was at a crucial stage. Subjects were in short supply. A major project was in danger of losing its funding, and it wasn't as though anyone was damaged.'

'Except possibly your subject, Mr Marks.'

'A convicted killer, Inspector Evans.'

'Want coffee? I'll hold it for you.'

'I'd love one, Joseph, but it's time to call a taxi.' Bradley held up her hands. 'I have to go to the hospital now. My dressings need changing.'

'In that case you may as well take the afternoon off.'

'I was going to, anyway. It was bloody agony the last time they did it. In fact it's bloody agony all the time. I don't think I've slept all through a night since it happened.'

'Could be because you're sleeping in Collins' flat.'

'I don't think so. The man's a pussycat in my hands.'

'You've pulled his claws?'

'And he hasn't even noticed. Do you know what sounds

absolutely irresistible to me at this moment? A couple of tranquillisers, a good video, a bottle of wine, and fish and chips.' She grinned at him. 'They promised to free my thumbs today, so I should be able to grip without getting my bandages filthy.'

'Grip what? Collins' neck?'

'Hopefully, with plastic bags over my hands, a bath sponge.'

Joseph left his desk. 'I'll run you to the hospital.'

'There's no need. The taxi service is pretty good.'

'I don't doubt it, but after a morning spent in this place, I'm ready for a break.'

'Did you discuss this first transplant with anyone, Mr Marks?'

'Like who?'

'Your colleagues? Your uncle?'

'Not everyone forgets what they've already said, Inspector. I told you my uncle knew nothing of this; however, my colleagues knew of my success. I prepared and delivered a full report on my initial transplant to the firm sponsoring the programme, and to medical representatives from rival programmes.'

'They accepted it?'

'Of course. I took care to see that my work was properly documented, and photographed.'

'Photographed? There were no photographs in the file we saw in the burns unit back in England.'

'There wouldn't have been. I explained that, in order to comply with the wishes of both parties, it was necessary to conceal both the subject's and the donor's identities. Only the sponsors were allowed to see the full photographic evidence.'

'And your sponsors were satisfied with your explanation?'

'They had no reason to be otherwise. I'd accomplished what no other surgeon in my field had done. I was the first to prove that a successful face transplant could be carried out with minimal scarring, and believe me, Inspector, many people have had good cause to be grateful to my trail-blazing since,' he added smugly.

'You say the procedure was fully documented. Did that

include release forms giving both the subject's and the donor's permissions?'

'The documents included copies of Anthony George's donor card, and the subject's medical release forms.'

'For that specific surgery?'

'For general medical research.'

'You removed the donor face?'

Marks remained obstinately silent.

'Where was it kept until the transplant took place?'

'In ideal conditions in the clinic, until I was ready to use it. I admit I transported it there myself. There's very few problems – medical ones that is – that don't disappear if you throw enough money at them.'

'So you carried out the transplant. And afterwards?'

'Afterwards?'

'Post-surgical treatment?' Evans pressed.

'I kept the subject heavily tranquillised in order to minimalise damage from inadvertent movement during the healing process. I saw him daily for a week after the operation, and on a twice-weekly basis for three weeks after that. By then the man had made a full recovery. I then left the country.'

'And the man?'

'I never saw him again.'

'You didn't arrange for him to be returned to prison?'

'I can't be expected to keep tabs on all my ex-patients.'

'Not even a guinea-pig of such importance?'

'As I said,' Marks' patience was clearly wearing thin, 'the last time I saw my patient was a month after the transplant. I then left the UK to deliver notes and details of the surgical techniques I'd pioneered to the programme sponsors. As a result, I was offered the position of director of the programme here in the States. Not unnaturally, I accepted it.'

'And you never checked your subject's reaction to your "pioneering surgical techniques".' Evans' voice was heavy with irony.

'I followed his case for a month afterwards, no longer.'

'Dr Randall, who works on a similar programme to yours, told one of my colleagues that patients frequently develop problems of adjustment after a face transplant.'

'I would say inevitably rather than frequently.'

'Yet, knowing this, you didn't arrange for your guinea-pig to receive post-operative psychological evaluation?'

'I carried out the procedure on an experimental basis, and on a volunteer.'

'Who, in your opinion, clearly had no rights?'

'Convicted murderers have few rights in the eyes of the law.'

'Did you prescribe any drugs for him?'

'The usual. Painkillers, tranquillisers . . .'

'Enough to turn him into a junkie?'

'I resent the inference, Inspector.'

'This man' – Evans held up the photograph of 'Tony' again – 'was filmed by a television crew less than a month ago. He was showing clear-cut signs of substance abuse.'

'You can hardly blame me for the state of a patient two years after my last professional appointment with him.'

'When you left the country did you arrange for your patient to receive any further treatment at all?'

'The surgery was successful, the subject made a full physical recovery.'

'And that was it: the end of your involvement?'

'I have told you all I know, Inspector. This interview is at an end. May I remind you that I still have the original donor card and medical research consent forms. Should you ever try to prosecute me, I will counter-sue. You can count on that.'

'You arranged for a perfectly healthy man to be spirited out of prison, peeled off his face and transplanted a dead man's face on to it, for no reason other than the fact that you wanted to see if it could be successfully done?'

'I was certain it could, and my surgery's success vindicated my earlier belief in the procedures.'

'And like Dr Frankenstein you created a monster? Possibly one that murders.'

'You gave me your word. Immunity in exchange for information.'

'So I did, Mr Marks. But I didn't give my word that I wouldn't file on a charge of aiding and abetting a prisoner to escape.'

* * *

'Collins, it's Evans here. No doubt about it. Adam Weaver *is* wearing Anthony George's face. I've had confirmation from the surgeon who carried out the operation.'

'He talked to you, then?'

'Eventually. So pull all the stops out on trying to bring Weaver in.'

'We have been,' Collins answered irritably.

'I'll be back with you tomorrow.' The line went dead.

Collins looked at Mulcahy. 'That was the Inspector, our man is definitely Adam Weaver.'

'I thought we knew that before Evans went to America?'

'We did, but now we have full confirmation.'

'What did he say about the Marks connection?'

'Nothing, but he'll be back here tomorrow.'

'Then you'd better have Adam Weaver ready and waiting for him in a cell, Collins, hadn't you?' the Superintendent muttered darkly.

After dropping Anna Bradley off, Joseph felt at a loose end. There were any number of places he could go, any number of things he could do. Conscience told him he should return to the police station to check if Evans had telephoned from the States, or see if Collins had found anything in that skip. But Trevor felt too restless to sit behind a desk coping with the boredom of routine police work. That might be the technique that eventually caught most killers, but it was generally as tedious as hell.

Or he could go down Jubilee Street and talk with Tom Morris, Sam Mayberry or Captain Arkwright, but there was no reason to suppose that they'd have anything more to report than previously. He could even take an hour out, as there was no one to shout at him – not that Evans ever really shouted.

Trevor glanced at his watch: a quarter to twelve. There were only two places Lyn was likely to be at this hour: the hospital or her parents' home. He could offer to buy her an early lunch, take her somewhere cosy, find a quiet table, talk reconciliation ... for a few moments he thought about it, really thought about it. Even if he did manage to persuade her to move back in with him, nothing else would change. Depending on what was waiting for him at the station, he'd be spending that evening either waiting inside for Evans' return, or out combing the streets for 'Tony' again, in an attempt to stop that lunatic from killing someone else. So taking Lyn out to lunch now wouldn't solve anything. If anything, it would only create a whole new set of problems for them both.

Trevor gazed at the towering pillars of the new burns unit which soared behind the casualty section. He could always offer to take Daisy to lunch instead – no strings attached, of course. But there was no 'of course' about it.

Daisy had become a drug he couldn't get out of his system. But then she'd only ask him about Lyn. Daisy didn't want to complicate things. So nothing in his life was resolved. Nothing at all, he reflected, as he turned his back against the skyline and climbed into his car.

Chapter Fourteen

'Evans phoned,' Collins greeted Joseph as he appeared in the office carrying a burger-bar takeaway. 'He confirmed that Adam Weaver is wearing Anthony George's face.'

'Good,' Joseph murmured, absently dumping his food on Bradley's desk. He sat down behind it and opened the bag.

'Little woman isn't going to like you eating junk food,' Collins taunted.

'The little woman isn't around to object,' Joseph retorted unthinkingly.

'You let her go?' Collins began unwrapping the fish and chips he'd sent out for, on Joseph's desk top.

'It wasn't a question of letting her go. She just went.'

'What did you do to her?'

'Nothing.'

'Nothing to try and keep her either. You're a bloody idiot, Joseph. Don't you realise that girl was the best thing that ever happened to you?'

'Best thing? To go home every night to nagging? For the first time in eight months my life is peaceful, and I like it that way. I can walk into my own house without anyone asking me where I've been, what I've been doing, and how late I'm going to have to work tomorrow.'

'She's concerned about you.'

'Concerned! Can this be the same man who told me six months ago that all policemen should live alone?'

'I was talking about myself.'

'Really? Great advice, Collins, especially considering that at the moment you're as good as living with Bradley.'

'That's none of your business.'

'Neither is Lyn yours.' Joseph took out the cardboard beaker of Diet Coke he'd bought and ripped off the plastic top.

'It's Daisy, isn't it?'

'Lyn *was* getting jealous of Daisy,' Joseph admitted reluctantly.

'So, when is the lady doctor moving in with you?'

'No chance. She doesn't want to get involved in a break-up between Lyn and myself.'

'But you did ask her to?'

'No, of course not! Lyn only moved out the night before last.'

'But you still imagine you're in love with Daisy?'

Trevor slit the paper bag along one side and spread it out on the desk. Opening a yellow polystyrene carton, he took out a chicken burger and bit into it.

'Well?' Collins demanded.

'I don't know,' Joseph answered irritably.

'What about Lyn? Doesn't she deserve something from you after all the months you've lived together?'

'Like what? A brass medal? I've just told you, my private life is none of your damned business.'

Collins shook his head. 'The trouble with you, Joseph, is that you never *have* realised when you're well off.'

The light was beginning to fade as he woke. Something had disturbed his sleep – but what? He lay still, heart pounding, tensing his body in readiness to flee – or fight. Grit dug painfully into his shoulders and the backs of his thighs, through his jeans and the thin shirt. He could hear children playing close by. How close? He reached out, parted the spills of the blinds with the tips of his fingers, and peered through the gap. Wherever those children were, they weren't in this garden.

Clambering to his knees, he slid back the door of the greenhouse. It grated with a rasping sound he was certain could be heard at the end of the street. Cold air rushed in to dispel the warm, musty smell of wet earth and potting compost. The wall dividing the garden he was in from that of next door was barely four foot high. He slithered out, crawling like a commando over the concrete path. He cried out involuntarily as something sharp and heavy landed on his back. A cat shot over his head and up a fence post.

Trembling, he closed his eyes and lay flat, hoping against hope that no one had heard his cry. Minutes stole past before he opened his eyes and rolled over. Washing still flapped on the line above him. He eyed a pair of men's jeans, then a check shirt and a pullover. They all looked too wide for him, but beggars couldn't be choosers. Rising to his knees, he reached up and tugged. The pegs securing the jeans snapped on the third yank. The shirt and pullover were easier to dislodge. He watched the washing line bounce backwards and forwards, before retreating into the greenhouse.

Changing quickly he bundled his filthy discarded clothes under his arm, as he couldn't leave them here. If the theft from the line was reported and the police came nosing about, they might easily put two and two together. Possibly even using prime sniffer dogs, as his series character had once done when investigating a burglary. Looking around to check that he hadn't left anything, he spotted a pair of garden shears. He picked them up, opened out the blades and ran his fingers along the well-honed edges. Pulling his long hair to one side of his head, he began to hack at it. Then he tucked the severed mane into his bundle of clothes, and pushed the shoulder-length remains inside his collar, away from his face. As an afterthought he also concealed the shears inside his bundle. Ready as he'd ever be, he left the greenhouse.

He eyed the outside tap but decided not to risk having a wash. The children's voices still drifted over the wall. The sooner he left this place behind him the better.

Joseph handed Collins the report Evans had faxed from New York.

'The Inspector *has* been thorough,' Collins said, as he scanned the pages.

'Would you expect anything else?'

'No. But one thing is clear.' Collins handed the final page back to Trevor. 'Our next stop has to be Brian Marks.'

While Joseph dialled for an outside line, Collins sat back to eat his fish and chips and indulge in carnal thoughts of Anna Bradley. All available personnel were scheduled to scour the town again that night for 'Tony'. The prospect of another non-productive night out on the streets sickened him. Sometimes it seemed as though he had wasted his entire life peering into the seamier side of things. He was tempted, just this once, to make himself unavailable. To plead sickness, pick up Bradley, and take her somewhere special. Wine and dine her and, at the end of the evening, ask her to move in with him. It had been a long time since a woman had excited him the way she did and, although sex was certainly a motivating factor, he knew already that with Bradley it was only a part of their relationship. They were friends as well as lovers – something that had never happened with a woman before. He actually enjoyed talking to her. On the down side, he knew she'd be absolute hell to live with for someone with his orderly habits. But, then, he wasn't too old to change his ways. Not when the prize was someone like that, he reflected, remembering just how good that lunch-hour spent between the sheets had been.

'Collins? Collins!'

He glanced across the office, and saw Joseph had replaced the telephone receiver.

'I was miles away.'

'So I see. Our man's away until next week.'

'Who?'

'Brian Marks,' Joseph supplied testily. 'So his secretary has pencilled us in for eight-thirty next Thursday morning. That's the day she's expecting him back, and it's the only time free in his diary.'

'We going to need a warrant?'

'I doubt it. Solicitors are generally far too astute to leave anything incriminating lying around their office. But I'll check with the Inspector when he gets back tomorrow, to see which way he wants us to play it.'

'Did his secretary say where Marks was?'

'She doesn't know. He told her he'd be away on private and urgent business, and couldn't be contacted.'

'How very convenient for him.'

'But not for us,' Joseph mused.

The taxi that had collected Anna Bradley from the outpatients' clinic deposited her outside her own front door at three in the afternoon. She paid the driver, stuck her key in the door and, after some painful manipulation of her bandaged thumbs, she finally succeeded in turning the lock. She slammed the door behind her and dropped her coat, bag and keys on the floor.

Staring at the mess in her living room, she decided Collins was right. It *was* disgusting. Too lethargic to even attempt clearing up, she climbed the stairs and went into the bathroom. Wincing, she turned on the basin tap with her heavily bandaged hand and managed, by gripping her toothbrush between forefinger and thumb, to awkwardly clean her teeth. Turning off the water, she proceeded into her bedroom: the only place in the house she'd actually finished decorating to her taste. The brass bed-head gleamed with the lacquer she'd applied so that it wouldn't need polishing. The Tiffany-style lamp on the bedside table was a dull bronze, the bedspread and matching curtains old gold lace. Making a mental note to invite Collins up there soon, so he wouldn't think she was a complete slob, she moved a pile of clothes from the bed on to a chair, and switched on the television she'd hung on a bracket high on the wall in a corner of the room. Picking up the remote control, she lay on the bed and flicked through the channels. Two were horse racing, one was a very bad American soap opera. Turning the sound down low, she lay back on the pillows and watched as a young man with a most improbable hairstyle knocked at a flimsy plywood front door. She didn't see much more than that, as the combination of the painkillers they'd fed her in the hospital and the softly murmuring television proved too much. The soap opera gave way to a news bulletin, which in its turn was supplanted by a cartoon . . . and she continued sleeping through them all.

'You wanted a list of break-ins, sir.' Chris Brooke placed the details on Trevor's desk.

'I did.' Joseph pushed aside his uneaten chips, and stared at the sheet in dismay. 'Seventy-two?'

'About average for a Friday night in the streets central to town, sir.'

Joseph looked across at Collins who, lump of fried fish in hand, was studying his own copy.

'Fingerprint squad been out on all of these?' he mumbled through a full mouth.

'They're trying to get around them, sir.'

'Well, we can discount some.' Collins picked up a pencil, and crossed off the first half a dozen addresses. 'There's no way our man would be removing antiques, furniture, paintings or silverware.'

'What about videos and televisions?' Joseph suggested. 'He's been living on the street a long time, so he could have made appropriate connections.'

'No fence I know is going to risk taking goods off a murder suspect, and with the publicity we've put out on him, I doubt there's any villain in town who doesn't know who he is by now. No, what we're looking for is a break-in with removal of food, money and possibly clothes.'

'And that restricts this list to . . .?'

'Just five.'

'Six,' Joseph corrected.

'Hardly Nasturtium Drive, he'd stick out like a sore thumb up there.'

'I would say he'd stick out like a sore thumb everywhere, but he seems to be evading us very neatly at the moment.'

'Number 12 Nasturtium Drive: freezer emptied, approximately two hundred pounds' worth of food,' Collins read. 'Come on, Joseph, I can't see our man staggering around with a huge sack of frozen food on his back.'

'He could have carried it to his new squat. Three bottles of whisky have gone . . .'

'But no clothes, no blankets. We know he left everything behind in that factory.'

'OK, scratch it. Let's move on.'

Uncertain whether he was expected to stay or not, Chris Brooke leant against the door and waited, watching the two sergeants as they worked their way down the list.

'This is more like it: pork pies and cans of beer.'

'From a student hall?'

'He'd fit in.'

'None of the ones I've seen are *that* filthy.' Trevor concentrated his attention. 'That's the one.' He stabbed the paper with his pencil. 'Balaclava Street.'

'Sink damaged, a blanket taken, a glass found near the sink – you ordered the glass to be printed?' Collins demanded of Brooke.

'I don't think they've got to it yet, sir.'

'See that they do, right away.'

'Yes, sir.'

'Let's face it,' Joseph said irritably, after Brooke had left, 'even if it was him in Balaclava Street last night, he could be anywhere by now, and we still haven't a clue where to start looking.'

'Is that defeatism I hear, Joseph?' Collins lifted his anorak from a peg on the back of the door. 'Come on, let's take a run down Jubilee Street and talk to Sam Mayberry and Tom Morris.'

'Why? They won't have any further news, and both of them are sick to death of the sight of us.'

'Tactics, Joseph. After a couple of hours with them, we'll deserve a meal break before kicking off our search in the streets.' He was still planning a romantic dinner with Bradley. 'And this time may I suggest we use a car. I don't know about you, but I was bloody frozen last night.'

'And so life goes on.'

'But not all night. We'll need to be alert for the Inspector's return tomorrow, so I suggest a twelve o'clock curfew, but only for the sergeants.'

'And if Mulcahy finds out?'

'He can scream all he likes. I need my beauty sleep.'

'I'll be with you in a moment. I've just one call to make. I'll use the other office.'

Joseph closed the door behind him, sat himself in the Inspector's chair, pulled his diary from his pocket, checked the number and dialled. It rang six times, and with each ring he started nervously. It would be easy to replace the receiver now, before the call was answered. Much easier than searching and stumbling over words in which to convey his confused emotions.

'Hello.'

Trevor recognised Lyn's brother's voice. He wondered why he wasn't at work, then he remembered it was Saturday. The weekend was just one more thing he tended to overlook when immersed in an investigation.

'Simon, it's Trevor Joseph.'

'I was wondering when you were going to ring.'

Was it animosity that made his voice sound brusque, or was he simply in a hurry?

'Can I speak to Lyn, please?'

'I'll get her for you.' There was a dull clunk as the receiver was set down on a hard surface. Joseph could hear voices in the distance. Faint, but not so faint that he couldn't detect an argument. Finally Simon shouted, 'He's *your* boyfriend, so you bloody well tell him.'

'Lyn speaking.' Her voice was sharp. Not a good tone to begin a reconciliation.

'I was wondering if you were all right?'

'Perfectly well, thank you. Why shouldn't I be?'

'Look, could we meet somewhere. Have dinner perhaps?'

'You're not working tonight?'

'I am, but I can take a couple of hours off.'

'Let me know when you can spare a whole evening.' She slammed down the telephone, and he held the empty receiver until it began to buzz. Hanging up, he pulled out his book again, and dialled the number of the local hospital. He had to go through two switchboards and three secretaries before he finally reached Daisy Randall.

'It's Trevor Joseph here. I wondered if you'd like dinner tonight? Just dinner,' he added flatly. 'I have to work afterwards.'

'What about—'

'Lyn left me yesterday.'

'And you're phoning me *today*?'

'Just dinner. Conversation. Nothing more.'

He sensed her hesitation, as he willed her to give him the answer he wanted.

'I won't finish here until half-past seven.'

'I'll pick you up in the foyer.'

'But I won't have had time to change.'

'We don't have to go anywhere smart. What about the pub around the corner?'

'No, not there,' she said quickly.

Trevor racked his brains, trying to think of a place where neither of them was likely to run into anyone they knew.

'What about that Turkish restaurant?'

'No,' she answered, remembering the hospital crowd, 'the Chinese.'

A lot of the police force ate in the Chinese, but he'd rather put up with their comments and enjoy eating with Daisy than eat alone. 'See you at half-past seven.' He hung up before she had a chance to rethink her decision.'

The telephone woke Anna Bradley. She opened her eyes and reached out, grimacing as her hand closed painfully around it. She glanced up as she carried the receiver to her ear. A quiz show was now playing on the television: a row of earnest young men sat opposite a row of equally earnest-faced young women, watching a presenter pull questions out of a rotating drum.

'Bradley,' she answered abruptly, her voice hoarse from sleep. She could hear breathing, slow and steady, and the faint hum of traffic. 'Bradley,' she repeated irritably, wondering if she'd picked up a pervert on her line.

'Anna . . .'

The voice was faint, but she thought she recognised it. 'Adam?' she questioned tentatively.

'Anna, I need help.'

'Half the local force is out searching for you. You have to give yourself up.'

'Not yet, Anna. I'm innocent. I swear it. I just need help.'

'Adam . . .'

'Anna, please, you have to believe me.'

'I believe you.' She meant every word.

'I haven't anywhere to go.'

'Come here, then.'

'You won't tell anyone?'

'I promise. We'll talk – decide what to do next after you get here.'

'I saw you with the police last night.' His voice was growing fainter.

She almost said *I am the police*, then she remembered him, the time they had spent together, the way he had made her feel. How, night after lonely night, she had dreamt of this sort of thing happening. Of him coming to her, needing her – only her.

'You live in Mitre Gardens.'

'How do you know?'

'It doesn't matter. Do you live alone?'

'Yes.' She wanted to explain there hadn't been anyone after him. No one since he had walked out on her.

'I'll come to you, soon. If any one else is there, I'll know, and I won't come in.'

The line went dead. Anna Bradley sat still on the bed, clutching the receiver, oblivious to the noise echoing down the line. She knew what she *should* do. Contact Joseph, and contact him immediately. But that familiar voice had worked its old familiar charm. Adam Weaver. Was it possible that she still felt something for him? He'd sworn he hadn't done anything criminal. Somehow she'd believed him when he'd told her that. Did she really believe him? What evidence – real, hard, concrete evidence – had she seen or heard to prove his guilt? After everything they had once meant to one another, the least she could do was listen.

'You said you had to work later?'

'Probably all night.'

'Still looking for your arsonist?'

'Even if he isn't the same one who set fire to that man in Jubilee Street, he's a murderer, with ten dead . . .'

'Eleven,' Daisy said grimly. 'Another one died this afternoon over in the burns unit. I'm sorry, I thought you would have known that.'

'After the initial flurry, no one bothers to tell the investigating coppers anything further, and we always seem to be too damned busy to read the papers – except when "upstairs" sends down copies marked for our attention because some reporter has decided it's open session on the police. Who was the victim?'

'Fifteen-year-old runaway. A boy. One of his friends told us his real name, so at least his parents were there at his bedside.'

'Some comfort.'

'Trevor, not even you can blame yourself for this.'

'If I hadn't gone in there that morning, none of it would have happened.'

'Maybe not that night, but certainly another time. The firemen all agreed that old factory was a disaster waiting to happen.'

'I've seen a lot of those around. Not all of them go up in flames.'

'Those people had nothing, and nowhere to go. You were looking for a murderer . . .'

'And we succeeded in turning him into a mass-murderer.'

'Two years ago I suspected you were too sensitive for this job. Now I *know* you are.'

He looked into her grey eyes. They glittered like diamonds in the light of the small lamp that burned on the table.

'You never told me that.'

'I'd just given you the brush-off. You probably wouldn't remember.'

'I was stretched out in casualty, battered and bruised, after a dealer had run his car straight into me. You were the junior doctor on duty. I asked you for a date, and you said, "Thank you, but I have more man in my life than I can handle right now, Sergeant Joseph."'

'You *do* remember.'

He leant back, away from the table, as the waiter brought their dishes: sweet and sour pork for him, prawn fried rice for her.

'I remember everything about *you*,' he murmured huskily.

She looked at him. 'Eat up.'

'Why? So I can get back to work early?'

'No, so we can have coffee afterwards in my flat.'

'Daisy . . .'

'Anyone who's carried a torch as long as you have, Trevor, deserves something in exchange.'

'Throw the dog a bone?'

'You know, the trouble with you is that you always *have* talked too much.'

Bradley checked her bedroom and bathroom, then went downstairs. She straightened the throwovers on the old couch and chair. Slipping plastic bags over her bandaged hands, she tried to clear the kitchen of dirty dishes, but after smashing three she gave that up as a hopeless task. The downstairs curtains were still open. Usually she closed them as soon as dusk fell, so the neighbours couldn't see the mess inside, but tonight she decided to leave them open. One thing about her starter home, with the windows uncovered anyone looking in from the outside could see right through the living space from front to back, so Adam could check for himself that she was alone.

Switching off the main light, she lit an Indian oil-lamp in the corner. On the rare occasions when she had an evening free and spent it at home, she stayed upstairs in her bedroom. That's why she'd set up her TV and video there. She even ate her meals upstairs, although she was careful to take all her dirty dishes back down to the kitchen. It was easy to put up with the downstairs chaos since she only ever walked through it on her way out of the front door.

The phone rang again and she jumped.

'Hello, gorgeous. Did they treat you very badly in the hospital?'

'Collins?'

'Expecting the bogeyman? Fancy coming out to dinner? I'll feed you with my own fair hand.'

'Thanks, but I couldn't face it. They really pulled me about this afternoon. My hands hurt like hell.'

'Then I'll bring around a takeaway and a bottle of wine.

What would you like: Indian or Chinese? White or red?'

'Please, Collins, can we possibly make it another night.' She tried to soften her refusal. 'I've taken a painkiller and a sleeping tablet. I'm already in bed.'

'I have a couple of hours before we go out on the night-shift, I could come and warm you some milk, and clear up that mess downstairs.'

'No! I feel like throwing up, and that's one thing I'd rather do in privacy, if you don't mind.'

'Fine.' There was a very definite edge to his voice.

'Maybe tomorrow, Collins. I really do feel lousy tonight.'

'Whatever you say.'

'Collins?'

He'd already hung up.

It wasn't easy to move through the town without being noticed – particularly for someone as scruffy as he was. But his shorter hair and his clean clothes had given him new confidence. Head up, he walked briskly down a side street immediately behind a crowd of students. Despite his ill-fitting clothes and sparse, scraggy beard, he obviously didn't look different enough to warrant any curious glances. The police were searching for a man dressed in black, with long, matted hair. Someone homeless and furtive, not a confident though scruffy mature student.

For the first time he was grateful for all the time he'd spent out on the streets, as he knew the town lay-out well. It was quite a distance yet to Bradley's house, but he dare not risk hitching, and didn't possess a penny piece towards a bus fare, so he had no other option but to walk. Strange, a week locked up in that factory, followed by a couple of days on the run, had cured all craving for alcohol and the pills for which he had exchanged most of his dole giros as soon as he had cashed them.

The gang of students turned into a pub, and he dived in after them, heading straight for the gents, where he looked in the mirror. His face was filthy with ingrained dirt that highlighted every crease and line. He placed a grimy hand beneath the soap dispenser and pressed it half a dozen times. Eventually he used all the soap and half the paper towels before he was satisfied. A man walked in and stared at him, before he made his way to a cubicle.

As he ducked out quickly, and back into the street, a woman holding a Doberman on a lead walked out of a house in front of him. When the dog snarled, she began to apologise. He merely smiled and walked on. The act of smiling felt peculiar, alien. He wondered if it was the first time he had tried it with this new face. He slowed his steps and glanced back. The woman was walking away in the opposite direction. Two more miles now; that's all he had to negotiate. And then, if Anna Bradley kept her word, he'd be safe – for a time.

'Home.' Daisy shut the front door of her flat behind them and tossed her keys and handbag on to a chair. 'Do you really want any coffee?' she asked, turning to face Trevor.

He shook his head. He felt as awkward and embarrassed as he had when he'd been a teenager taking a girl out for the very first time. He wanted Daisy, had fantasised about her for what seemed like forever, but he had always envisaged their meeting again in glowing, sunset-tinted, romantic scenarios. Somewhere exotic like Tahiti, not an impersonal environment like this hospital flat.

'Daisy, we don't *have* to do this.' He looked away from her, down to the worn carpet.

She shrugged her arms out of her coat and dropped it on top of her keys. Then she walked towards him. Two steps, and her arms were around his neck.

Reaching up, she ran her fingers teasingly, tantalisingly down the side of his face, from temple to jaw. He locked his arms around her waist and pulled her close. Bending his head, he brushed his lips tenderly over hers. His touch was so brief, so light, she couldn't be sure afterwards that their lips had actually met.

'I'm here, I'm real, and I don't break easily.'

'After all this time, I'm having trouble believing it.'

'Then I'll just have to take the initiative.' Lifting her face to his, she kissed him with a fervour that bruised his mouth and took his breath away. He moved his hands around to her breasts, caressing her tenderly, as though still afraid of hurting her. She moved away. Taking his hand, she led him through the door of the bedroom.

'Daisy . . .' He tried to catch her eye but she refused to meet his gaze.

'I said *no* words, Trevor. If we start talking, we'll never stop. And you have to leave soon.'

'Only for tonight. Neither of us is going away. We've all the time in the world. We've waited so long already, a few more days aren't going to make any difference.'

She walked ahead of him towards the bed, kicked off her shoes and unzipped her skirt. 'I just hope that, after all that waiting, I live up to your expectations.'

His mouth went dry as he watched her unbutton her blouse. He wanted to tell her he loved her – had loved her since the first moment he'd seen her. He tried but, after she had slipped out of the last of her clothes, she laid a finger over his mouth.

Lights burnt at regular intervals in the windows of the houses. He tried to check the numbers, and failed. The houses were small, yet most had names which left no clue as to their position in the street. Then he found two consecutive numbers halfway down that told him odds were one side of the road, evens the other. He crossed the street, his broken shoes soaking up the rainwater from a puddle that had collected in a patch of sunken tarmac. Stepping back into the shadows of a garage, he glanced up and down.

She must have been watching for him. The front door opened even before he knocked. He stepped swiftly inside. Half hidden by a decorated screen, he waited just inside the door while she drew the curtains at both the front and the back of the house.

'Anna, I'm sorry. But I had nowhere else to go.'

She'd tried to prepare herself, but none of her most vivid imaginings had equipped her to deal with this reality. The voice, unlike the one heard on the video, was definitely Adam's. The stance and also the walk were his. He was a good deal thinner than she remembered, and that she could cope with. But not the face. Even in the subdued light of the oil-lamp, it was so very different. She turned aside quickly, hoping to spare him her shocked reaction.

'I left the curtains open so you could be sure there was no one here except me. You must be cold, so why don't you go up and have a bath while I get us something to eat.'

'You haven't changed, Anna. I see you're still as domesticated as ever.' He looked around the room.

'Yes,' she agreed dully, suddenly remembering more than she wanted to. 'I must have been hell to live with.'

'No more than I was.'

Those eyes, those startlingly dark eyes. She would have recognised them anywhere. 'How hungry are you?'

'It's so long since I've eaten, I can't be sure.'

'I'll send out for whatever you like. Chinese takeaway, a pizza . . .'

'Same old Anna, always knows where to buy, but never how to cook.'

'The bathroom's on the left at the top of the stairs. There's a clean robe and a towel laid out.'

'And I thought I looked quite presentable.'

'You don't *smell* presentable,' she answered bluntly. 'Well, what's it to be? The food?' she reminded him, in response to his blank look.

'Whatever you've got in your kitchen cupboard.'

'Nothing?'

'In that case whatever *you* want. You swear you won't tell anyone I'm here?'

'Not until we've had time to talk. Go on. Get upstairs.'

He turned away, and she leant weakly against the wall to take a deep breath. The telephone faced her. She knew what she should do – pick it up and call the station. Then ask to be put through to Mulcahy. Instead she walked across to her wall board, read the numbers written there to remind her, memorised the number of the local pizza house, and dialled.

Chapter Fifteen

The bedroom was quiet. From outside came the whine of an ambulance siren heading for casualty, and the clicking footsteps of nurses leaving the hostel next door to begin their night shifts. Trevor lay next to Daisy in the small bed and stared at the ceiling, watching the patterns the car lights made on the swirls of artex. Carefully, so as not to disturb her, he raised his arm and glanced at his watch.

'You have to go?'

He turned his head on the pillow and faced her. 'I'm sorry.'

'So am I.'

'I wanted it to be wonderful – special between us.'

'Perhaps you wanted too much, Trevor. As you've found out, I'm rather an ordinary woman, and at the moment a rather tired one. Hardly the dream person you built me into.'

'I love you, Daisy. I always have. I—'

'No, Trevor.' She laid her finger across his lips to silence him. 'I think you were in love with the idea of me, not the reality. You don't know me, not really. But you do know Lyn. No, let me finish,' she continued as he tried to interrupt her. 'I remember you as an honest and decent man. So you wouldn't have asked her to move into your house unless you believed yourself to be in love with her.'

'She helped me. She was my nurse. I was grateful to her.'

'You didn't love her?'

'I thought I did at the time,' he admitted dismally.

'And you don't now?'

'I'm not sure *what* I think any more.'

'Your uncertainty set in when the honeymoon period ended and boring, mundane, day-to-day living began?'

'How do you know?'

'Because I've been there. Because I used to shout at Tim every time he failed to organise his free time to coincide with my own. Because I know how foul it is to love someone, really love someone, the way that girl loves you, and not be able to see them for more than a few minutes from one week to the next. Don't you see, Trevor, you couldn't make love to me because you feel guilty about her? And that has to mean you still feel something for her. Knowing about Lyn, I was a fool to drag you back here, and a bigger fool to suggest climbing into bed. I should have made my own way back from that restaurant.'

He sat up and swung his legs out from the tangle of sheets. Running his hands through his hair, he turned to look at her. 'It's not your fault. It's mine. I've made a right bloody mess of things.'

'Perhaps if we try laughing about it, we can at least salvage our friendship.'

He smiled. 'I was right all along: you're a very special lady. Whoever gets you is going to be a lucky man.'

'No, he isn't,' she contradicted soberly. 'Everything I have, everything I am, I've invested in my career. There's nothing left for a private life.'

'One thing I've learned the hard way is that a career isn't enough of an excuse for living.' He reached for his trousers.

'It is for me. It's had to be. Since Tim died I haven't really felt anything for anyone. Most of the time I'm completely dead inside. I don't feel sorrow, or joy, not even for the patients. Only a sense of professional satisfaction when an operation is a success. I never talk to another man, let alone go out with one, without thinking of Tim. Even when I was with you tonight in the restaurant, I watched every move you made, studying the way you ate, your conversation, the way you comb your hair – contrasting everything with Tim, and the way he used to do the selfsame things.'

'Just as I've done with every woman I've spent time with since I met you.'

'And now?'

'Now?' He looked at her in bewilderment.

'Tell me, have we succeeded in finally laying this ghost from your past to rest?'

He left the bed and pulled on his shirt. 'It was a comforting ghost. It gave me something to cling to, something to hope for – a reason to go on when I felt low.'

'Go and see your Lyn, Trevor. She'll give you a better reason. One made of flesh and blood, not wishful thinking and memories that never were.'

'Where the hell have you been?' Collins demanded testily, as Trevor pulled up outside the Catholic hostel in Jubilee Street.

'Checking our leads.'

'I bet. You've got lipstick all over your face.'

Joseph looked in the rearview mirror of his car and rubbed his cheek vigorously. 'Any sign of our man?' he asked in an attempt to divert Collins' attention.

'No bloody sign at all. Murphy and Brooke are fed up to the back teeth.'

'Aren't we all?'

'Not you, apparently. Which one did you lay? The doctor or the nurse?'

Ignoring Collins' question Trevor left his car. 'There has to be somewhere else that we can look now?'

'Obviously. Wherever the bastard is hiding out would be a good start, but *you* tell me where that is. He could be in any bloody street in this town. If he noticed someone leave their home in an airport bus, he could be holed up in their house even as we speak. With all mod cons to hand, too: food, fridge, freezer, heating, television . . .'

'Sooner or later he'll have to come out.'

'For what?'

'To vacate the place when the owners came back.' Joseph locked his car.

'I suppose we'd better go down Jubilee Street.'

'Again?'

'We could start with Tom Morris's place for a change.' He glanced at Joseph as they headed down the street. 'Well, come on. Tell Uncle Peter all. You make it up with Florence Nightingale, or not?'

Trevor filched a cigar from Collins' top pocket. 'Haven't seen her.'

'Then you've finally succeeded in bedding the delectable Daisy?'

'Mind your own damn business.' Trevor stared determinedly in front, at the doorway of the council hostel.

'You know she's way out of your class, don't you?' Collins needled. 'Women like her marry into money, or their own kind. Tim Sherringham qualified on both counts – you don't. You haven't the one, and you certainly aren't the other.' He pulled a lighter out of his pocket to light the cigar Joseph had pushed into his mouth. 'You're even more of a bloody fool than I thought. You've exchanged the kind of domestic bliss every man dreams of for a quick roll in the hay.'

'What I do is my own affair.'

'Not when it affects your moods, and I have to work with you. Sometimes I think you shouldn't be allowed out without a minder.'

'Damn it all, we're in the middle of a case,' Joseph shouted, furious with Collins for suspecting so much of the truth.

'That's the bloody trouble with us, Joseph. We're always in the middle of some fucking case.'

'More pizza?' Anna Bradley was seated next to Adam Weaver on her bed. The television set flickered silently in the corner as they waited for the late evening news.

'No thanks.' Adam wiped his hands on a paper napkin supplied with the boxed pizza, and leant back against the headboard, kicking his bare feet up on to the bed. Despite a long soak in the bath, his legs still didn't look entirely clean. The clothes he'd stolen earlier from the washing line were already whirring around in the machine downstairs, in a double dose of powder liberally laced with disinfectant. Bradley felt she should have done the same with Adam himself, if it had been possible.

'I couldn't eat another thing.' He dumped the last crust on his plate, and looked around the bedroom. 'I take back what I said about your place. This is really rather civilised.'

Bradley closed the empty pizza box, and carried it downstairs with the dirty plates. She returned with two cans of cold lager, handing one to Weaver.

'Adam, we have to talk. Do you actually know what I do for a living now?'

'Let me guess. You're a newspaper reporter?'

'Try again.'

'You were hanging around with the police last night.'

'You were close enough to see us?'

'Us? You're with the police? Shit!'

'I got fed up with always being broke. Not all actors get as lucky as you.'

'Lucky!'

'You had your own series.'

'Oh yes, I had it all, didn't I?' he countered bitterly. 'Fame, fortune, a sexy wife, a beautiful child.'

'Did you kill her?' Bradley interrupted softly, needing, wanting, to hear a denial from his own lips. The silence in the room seemed deafening – crushing in its intensity. He stared at her through dark eyes flecked with gold. Eyes she remembered so well.

'No, Anna.' He spoke resolutely, telling her what she wanted to hear. 'I didn't kill Laura.'

'You had a fair trial. The jury convicted you.'

'Because someone set up all the evidence to point my way. I was the patsy, the fall guy . . .'

'You had no alibi.'

'I wasn't anywhere near that cottage when it happened. I was up in London, drunk and alone for most of the evening in my flat. If I'd known I was going to *need* an alibi, I'd have been more careful to provide myself with one. Gone somewhere other than an off-licence where the assistant was more interested in the book he was reading than the customers he was serving.' He smiled grimly. 'Come on, Anna, give me credit for some intelligence. If I'd wanted to kill Laura I would have planned it better.'

She pondered on what he was saying. It did make sense – unless it was, as the prosecution had successfully argued, a premeditated crime made to look as though it was committed in a single murderous moment of passionate insanity. The doubt still remained, small and gnawing, at the back of her mind.

'Laura was having an affair,' he added.

Anna remembered what the victim's sister Blanche had said. 'Who was he?'

'I wish I knew. She taunted me with all the sordid details except his name.'

'You must have had your suspicions. There was gossip about that game-show host she worked with . . .'

He laughed mirthlessly. 'Seb? It was I who introduced him to his boyfriend.'

Anna swallowed hard and forced herself to meet his gaze, believing she still knew him well enough to tell whether or not he was speaking the truth. 'Did she start an affair in retaliation for your own exploits?'

'How well you know me,' he said acidly, 'even after all these years.'

'I do know that, in all the time we lived together, only one of us was faithful.'

'I've never made a secret of the fact that I consider monogamy an absolute swine of an institution to impose on any normal healthy male.'

'This is one situation your naive, boyish charm won't get you out of, Adam. But, then, you always were too good-looking for your own good.'

'Not any more,' he retorted savagely.

'So you were *both* having affairs,' she continued, in an attempt to draw the full story from him.

'Yes. But you have to realise what it was like for me after I started with that series. It all came so quickly, so easily – it seemed like I was created overnight. I now know that it happened too quickly for my own good. One minute I was broke, living with Laura and the baby in a grotty, rented flat; the next I had access to everything I'd ever dreamed of, and a whole lot more besides. Unlimited drink, women throwing themselves at me wherever I went . . . I won't deny I loved every minute of it. But then there was Laura.' He looked intently into her eyes. 'You were right, Anna. It wasn't much good between Laura and me from the start.'

His reply grated on her, like a speech from a bad soap opera.

'I've been an actress, too, Adam. So I can see through a hollow performance.'

'All right, the bottom line. It was bad, very bad. The only thing we had in common was a desire to torment one another – and, of course, Hannah.'

'Your daughter!'

'Have you seen her?'

'Yes.'

'How is she?'

For the first time Anna sensed real anguish.

'Remarkably sane and well-adjusted, considering what she's been through. Her aunt Blanche told us that she still talks a lot about you. She noticed you watching her in the playground that day.'

'I know. I tried to keep out of sight, but one of the other kids spotted me.'

'And thought you were a dirty old man.'

'Understandable, I suppose.'

'Let's go back to the beginning, Adam. Somehow you escaped from prison.'

'I'd have done anything to get out of that place. You have no idea what's it's like.'

'I have every idea,' she said firmly. 'I've toured enough of them.'

'So, you've walked down those smelly corridors, seen the spyholes the warders use to watch every move the prisoners make inside their cells – dispelling every notion of human dignity. I couldn't even take a piss without someone watching. Can you imagine what that's like? Or the stench in those cells after hundreds of men are locked up for hours on end like animals.'

'I told you I've seen them.'

'For how long? A couple of hours? But all the time you were breathing in the stink of sweat and urine, you knew that, any time you wanted, *you* could go outside and breathe in good clean air. It's not the same, Anna. No brief visit can begin to tell you what it's like to be incarcerated for hours, days, weeks on end with only your cellmate to talk to. Something you have no control over choosing. And, as if all that wasn't enough, you have to put up with an endless parade of shrinks trying to get inside your head.'

'Who helped you escape?'

'I don't know.' He left the bed and walked to the curtained window. 'Do you have a cigarette?'

'I don't smoke. You must have seen someone unlock your cell door?'

He opened his can of beer. 'All I can tell you is that one night after lock-up, not quite a year into my sentence, a warder came and took me out of my cell. I asked him where we were going, and he said solitary. I asked him what I had done, and he told me that the governor would explain in the morning.' He drank deeply from the can. 'There wasn't a morning. Not one that I can remember anyway, and crazy as that sounds, I swear it's God's own truth.'

'So one of the warders let you out?' Anna forced him back to hard facts. 'Who was he?'

'I don't remember a name. He was just one of the screws. I recall looking at my watch; it was early in the morning. One – two o'clock, somewhere around that time.'

'How long were you in solitary?'

'I'm not sure. A doctor came to see me just after the screw left. At least I think he was a doctor. He was wearing a white coat.'

'The prison doctor?'

'If he was, I hadn't seen him before. He reminded me that I'd volunteered to take part in a research programme, and asked if I'd had any second thoughts. I told him I hadn't.'

'What kind of research programme?'

'Medical. Colds, drug testing that sort of thing. One of the old lags suggested I volunteer just after I began my sentence. He said it would gain me brownie points with the screws, and better and extra food. I thought why not? I had nothing else to do with my time.'

'The doctor?' she prompted, ignoring the hint of self-pity.

'He gave me an injection. Told me it was influenza. Influenza my arse. Whatever it was, it knocked me for six. I remember my eyelids being too heavy to open. Feeling too sick to move. My legs and arms lying like dead weights on the mattress.'

'You were moved out of the cell?'

'Not that I can recall. Between that injection and the streets, everything's hazy. There was a room, a white room with tiled walls and lots of shining chrome on the walls. It could have been a room in the prison, it could have been anywhere. I don't know how I got there. I was lying in a bed, there were more injections. Once I thought I was strapped down, but I can't be sure whether that was real, or I dreamt it.'

'You must remember something more than just the odd impression?' she snapped.

'Do you think I haven't tried?' he shouted savagely. He turned to the wall and she caught a glimpse of tears trickling down his face. 'Oh God, Anna, I'm sorry,' he murmured. 'I know you're only trying to help. It's just that I've had two years with nothing better to do than go over this, and I know no more now than I did when it was happening.'

She sat in silence and waited for him to continue.

'There are a few images, and some must have been real,' he muttered when he had regained control of himself. 'Bandages covering all of my face, even my eyes. People removing them and swabbing my skin with cool lotions. Now' – he touched his face with his fingertips – 'I know *they*, at least, were real. The others I can't be too sure of. Like the straps, I don't know if they were there or imagined. I think there was an older woman with dark hair dressed in a white overall. She washed me, changed my sheets, but she never spoke. Not once, although I tried to speak to her, and when I tried, she just gave me an injection. There were others in surgical masks, and more injections – lots of injections. Those at least were real,' he added ruefully, rubbing his arm. 'The pin-pricks were visible for months afterwards.'

'Afterwards?'

'When I was on the streets.'

'How did you get there?'

'One morning I came to wrapped in a blanket in a car park. I had the clothes I stood up in, and the blanket – that was it.'

'No money?'

'Ten pounds in an envelope marked "Tony". That soon went.'

'Nothing more?'

'Nothing, except a new face. I freaked out the first time I saw myself in a mirror in a gents'. I wondered if I was going mad. If I was who I thought I was, or if I'd dreamt up my entire life.'

'The car park you were left in?'

'Was on the outskirts of London. When I calmed down, I visited a library, looked through the newspapers – read about my supposed escape from prison. Then I decided to make for this town, because Hannah and Blanche were here. I had to find out if I was Adam Weaver – if my memories were real or just figments of my warped imagination. At that time I was prepared to believe almost anything. I couldn't even be sure I was sane.'

'It's a long way from London to here.'

'I found a main road and hitched a ride. The lorry driver who picked me up had been down on his luck once too, so he dropped me off at the docks. With no money, there was only one place to go. Jubilee Street. You know the rest.'

'I only wish I did.'

'Life on the streets isn't very interesting.'

'Look at it from my point of view. The team I'm working with has been assigned a murder case. One that wouldn't warrant a byline in a newspaper if it hadn't been for the particularly brutal way the victim was killed. Then suddenly we find ourselves examining pictures of a man who supposedly died of natural causes two years before our murder took place. A man who apparently was our victim. Then we discover the man we originally thought was the victim is still alive, and what we have is . . .'

'How did you find out that it wasn't "Tony" who died?'

'Someone saw you after the murder.'

He nodded sagely as he opened the second can of beer.

'How did you get the real victim to swap clothes with you?'

'That was the easy part. Favours come cheap down Jubilee Street. At the right time of day a bottle of cider will buy a man's soul.'

'Why did you do it anyway?'

'Because those kids and teachers in Hannah's school had seen me. Because I knew they'd remember those bloody red baseball boots. Because I didn't want to be picked up as a potential child-molester and have my fingerprints taken, only for the police to discover who I really was.'

'Would that have been so terrible?'

'I didn't want to go back inside, not at any price.'

'Even shooting a policeman?' She raised her eyes to his. 'I was there when you tried to kill him, Adam.'

'Policeman or not, he shot at me.'

'His gun was never fired. Adam, I saw you . . .'

'I've never had a gun, Anna. Think about it. Where in hell would a man living on skid row find one? Look.' He pulled back the sleeve of the towelling robe he was wearing so she could examine the wound on his arm. It was still raw, infected with pus. 'He shot me there.'

She'd seen gunshot wounds before, and there was no mistaking the origin of his injury. She tried to remember. She'd seen Collins' gun afterwards, but was convinced he hadn't fired it. There hadn't been time for him to pull it out of his shoulder holster. And surely no man, not even one as desperate as Adam Weaver, would shoot himself willingly.

'Let's forget about the shots for a moment,' she said, unable to make sense of what he was saying. 'There's still the fire that was deliberately started in that building.'

'Not by me. It was already burning as I ran down the stairs.'

'Eleven people died as a result of that blaze. And the injured are still in hospital.'

'The fire wasn't started by me, Anna.' He looked at her earnestly. 'You do believe me, don't you?'

'If you were innocent, why did you run?'

'Because someone was taking potshots, and I was in the

firing line.' He returned to the bed and sat on the edge. 'Because even half a life in Jubilee Street is better than no life. Because I'm terrified of being locked up again. Because I need to find Laura's killer.'

'You know who killed her?'

'I know he must live somewhere close to this town, because she was forever driving over here to leave Hannah with her sister.'

'That's all you have to go on?'

'Someone *must* have seen them together. When I first arrived in this town, I tried going around the nightclubs, asking questions – but after a while living rough no one would talk to me.'

'I'm not surprised, if you behaved like you did on that video.'

'What video?'

'You don't remember a television crew filming you in Jubilee Street?'

'Oh my God!'

'You were stoned out of your mind.'

'Red wine and amphetamines.'

'Remind me not to try it.'

'Anna, you have to believe me! I've put all that behind me. I'm not a junkie. Just a man who looked for an occasional high-flying trip when he'd hit bottom. Sure I popped the odd pill when I could afford them, but I never injected. I haven't got AIDS. Anna, you're all I've got. You know me. We lived together. I confess I'm a womaniser. I've been a drunk and, worst of all, I've been a bastard to you and all the other women who were foolish enough to tell me they loved me. But I could never murder anyone. Look at me,' he pleaded. 'Look into my eyes and tell me if you think the man you're looking at could kill *anyone*, much less the mother of his child.'

She looked away, her emotions in turmoil. All she could be sure of was that once – what now seemed a very long time ago – she had loved Adam Weaver. Perhaps enough for a small part of her to always love him. And, even wearing a dead man's face, he was still Adam. She could hear it in the inflection of his voice – his rich, resonant voice – and see it in the way he moved his hands, in the depths of his eyes when he looked at her.

'Anna' – he reached out and took her hand – 'please, I know I'm asking a lot, but if you'd just allow me to stay here for a day or two, it will give me the breathing-space I need to find Laura's real murderer.'

'How could you even start looking, with all the publicity? "Tony's" face has been on the front of every local and national newspaper.'

'No one's caught up with me yet.'

'Adam, if you give yourself up now, tonight, I'll try to get Laura's case reopened. I have influence. I'm with the Serious Crimes Squad.'

'No!' The cry was intense, savage. 'No, Anna,' he repeated in a whisper when he realised he'd screamed at her again. 'Don't you see, this is my last chance. I can't – I won't go back to gaol. I'd kill myself first.'

Her initial reaction was to dismiss this threat as theatrical ravings. But something in his eyes left her uncertain. If he had moved any closer, raised a hand or tried to seduce her with the same old techniques he had once employed to silence her rantings about other women when they had lived together, she would have picked up the telephone and dialled the police station. But seeing him now sitting on the end of her bed, clutching her hand like a child and looking lost, alone and broken, made her believe in him as nothing else could.

'I've only one bedroom and one bed – and you're looking at it. But I've an extra duvet. If we roll it up and put it down the middle, we can both sleep here. I'm on early morning shift, so I'll see what I can find out. We can talk again tomorrow night.'

'Anna . . .'

'Don't thank me. Not yet, Adam. I may have to help arrest you.'

Chapter Sixteen

'Jet lag?' Collins enquired of Evans, who was stifling an enormous yawn.

'Just sheer bloody exhaustion.'

'Now that's something I *do* know about.'

'You get my fax?'

'Yes,' Joseph replied.

'You've interviewed Brian Marks?'

'Can't,' Collins interrupted. 'He's away, and won't be back until next week.'

'He must have left a number in case of emergency.'

'Nothing. He lives alone, but his secretary checked with the housekeeper. He's locked up his house, switched on the burglar alarms, and given the help a fortnight's paid holiday.'

'Then get on to the local force. Arrange a search warrant. See if there's an address in the house. We've got to be seen to be doing something other than sitting around on our arses.' Evans looked over at Bradley, who was silently flexing her damaged hands. 'You've been taking it easy, I hope?'

'Any easier and I'd be sleeping.'

'I've got a job for you, and the Super's agreed you can have Sarah Merchant to assist you.'

'The girl on the switchboard?'

'She's a whizz with computers, and the sooner we computerise all our information on this case, the better. I want you to concentrate on Adam Weaver. I want the name and address of every friend, every relative, every acquaintance, and any and every hole he could possibly bolt to, all available at the touch of a finger. The man has to be somewhere, and it's my guess someone is shielding him.'

'Little green men in a spaceship?'

'Was that intended to be a serious contribution, Collins?'

'You're beginning to sound like the Super,' Collins grumbled. 'We've searched every inch of this town, from one end to the other.'

'Then search it again,' Evans demanded mercilessly.

'Have a heart. During the last week I've spent more time in Jubilee Street than I have in my own bed. We've checked the dossers, we've checked every burglary . . .'

'And?'

'He broke into a terrace house in Balaclava Street the night before last. Took a blanket and drank a glass or two of water.'

'Then he's still got to be out there on the loose. Joseph, you concentrate on tracking down Brian Marks. Collins, check out all the pushers. If that video meant anything, Weaver has a habit that needs feeding. Tonight we all go out again. Except you, Bradley.'

'Thank you, sir.'

Collins frowned, wondering if Bradley was sicker than she was letting on. Normally she would never have allowed herself to be sidelined on a case.

'For all our sakes, something has to break soon.' Evans reached for his peppermints. 'And for my money the most likely leaks are going to stem from "Tony" or Brian Marks.'

'Sir,' Bradley ventured. 'Is it worth pulling the records on the murder of Weaver's wife?'

Collins groaned. 'For the love of Mike, we're already investigating a convicted killer on the run, the murder of an army deserter, arson with eleven related deaths, besides a crooked solicitor and a suspect doctor. Why in hell do you want to dig up what's over and done with?'

'Just an idea.'

'Any reasoning behind it?' Evans asked.

'Weaver always protested his innocence. What if he was?'

'Come on,' Collins scoffed. 'He had his trial.'

'And was convicted on circumstantial evidence.'

'Circumstantial traces of his blood were found in that cottage bathroom.'

'It was his bathroom, he had recently suffered a deep cut on his hand.'

'Sustained when he chopped up his wife?'

'Sustained on a set a week before Laura Weaver was murdered,' Bradley contradicted. 'The director testified that he bled like a stuck pig for two days.'

'How come you know so much, Bradley?'

'I asked records for the newspaper clippings.'

'Why?'

'Background on Weaver.'

'And now you think he's innocent?'

'I don't know. It's just that some things don't quite add up.'

'Like your schoolgirl crush on him?' Collins sneered.

'I outgrew that a long time ago. Something Blanche Davies said set me thinking.' Bradley paused, desperately trying to sift the information the woman had given her from the story Adam had told her the night before. 'She suggested that Laura Weaver was having an affair.'

'And you think the lover could have killed her?'

'It's a possibility.'

'Tell me, why would any man kill his bit on the side?' Collins asked.

'Jealousy – greed – fury – who knows? Perhaps she'd just told him it was over.'

'I don't buy it. Not another man's wife.'

'All I'm saying is that it has to be worth looking at.'

'No innocent man would undertake an escape from gaol that involved something as drastic as a complete face change. Look at the facts, Bradley. Weaver's life was wrecked. He went from being a rich, successful actor, with a family, to less than a penniless nobody in Jubilee Street. If he'd really been innocent he would have stayed in prison and written letters to the newspapers, to his MP, gone on hunger strike, got his solicitor to lodge an appeal.'

'He did all of that except the hunger strike, his efforts just weren't that well reported. The thing is he got nowhere, and now he could be trying to find the real killer.'

'That's one hell of a supposition – that first he's innocent, and now he's playing Sherlock Holmes.'

'What if the real killer knows that "Tony" is Adam Weaver,' Bradley proposed uncertainly.

'How would he?' Collins demanded. 'It took us long enough to find out.'

'But what if he had something to do with Weaver's metamorphosis into "Tony"?'

'Phillip Matthews died, not Weaver,' Joseph pointed out, wondering where exactly her train of thought was leading.

'He died because he was wearing "Tony's" clothes,' Bradley argued stubbornly.

'You can't have this both ways,' Collins said shortly. 'Even if Weaver's wife was killed by someone else, and that someone else is now after Weaver, which I don't buy for one minute, I still can't see how the killer would have realised that Weaver was the same as "Tony". And, if, by some miracle, I'm wrong, and the murderer *did* know, why did he set fire to the wrong man in Jubilee Street?'

'He went by the clothes. It was dark . . .'

'Close up, Matthews looked nothing like "Tony". And he must have seen him clearly enough. There's lights in Jubilee Street,' Joseph pointed out.

'Bradley, you can't get away from the fact that Adam Weaver shot me, and then set fire to the factory. Even if he didn't murder his wife, he's a killer now, all right.' Collins lifted his feet on to the desk, and linked his hands behind his head. 'Whichever way I view that man, I see a psychopath.'

'You're probably right, Collins.' Bradley left her desk and headed towards the door. Collins was pigheaded, abrasive and chauvinistic, but what he was saying made sense. Exactly the same kind of sense that Adam's story also had made, in her bedroom the night before.

Collins picked out a pale grey leather jacket from his wardrobe. He slipped it over the black silk shirt he was wearing, and walked into his living room.

'What do you think?' he asked Trevor Joseph, pulling the sleeves down with his thumbs. 'Fairly prosperous dealer?'

'Mafia hood, more like it,' Joseph retorted.

'Something tells me you're not looking forward to our little night on the town.' Collins turned to switch off the bedroom light. 'Station first, for the briefing, then where do you reckon we start: the clubs or the pubs?'

'The clubs.' Joseph buttoned his jacket.

Collins surveyed him critically. 'That suit was never wonderful, but a pressing might have toned down the dog-eared look.'

'It's the new, lived-in, crumpled style. Haven't you heard of it?'

'You know something, Joseph' – Collins couldn't resist one last glance in the mirror – 'you make a more convincing down-and-out than you do a prosperous villain. Rags suit you better.'

'You all right?' asked Sarah Merchant. She and Anna Bradley sat side by side in front of a computer screen that rose like an island out of a multi-coloured sea of files on the desk all around it.

'Not really,' Bradley said flatly, trying to pick up one of the files between her wrists.

'Now we've collected all the information, I can carry on just as well without you,' Sarah said kindly. 'Inputting data is a one-man job.'

'You sure?'

'Absolutely. Want me to check if there's a car free to take you home?'

'Please.' Bradley sat back in her chair as Sarah picked up the internal telephone. 'At this moment my idea of heaven is to stick plastic bags over these' – she held up her bandaged hands, 'then have a hot shower and crawl between the sheets – before carrying on with this lot.' She indicated a further pile of files at her feet.

'That sounds like a sure recipe for sleep.'

'It probably will be.'

As Collins stuck his head around the door, Bradley stared at his well-groomed hair and wide-boy outfit. Merchant's response was a wolf whistle.

'This is nothing,' he winked. 'Wait until you see Joseph. He's actually wearing a suit and tie.'

'No shirt?'

'That, too. You were ringing for a lift for the invalid here?'

'I can get a taxi,' Bradley interposed hastily.

'No need.' Collins wondered if it was his imagination, or if Bradley was deliberately trying to avoid him. He racked his brains to think of something he might have done to upset her. 'We're going your way.'

'It's all right, really . . .'

'Look, woman, for once do as you're told.' Collins knelt and scooped up the files heaped at her feet. 'These going with you?'

'Yes, but—'

'No buts. Into my car.'

'Really I'd rather—'

'I've got your coat.' Trevor was standing in the doorway.

Merchant sniffed. 'You two should have co-ordinated. Your colognes fight something dreadful.'

'Only Joseph's,' Collins agreed. 'He has no taste. You getting off that chair, Bradley, or do I have to carry you out?'

Bradley stood and allowed Trevor to drape the coat over her shoulders. All she could think of was Adam Weaver. She'd warned him to stay out of sight, and hoped he'd have the sense to do just that until she had thought everything through.

'How about inviting us in for a cup of coffee?'

'This is the house you're afraid of catching the plague in, remember?' Bradley pressed down the door handle of the car with her elbow.

'We're prepared to risk it, aren't we, Joseph?'

'I really am feeling tired . . .'

'You can't stop me carrying the files for you.'

'I can manage.'

'Just as far as the door, for Christ's sake.'

Joseph stayed in the car, watching as Collins gathered up the paperwork to follow her. Bradley ran ahead to unlock the door, then swivelled round to block Collins' access. He dumped the files unceremoniously in her arms and turned on his heel.

'What have you done to upset the lady?' Joseph enquired, as

his colleague climbed back into the driving seat.

'Nothing much as yet, I'd have thought.'

'Perhaps it's the "as yet" she's wary of. She could have a closet lover holed up in there.'

'Bradley!'

'Some police have private lives.'

'And some make a total balls up of them, even when they're lucky enough to find an ideal partner,' Collins bit back viciously.

Anna Bradley walked straight through her living room and into the kitchen area. She'd left the curtains drawn shut that morning, and Adam hadn't opened them, but he had cleaned up. The kitchen floor was sparkling, the air smelled strongly of soapsuds, disinfectant, and something warm and appetising. She opened the oven door to find a casserole bubbling. Closing it again, she dropped her shoulder bag on to the table and went upstairs. The bed was made, the furniture dusted, but there was no sign of Adam himself. She tried the bathroom door, but it was locked. She knocked quietly.

'Adam. Are you there?'

When there was no answer, she murmured, 'I'm alone.'

'I heard voices,' came a muffled reply.

'A colleague brought me home. I can't drive with these hands, remember?'

'I heard him. He didn't seem anxious to go.'

'He's concerned about me, that's all. He was the one with me in the old factory when I got hurt.' As he opened the door, his eyes held the fear and wariness of a cornered animal. 'I wasn't sure you'd be here when I got back.'

'I nearly took off,' he admitted. 'When you were here last night, I felt I could trust you. After you left this morning, I couldn't be sure.'

'You thought I'd remember that I work for the police and come with a posse to arrest you.'

'Yes.'

'That's what logic tells me I should do.'

'But you haven't told anyone?'

She shook her head. 'This is the hardest decision I've ever

made. You've no idea of the time, money and manpower that's been expended in the search for you. All day I've sat in that station listening to people talk about you – hazarding guesses as to where you could be holed up . . .'

'I'm grateful, Anna. Believe me, I know what this must be costing you.' He laid a hand on her shoulder, till its warmth penetrated the sweater she was wearing. Keeping her eyes on a level with the top button of his checked shirt and standing close to him on the cramped landing, listening to his familiar voice, she pictured him again as he had been all those years ago. With his own face.

'Adam, we have to talk,' she pleaded.

'I made a casserole with some beef I found in your freezer.'

'I saw it in the oven.'

'I came across a few bottles of wine when I was cleaning under the stairs.'

'There's even a Rioja, I think.'

'You remember?'

'I remember a great deal too much.'

It was a long night, going from backstreet dealer to the clubs, to the pubs, to the alleys, to the all-night shops that had much more on offer than the sweets and tobacco innocently displayed on the counter.

'If we were awarded medals for busting small-time dealers, we could be everyone's blue-eyed boys tomorrow,' Collins remarked, as they clanged out of a boarded-up shop on the fringes of a vast council estate.

'All units . . . all units!'

'That's us.' Joseph picked up the radio transmitter from the dash.

'We're on special duties now.'

'The call was "all units".'

'Knife fight in casualty at the General.'

'I'd forgotten it was Friday night.'

'Saturday,' Joseph corrected, as Collins completed a hazardous U-turn in the middle of the street.

* * *

She checked that the curtains were fully closed for the fifth time since she'd come home, before starting to lay the table. After lighting the oil-lamps, she sat down at the table, opposite Adam.

'Can we start again at the beginning?' she asked, as he ladled steaming casserole on to her plate.

'What beginning?'

'Laura's murder.'

'It goes back further than that. You knew I was already having an affair with her when you and I were living together.'

'Yes.' Anna stared resolutely at her plate.

'I know it hurts . . .'

'Stick to the facts, Adam. I'm finding this whole situation difficult enough without you raking over your colourful past.'

She was angry with him for trying to make love to her – but she was angrier with herself for almost succumbing to his approach.

He laid his fork down on the tablecloth. 'I married Laura because she was pregnant with Hannah, and that was the only reason. You knew me in those days. I wasn't out to marry anyone.'

'The days of shotguns held to bridegrooms' heads are long over.'

'I was besotted with the thought of becoming a father – I really thought she was carrying a son in my image.'

'But you got a daughter.'

'I wasn't disappointed. Not once I'd seen her. And Laura got what she wanted, too.' He picked up his fork and stabbed at a sliver of beef. 'She set out to catch me, and she did it with the oldest trick in the book. Not that I'm complaining. She was beautiful, good in bed, I wanted her, and she wanted my success. I think she hoped some of it would rub off on her. But I was never really happy with her – not in the same way I'd been with you,' he added softly.

'And half a dozen others too,' she snapped harshly, swiftly dispelling the romantic atmosphere he was trying to create.

'I'm not making any excuses. As I said last night, the success of the telly series made me a desirable commodity, socially, financially, sexually. I lost my head. Then, in the middle of it all, Laura told me she was pregnant. It came as a shock, but after all that partying, the prospect of stability – family life and kids – suddenly seemed attractive. We married. I bought the country cottage and the lease of a flat in London. I was riding the crest of the wave and, even if I worked long hours, there were compensations. Laura never knew how many hours of "filming" were stretched out to accommodate a willing fan or an actress colleague.'

She blurted out. 'So you weren't faithful to her either?'

'I can't remember being faithful to anyone – except perhaps you.'

'Bullshit!'

'If you'd allow me to continue, I was going to add that was true in the early days when we were both broke. You need money to be unfaithful, even it's only for the bus fare.'

This time she laughed, in spite of the pain.

'To say I didn't pay enough attention to Laura and Hannah would be an understatement. Just after I filmed that last series, we decided to take a break and spend most of the summer together in the cottage. It was about that time I realised Laura had found someone else. At first I couldn't be sure. There were a lot of wrong numbers. Callers hanging up as soon as I answered the phone. Good jewellery appearing on her dressing-table that I'd never seen before. And she wasn't the sort to buy gold pieces for herself. Fake yes, but not the real thing. Then there were all those weekends spent at her sister's. I'd ring up to talk to her, but Blanche and Hannah would usually be there alone. To be honest' – he pushed his plate aside – 'after the initial shock, I wasn't too upset about it. I was playing around myself.'

'With how many?'

He lifted his eyebrows. 'You know me.'

'Stick to the story, Adam.'

'It was a Wednesday. We were due to drive down to the cottage at the weekend. I'd finished filming at midday, and the costume fittings for the next series had been put off until the following week. I got back to the flat early to find Laura packing – just her own things. She told me she was off to stay with Blanche again. I was furious because Hannah still had a couple of days of school term left. She wanted Laura and me to come to her end-of-term concert. It was very important to her. And there was Laura clearing off the day before, just because she wanted to screw her lover. We argued, and it was quite a row. I'd had a couple of drinks to celebrate the end of the series, so I wasn't entirely rational. To cut a long story short, I hit her.'

'Hard?'

'Hard enough. She stormed out, telling me I'd never see her again as long as I lived. She also said she'd fight to get custody of Hannah and, given my record of drinking and violence, she'd get her. That was the last time I saw Laura alive.'

'You didn't follow her down to the cottage?'

'I told you, I'd been drinking. Far too much to drive safely.'

'The police reports say that your car had some mud on it.'

'I've never washed a car in my life. You know that.'

'Mud in London?'

'We'd spent all week filming on Wimbledon Common. It could have come from there.'

'You really didn't go anywhere near the cottage?'

'I'd no reason to. I had no idea where Laura had gone. Even in my fuddled state, I didn't believe her story about going to visit Blanche. To be honest the cottage barely crossed my mind, as I assumed Laura was going to *his* place, wherever it was. Look, if you've read the case files you'll know that the police didn't find one shred of evidence in that cottage to prove I'd been there that night. They couldn't even match the mud on my car to the soil around our cottage.'

'You'd played the detective part long enough to know you'd have to wear gloves . . . overboots . . .'

'Where were they then, when the police did their search?'

'Bottom of a lake or river.'

'You don't *want* to believe me.' He poured out more wine with an unsteady hand.

'Damn it all, Adam, I do want to believe you. But I'd rather know the truth. That's why I'm sitting here, asking you all these questions instead of phoning my superior.' Using the heel of her palm, she pushed her own wine glass down the table towards him. He filled it and carried it back to her. 'But you did leave the London flat that night, after Laura had gone?' she continued.

'After she left, I lay down on the bed. I think I probably slept for quite a while. The next thing I really remember was waking up in the dark. I telephoned Hannah to wish her goodnight.'

'Where was she?' Anna already knew from the files, but she wanted him to tell her.

'With a friend from school. It was a special occasion: a birthday.'

'And after you phoned?'

'I showered, and changed my clothes. But then you must know that already. The prosecution lengthened my trial by two days by concentrating on the importance of my changing clothes.'

'You changed because they were covered in mud?'

'From Wimbledon Common,' he replied steadily. 'I had a hangover from the afternoon's drinking. I wasn't feeling too hot, so I decided to go for the hair of the dog. All I could find in the flat was half a bottle of wine. I wanted something stronger, and went out to get it.'

'You took a cab?'

'To the off-licence?'

'So you walked, and no one saw you go out?'

'The porter; he testified at the trial.'

'But he couldn't put a definite time on when you left, and he didn't see you return.'

'So I was convicted on the deficient memory of a geriatric.'

'No, you were convicted on the evidence put forward by the prosecution.'

'All of it circumstantial.'

'You went to the off-licence?' she prompted.

'Ten minutes' walk away.'

'And you saw no one on the way?'

'Of course I did. There were people around. It wasn't that late.'

'But not one of them could recall seeing an actor who was a household name, and face.'

'I can't explain that, other than to say it was dark. The weather was foul. I'd turned the collar of my coat up, I was carrying an umbrella . . .'

'The eternal cry of the TV personality is that they can't step out of doors without being mobbed.'

'For once I wasn't.' His voice was brittle with irritation.

'And when you reached the off-licence?'

'I bought a bottle of whisky.'

'What brand?'

'How in hell should I remember?'

'Because it's important.'

'It wasn't at the time, because I didn't know I was going to be charged with killing my wife that night.'

'The assistant didn't remember seeing you.'

'No, but I was able to testify that he'd had his nose glued to a book.'

'But you couldn't say what that book was.'

'Because it was opened out flat on the counter. I handed him the whisky, he took my money, gave me my change . . .'

'But no receipt.' Bradley had studied the files thoroughly.

'He might not have given it to me.'

'It was company policy to give all customers receipts.'

'Then I must have dropped it.' He felt as though she had placed him in the dock all over again.

'There were no receipts found in the rubbish swept from the floor of the shop that night. None in the flat, in your car . . .'

'But a half-full bottle of whisky with a price tag bearing the name of the off-licence was found on my coffee table.'

'A bottle which could have been bought at any time. Look at it from the prosecution's point of view, Adam. You were seen leaving the flat. No one remembers seeing your car in the garage of the flats that night . . .'

'No one remembers not seeing it either. Half the people who lived in that apartment block were dead from the neck up. They'd do anything not to get involved, especially in a scandal or crime, and I found myself embroiled in both.'

'No one saw you walking to the off-licence. The assistant didn't remember serving you. No one saw you walking back,' she continued mercilessly.

'I watched television. I told the police what I saw.'

'A four-year-old film. You could have seen it in the cinema or on video . . .'

'Please, spare me any more,' he cried out angrily. 'I've been through all this a hundred times and more.' He pushed his food away and sunk his head down on his arms.

'You really have no idea who Laura went to meet that night?' she asked quietly when the silence grew too much to bear.

'Do you think I'd have gone to prison if I had?' he mumbled miserably.

'Come on, Adam, she was your wife. You must have had some idea who her friends were, and where she went when she wasn't with you.'

'She spent quite a few weekends with Blanche, or claimed she did. She had lunch with friends in London now and again, but the police checked out everyone I knew about. They were all noted in her address book, anyway. Laura never really got back into mainstream acting after Hannah was born. Those naive-young-girl parts she'd been landed with dried up as she grew older. You know what the business is like.'

'I also know that, on what little you've told me, we could spend ten years trying to track down Laura's murderer, and get no closer.'

'But we've got to try!' He crashed his fist down on the table, clinking the crockery. 'We have to try,' he repeated insistently. 'If we don't, I'll be sent back to prison, and I couldn't stand that. I'd go mad. I wouldn't last there a week. I'd kill myself! So help me God, I'd kill myself.' His voice dropped to a whisper.

He sat before her, eyes staring, hands fidgeting. Such was his emotional intensity at that moment, she believed him capable of anything – even murder. She thought guiltily of the Super, the Inspector, of Joseph, Collins and the whole of the police force now concentrating all their resources and energy on finding this man, when he was sitting here in her house. If any of them ever found out she'd sheltered Adam Weaver, it wouldn't just be her job on the line. She'd end up in a cell with all of them throwing the book at her. As she pushed her empty glass back towards him, she made a mental note to check the maximum penalty for harbouring a felon.

Chapter Seventeen

Joseph and Collins weren't the first police officers to reach the General Hospital. Brooke and Murphy were already there, dealing with a fracas off the main waiting area.

'Just a domestic, sir,' Chris Brooke shouted across to Joseph above a sea of heads, as he handcuffed a fair-haired, stocky man with blood streaming from a cut above his eye.

'No wife of mine is going to sleep around like a common slut and get away with it. Not while I've breath in my body,' Brooke's prisoner roared.

A woman with skinned lips, bruised mouth, and a bloody gap where her front teeth should have been, screamed at him from Murphy's restraining arms. 'I divorced you six months ago, you bastard.'

'Happy families,' Collins murmured. 'Why can't they beat each other up *off* my shift.'

'There's another one in theatre.' A sister bustled in with a tray of plastic sutures and scissors. 'The wife's new boyfriend.'

'Three of them did all this!' Joseph looked back at the waiting-room, which was littered with upturned chairs and delicately patterned sprays of blood.

'Emergency!' A paramedic crashed along the corridor behind them, preceding a trolley being pushed at speed by his partner.

'That's all we need. You know what Saturday nights are like here. Couldn't you have taken this one up the road? Just this once?' the sister joked poorly.

The paramedic took the sister to one side of the passage and began relating as much of the case history as he knew in an urgent, low-pitched whisper. After briefly examining the elderly man on the stretcher, the sister eventually called for a nurse.

265

'Unless you want to do otherwise, Sarge, we'll take this lot down to the station and charge them, as soon as they're bandaged up.'

'That's fine by me,' Collins answered Brooke. He turned to Joseph and nodded towards the door. Only too glad to leave the noisy chaos behind them they started down the main corridor. Halfway along, Joseph realised that Collins was no longer with him. Looking back, he could see his partner standing over the trolley that had just been brought in.

'It's Marks,' Collins announced.

'Brian Marks, the solicitor?' Joseph asked.

Collins looked up at him. 'Where in hell did that sister go?'

Anna sat with her chin supported on her hands. She'd drunk too much. The one bottle of wine had turned into four. She'd barely touched the casserole Adam had cooked, and the alcohol, mixed with the painkillers she'd taken to see herself through the day, had muddled her senses to the point where she was no longer capable of evaluating anything Adam said to her.

The room swam headily before her eyes as his exquisitely regulated actor's voice droned on softly in the background. She was conscious of its soothing resonance, the contrived poetic harmony, but she could no longer decipher the meaning behind his words. All evening they'd talked, but she was, if anything, more confused now than when she'd left the police station that afternoon. Hours ago the trained detective in her had reasoned that Adam hadn't presented her with a single convincing detail to support his innocence of any of the crimes he had been, or could be, charged with the moment he was picked up. His alibi for the night of his wife's death sounded no better now than it had done two years ago. His explanation for changing clothes with the army deserter who'd subsequently burnt to death was shaky to say the least. If those red boots had worried him that much why hadn't he simply dumped them and salvaged another pair from one of the skips installed to collect clothing for the charity shops? And the damning evidence regarding the factory fire – she had witnessed it with her own eyes.

Collins was right. Adam had received his day in court. He'd

had a fair opportunity to clear himself, but had been convicted. Found guilty of the most heinous crime of all: murder. And since his escape from prison he'd wrought death and destruction on everyone and everything he'd touched. Why was she sitting here listening to him now, when she should have got on the phone to the Superintendent straight away?

Was it simply because of an old love that should have died years ago? Or was there something else – an innocence in Adam that she sensed against all logic. An innocence she wanted to believe in despite hard evidence to the contrary.

'Adam, do you realise that just sitting here in the same room with you means I'm committing a crime?' she interrupted harshly. 'It's called harbouring a felon. I could go to prison, lose my job . . .'

'As a cop?'

She detected the sneer. 'I'm a good officer,' she slurred defensively. 'Going undercover is not that different from acting. It's taken me a long time, but I've finally found something I can do well. My work means everything to me now. I've built a life for myself around it. Not much of one perhaps by your standards' – she gazed defiantly around her shabby living-room – 'but it's all I've got. No!' She held up her hand. 'Let me finish. If I could see a way to help you prove your innocence, I'd say stay here and I'll help you. We'd work at it together. But from what you've told me, I can't see any point.'

'But there's still Blanche! She has to have some idea who Laura was having an affair with,' he continued unrelentingly.

'She's already told us she didn't. It's not that I don't believe you, Adam. It's more like I can't. I'm not the same person you used to know. I'm police officer first now, Anna Bradley second.'

'You're not that different.' He dumped the used plates on the draining board and turned to face her. She rose from her chair and moved towards him, her emotions in complete turmoil.

Wrapping his arms around her shoulders, he bent his head and kissed her gently. His lips – Anthony George's lips – grazed her own. She closed her eyes so she didn't have to look at his face. She reached up and clasped her hands around his neck.

No! This was all too familiar, too dangerous. She pushed him away.

'I'm sorry, Anna. I hurt you once, and I'm hurting you again. I have no right to ask anything of you. I'd better get going but before I do I want you to know that, whatever happens, I won't reveal to anyone that I was here, or that you helped me out.'

'Where will you go? No, don't tell me.'

This time she was the one who kissed him. That kiss led to another – and another. Slowly they climbed the stairs. She felt too tired, too muddled by a heady mixture of wine and emotion to think clearly. Tomorrow . . . she would think about everything in the morning. Things always seemed better in the morning. One night couldn't make any difference to the police search, and for the first time in years Adam was entirely hers. She had the night, and she had him. For now, she would shut out everything else except that.

'You sure that was Brian Marks?'

'I interviewed him once, remember?'

Collins continued to pace the length of the side room the sister had shown them into. The door opened, and a young woman walked in, wearing a white doctor's coat.

'You the ones waiting for news of Mr Brian Marks?'

'Yes.'

'Relatives?'

'Police.' Collins pulled out his identification.

'I'm the houseman. If Mr Marks has a family, they should be contacted.'

'I'm not sure there's many of them left, love,' Collins said flatly. 'What's wrong with him?'

'Paracetamol overdose.'

'Serious?'

'I'm afraid so, but for the moment Mr Marks is quite lucid. He told us he booked into a hotel room three days ago, and swallowed an entire bottle of forty tablets. He's surprised to be still alive, and frankly so are we. But as the drug has now been in his bloodstream for more than forty-eight hours, the damage to his organs has already been done. There's very little we can do except make him comfortable and wait for the inevitable.'

'How long?' Collins asked bluntly.

'Any time. There's massive damage to his liver. It's a pity, but he obviously knew what he was doing. And, in my experience, if someone is really serious about suicide, they generally succeed. He wouldn't be here now if it hadn't been for the efforts of a persistent chambermaid who opened his door with a master key.'

'Is he capable of answering some questions?'

'For the moment, yes.'

'Can we talk to him then?'

'Only if he wants to talk to you. We're going to move him up to a ward shortly. But I warn you now, with such massive internal damage, his condition could become extremely unpleasant at any moment.'

The young doctor ushered Joseph and Collins into the cubicle where Brian Marks was still lying flat on the trolley he'd been brought in on. His skin was the colour of wax and he was trembling uncontrollably. His eyes, dull, glazed, had trouble focusing as he turned to look at them.

'Is there anyone we can send for, Mr Marks?' Joseph asked.

'No one. I live quite alone . . .' His voice faded to an almost inaudible whisper.

'What about your nephew in America?' Collins suggested.

'It will be over before he could get here.'

'We've been looking for you,' Collins divulged. 'One of our colleagues went to the States to interview your nephew, Laurence Marks, in connection with a case involving multiple murder and arson. As a result of that interview, we have reason to believe that both the murders and the arson attack were carried out by one Adam Weaver, who was represented by your firm when he was charged and convicted of murdering his wife. We now also know that, courtesy of your nephew's surgical skill, Weaver is wearing the face of one Anthony George, now deceased and also an ex-client of yours. Would you like to tell us what you know about these crimes and Adam Weaver's current whereabouts? However, if you do so, I have to caution you that anything you say . . .'

'It's too late for that to matter . . .' Marks closed his eyes. If it hadn't been for the occasional slight movement of the blanket covering his chest, Joseph could have believed him already dead.

'Would you please tell us, sir, why you arranged for Adam Weaver to receive another man's face in a transplant operation?' Collins pressed.

'I didn't. Laurence did it all. He told me about it afterwards. By then it was too late.'

'Too late?' Collins pressed insistently, moving closer to the trolley so he wouldn't miss a word.

'Laurence thought I'd be pleased. That I'd take Weaver to Emma . . .'

'Emma?' Collins demanded. 'Who's Emma?'

'George's mother. You see Laurence knew I loved her. But she was already . . .' His voice tailed off as his eyelids flickered.

'Dead?' Joseph prompted.

The old man moved his head slightly. 'I told Laurence he was mad. He could never have fooled a mother about her own child.' Marks' voice was growing frailer, more feeble by the second.

'Did you arrange Adam Weaver's escape from prison?'

'No. I didn't know anything until it was all over. *Fait accompli.* You see . . . Laurence . . .' The old man finally managed to open eyes that were already cloudy with death. 'He would never have admitted it, but he was afraid the operation might go wrong. I blame myself for not going to the police when Laurence first offered me Anthony. Lazarus returning from the dead . . .' The sentence ended in a croaking gurgle. Collins thought Marks had laughed, until he saw the bubble of bloody froth burst on the old man's lips.

'The whole thing was so preposterous . . .' Marks reached out and gripped the sleeve of Joseph's coat. '. . . I thought no one would believe me. And Laurence wouldn't tell me what he'd done with Weaver.'

'But you knew Weaver was "Tony" when I interviewed you in your office?' Collins demanded.

'I suspected that Laurence had killed him. I had no idea he

had set him free . . .' Marks' voice was now so low that Collins and Joseph had to bend their heads to hear what he was saying. 'I didn't think he'd kill again, but I should have known . . .' The old man's eyes closed again.

'What should you have known?' Collins urged frantically.

'I saw the photographs of what he'd done to his wife. All those people dead, and I'm to blame because I kept my silence.' Marks gripped Joseph's sleeve tighter and sat up suddenly, his eyes no longer dull, but burning feverishly. 'In court he swore he was innocent, and I believed him. There are plenty of innocent people in our prisons. We all know that.'

'More than is generally realised,' Joseph agreed in an attempt to soothe the troubled old man as he pushed him gently back down on to the trolley.

'He once said he would do anything to get out of prison and prove his innocence. And he did, didn't he? He even exchanged his face for a dead man's. He said . . . he said . . .' The effort proved too much. Marks sank down on to the trolley, his hand swinging heavily at the side. A nurse, who'd been standing unnoticed nearby, stepped closer. She gently picked up the hand and laid it on his chest.

'We're going to have to move him up to the ward now.'

'Can we stay with him?'

'I'll have to ask the doctor, but I wouldn't waste your time.' She blotted the bubble of frothy blood from Marks' lips with a tissue. 'The end is very close. I doubt he'll come around again.'

Anna Bradley opened her eyes and sensed something was wrong. She stretched out her hand to find the other half of the mattress empty and cold. Had Adam gone without saying goodbye? Heart pounding, she slid out of the bed and switched on the light to check the clock. Half-past three in the morning.

Slipping on her dressing-gown and holding it closed with her bandaged thumb, she first checked the bathroom. Empty. Shivering, uncertain whether she even wanted Adam to be still in the house, she went downstairs. All the curtains were closed and several lights were switched on.

Adam was sitting at the table, his back towards her, a pen in his hand and a pad of notepaper in front of him. He turned, and she gasped. He'd cropped his hair to within half an inch of his scalp – with her nail scissors, judging by the unevenness of the cut. The poor remains he'd bleached with the peroxide she used on her own hair. He'd applied a tan make-up to give his face some extra colour, and painted a very credible scar down his left cheek, using a mixture of clear and red nail varnish. An actor's trick they'd been taught in college.

'I didn't want to wake you, but I've got to go now. I've taken five pounds out of your purse. I've left an IOU. To be honest, I've no idea when I'll be able to pay you back.'

'Don't worry about it.' She'd noticed her sharpest kitchen knife lying on the table next to him. It was the large one she used for slicing frozen food taken from the freezer. As he picked it up, she shrank instinctively towards the door.

'I made toast. Do you want some?'

Walking backwards, she shook her head as she crashed her spine painfully into the newel post at the bottom of the stairs.

He gestured to the notepad. 'I'm writing a letter to Hannah.' He turned back towards her, his hand closed lightly around the knife. 'You'll post it for me, won't you?' he pleaded.

'Of course.' She began to retreat up the stairs.

'Anna . . .?'

'I have to go to the bathroom.' She turned and raced up the last few steps; diving into the room, she closed and bolted the door behind her. Sitting on the edge of the bath she stared at the flimsy bolt, wondering how long it would hold if a man the size of Adam Weaver applied his shoulder to the door. Not long at all.

'Damn him for pegging out before he told us the whole story,' Collins complained angrily, as he and Joseph stepped out of the entrance to the casualty department.

'I don't think there was much more he could tell us. I doubt he ever saw Weaver again after the man left prison.'

'You're probably right. But where does that leave us now?'

'Where we were this morning. Nothing's changed except we now know a little more.'

'Like?'

'Like the guilt an old man carried around with him for keeping his mouth shut.'

'Has it occurred to you that Philip Matthews and those kids who fried in that old factory might still be alive if Marks had come to us when he first found out what his nephew had done to Weaver?'

'Yes. But the thought doesn't bring us any closer to finding Adam Weaver now.'

'No, but it does bring us nearer to Blanche Davies.'

'You reckon she knows something?'

'She knew Brian Marks fairly well.'

Joseph glanced at his watch. 'It's four o'clock in the morning. We can hardly go banging on her door at this hour. I'm for bed, even if it is only for an hour or two. Want to come back for a nightcap? If you have one too many, I've even got the spare bed made up.'

'I wish I could say I've somewhere better to go to but, seeing as how I haven't, thanks.'

'You two look as though you've had a night on the tiles,' Evans commented, as Joseph and Collins strolled into the office, yawning and bleary-eyed, at ten o'clock.

'A night in the hospital more like. We found Brian Marks.'

'What was he doing there?'

'Being a patient – attempted suicide.'

'Why didn't you contact me?' Evans walked around Bradley's desk, where Sarah Merchant was working on the computer.

'There wasn't time, as he very inconsiderately died soon after we found him.'

'Then it wasn't attempted suicide, was it, Collins? It was successful.'

'He was still alive when we first saw him.'

'It was paracetamol poisoning,' Joseph interrupted. Collins in this pedantic mood was more than even he could take. 'But we did manage a few minutes with him, and he corroborated everything Laurence Marks told you. He also revealed to us that Laurence Marks told him about Weaver. He blamed himself for not coming to us sooner.'

'As well he might.'

'But none of that gives us a day off from playing "Hunt the Weaver",' Collins griped.

'I've got every available man already looking, and I see no reason why you two shouldn't join them. Oh, and while I think of it, either of you heard from Bradley?'

'No, why?'

'She isn't answering her phone. Could she be staying with friends?'

'No one I know anything about.' Collins frowned.

'I'll send a car round there just in case she's been taken worse.' Evans picked up the phone.

'Don't bother with a car. Joseph and I will call in on our way over to see Blanche Davies.'

'Haven't you and Bradley already interviewed her?'

'That was before Brian Marks died.'

'That's right. Marks was her solicitor too, wasn't he?'

'And very good friend.'

'Just don't get side-tracked on some wild-goose chase. The Super's already moaning about the cost of this investigation. If we don't come up with Weaver in the next twenty-four hours, he intends to cut our manpower.'

'There's just a chance that Blanche Davies might think of someone from Weaver's past who may be sheltering him.'

'I haven't come up with a single lead that hasn't already been checked out clear.' Merchant pressed a button on the computer, and set the printer spewing out paper.

'That bothers me.' Joseph picked up the first sheet. 'Here we have a man who gives up his identity for a new face, only to end up as a down-and-out. If he'd had someone to fall back on, you think he would have gone to them in the first place, rather than rough it on the streets.'

'You know, I feel sorry for Weaver in a way,' Merchant said absently, as she tapped into a search programme. 'He was an extremely good-looking fellow. It must have been a shock when the bandages came off and he saw this rather ordinary face staring back at him from the mirror.'

'You're still not entirely convinced that Weaver is our killer, are you, Joseph?' Evans dropped the file he'd been studying on to the desk.

'I don't think the facts in this case quite add up, that's all.'

'Why the hell are you trying to complicate an open-and-shut case?' Collins demanded irritably. 'You're as bad as Bradley.'

'Just trying to get at the truth.'

'Well, don't. It confuses the investigation and makes for yet more work. Let's look for Weaver, find him, charge him, and get back to normal.'

'What's your idea of normal, Collins?' Evans smiled.

'Unfortunately for me, it's now the quiet celibate life of a monk,' he replied, winking at Merchant.

'Monks don't tend to drink as much as you do.'

'I didn't say which religion I followed.'

'Her curtains are still shut,' Joseph observed as they drew up outside Bradley's house.

'That doesn't mean anything. She often keeps them closed so the neighbours can't see the mess in her living-room.'

'Then you have ventured into the lady's den.'

'Once.'

Joseph winced as Collins banged the passenger door shut. He watched him walk to the front door and ring the bell. Collins pressed it six times, each time more impatiently, but each time to no avail. Eventually Trevor switched on the ignition and touched the button to lower his window.

'Like the Inspector said, she could be away somewhere.'

'Without telling anyone at the station?' Collins walked along the front of the house and tried peering through the curtains, but there were no gaps. He returned to the front door, and confirmed that it was locked. 'I'm going around the back.'

'I'll come with you.' Joseph raised the window again and locked the car, before following his colleague around the house. He found him staring at a bloody hand-print on the glass panel of the back door. Joseph glanced down at the ground. Red footprints ran in a cartoon trail up the garden path. A pair of bloody garden shears lay discarded in the middle of the lawn.

The prints themselves ended abruptly before a four-foot fence that marked the boundary between Anna's small garden and the woods behind.

Silently Collins pulled a handkerchief out of his pocket. Wrapping it around his fingers he depressed the handle of the back door which opened, swinging inwards.

'Bradley!' he cried. It was the first time Joseph had ever heard fear in his voice.

She was lying face-down on the vinyl, wedged between a row of kitchen units and the table. Her right arm was folded beneath her head. The black hilt of a carving knife protruded from the crook of her elbow. Her short blonde hair was stained crimson, soaked by the blood that had formed puddles on the brown-and-white chequer pattern on the floor.

Collins backed out through the door. Joseph could hear him vomiting into the drain as he himself crouched to lay his fingers on Bradley's neck – where a pulse would have throbbed, if she'd still been alive.

Chapter Eighteen

'Weaver's fingerprints are all over this place, Superintendent.' The forensic scientist who greeted Mulcahy as he parked outside Bradley's house looked like a pantomime snowman in his white hooded suit, mask, gloves and boots. 'We found them in the living-room, the bathroom, the bedroom. Even under the stairs.'

'You sure?' Mulcahy demanded.

'No doubt in my mind, sir. We brought a 'scope and a current file for on-the-spot comparisons, but I'll do a double-check back in the lab.'

'Anything else?'

'Give us a chance. We've only been here an hour. We're still working on it, but there's semen stains on the sheets on her bed. We'll have DNA and blood grouping for you later.' The man pushed a box containing an array of clear plastic bagged items, including a bundle of lace and bedding, into the back of his van.

'Then the bastard raped her.' Unwilling to leave, but excluded from the crime area by the forensic team, Collins, shell-shocked and stern-faced, leant against Joseph's car. Trevor stood next to him, although he would have preferred to drive Collins back to the office. The atmosphere was electric.

Everyone was trying desperately to remain professionally detached, attempting to treat this crime scene like any other. And everyone – including the forensic team – was failing miserably. Bradley had been that rare officer: a woman who could be tough when she needed to be, yet universally liked by the men on the force.

'There's nothing for either of us to do here, Collins,' Joseph suggested quietly. 'Why don't we let the forensic boys get on with it. We'll find out what we want to know when they put their report in.'

If Collins heard him, he made no sign of it.

'I won't be able to confirm anything on potential rape until I get her back to the mortuary and do a full PM,' O'Kelly informed Mulcahy. He nodded to the police photographer, who stepped past him and headed along the outside path leading to the back door. They followed him. Soon a series of flashes illuminated the wooden fence and concrete posts beyond, lightening the gloom of the grey, overcast morning.

As the photographer stepped away, O'Kelly beckoned to his assistant. 'Erect the screens around here, then give me a hand to turn her over.' He glanced at the photographer. 'Don't go too far away.'

'Give me a shout as soon as she's ready.'

'She! *She* had a name,' Collins cried, finally showing signs of breaking.

'Steady. Everyone's doing all they can.' Joseph laid a sympathetic hand on Collins' shoulder.

Evans moved around from the back garden to stand on the paving in front of the house. His enormous figure was covered by a flimsy, flapping paper overall; his hands and feet were swathed in plastic gloves and overshoes. A paper hat, similar to the ones worn by catering workers, covered what was left of his hair. He looked ridiculous; a comic, theatrical figure, but no one smiled.

'I've sent for the dogs, sir,' he informed Mulcahy. 'There's a trail of bloody footprints leading out through the back door and up the garden. We found a pair of bloodstained shears on the back lawn, which I've bagged and handed over to the forensic boys. Looks like he dropped them before he climbed over the fence and into the woods.'

'You think he's still in there?'

'If he is, the dogs will soon sniff him out. One thing's certain, he won't go far without being noticed. Judging by the footprints, he must be soaked in blood.' The Inspector turned to his two sergeants. 'Why don't you go back to the station, Collins,' he suggested gently. 'You could co-ordinate the search for Weaver.'

Collins' hand trembled as he gripped the cigar nestling in his top pocket. 'Bradley meant something to me. Really meant something. Do you understand what I'm saying?' His voice rose alarmingly as he crushed the cigar. 'She wasn't just a colleague, just one more copper killed in the line of duty. I . . . I cared for her. I've more right to be here than the rest of you.'

'No matter how close, if you were Joe Public, you wouldn't be allowed anywhere near this house right now. You know that. Come on, the Inspector's right. We need to pick up Weaver before he kills someone else.' Joseph opened his car door. 'Let's go.'

Collins turned on his colleague furiously. 'You can go sit on your arse in the bloody station if you want to. I'm not Joe Public, to be fobbed off with platitudes and parked in a waiting room. I'm a copper, and I'm going to do what coppers are trained to do. I'm going out with those dogs, and I'm going to catch that bastard.'

'Collins, you're not helping us, or doing yourself any favours,' Mulcahy began testily.

Collins turned his back on them. Placing his hands on the bonnet of the car, he leant heavily forward, staring at his distorted reflection mirrored in the paintwork. 'I want to see her,' he demanded softly. 'Just one more time. Then I'll go.'

'I don't think that's a good idea,' Evans broke in.

'Wait until we get her back to the mortuary,' Mulcahy suggested.

'So O'Kelly can clean her up and lay her out all peaceful and smiling. No! I want to see her the way she is now. I want to see . . . and remember.'

'Shouldn't you go and telephone her family?' Joseph interrupted, in the hope of distracting him.'

'Who? Her sister in Canada? Her brother in South Africa?'

'We'll go back to my place. You can use my phone,' Joseph offered, ignoring the biting sarcasm.

'I want to see her again – and I want to see her now! Exactly as she looks now.'

Evans recognised the irrational hysteria mounting in Collins' voice. He nodded to O'Kelly, who had just walked out of the kitchen and was standing inside the inadequate cover of the waist-high screens his assistant had now erected outside Bradley's back door.

The pathologist stepped inside the house again, and Collins followed him, Joseph close behind. Through the open door he could see that the whole house was a hive of activity. Paper-suited and masked figures seemed to be crawling over every inch of the living-room, but their activity stopped short several feet away from the broken figure that lay on the floor between the table and the door.

'I really wouldn't, if I were you, Sergeant.' O'Kelly laid a restraining hand on Collins' arm as he stepped past Joseph.

'I want to see her. I want to see exactly what he did to her, so I can remind the bastard of every blow – every mark, every wound – when I catch up with him.' Collins trod blindly forward.

'No further. Not without sterile overalls.' O'Kelly's assistant blocked Collins' path as he tried to move beyond the doorstep. They'd turned Anna over. Joseph took just one look before retreating, remaining outside the house but inside the inadequate cover of the screens.

That brief glimpse lingered, blotting all else from his consciousness. Bradley's face had been unrecognisable – hardly even human. He closed his eyes but the image intruded, filling his mind. Jagged strips of skin lying over deep, blood-soaked gouges running horizontally from forehead to chin. One ear, completely severed, swamped by a sticky pool of drying blood at the side of the head, the carving knife embedded in the face; its blade buried in the socket where her eye had been.

Collins stumbled forward. He would have fallen on to Anna's body if O'Kelly's assistant hadn't stepped forward to hold him upright.

'Take him away,' O'Kelly shouted, turning to Joseph. 'Now!'

Everything seemed red. The grass around him. The damp turf he lay on. Even the filmy mist that covered his eyes and clung to his lashes. All steeped in the blood that had soaked into his shirt and trousers and was now smeared over everything he touched. He could feel it sticky, wet as it trickled over the skin on his chest. He screwed his eyes shut and shuddered, seeing again those great gaping wounds . . . hearing her screams . . .

He tried to close his mind to the awful scene. He desperately needed to find water. Running water where he could scrub away these stains once and for all. Then perhaps he'd feel clean again . . .

He'd crawled through the fringes of undergrowth bordering the woodlands behind Anna's house. He'd kept on crawling, through the darkness, through the false dawn – and the real one. He had no idea of the time, other than it was day because it was light. It could just as well be early morning or late afternoon. The atmosphere was misty, grey – close to dawn or dusk.

He'd never liked the country, and now he knew why. Every rustle in the undergrowth sent his pulse-rate soaring. Every animal screech sent his hands protectively to his head. The mist that concealed him, far from comforting, was pregnant with unseen, unknown dangers. And God alone knew what evils lurked within the grey-green distant shadows his eyes couldn't penetrate.

He urged himself to go on – keep running. But not through the streets. Not yet. He couldn't venture into town looking the way he did. And he hurt – all over. He tried to lift his right arm, but it wouldn't move. He looked down to see it hanging uselessly at his side. The sleeve of his shirt, once bright check but now crimson, was rent from shoulder to wrist, covered with blood. He couldn't see a break in his skin, but he could see a misshapen lump where the bone had snapped above the elbow. And the pain was excruciating. He bit at the torn sleeve, tearing the cloth further with his teeth. Freeing a strip, he tried to bind the arm to his chest, but the cloth was slippery and too short. A wave of blissful nothingness engulfed him, he had no means of knowing for how long. When he came to, he began retching. He couldn't lose his grip. Not now. He had to find water, and another washing line to rob. And afterwards?

Back to the streets, to running, hiding – staying one step ahead. Until the next time.

Bundling Collins into the car, Trevor drove him to his own house. He couldn't think of anywhere else. He couldn't face the embarrassed sympathy of their colleagues in the police station. They both badly needed a drink but a pub would be too public. As soon as they got inside, he poured out a couple of stiff brandies. Leaving Collins alone in the living-room Trevor phoned through to the station and spoke to Merchant, telling her where they could be found, if needed. Cutting short her condolences, he then hung up.

'This isn't doing anything.' Collins downed his brandy in one gulp. 'We shouldn't be sitting here on our backsides. We should be out there looking.'

'With the numbers Mulcahy put out on the streets this morning, our absence isn't going to make any difference.' Trevor knew Collins couldn't be thinking straight. Soon, very soon, either Mulcahy or Evans would be taking him off the case. That was standard procedure with any officer emotionally involved with a victim. Especially a murder victim.

'I can't just sit here getting plastered,' Collins countered savagely, tossing back the second brandy Joseph had poured for him.

Trevor didn't answer. He simply refilled both their glasses, sat back and prepared to listen.

Sarah Merchant was still patiently inputting information on to her computer when Dan Evans and Bill Mulcahy returned to the station. She took one look at their faces and went out to get them some coffee.

'If there is anything I can do to help, sir, I'd be only too glad to,' she said, returning with a loaded tray. 'And if it's a question of overtime, I really don't mind.'

'I'd like you to attend the case conference this evening. At eight sharp,' Mulcahy answered. 'We should have some results from O'Kelly and the forensic teams by then.'

'Come up with anything on the computer yet, Merchant?'
Evans asked.

'I'm still inputting information, sir, but Sergeant Bradley
and I went through it all yesterday. Neither of us could find any
close contact that we hadn't already checked out.'

'Well, we now know where he was last night . . .'

'Early hours of this morning, at least,' Mulcahy corrected as
Merchant left the inner office. 'You probably noticed that the
face on Bradley's watch was smashed. The hands had stopped
at five o'clock. He picked the lock on the back door.'

'Forensic team did say they weren't too sure about that.'

'It was lying open, wasn't it?' Mulcahy demanded irritably.
'Isn't that enough evidence. The rest of the house was sealed
tighter than a drum.'

'It does look like he might have come in that way.' Evans trod
carefully. His own emotions were in turmoil, but he was doing
a better job of keeping them in check than any of his colleagues.

'So he broke in, and presumably made some noise. She came
downstairs to check – and he attacked her.'

'Let's wait until we talk to O'Kelly again. This is one
investigation I don't want to predict.'

'And one postmortem I never thought I'd have to witness.'
Mulcahy slammed his fist into the desk.

'Do you want me to go?' Evans asked. 'After all, she was my
sergeant.'

'You sure you can cope with it?'

'I'll ring O'Kelly and ask what time he's performing it.'

'In that case I'll stay here and co-ordinate our search for
Weaver. If you've time before the postmortem, I'd appreciate it
if you'd track down Collins and tell him you're taking him off
the case.'

'Completely?'

'I don't want him any closer to it than Merchant's computer.
And that's an order.'

Head lowered against the wind, Adam Weaver jogged along a
narrow street of terraced houses. The black tracksuit pulled off
yet another washing-line couldn't have emerged from the

washing machine too long before he'd snatched it. Soaking wet, it clung to his limbs, which were still shivering after his icy plunge into a farm-polluted stream.

On leaving the cover of the woods he found himself closer to the town centre than he'd expected. He knew this area well, and all the short cuts it offered, including an alleyway that led down to the bottom end of High Street – the decaying end. He knew about the floor-level window that opened into the men's toilets of the old cinema. Two nights ago, while hiding in the skip, he'd watched the police check out the cinema thoroughly. Afterwards he'd seen workmen board it up, and even later he'd observed a couple of homeless kids prise one board off with a claw hammer – hingeing it so it would stand a quick careless inspection – like the one that had given them access into the old factory. He had to get off the streets quickly and could think of no better place to go.

His blood ran cold as a police car drove slowly alongside. Its window whirred softly downwards, and a uniformed officer hailed him.

'We'd appreciate your assistance, sir.'

He had no other choice, so he stopped running. Turning slowly, he placed his hand on his knee, and leant over with his head down, as though out of breath.

'Have you seen this man, sir?' The young policeman flashed a photograph of "Tony" taken from the video.

He took it from the policeman's hands, and held it for a few seconds, then shook his head.

'I've not seen him at all,' he lilted in a credible Irish accent – always one of his best.

'If you do . . .'

'I've seen the posters, with the number to call. I'll get in touch.'

'Thank you, sir.'

The car sped on past, and Adam began to breathe again. Just a few more yards, then he'd be in the alleyway. There was a room right at the back of the cinema, which few others knew about. He'd kipped there for a couple of nights last winter, before the building's owners had cleared the place out the first time. It had originally been the projection booth, and seemed warmer than the huge rat-infested auditorium. And what he craved most now was warmth. Dry warmth – and a deep black sleep that would enable him to forget Anna.

'We were originally on our way to see Blanche Davies.' Despite the brandies he'd swallowed, Collins still appeared stone-cold sober.

'We've both been drinking since,' Joseph pointed out, as he dipped into his third brandy.

'I'll drive if you can't manage.'

'Collins, it can wait.'

'No, it damn well can't.' He was out of his chair before Trevor had time to put down his glass. Cursing, Joseph followed him to the front door. Collins had picked up his keys, and was soon turning over the engine of his car. Joseph slammed the house door shut, flicked up his jacket collar against the onset of rain, and climbed into the passenger seat.

Blanche Davies' house was warm and fragrant with the rich cooking odours associated with a traditional English Sunday lunch. Yet the smell, after seeing Bradley's hacked body, made Trevor's stomach heave and his head swim.

'Sergeant Joseph?'

'And I'm Sergeant Collins.' He pulled out his identity card.

'I wasn't expecting you.'

'May we come in for a few minutes?'

Blanche Davies opened the door and led them into the living-room, which was more cluttered than the last time Trevor had seen it. The supplements from one of the larger Sunday newspapers were scattered over the floor, the children's comic section uppermost.

'Hannah?' Blanche interrupted her niece's reading. 'Would you please check the meat and potatoes for me.' The child went into the kitchen, and Blanche closed the connecting door. 'How can I help you?' she asked, glancing from Joseph to his companion, white-faced and tense. The look in Collins' eyes sent a chill through her veins.

'I'm afraid we have some bad news for you, Miss Davies,' Trevor broke in, taking the responsibility away from Collins.

'Bad news? About Adam? You've found him?' She sank down on to the sofa.

'No, not Adam Weaver. About your solicitor, Brian Marks.'

'Mr Marks?'

'He died in the early hours of this morning in the General Hospital.'

'Died? He always seemed so fit. Was it a heart attack?'

'No,' Collins broke in abruptly. 'Suicide. He took an overdose of paracetamol.'

'Mr Marks killed himself?' she murmured in a shocked whisper.

'I'm afraid so,' Joseph confirmed in a kinder tone.

'But why? Why on earth . . .?'

'Guilt!'

Joseph gave Collins a cautionary look. 'We have reason to believe that Brian Marks knew who arranged your brother-in-law's escape from prison.'

'Surely if he'd known that he would have gone to the authorities?'

'Apparently not.' Joseph watched Blanche slump back into the sofa.

'We also have reason to believe that Brian Marks was aware that Adam Weaver received another man's face in a transplant operation carried out shortly after his escape.'

Blanche stared at Collins uncomprehendingly. 'A transplant? Are you saying that Adam has another man's face? That photograph, it didn't look at all like Adam, but,' she appealed to Joseph, 'you and Sergeant Bradley said something about plastic surgery . . .'

'We said something *like* plastic surgery.' Joseph corrected, noticing the tense muscles knot on the back of Collins' hands at the mention of Bradley's name.

'The newspaper reports I've been reading?' Blanche asked. 'Was it Adam who murdered that poor man down the docks?'

'We would like to question him about that – and the arson attack at the old factory,' Joseph replied noncommittally.

'Do the police ever give a straight answer to a straight question?' she bit back antagonistically.

'We can only tell you what we know ourselves.'

'It's just that Adam . . . I found it hard enough to believe that he killed Laura, but this . . .'

'Have you or your niece seen this man' – Collins produced the dog-eared photograph of 'Tony' from his inside pocket – 'since he was seen loitering outside Hannah's school?'

Blanche shook her head.

'Did Brian Marks ever talk to you about your brother-in-law?' Collins continued ruthlessly.

'Of course, during the trial . . .'

'Not during the trial, afterwards?' Collins persevered. 'Did he ever mention Adam Weaver's name *after* he escaped?'

'Not that I can remember, other than to ask what I'd do if Adam ever tried to contact Hannah.'

'And what would you do?'

She looked Collins in the eye. 'I'd contact the police, of course. For Hannah and Adam's sake as much as anyone else's.'

'Adam's sake?' Joseph questioned.

'I don't know whether he's guilty or innocent. But I do abhor violence of any kind. I couldn't bear to live with the thought that I contributed in any way to someone's death. And I wouldn't take that risk by trying to shield Adam.'

'Then you do think he's capable of carrying out these crimes?' Collins homed in on every scrap of information.

'I don't know,' she cried. 'I don't know anything for certain about Adam, not any more.'

'Marks never mentioned your brother-in-law after the trial, other than to ask what you'd do if he contacted you?' Joseph persisted in a softer tone.

'No.'

'And you had no further contact with your brother-in-law. You didn't visit him . . .'

'No. But I wrote to him and, after Adam was convicted, Mr Marks passed on some letters that Adam had written – one to me and one to Hannah.'

'What did these letters say?'

'Personal things. In mine there were things he wanted me to tell Hannah about him – and Laura – while she was growing up. And how sorry he was that I'd been left to pick up the pieces.'

'Did he claim he was innocent?' Joseph asked.

'Not in that letter, but then he'd protested his innocence all along.'

'Did he mention any names? Any friends you might go to if you were in trouble?'

Blanche shook her head as she pulled a handkerchief from her pocket.

'Is there anyone you can think of who might shelter him?'

'Don't you think I would have told you by now if there was?'

'What was in Hannah's letter?' Collins charged.

'It hasn't been opened yet. Adam didn't want her to read it until she was older, but I'm sure there's nothing in it that will help you find him . . . Oh God!'

The tears that had been hovering close to the surface since they had told her about Marks finally began to fall.

'I'm sorry. It's just that I'm going to miss Mr Marks,' she apologised.

'I'm sure there'll be someone else in his solicitors' firm who'll be able to pick up where he left off.' Joseph suddenly felt unequal to dealing with Blanche Davies' grief as well as his own.

'You don't understand, it's not just his firm. He was much more to us than our solicitor.'

'Auntie Blanche?' Hannah stood in the doorway, looking very small and alone. 'I heard you crying,' she explained, giving Trevor a reproachful glare.

'Hannah, come here.' Blanche held out her arms.

'It's Daddy, isn't it?' As the child warily backed away, she rammed a fist into her mouth.

'No, Hannah, it's not Daddy. It's Uncle Marks. He died last night.'

'He was old, wasn't he?' the child said practically.

'Yes.' Blanche valiantly attempted a smile. 'He was old.'

'Well, if he was good, he'll go to heaven.' Hannah turned to

Trevor Joseph. 'Have you come to talk to me about that man outside the school.'

'No, Hannah, not this time. Not unless you've seen him again?'

The child shook her head.

Joseph looked down at the floor. He was finding this visit extremely difficult. The last time he had been in this room, he had been with Bradley. Collins wasn't the only one who was going to miss her. Life was so fragile, so bloody unfair. One minute you were *there*, a living, breathing entity going about your business, trying to enjoy yourself as best you could. Then, wham – nothing! Unable to stand still a moment longer he went to the door. 'I think we'd better be going. Sorry to have to bring you bad news, Miss Davies.'

Tight-lipped, Blanche nodded.

The child went to Blanche and caught her hand. 'Shall I telephone Uncle Nigel?'

'Uncle Nigel?' Collins looked to Blanche, but it was Hannah who continued.

'He's our best friend.'

Collins looked swiftly at Blanche Davies over the child's head. 'Who exactly is this Uncle Nigel?'

'You heard Hannah, a friend,' Blanche said testily. 'A very old friend.'

'Of the family?' Joseph asked.

'He was in school with Laura, and college after that.'

Joseph could have kicked himself. Blanche Davies was a stunning woman – one who looked remarkably like her sister. Why hadn't he thought of checking out her men friends to see if there was any connection between them and Laura Weaver's mysterious boyfriend.

'What does he do?'

'He's a freelance film director.'

'Nigel Valance?'

'You know him?' Blanche asked Collins, clearly surprised.

'We have to go.' Collins turned and let himself out of the front door, leaving Joseph to apologise for their intrusion and say their goodbyes.

'Valance was filming down in Jubilee Street for days before that down-and-out was torched,' Collins began, as soon as Blanche had closed the door on them. 'He got to know a lot of the vagrants when he was making that documentary.'

'And he was filming the fire over in the old factory before any of the emergency services even got there. I saw him there with his camera myself. Mulcahy and the Fire Chief were cursing him.'

'Then he could be connected?'

'All we've got is a series of coincidences.'

'I gave up believing in those a long time ago,' Collins said sharply as they reached the car. 'Think about it. Weaver escapes from prison, then he goes missing. He disappears into the one world where newcomers don't have to explain themselves. Then, nearly two years later he resurfaces here. He can't resist going to see his child, but she talks – she tells this Uncle Nigel . . .'

'But Hannah said the man's face wasn't her father's.'

'Valance would know Weaver was an actor. That he could change his appearance . . .'

'So much his own child doesn't recognise him? All right' – Joseph shelved the question – 'what do you want to do?'

'Radio in – put out a warrant on him.'

'We haven't got enough evidence for that.'

'Then ask for a car to watch this place. We'll use the excuse that Weaver's likely to turn up any minute. We can then brief the driver on Valance . . .'

'Are you finally accepting the possibility that Weaver might be innocent.'

'Possibly of killing his wife. But not Anna.'

'Collins, it doesn't add up.'

'Nothing bloody well adds up. It hasn't since this case started. If we take a detour past the television centre on our way to the station, we can get Valance's home address. A couple of hours of hard work and some luck. That's all we need to bury Weaver and, if need be, Valance alongside him. I always knew there was something perverted about the little shit.'

Joseph eyed Collins warily as he pulled his keys from his pocket. He wondered if Collins had handed back the gun he'd been issued before going into the factory. Or if he meant to bury Weaver and Valance – literally.

Tom Morris sat next to a youngster hunched over a bowl of cornflakes on the most distant table from the counter in the hostel dining-room. 'Tell me, have those squatters who were burned out of the old factory found anywhere else to move on to?' he asked.

'Nowhere I've heard about.' The boy carried on crunching.

'You sure?'

'I don't know, do I? Look, Mr Morris, if we didn't have to pay for this place, more of us would come here. It's hard to find what you lot charge for a night's kip.'

'Not if you lay off the drink and the drugs.'

'I'd like to see you try it, Mr Morris. See how far you'd get out there without something extra to keep you warm at night.'

'Mr Morris?' A young boy stood shuffling awkwardly in front of their table.

'Yes,' Tom answered impatiently.

'Can I have a word with you, sir, in private? It's important.'

'Go and wait outside my office, and I'll see you there,' Morris ordered.

Tom was surprised to find the boy still waiting when he finally climbed the stairs a quarter of an hour later.

'Come in,' he muttered irritably, checking his watch and noting that he was going to be late for lunch with his wife and her parents, if he stopped off to shower and change first. That was something he did routinely every time he left the hostel, as if the place contaminated him in some way.

'It's like this, Mr Morris. I saw him, and I didn't know who to tell. I can't go to the coppers, because I shouldn't have been there. But it's still cold at nights . . .'

'Who did you see?' Tom Morris demanded, cutting through the boy's ramblings.

'That man the police are after. The one whose pictures are up everywhere. He looked a bit different, but I saw him once when he was dossing down here, so I'd recognise him anywhere – even with blond hair. He was climbing into the old cinema. Looked like he'd hurt his arm. He fell down twice.'

'The old cinema's boarded up.'

'Not completely. Jason hooked one board open – just like he did in the factory.'

'When did you see him, Robert?'

'This afternoon. I was going to save my doss money by sleeping in the cinema tonight. But I won't, not now. I was in that old factory when it went up, and I don't want to get caught twice. But there's others in that cinema, Mr Morris, sir. They should be warned. I didn't know what to do, then I thought of you. So I came right here. Everyone says he's the one who burnt that man to death and set fire to the factory. If he torches the cinema, he'll kill everyone inside. But I can't go to the police. They'll try to stick me back in care . . .'

'Don't worry, Robert. You won't have to tell them anything.' Tom Morris picked up the telephone. 'If you run along now, no one's going to know that you've even spoken to me. I won't mention your name.'

'You'll say *you* saw him, sir?'

'That's it Robert. I'll say *I* saw him.'

Chapter Nineteen

'Don't you see, it all fits?'

'You've got one hell of a lot of suppositions there,' Evans pointed out mildly.

'Look, Nigel Valance is a friend of Blanche Davies. He was in school and college with Laura Weaver. What does that tell you? Laura Weaver was having an affair with him, right?'

'I'll go that far as a possibility, but to jump from there to Nigel Valance killing her . . .'

'You were the one who believed Weaver was innocent, Joseph,' Collins rebuked.

'All I ever said was that the evidence didn't quite add up.'

'Nigel Valance is Blanche's friend, right,' Collins lectured heavily. 'From the way she talked about him, a *good* friend. He obviously visits her and Hannah. Supposing Hannah mentioned the man outside her school, and said that the man looked like her father . . .'

'From the back,' Joseph interposed.

'Don't you see. If Weaver changed clothes with Matthews, the same description would have fitted both. Tall, dark, thin, wearing red baseball boots. Matthews could have been killed by Valance in mistake for Weaver.'

'Two questions, Collins.' The Inspector stared thoughtfully at the photographs pinned on the cork board. 'One, how did Valance know about Weaver's face transplant, when we only just found out about it ourselves?'

'Weaver successfully evaded capture for two years after his prison escape. Valance would have guessed that Weaver had changed his appearance. And Valance knew Weaver was an actor, skilled at changing his appearance . . .'

'Come on, the man had his own television series a couple of years ago. His picture was on the front page of every newspaper at the time of the murder. Tony looks nothing like Weaver.'

Collins thought for a moment. 'It is possible Marks told him. Marks knew about the transplant, he was also concerned for Blanche Davies and the child. Who better to confide his secret to than Blanche's boyfriend, a man in a good position to protect them.'

'Now you're into maybes as well as suppositions,' Joseph protested.

'Valance and Blanche are obviously an item,' Collins continued to argue, sounding a little too calm and rational for Evans' liking, for a man who'd just seen his girlfriend's knifed and battered body. Evans was on tenterhooks, waiting for the full flood of emotion to burst, after those first few eruptions at Bradley's house. 'And if you want to find someone prepared to put their all into protecting a woman and child, who better to approach than the man who's knocking off the woman.'

'He was certainly hanging around during the fire at the factory and, from what we know, practically the first on the scene.'

'It's beginning to fit for you, too, Joseph?'

'The second question is, if Valance is our villain, why are Weaver's fingerprints all over Bradley's house?' Evans asked.

'Weaver's a man at the end of his tether. He broke in . . .' Collins struggled to keep his voice steady. 'Bradley recognised him. He went berserk.'

'So we have two killers on the loose?' Evans suggested.

'It's happened before,' Collins asserted forcefully.

'I wish we had Weaver in custody,' Evans breathed vehemently. 'Something tells me that, guilty or innocent, he's the only one who can help us clear this mess.'

'Poor bastard, if he is innocent,' Joseph murmured.

'Collins, chivvy Merchant. See if she can come up with a list of people who were in drama college with Laura and Adam Weaver, and also the actors they worked with afterwards,' Evans ordered, wanting to keep Collins busy. 'It might help if we find Valance's name on that list. Joseph, you check with control and put out a "pick up on sight" on Valance. Assistance-with-enquiries will have to do until we have enough evidence for a warrant. As soon as he's found, I want him brought in. The Super and I will question him. And you two,' he looked sternly at Collins and Joseph, 'will stay safely on the other side of the glass. And that's an order.'

'Files from Sergeant Bradley's house.' Chris Brooke dumped a pile on the desk that had been Bradley's, and was now Merchant's. 'They've been passed on by forensics.' He cleared his throat awkwardly as he glanced at Collins, who was slumped on a chair reading the computer printouts as they spewed from the machine. 'I . . . we . . . I mean all the boys, sir. We're very sorry about Sergeant Bradley. We want you to know that.'

Collins continued to thumb blindly through the printouts. If he'd heard Brooke's condolences, he made no acknowledgement. 'Any news on Valance yet?' he enquired coldly.

'Not yet, but we know he's expected at Miss Davies' house any minute. It can't take much longer.

'Just see that it doesn't.'

'Yes, sir.' Brooke backed out of the door.

'That drama college phoned back yet?' Collins continued.

'You know they haven't. You're sitting right next to the phone,' Merchant retorted with unintentional sharpness.

Her reply sounded too like the one Bradley would have made. Hurting more than he would have ever believed possible, Collins picked up one of the files Brooke had left on the desk. A file Bradley had looked at only yesterday. As he flicked it open, newspaper cuttings and lists spilled out, falling to the floor.

'Sergeant Bradley was evaluating and collating the information collected by the team who originally investigated Weaver's escape from prison,' Merchant explained.

'No doubt they, like us, were looking for possible holes he might have bolted to.' Collins picked up a sheaf of yellowing pages clipped from a stage magazine, and began reading.

'*Student play attracts interest of Film-maker*' was the first heading that seized his attention. Underneath it was a rambling article about a girl whose name Collins didn't recognise; above it a photograph showing a group of young people dressed in seventeenth-century costume. The girls wore long, lace-trimmed dresses with plunging necklines, the men had knee-breeches, flowing shirts and thigh-length embroidered waistcoats. He studied the faces, picking out Weaver's at once. He stood centre-stage, holding the hand of the leading lady, the same one who had supposedly attracted the film-maker's attention. Relegated to the second row, behind him, Collins recognised Laura Weaver's pert and pretty face framed by an elaborate wig festooned with ringlets. He had to search hard to find Nigel Valance. He finally found him at the end of the last row, dressed in the rough apron of a blacksmith. He stared long and hard at the features of the girl next to him. There was no mistake. Anna Bradley smiled out from under the white mob cap of a maid.

He remembered her transformation when they had gone undercover into the factory.

"I was an actress. I have a college certificate to prove it. A season in a chorus . . ."

He tossed the photograph over to Joseph. 'End of back row. Looks like Bradley took care to keep all evidence of the connection between herself and Weaver well away from the computer.' With shaking hands he picked out a typewritten sheet from the pile of clippings, which proved to be a list of names copied from the drama college's student register.

'Then Bradley knew Weaver?' Joseph murmured after reading the name captions below the photograph.

'Looks like it.'

'I had no idea.'

'It seems to me she took care to see none of us did,' Collins said abruptly as he scanned down the list of names. As the list was alphabetical it didn't take him long to find the ones he wanted. Bradley's name came first, Laura Davies' second, and Weaver's halfway down the list. And close to the bottom was Valance, Nigel. Four people tied together by murder, ten years on.

'No wonder she wouldn't let any of us near her house for the last couple of days,' Collins said savagely.

'You can't think she was sheltering Weaver?'

'What else could it be? The only wonder is we were too bloody stupid to see it before now. Forensic said his fingerprints were all over the place. The bedroom, the bathroom, the living-room, under the stairs . . . semen stains on the sheet. How many murdering rapists would stay in a house long enough to leave their fingerprints everywhere, and then rape a woman upstairs on her bed before dragging her downstairs into her kitchen to kill her?' Collins said bitterly.

'He's here.' Murphy stuck his head around the door of the incident room where Joseph was sifting through papers.

'Valance?'

'In room two. The Super's in there with the Inspector now. All the man's done since we cautioned him is squeal like a stuck pig for his lawyer.'

Joseph dropped the file he was holding, and joined Murphy in the corridor. 'Told Collins?'

'Not yet.'

'Tell him I'll see him in the viewing box.'

Murphy hadn't exaggerated Valance's hysteria. He was sitting, purple-faced and seething with indignation, down table from the Superintendent, who was leaning over – outwardly relaxed and comfortable – with his arms crossed in front him. A WPC and a uniformed constable stood guard in front of the closed door.

'Solicitor here yet?' Murphy asked, joining Trevor in the viewing room.

'No.' Joseph looked over his shoulder as Collins walked in with Brooke. Sitting down silently in one of the chairs, he removed a pen from his top pocket and began to tap it against the table top. Time crawled. The high colour drained from Valance's face as his fury subsided, but no one in the interview room or the viewing box said a word.

Eventually a short, tubby man wearing a creased shiny suit bustled into the interview room with a bulging briefcase.

'Sorry I took so long to get here,' he apologised to Mulcahy and the room in general.

'Turn the sound up.'

Joseph leant forward and did as Collins asked.

The solicitor sat down at the table, between the Superintendent and his client. He looked up expectantly as Evans began to read the charges, beginning with the arson attack on the old factory. Evans didn't get any further. Loudly protesting his innocence, Valance rose from his chair and tried to make for the door. His solicitor urged him to return to his seat, Evans attempted to continue reading, but the commotion Valance was making drowned them both out. Waving his arms threateningly, Valance demanded to know what evidence they had to charge him. It took the combined efforts of Evans, the constable and the solicitor to return Valance to his seat and quieten him sufficiently so Evans could continue.

Nerves jangling at breaking point, Trevor watched Collins gripping the pen on the table in front of him. He ran his fingers from the bottom to the top, turned the pen over and repeated the performance – again – and again – and again. And all the while, first the Inspector, then the Superintendent, continued to grill Valance. About the fire in the factory, and his speedy appearance on the scene. They delved into Valance's relationship with Blanche Davies and her niece. Unnaturally composed after his earlier outburst, Valance fielded every question with a cool confidence that exasperated the officers in the viewing booth.

'Damned actors,' Joseph swore angrily. 'It's impossible to know when they're telling the truth and when they're lying through their teeth.'

Without any warning, Mulcahy switched technique. Instead of laying emphasis on the reported facts, he concentrated on insinuation and innuendo; hinting that Valance might have had an ulterior, possibly perverted motive for continuing his friendship with Blanche Davies and her niece after Laura's murder.

If Mulcahy had hoped to provoke an emotional response, he succeeded. As Valance's veneer of self-control finally cracked, he once again became the ranting, raving, screaming lunatic he had been when Evans had first begun to read the charges. Another ten minutes were wasted while they attempted to calm him so Mulcahy could continue. Then a tray of tea and biscuits was brought in and everyone returned to their seats at the table. Mulcahy shuffled his papers, and finally began again.

'Let's go back to the beginning, Mr Valance, shall we?' The Superintendent produced the college photograph Collins had found in Bradley's files, and pushed it across the table. 'You studied drama alongside Adam Weaver and Laura Davies.'

'I've never denied it.'

'A simple yes or no will suffice, Mr Valance.'

'You subsequently had an affair with Laura Weaver?' Evans picked up the questioning.

He looked at his solicitor. 'Do I have to answer that?'

'You don't have to answer anything you don't want to, Mr Valance.'

'But if you don't answer us, Mr Valance, you leave us to draw our own conclusions.'

'So I had an affair with Laura Weaver?' he contended arrogantly. 'So what? Her husband was sleeping with half of London, and Laura wanted to get her own back. I wasn't the only one she was bonking on the side.'

'Are you saying that Mrs Weaver had other lovers beside yourself?'

Suddenly Collins leaned forward in his chair, his hands closing around his pen.

'Dozens who didn't matter to her, and one who did. She threw me over for him, but he didn't really want her. I tried to tell her, but she wouldn't listen. He was happily married before she came on the scene. He saw her as a bit on the side – nothing more.'

'Do you know this other man's name?'

'Of course. She used to tell me everything. It was all a big game to her. If Adam Weaver slept with twelve girls in one week, she'd want thirteen men. And I was happy to be one of the crowd, until *he* came along and she became infatuated with him. It made no difference that he wanted a fling and nothing more. She became totally obsessed with him. Probably because he was the one man who tried to leave her. When he first told her he wanted to break it off, she began telephoning him at all hours of the day and night. At home, in work – it made no difference that his wife was the jealous sort, or that Laura was ruining his career. If anything it added spice to her obsession. I think he must have been the first man to ever turn down what she had to offer.'

Valance shook a cigarette out of a packet and pushed it between his lips. 'His name was Morris – Tom Morris. She met him through her sister Blanche. I think at one time he and Blanche worked together. Like Blanche he was a social worker. That was one of his attractions. Unlike the rest of us he did a *serious* job, infinitely more worthwhile than entertaining the masses. The first time Laura set eyes on him, he'd just come back from his honeymoon. But, as I said, that made no difference – not to her. She saw every man as fair game. She wanted him, and she got him – for a while. But I think, when she fell in love with him, they both got a lot more than they bargained for.'

'What exactly do you mean by that, Mr Valance?'

'It's obvious isn't it? Two weeks before she died, she told me it was all over between us. That she couldn't continue living the same empty way that she had been any more. That Morris had shown her that there was more to life than drink, parties and bonking. That he was the first man she'd ever really loved. Enough to give up all other men, her career, Adam, even her daughter if need be. She told me she'd finally persuaded him to leave his wife and go away with her, but the next thing I heard, she was dead.'

'Your name doesn't appear among the list of witnesses at Adam Weaver's trial.'

'Why should it? There's nothing I could have said about the night she died. I did wonder if she told Adam what she was up to, and he lost control. Their fights were legendary, even in college. I've seen both of them wearing shades to hide the black eyes they'd given one another.'

In the viewing room, Murphy murmured, 'Which ladykiller

are you going to put your money on? Weaver, Morris or Valance?'

'Perhaps Morris decided he wanted to stay married to his wife,' Brooke suggested. 'And perhaps the mistress threatened to tell the wife the full story.'

'Women *have* been killed to keep them quiet,' Murphy agreed.

'Morris was in Jubilee Street the night Matthews was murdered.'

'And in the old factory the night it burnt down.'

'What do you think?' Brooke asked. 'Another warrant?'

'That's up to the Super.'

Joseph looked around for Collins, but the door to the viewing booth was swinging on its hinges. He'd already left.

Collins entered the top end of Jubilee Street at twice the speed limit. Slamming on the brakes, he screeched to a halt, abandoning his car a good foot from the kerb. He flung open the door and jumped out without removing the keys from the ignition. Joseph, who'd raced after him to the station car park, extracted them before climbing out too. He pocketed them, after using the radio and locking the doors, determined that Collins would not be driving again that day. He then followed Collins into the Council hostel, just in time to hear Collins bang loudly on Morris's office door.

'He's not in,' an attractive blonde volunteer called down from the landing above.

'Do you know where he went?'

'No idea. But he usually takes Sunday afternoon off.'

Collins trailed back down the stairs, bumping into Trevor on the way.

'I put out his description on the radio, but Merchant told me Evans got there before us. It's already gone out to all cars and beat constables.'

'I'll kill the bastard. So help me God, I'll . . .' Collins kicked the front door savagely aside on his way out.

'We still can't be sure it was him. Come on, we'll call in on Sam Mayberry – see if he has any idea where Morris usually spends his Sunday afternoons. If we do find Morris, we'll take him in, and let the Inspector question him.' Rightly or wrongly

Joseph decided that the best course for both himself and Collins was to keep busy, hopefully until Bradley's killer – whoever he was – was safely in custody. But he dreaded the aftermath when his colleague's anguish and mourning would inevitably break loose.

'Gentlemen, it's good to see you. Any progress on your missing man?' Sam Mayberry had stopped them in the street, his arms loaded with plastic carrier bags containing donations of food from the local church congregation.

'We think we're getting close, Sam,' Joseph answered quickly, taking the car keys from his pocket.

'You're here. You're not there?'

'You said something?' Joseph turned to the tall, gangling youth with yellow hair and missing front teeth who'd been walking along behind Sam.

'I thought you'd be with Mr Morris.'

At the mention of Morris's name, Collins swung around.

'Why should we be with him?' Joseph asked.

'Because . . . because . . . It's a secret,' the youth mumbled, taking a step backwards, away from them.

'You can tell us your secret, lad. It will be safe with us,' Collins urged.

'You'll arrest me. You'll lock me up,' the boy began to gibber.

'I promise you, we won't.'

'Tell the sergeants what you know, Robert,' Sam reassured him. 'Then you can come with me and we'll make ourselves a slap-up meal. I've got all the ingredients.' He held up a carrier bag. 'Now, about this secret?'

'You promise I won't go to gaol?'

'We promise,' Joseph assured him solemnly.

'I saw him.' The boy smiled tentatively. 'The one everyone's looking for.'

'This man?' Collins pulled the 'Tony' photograph out of his pocket.

'Yeah, that's him. Only he doesn't look like that any more. His hair is short, and yellow like mine. And he's hurt bad. There's blood on his face and all down his arm.'

'Where did you see him?' Joseph cut in swiftly.

'I told Mr Morris to tell you because I shouldn't have been there. That's why he said he'd tell you for me.'

'Where shouldn't you have been?' Collins demanded furiously, his temper breaking.

The boy began to blubber.

'Robert, this is important. You must tell the policemen what you know.' Mayberry dropped one of the bags, and put an arm around the boy.

'The old cinema.'

'The one at the bottom end of High Street?' Trevor already had the car door open.

'How did you get in there?' Collins asked as he ran towards Joseph's car.

'There's a window. It looks all boarded up but it isn't. Toilet window at the back.'

'I'm sure Tom Morris would have phoned the station if it seemed important . . .'

Sam was speaking to the rear end of Joseph's car as it sped up the street.

Joseph picked up the radio receiver.

'Don't request back-up.'

'Why not? If he's really in there . . .'

'He might not be. That kid's obviously not sixteen ounces.'

'Collins, this is one time everything should be played exactly by the book – for all our sakes, including Bradley's. Look what happened to her.'

'You leave Bradley to me!'

'Bradley was *my* friend, too. We both owe it to her to see that this thing is dealt with properly and thoroughly.'

'And the bastard who turned her into mincemeat?'

'I want to make sure that when we get him to court, he won't walk free. And he will if we make a balls-up now.'

'That's always supposing he ever reaches court,' Collins muttered darkly.

Most of the buildings in Park Street were pre-First World War.

More than half of them were boarded up and decaying. Two of the pubs still had their doors open, but they were the sort of places that bikers rode into on their machines. A vast warehouse, belonging to a retail chain that had moved out of town years ago, stood shuttered and closed next to the grimy but ornate art-deco facade of the old cinema. Two uniformed constables had responded to Joseph's calls for assistance and were already waiting for them in the alleyway.

'There's a window around here that's been prised open.' Joseph left his car and studied the back of the grey brick building.

'Shouldn't we wait for a warrant, sir?' one of the constables suggested.

Collins gave him a withering look. 'How long you been out of college, boy?'

'Six weeks.'

'Any more questions like that and you'll wish yourself back there.'

They followed Collins round to a row of three windows set quite close together. He took a penknife from his back pocket and, slipping the blade beneath the first panel, he levered upwards. It remained obstinately fixed. But when he tried the second, it swung upwards easily.

Joseph turned and saw to his relief that the rookies had been joined by Brooke. 'Wait here, Brooke, until either Sergeant Collins or I call you.' He turned to the rookies. 'You two guard the entrances to this alleyway, one either end. The slightest sign of trouble, you radio for help.'

'Yes, sir.' They ran obediently to their posts.

'We're going to need torches,' said Joseph as he peered under the board.

'And a gun,' Collins added.

'Brooke, radio back and tell the station what we need. Collins, there's no point us going in until we get hold of a weapon,' Joseph shouted as his colleague swung back the panel and started heaving himself up on his arms.

'There's every point. If Weaver is in there, and Morris has gone after him, Weaver's as good as dead. And with him gone, we may never know the bloody truth.' He disappeared behind the board leaving Joseph no option but to follow.

It was as dark in the old cinema as it had been inside the abandoned factory.

'Bloody hopeless,' Collins growled, blundering straight into a stinking urinal as the board swung back after Joseph had entered.

'Torches, sir.' Brooke slid open the board and handed in two heavy-duty models.

'Where did you get them?'

'Sent one of the lads to borrow them from a garage around the corner.'

With the light switched on, Collins stepped forward again, splashing through the foul-smelling mess on the floor. 'They could have found a better bloody way in.'

Joseph swung his torch beam upwards until the light settled on an automatic door-closing mechanism close to the ceiling. He pushed on the wooden panel beneath it. It swung open to reveal pitch-black, musty nothingness. As he swept the beam from side to side, torchlight glinted back at him from the glass panel of a booth that had once dispensed tickets and sweets to the patrons. Beyond the booth, a corridor opened into a long, narrow hallway, ending in doors at either end.

By tacit agreement Collins took the right-hand door, Joseph the left. They emerged simultaneously in a vast auditorium. Blackness closed in on them, crushing, absolute and silent, from all sides. The patter of tiny feet indicated the presence of rats. Pointing their torches downwards they both stepped forward, walking in unison. One step at a time, they shone their lights along the row of seats, waiting until their beams met in the centre. Then they turned their backs and scanned along the side rows until the light hit the far walls. Thus, infinitely slowly and torturously, they covered every inch of what was left of the original seats. Pools of light illuminated piles of rotting rubbish, food cartons black with mould and chewed by rodents, broken springs sprouting from mouldering crimson velour upholstery.

Finally they reached the front row. Below the tattered gold silk curtain that once rose and fell in front of the screen, the raised platform was heaped high with empty food tins, old newspapers, and cardboard boxes. Keeping their torches trained low, they played their lights around the front area. Doors stood either side of the wide curtains. They were both heading towards the right-hand one, when Joseph halted in his tracks.

'See that?'

Conscious that another light had flickered from the back of the hall, they both looked up quickly.

'The projection booth,' Collins whispered, and they sped back up the aisle.

They could smell the petrol long before they reached the projection room. Joseph put a shoulder to the door and heaved against it. It wasn't locked and the door burst open, pitching him forward. As the torch rolled from his hand, its light settled briefly on Tom Morris, who was standing there, petrol can in hand. On the floor before him lay Adam Weaver, gagged and bound. His elbows were tied together at his back, his wrists, knees and ankles trussed like a turkey's.

Momentarily fazed by the intrusion, Morris appeared disorientated, but only for as long as it took for him to register Joseph's presence. With one swift movement he pulled a gun from the inside pocket of his coat, and fired.

Joseph cried out and slumped heavily to the floor alongside Weaver. Out in the passage, Collins switched off his torch and ducked behind the door.

He peered cautiously around the corner. Joseph's torch lay on the floor of the booth, as did the light Morris had been using. They illuminated Weaver's feet, encased in a pair of shabby trainers, and the back of Joseph's head lying very still.

Collins closed his eyes for a moment. Now was not the time to worry about Joseph. He had to think of Morris – and himself.

Hearing a whisper of movement, he opened his eyes. Morris's hands and arms slithered into view, as he crept forward on his stomach. Morris was heading for the door – and the passage where Collins waited. He was holding something in one hand. Collins recognised the gleaming silver mechanism of a cigarette lighter, as Morris flicked it on and edged the flame towards Weaver's petrol-soaked body.

Collins saw Weaver's eyes grow wide in terror. Aiming carefully, he hurled the only thing available. His precious torch. It caught Morris's hand, and the lighter flew backwards out of Morris's fingers, landing on a pile of rubbish over in the corner. The flame flickered for the briefest of seconds, but it was enough to set some papers piled over rags alight.

'Morris!' Collins shouted. 'Drop your gun. I'm arresting you.'

'You didn't see what this bastard did to Laura . . . You didn't see what he left for the police to shovel out of the bath!' Morris screamed hysterically.

'It's over, Morris,' Collins yelled, conscious of the flames licking ever closer to Weaver and Joseph. 'We know you killed Laura Weaver.'

'She had it coming.' Morris's voice dropped to a whisper. 'She was going to tell my wife. I couldn't let her . . .'

Adam Weaver suddenly took advantage of Morris's distraction. Throwing his weight sideways he squirmed across the floor, propelling both Joseph and himself into the far corner, as far from the rapidly spreading fire as was possible in that confined space.

Morris's gun flashed again. Collins threw himself back out of the doorway. The bullet whistled harmlessly overhead.

'Brooke?' Collins screamed, hoping against hope that the constable could hear him. 'Send up the reinforcements. Now!'

'When Blanche told me Hannah had seen some down-and-out she thought was her father, I knew he'd come back. I had to kill him. I'd built a life for myself. A good life. I had work, important work, and a good wife who loved me. I couldn't give that up, not for him, and not for a tramp like Laura.'

'You killed her because she was a tramp?' Collins called out in an attempt to distract Morris, as he inched nearer to see how close the flames were getting to Joseph and Weaver.

'I didn't want to. But she was going to tell my wife. And afterwards, just when I thought it was all over, Weaver escaped from prison. Then Marks warned me Weaver looked different. He knew I was a friend of Laura's. A trustworthy, happily married friend. Not some boyfriend she could get tired of at any moment. I promised Marks I'd take care of her, and Hannah. And I tried. I thought I'd killed him down on the docks. Only it was someone else. I didn't even succeed in smoking him out of that factory, and all those other people died,' Morris moaned, sitting with his gun cradled in his lap between the fire and Weaver and Joseph. 'They didn't deserve to die. But it wasn't my fault, it was his.' He pointed his gun at Weaver. 'He made Laura neurotic. He married her but he didn't love her. That's why she wouldn't leave me alone, even when I told her it was finished between us . . .'

'And Anna Bradley?' Collins demanded.

'There was no Bradley!'

'12 Acacia Drive,' Collins said.

'I have a good network. Better than the police's. One of my boys saw him going in there. You see, they tell me everything. She got between me and Weaver . . .'

Collins kicked the door wide open. The draught fanned flames were already consuming the floorboards beneath the rubbish. Smoke billowed out into the corridor. Morris pointed the gun at the door and fired – again and again. Collins flung himself to the floor. Once the bullets stopped flying and the gun clicked empty, he inched slowly forward. Weaver lay in the corner huddled up against Joseph, who still hadn't moved despite all the noise.

Morris was scrabbling at the edge of the fire. Picking up a burning rag, he flung it straight into Weaver's face before darting out the door.

Weaver screamed.

Horror-struck, Collins rolled out of Morris's path. Then, heaving himself to his feet, he plunged into the smoke-filled inferno of the projection booth.

Petrol burnt blue over Weaver's face, blistering his skin, as Collins stripped off his coat and thrust it down over the bound man's blazing head, smothering the flames with the cloth. Grabbing Joseph's legs he hauled him out into the corridor.

Feet thundered down a passage behind him.

'Watch out for Morris. He's got a gun,' he shouted as Dan Evans hurtled into view. Morris's gun flashed up the corridor, from the direction of the auditorium. The Inspector whirled around and fired at the flash. The bullet homed in, eliciting a long drawn-out screech.

'Call an ambulance!' Collins was now heaving Weaver out of the projection room. He pulled his coat away from the man's face, to see that Weaver's skin and hair was a brittle, blackened mess. Even the gag Morris had wound around his mouth was burnt through.

Collins pulled the flick-knife from his shoe and cut through the ropes binding Weaver's arms and feet. 'It's all right, mate,' he murmured to Joseph's inert body. 'Help's on the way.'

Epilogue

It was raining. The grey-stone crematorium glistened darkly as the mourners, heads bent, filed slowly out through the exit doors. Collins paused to view the sodden wreaths laid out on the lawn. His own cushion of white carnations and red roses already looked tired and weather-beaten, and the ink on the card had run beneath its inadequate plastic slip, making his message indecipherable. That probably was just as well, as he hadn't wanted anyone else to read his personal goodbye to Anna Bradley.

'I'm sorry, Peter.' Lyn Sullivan walked towards him, soberly dressed in a long, dark, hooded cape. She held out her hand. 'I'm really sorry,' she repeated. 'I know how much Anna had come to mean to you. And to everyone else on the force.'

He turned his anguished face to hers. His cheeks were damp, but she couldn't tell whether from rain or tears. Lyn faltered, searching for something else to say that would help ease his pain. Feeling utterly impotent in the presence of such intense grief, she moved on.

Trevor Joseph was standing to one side with the vicar, thanking him for his sympathetic handling of the service. She stood back and waited for him to finish, watching the mourners walk slowly past the assembled wreaths. Finally he came over to join her.

'I went straight down the station when I heard that one of the sergeants had been killed and another injured.'

'I know. Sarah Merchant told me you'd been in.'

'You were hurt?'

'Not badly.'

'Trevor . . .'

'It's not Daisy. It never was,' he interrupted.

'I know. She came to see me. Told me what a lucky girl I was.'

'There's a lot who'll disagree with her on that.' He smiled grimly.

'Not me,' Lyn murmured, lowering her eyes.

'Just as well Daisy's working in this town,' he said, wanting to switch their conversation to the commonplace, anything that wasn't personal. He couldn't deal with emotion now – not with Collins standing only a few feet away. 'Adam Weaver's face is going to need rebuilding again.'

'At least his name is clear and he has his daughter back.'

'When I last saw him, he seemed happy with that much.'

'Trevor, couldn't we could try again . . .' she ventured tentatively.

'No. I don't think that would be a good idea. It's not that I don't want to.' He shrugged his shoulders in the long black uniform coat taken out of mothballs for the occasion. 'But you know me, I'd make a whole lot of plans with you, give you a lot of promises I'd keep only as long as it took for the next investigation to get underway. You were right all along, Lyn. Policemen shouldn't have girlfriends or wives. When they've already made a commitment to the job there's simply no time left for a personal life.'

'But this case is over, now,' she pleaded stubbornly. 'You've caught your killer. Anna can rest in peace. We'd have a little time, surely.'

'Not much before another case breaks.'

'Enough for me to show you how sorry I am.'

'Lyn' – he thrust his hands deep into his pockets – 'please, do yourself a favour. Walk away now. Before I say yes, and ask you to move back in.'

'If there's a chance, I'm not going anywhere.'

'Can't you see what this is doing to me?' he begged. 'I'm not that strong, and it's not me that will be hurt – it's you. Collins has been switched to the Serious Crimes Squad. He's going to need someone around, so I've asked him to move in with me.'

'I could live with both of you.'

'No.'

312

'Are you really saying you've asked him to live with you to keep me at bay?'

'Maybe to keep all personal emotions at bay,' he said coldly, eyeing Collins. Better never to feel anything for another person ever again than suffer what Collins was going through over Bradley.

Evans walked up.

'We're all off to the Black Lion as a sort of wake. Would you like to join us, Lyn?'

She shook her head, biting her lips to hold back the tears.

Daisy appeared at Evans' side and held out her hand. Joseph took it first. When he released it, she offered it to Lyn.

'You look frozen, Lyn,' she admonished. 'Why don't you take her home now, Trevor?'

'Collins . . .'

'You can't possibly know what he is going through, or what he needs right now. But I do. I've been there, remember. So leave him to me.' Daisy left them and went over to Peter. Wrapping her arm around Peter's shoulders she spoke softly to him. Then she turned her head in their direction. 'If you're going to the pub, we'll see you there,' she called back to Trevor and Lyn, as she and Collins walked away together.

'Conspiracy?' Trevor asked Lyn.

'Not one I know about.'

'I'm sorry . . .'

She slipped her hand into his. 'Please, no more recriminations.'

They watched silently as Daisy and Peter joined the other mourners gathered in the car park. Within minutes they were lost to sight among the crowd of uniformed officers who'd closed ranks to shut out the civilians.

'You were right, Trevor,' Lyn admitted. 'I didn't understand. Not until today. Coppers are different, and they've every right to be when just wearing a uniform makes them such easy targets.'

He turned to face her. 'Want to go to the pub, then?'

'Yes, please.'

'And afterwards, you go home?'

'Yes, I'll go home with you,' she said, deliberately

misunderstanding him. 'I know this isn't the time or the place. But we have to make plans. For our baby.'

He stared at her in disbelief. 'Lyn . . .?'

'Just make sure you book a day off for the birth,' she said firmly. 'I think I can learn to forgive you almost anything. But that's one thing I don't want to go through alone.'